Cross-Dressed to Kill

By

Andrew Lucas

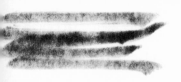

This is a work of fiction.
Names, characters, places, and incidents either are the product
of the author's imagination or are used fictitiously. Any
resemblance to actual persons, living or dead, events, or locales
is entirely coincidental.
This work is not autobiographical.

Published by The Y*e*S Press Ltd.
June 2011

With thanks to
Victoria Orr-Ewing
Sarah & Neil Starsmore
&
One or two others.

~oOo~

For
the four
most important,
and the one
most special.

About the Author

Andrew Lucas lives a mile or so off the south coast of England on the Isle of Wight and is currently working on the follow-up to CD2Kill and a new novel, 'Reunion', both due for publication late summer 2012.

Andrew likes Arvon....

Prologue

I am a murderer.

This is a fact that I cannot deny.

I have heard evidence and I have read stories about me that leave little room for doubt. I have been judged and found guilty by a dozen of my peers. I understand that people have died. Yet still, despite these sad realities, as a reasonable member of the human race I find it hard to believe that I have committed a real crime. However, if I am the wicked man, as has been reported, then it never seemed that way at the time. At the time, or times (and I am afraid there have been a few), the feeling I most remember was surprise... whoops.

'I am a murderer.' it's a simple statement, which these days seem to slip almost casually from my tongue. Maybe if I had been an archaeologist or a gardener I could say just as easily 'I am a digger'. I have dug of course, holes, quite a few of them over the years, for a variety of reasons and in a variety of shapes and sizes. I have dug big holes and small holes, short trenches and shallow furrows, in my garden mainly, but just not enough to earn the label 'serial digger'. The question I suppose, were I to wear that tag, would be; does the label alone define me? Should I pass someone in the street who recognised me, would they stop and stare, and believing that shovelling was my solitary obsessive passion in life, point a finger and shout? 'Look, there goes the digger... oh those poor holes... watch out for your gardens'. Would I be forever tarred with that burdensome brush? I understand that labels are important of course, words like, innocent, victim, guilty, and killer, but once tagged is that all we ever are?

Am I sorry? Do I feel remorse? I could give a dozen answers. Sometimes yes, although often no. Instead, I shall say simply that to anyone adversely affected by my actions, I apologise, but to those who I have relieved of their troublesome and often irritating lives... today, I do not.

However, I recognise that people have died and I have been tried and convicted of the most serious of all crimes, and so I can quite definitely say, that in the opinion of a great many people, and in particular, in the eyes of the law, I am now and I will always only ever be a murderer.

CHAPTER ONE

I knew that I was in trouble when my reflection looked back at me and winked.

Almost every day for almost thirty years, I'd stood behind a chair staring into a mirror, carefully studying the reflections within, and I'm pretty certain that I'd never seen myself winking before.

At home on Gillycote Road.

I remember that the morning began reasonably well. I woke without needing the snooze button and the shower actually kept a steady temperature. Breakfast was okay, but then breakfast is always okay, coffee and Granola, I still like coffee and Granola for breakfast. Granola is great; it sets me up, keeps me going and clears me out all in one sitting. Coffee on the other hand is not so good. Caffeine argues with my herbal anxiety patch and makes me sweat. But hey, I like the taste of coffee and according to Homer (Simpson not the Greek chap) it does a man's soul good to take risks before lunchtime.

Up, fed and dressed, I grabbed my jacket and mobile phone and left the house a minute earlier than usual at 08:11, which was, of course, in itself unusual. I liked punctuality and routine; I needed punctuality and routine. Perhaps I still do. When I worked full time, I depended on being able to keep to my schedule, and that schedule depended on those around me being punctual. Even today, even in my present circumstances I try to keep to that good example.

I left home early because I am stupidly squeamish (a minor problem during my youth that in my later life became a positive handicap). The extra minute would get me to the bus stop in time to catch the 8.15 into town and thus avoid having to pass the gruesome corpse of a road kill badger. The luckless creature had been run over by something big and heavy and lay, squished like a half used tube of toothpaste, against the kerb of the pedestrian crossing at my end of Gillycote Road. I almost tripped over the wretched thing on my way home the previous evening. I reckoned it was a fair bet that neither the badger's appearance nor its smell would've improved overnight.

Alas my efforts turned out to be wasted, not because the number 17 bus was a full two and a half minutes late, which was bad enough, but because when the bus did arrive it was bursting with dozens of squealing pink piglets, each of the little sweeties garbed in foul shade of maroon and smelling of milk and Coco-pops. I took one look inside and quickly decided that confronting the festering Brock might not be so bad after all, walking to work in the quiet fresh air, I'd pinch my nose and squint.

It was only after I had decided against the bus ride that I realised what a beautiful morning I had woken to. The sky was blue, there was genuine warmth in the late October sun and a few of the local birds had come out for a twitter. I should have felt a spring in my step. I should have felt like Uncle Remus, *zippahdee doo dah*, deary me.

The walk from my home into town usually took about twenty-three minutes at a sensible pace. I'd managed it in eighteen minutes once but the exertion left me clammy round the armpits and made my knees ache for several days afterwards. Therefore, I set off with a moderate stride and my hopes for a good day still high. In the event, I passed the badger without too much trouble. The pedestrian crossing was busy with mothers and spotty children on their way to a local play-school and I was careful to avert both my eyes and nostrils at the crucial moment. I coped with the cries of 'Mum, its guts are hanging out' from the children, and only gagged briefly through my own ludicrous compulsion to turn at the last instant and confirm what I already knew. The remains of the badger looked absolutely disgusting. Why do we do that? I know it's not only me. Do we always need to prove the obvious, to sniff the mess on our shoe to know that dog-poo stinks?

Recovering my composure rapidly, I kept pace with myself perfectly for the rest of the walk, and at 08:26ish I rounded the corner onto the High Street. This wasn't my usual route to work. I would usually have taken a short cut behind the High Street, between the new St Mary's NHS medical centre and the courtyard development of town houses and smart apartments that adjoined the back of my salon. Today, however, I'd decided to reward my earlier fortitude with a treat from Starbucks coffee shop, a tall skinny latté' and large slice of sharp lemon cake. I cannot pretend that this was an entirely rare occurrence because it wasn't. However, I liked to reward my personal triumphs - however small they may be - with little treats. I confess, that since Starbucks opened in my town, the treats have become easier to earn and more frequently awarded than they probably should have been. I used to try to excuse my weakness by pointing out that I always drank my latté' skinny but then I started buying the cakes. The cakes were intended to be an occasional lunchtime indulgence. However, as I am being completely honest I will admit that, as I recall, only one slice of sharp lemon cake ever made it past elevenses, and there were odd days when I bought two slices and my latté was not so skinny.

In my town, Starbucks was small. I'd seen larger Starbucks in airport lounges and on railway platforms. My Starbucks had two two-seater settees, one three-seater settee and five tall bentwood chairs and that was it. There was almost always a queue, and if the queue consisted of more than six people then come rain or shine the seventh eighth and ninth queued outside. Therefore, as I walked along the High Street and approached my Starbucks, I was pissed off to see that there were at least ten people waiting in line. It wasn't that it was raining or even cold, the sky was still blue and the air was still fresh, but queuing outside a shop, worse, queuing outside a takeaway first thing in the morning. Forget the time it takes, it's just so demeaning, so bloody desperate. If Starbucks hadn't been the only supplier of sharp lemon cake, I would have taken my three pounds an eighty-five pence and marched straight to the Columbian Organic Coffee Kingdom, or whatever it's called.

Reluctantly, I took my place in line and wondered if Starbucks had a customer suggestion policy, they certainly should have had. Just standing there for those few minutes I came up with half a dozen solutions to their more obvious deficiencies. Simple ideas ranging from employing only

9

Japanese women who, in my experience, are always smiling, efficient, and wonderfully polite, to placing Starbucks kiosks outside Starbucks coffee shops so that we who are forced to queue can at least get a decent cup of coffee while we wait.

When my turn finally came, Colin, a young and sometimes surly lad with a country accent who had worked in the coffee shop for some time, smiled at me from behind the shiny Gaggia coffee machine while wiping down the froth-making-*doobreedangler*. Without any prompting at all (which quite took the wind from the wings of my intended whinge) Colin apologised for keeping me waiting so long and then asked me if I wanted my 'usual'. I remember feeling pretty cheesed off by his choice of words. Firstly, because I wanted Colin to be at his most arrogant and obnoxious best so that my irritation with the Starbuck Corporation could be properly vented, I enjoyed a good whinge, after the time I'd spent queuing, I deserved a good whinge. Secondly, how dare he suggest that I have a *'usual'*, I was a spontaneous, imaginative person… I did not have *'usuals'*. Favourites maybe, even preferred items but not *'usuals'*, *'usuals'* are for the hard of thinking regulars of the Old Nags Head.

Unfortunately before I had the chance to make my objections clear to Colin he was already wrapping me a large slice of sharp lemon cake and calling for a tall skinny latté'. I smiled back at him and said thank you.

Goodies in hand and my mood mellowing I left Starbucks at 08:42 or thereabouts and made straight for my salon.

Before nine o'clock and after five thirty my small salon could be a personal haven, my refuge from the world, but between those hours, when the doors are open to the public, my salon, like any other hairdressing salon took on a life of its own. On a Monday, it might be a theatre, full of life and laughter. On a Tuesday, my tilting hydraulic chair might double as a psychiatrist's couch. On a Wednesday, the reception area could become a ladies club, the washroom a dressing room for Prada or Gucci (*okay, in my town more likely M&S*), and, if I was feeling generous with my wine on a Friday afternoon, then there were times when the front of house made a good bar. At

10

least, I liked to think of it that way. My salon may have been small, but even when it finally became obvious to me that the business was slowly failing, I was happy to believe that it still retained a certain exclusivity, a professional 'je ne sais quoi' if you like, that other salon owners might yet envy.

Twenty years earlier, I might not have been quite so content. Twenty years earlier, I had grander plans. Plans to be the next Vidal Sassoon with a glittering career on TV and in the media. I would have been a Nicky Clarke. I had talent and opportunities; '*I shoulda been a contender*'. Not that I was bitter or disappointed... Good lord no! How could I have been disappointed? I still had a reasonable business, a beautiful home, a wonderful life... Why on Earth would I have begrudged my luckier contemporaries their more obvious successes?

I remember, as I turned the key in the lock, feeling disappointed that even so early the day seemed to be pushing against me. Something in the ether was nudging at my 'watch it' bump, fey and baseless perhaps but I am now, and I always have been, a sensitive soul, a chill here, a vibe there, the vaguest premonition and I'll feel it.

Struggling with my cake and coffee, I pushed at the door with my foot and was met by familiar air, a mixture of smells, of dusts and of moisture. Salons are like that, we hairdressers squirt lotions and potions at people and then wonder why our establishments smell peculiar. Publicans have the same problem with cheap food and beer slops, and hospitals with disinfectant, and the whiff of sickness and death.

At 08:46, now, remarkably, only one minute late, I stepped into my salon and took a bow. Of course, the salon was empty and from that point of view, my bow was an entirely redundant waste of energy. However, working mostly on my own by then, bowing to people who weren't there was just my way of starting the day, like singing in the shower; my bow was part of my morning ritual. Surely, most of us have a morning ritual, little things that we do either for luck or simply because it feels right and proper at the time. I knew a chap who cleaned his teeth obsessively on the tube from Willesden

Green to Baker Street every weekday morning, up and down on the London underground for twenty-three minutes... very pink gums. My brother used to fart in time to his favourite tunes on his car radio; he got quite good at it... *La Petomane* of the Watford Gap, he hated to run out of wind before the north Circular. And several years ago, I worked with a girl who'd spend the first half hour of every single morning sitting cross legged on her kitchen table with a magnifying glass and a pair of medical tweezers plucking her pubic hair. Her ex-boyfriend - actually, her very ex and bitter boyfriend - told me that if she hadn't dumped him in favour of his best friend (also now an Ex) he would have left her anyway because he kept finding the remnants of her pubic stubble in his shredded wheat.

So there we are... one of my little rituals was to begin each working day by bowing to a nonexistent audience, to my no longer employed staff, and to my not yet arrived clients.

...And that was when it happened.

At least that was when I first saw it, the wink, from my reflection in the mirror. It was just a casual glance as I walked past. I rarely looked at myself in the mirror back then. In fact, other than to check for the odd stray whisker or pickable spot unless I really have to I still don't. I suppose if you've spent thirty years looking at other people's reflections you stop bothering with your own. Besides, I knew what I looked like and hardly a day went by without some smart Alec reminding me of my resemblance to Paul Newman... I wish, I wish, I wish.

Although the wink caught me by surprise and I was fairly certain that my face hadn't moved, I wasn't unduly upset by seeing it, after all a wink is a wink, even if this one did come unbidden from my own reflection. I tried to put it down to some kind of numb spasm and almost managed to convince myself that I had winked involuntarily and simply not felt my eyelid move. Obviously, I know better now, but then hindsight is such a convenient thing. However, despite my denial I spent the rest of the morning trying to avoid catching my own eye in the mirror. In fact, it became a bit of a game and I scored well. By lunchtime, I'd cut and blow dried five heads of hair, and had even chatted with a couple of the more agreeable ladies, without so much as a twitch of an eyebrow. I felt pretty safe.

I ate my lunch, as I often did, sitting at the reception desk answering the telephone and studying the appointment book. About two thirds of the way through a scrummy Brie and bacon baguette, forgetting the wink for a moment, I began to realise that while the morning had been a straightforward snip and puff, the afternoon was likely to be more challenging.

I had run my modest but exclusive salon, complete with its tad of professional je ne sais quoi, for nineteen years before I saw that first wink. During that time, I passed from my twenties through my thirties and into my forties, I'd aged and most of my regular clients had aged with me. Over the years, I had built quite a following of gently maturing ladies who appreciated my creative tonsorial skills. Some of them were lovely, some of them were hideous, and many of them became good friends. I suppose it was a natural progression. After all, I spent a half hour or more, once or twice a week with most of them, gossiping about holidays and grandchildren, or Coronation Street and Golf, even wayward husbands and erstwhile lovers. I suppose I got to know many of my ladies pretty well. However, unlike most personal relationships, when things don't work out quite so nicely, where a lover might run for a bolthole, or a husband or wife might throw in the towel, remarkably, perhaps sadly, for the sake of a decent haircut, no matter what, some clients will always come back.

The day I opened my salon has etched itself into my mind for several reasons. It was the day that while shopping for a celebratory meal I discovered Marks and Sparks baked black cherry cheesecake tart. An indulgence that became my absolute favourite dessert of all time ever, and that was quite outrageously removed from my local M&S after only a year on sale (in their international stores they do still carry the blueberry version but it's a pale imitation). Opening day was also the last time I slept with a real live person, although, as that is a subject that may crop up later on, two words will have to suffice, 'disappointing' and 'uncomfortable'. But perhaps most poignant to this part of my story, July 17th was the day I met the evil widow, Mrs Marjorie Warton, a bumptious woman who unwittingly changed the path of my life.

Large and always over powdered the Wart hog…

A pause here - I should explain that when I had my own salon to help with my often appalling memory I would occasionally give my clients nicknames, some polite and some not so, but most reflecting either a physical characteristic or the general demeanour of the particular customer. In Minging Marjorie Warton's case, I managed both by focusing on a simple play on words and her uncanny facial resemblance to the less attractive members of the porcine family. Thus, after almost a whole minute of strenuous thought, I came up with the nicely unsubtle 'Wart…Hog'. Childish, but my inner rascal grinned victoriously whenever I thought of the truffle-snuffler. Where was I…?

Large and always over powdered the Wart hog lived in an expensive penthouse apartment adjacent to but high above my salon. Undoubtedly, a clever woman, she had built an impressive personal fortune through local business and real estate. Now in retirement, the Wart hog used the fruits of her labours to spoil and pamper herself, and was generally considered, by those who knew her best, to be a selfish, first class pain in the arse. Thankfully, as far as my business was concerned, Minging Marjorie was an atypical punter. A rare rogue client, who, convinced of her own supreme importance, bullied her way through the town and my salon, seeming to think that the best way to ensure good service was to moan and whinge and to be as thoroughly obnoxious as she possibly could be.

'Tell him I want to be seen straight away, I need to be out by three.' were the first words that I ever heard her utter. Alas, due to my need of new business at the time, they were words that would haunt me at 2.15 on every Tuesday and Friday from that day on… bugger.

The final mouthful of my baguette was a goody. I had carefully eaten around a large sloppy lump of brie and particularly crisp curl of bacon saving the best until last (this is not an indication that I have an unusually sharp memory it is simply something that I always would have done, I like the slurpy scrunchy bits of life).

I waited for Marjorie Warton to arrive. Her appointment was earlier than usual, at 1.45 for a permanent wave and a cut and blow dry, a nice little earner for me, that taking three hours would have been even nicer if it hadn't been for old misery guts. I just thanked god I'd not been born a chair, having to suffer those billowing buttocks wedge between my arms for one hundred and eighty painful minutes; my hydraulic lift would've wilted and probably dropped off. I'd taken the precaution of clearing my book around the appointment so that the Wart hog would be my only client, at least that way no one else would have to suffer her incessant whining.

Minging Marjorie arrived precisely to time, punctuality her only concession to my sensitivities.

'I'm here.' She shrieked, shoving the salon door so hard with her fat hip that it bashed into the reception desk. '...And you can have me all afternoon you lucky boy, I don't have to be out until five.'

'Marvellous.' I said, and then I screwed my lunch bag into a ball and threw it into the waste bin, adding under my breath 'bloody marvellous.'

I struggle to remember exactly how the rest of the afternoon played out. I'm sure that it would have been punctuated by grumbles and whinging, by 'Ooh that hurts' and 'Ah It's trickling down my neck' or 'I can afford the best you know I don't have to put up with this'. She was like the annoying creak from old central heating pipes, tic-tic-tic tut-tut-tut, they drive you mad but you need the warmth (or the dosh in the Hog's case) that they provide. Over the years, my brain had learned to switch off to most of the rubbish, self-defence I suppose. At some stage I must have wound curlers into her hair, and I'm sure that I doused her down with some foul smelling chemical solution, and I probably sat her under a dryer to speed things up a bit. I don't actually remember. However, I do remember the telephone ringing and after I picked up the receiver, I do remember listening for a long, long time. The caller was my uncle Bert, my mother's elder brother. Bert was one of life's good guys and although we rarely spoke whatever he might have been interrupting I'd usually have been happy to hear from him. However, that afternoon alas, Bert's call was one of those that most people dread. A familiar but solemn voice tuned to deliver bad news. Somehow, I knew what was coming... my Mother had died. It was awful. In her armchair watching Richard and Judy, just like that.

My Mum was the kindest loveliest cuddliest woman in the whole world and I'd sort of forgotten that she was gradually becoming an old lady and that one day she was going to die.

When Bert hung up, I stopped thinking in real time and forgot myself for a moment, and just stared out of the window, day dreaming half-lit pictures of my Mum's happy face in the sky. When a cloud bobbled by and took my pictures away, my eyes fell to the ground, to the pavement, to a couple of pigeons that were bickering over a scrap of burger bun that some careless slob had thrown into the gutter. When their fight didn't settle which of them should eat the bun, the blessed pigeons started to shag... sex... huh... always the easy option.

'Coffeeeee?' The pitch was ear splitting.

I don't remember whether the Wart hog asked politely (I doubt it), or whether it came squealed or as a barked command, but the shrillness of her voice snapped me back to that sour moment of reality. I grunted a reply and shuffled from my place by the window. If she'd only opened her eyes to someone else for more than a second she'd have known something was wrong. She'd have seen the enormous icicle sticking out of my chest. She didn't of course' Why should she, she was too busy thinking about herself... it's a popular hobby. Just a shame it wasn't Minging Marjorie Warton in that chair with Richard and Judy.

I made myself a cup of tea before I made the Wart hog coffee and I put four sugars in it, a cup of tea in my favourite mug, a cup of tea that I knew I wouldn't drink, I hate sweet tea... not like my Mum.

I gave myself a few minutes before I took the coffee out to the salon. I'd made it properly, no spit or bogeys. She

16

didn't say thank you and I didn't care. I didn't tell her my news.

I went through the rest of the hairdressing process that afternoon on autopilot. It was all simple stuff and a treatment that I'd performed a hundred times before. I cannot pretend that I was paying much attention, although when I began to rinse the perm solution out of the hair, I realised that I probably should have been. As the pink froth swirled away down the plughole, the warm water from the showerhead revealed a reddened scalp and matted clumps of hair that had turned into a squidgy pale lemon mush. My disgustingly expensive permanent wave had seriously over cooked... bugger.

Despite the fact that by any standard I was having a bad day, I tried to stay calm, and for a while at least I managed quite well. Once I'd rinsed the bulk of the nasty bits down the plughole, I made the few repairs that were possible at the basin, and then wrapped Minging Marjorie's hair in a towel, and led her to a chair as far from the shop window as possible. I sat her between a bushy variegated fig tree (itself in need of a haircut) and a large floor to ceiling mirror where I usually carried out the less glamorous procedures. The last thing I needed was for passersby to see what I had done to the wretched woman. Of course, she quickly guessed that something was wrong. She'd been visiting the salon twice a week every week for nineteen years by then for god sake. She knew that she always sat in the same place for a cut or a blow dry, in the chair by the window, my favourite chair, just as everybody else did. As soon as she sat down, she leaned forward, peered into the mirror, and started picking at her hair.

'It's yellow' she said coldly 'and it feels slimy.'

Of course, at that point, she still had no idea either how bad the problem actually was or whether I'd be able put it right, and to be honest, neither did I. While the sorry mess that I'd created could still be loosely described as hair, in that it still appeared to be reasonably well attached to the Wart hog's head and if left alone it would have probably continued to grow, what we both saw reflected in the mirror more resembled clumps of wet cotton wool.

Forget professional ego, I cannot pretend that I'd never had to deal with this sort of crisis before; nobody is perfect. Thirty years in the trade and of course I'd experienced the odd disaster… just never anything quite so obviously horrible.

I tried to bluff my way out of the situation but my voice was lost in a knot of acid and wedged somewhere between the pit of my stomach and my bladder. Instead, I reached for my scissors and comb and started to move Minging Marjorie W's head from side to side, studying her reflection carefully as if trying to decide on a new style. She might have bought into the ruse more readily if I'd had the sense to keep my comb away from her head. I barely flicked the thing at a knotty mass above her right ear and the whole piece of hair came away from the scalp.

'Good god,' she shrieked, 'you stupid, stupid man!'

'Shit!' I gasped and swiftly shook the offending tangle from my comb away across the floor. The slimy glob slithered into the skirting board with an audible splat, a noise that seemed to mark the moment of my doom.

A million useless excuses flashed through my mind, but none gave me a hope of escape. So I just stood there, staring into the mirror, with my mouth slightly open, and with the freakiest hint of a smile on my lips, and waited for the tirade to begin. Then, several things happened simultaneously. I felt a cracking sensation between my ears, like the sound an ice-cube makes when it's dropped into hot water. My vision seemed to shift very slightly sideways, to the left I think, and maybe up.

And then I caught my reflection winking again.

My comb dropped to the floor and my hands dropped onto Marjorie Warton's shoulders. Marjorie Warton's eyes seemed to freeze and then my reflection spoke to me.

'Who cares?' It said… or maybe I said. Whichever it was, I saw my lips move and the words reached my ears as clearly and as sharply as a dog barking on a winter night.

'No one cares.'

_____

18

Marjorie Warton was very still, I looked down at her head.

'I'm terribly sorry.' I said.

More of her hair had come away and some of the redness on her scalp had started to glisten. I couldn't believe that she hadn't noticed the chemicals scalding her. She was a tough old boot, but surely, it must have really stung. At the back of her neck, immediately below the hairline, the polished handles of my scissors stuck out like some crazy Frankenstein-esque body piercing, leaving four inches of razor sharp Japanese steel firmly imbedded between the bones. There was no blood, well… very little, not enough to turn my stomach. Just the polished handles and a trickle of pink that had all but soaked into the brown and tan chequered towel that I'd wrapped round her neck.

'It's such a nuisance.' I heard myself sigh. My hands were still on her shoulders and I was staring at my reflection. Staring into my own eyes, grey with a bit of blue and maybe some green… and tired, really very tired, I didn't wink.

I stood there for some time, twenty minutes, maybe more. I didn't dare let go. She was dead and I was petrified. If I'd moved away, she would have toppled to the floor.

Someone sent me a funny birthday card a few years before all this happened and for some reason I chose that moment to remember it. On the front cover was a gruesome picture of a maniacal dentist pulling at a huge molar in the mouth of a patient. Inside the card, and the dentist had finally pulled the thing, but attached to the root of the tooth was the patient's brain. A caption read simply 'Whoops'. It didn't seem so funny anymore.

'Bugger.' I sobbed.

19

CHAPTER TWO

Standing six foot seven inches and weighing in at over three hundred pounds, Tristan Blandy, the wild child youngest and 'bit-of-a-surprise' son of my eldest cousin was not the sort of chap you could easily miss. Tristan had lived in my neck of the woods since the day after his sixteenth birthday when his mother threw him out of the family home. She called me one day, completely out of the blue, saying that she couldn't cope with him anymore, that she'd found him a bed in a hostel close to where I was living, and was otherwise unleashing him on an unsuspecting world.

'He's just like his father'. She cried into the telephone 'He's a monster. He's always in trouble. If he ever goes to school, he comes home drunk, and if I try to tell him off, he just laughs at me. I've had enough'

Why on Earth she pointed her son in my direction I'll never know, but as I'm sure you will have already guessed, I was thrilled; it's not every day that one is sent a gorilla after all.

I wish I could say that I did my best for the lad, that as a good second cousin I tried to help the afterthought kid through those most difficult years. I'd like to be able to tell you that I was there for him when he needed me most and that I'd helped him settle down and become a worthy member of the local community. Alas, none of the above is particularly true. The reality is that at the first sign of trouble I threw in the towel and that for ten years, while Tristan grew from a wayward youth into a hopeless man, I kept my head very well down. Tristan's behaviour did nothing to weaken my resolve either, from time to time I'd spot a headline in the local newspaper, *'Fiend devours live pigeon in Library.'* or *'Drunken maniac survives electrocution; Police rescue local giant from top of lamp post.'* just a couple of his less offensive exploits. So long as no-one knew that Tristan was my cousin, tales of his wild antics made quite entertaining reading.

Therefore, I confess, that despite the plea from Tristan's mother, I hardly put myself out to help the lad at all. I never really did the right *family* thing. My guilty gene knows that I should have done more, but I was a busy chap back then and still suffering from the selfishness of youth myself. For me the situation was a no brainer. Tristan was a bad lad, he always had been and he always would be; blood-ties aside he was nothing to do with me.

Then one day, after a particularly nasty punch-up in a local nightclub, Tristan surprised us all. I've heard the story a dozen times. How he arrived late at the club to find his girlfriend of the day in a clinch with another man. I've heard how the fight started and why so many people became involved. I've heard who threw the first punch and who threw the last. And I've heard a dozen times at least how Tristan, after delivering a savage beating, looked into the bloodied face of his victim and in it met his own personal epiphany... and found God.

For the next five years, Tristan went to church twice a day every day. He became everybody's friend, everybody's helper, and everybody's favourite blessing giver. I suspect that since that wonderful day I have been blessed and forgiven tens of thousands of times by Tristan... the Christian. And please don't think that I'm not appreciative, because I am. Just as I am appreciative of fellow ex-smokers who insist that I remain pure to breathe and enjoy un-smelly air, or of ex-drinkers who need me to know that my triple vodka is actually a poison and will probably kill me... I like to be blessed.

So, when a large shadow crossed the front window of my salon and when the sound of the front door opening was followed by a cheery 'Hallooee', even in my state of panic with a very dead client sitting in front of me, I knew I was about to be *Tristaned*.

'Stop!'

I tried to yell.

'Do not move.'

Or at least to raise my voice.

'Stay exactly where you are.'

But the noise that came from my mouth.

'I am very, very, busy.'

Sounded more like an excited Stephen Hawking than a confident hairdresser dealing with a minor interruption.

'I think I can do that for you.' Tristan shrugged and then froze in an animated pose like a caricature statue of superman. I could see his broad mouth grinning in the mirror, although thanks to the bushy fig tree, he couldn't easily see me and he couldn't see Marjorie Warton at all.

'I'm sorry.' I stammered, desperately trying to pull myself together. 'My lady's dropped off to sleep,' I lowered my voice until it began to sound a touch more natural. 'I don't want to startle her. Look Tris, I really am a bit busy right now can you come back later on?'

'I certainly could old chap, half an hour okay?' He asked.

'That's great, I'll see you later.'

'Okeedokee, *see you later mashed p'tater...*' He sang, I heard the door click shut and then almost instantly click open again '...and God bless you man.' Tristan called back before I heard it finally close.

'I don't think he will.' I breathed. 'Not today... not now.'

Looking back, I could probably argue that Tristan's surprise visit was responsible, in part at least, for my present circumstances. I could suggest that if he hadn't turned up on that sunny late October afternoon the long chain of events that led to my arrest and incarceration might never have begun. On the other hand I'd have to admit that as just before he arrived I'd skewered one of my clients and I really didn't want to get caught, the seeds of those future events had probably already sunk a pretty firm root.

The Clunk of the front door closing sparked my system into what I now think of as my *self-preservation mode*, maybe a state of mind above or outside that which I'd usually consider either acceptable or entirely safe. Children know the place well; when the shit hits the fan, even the cutest of kids will deceive to survive. Civilisation and fear tame most of us by adulthood. In the 21st century, a jolt from our adrenal gland just leaves most of us feeling anxious or randy.

I looked up at myself in the mirror, my feet were braced well apart to the left and right of Mrs Warton, and my hands were resting on her shoulders, as if I had been pushing her down. I was sweating. Mrs Warton had slumped low in the chair. I needed to do something quickly. I needed to save myself. I reached under her arms and linking my hands across her chest, I heaved her back up into a sitting position. To hold the pose I slid the chair forward until her knees were wedged firmly against the wall, then I let go and stepped back. She didn't move. Apart from the state of her hair and the unfortunate protrusion from her neck, she looked fine.

Moving slowly and deliberately I closed down the salon. As I locked the doors and pulled the blinds the distant bells of St Michael's Church sounded four, a tad early to shut up shop but nothing that I hadn't done before. Despite the autumn sunshine, there weren't many people on the street outside, no one to nod to or who would notice if I were gone. I flipped the closed sign on the door and turned out the lights.

My salon comprised of two rooms each roughly twenty feet square. The front room was the main working area, 'the salon', while the back room was divided into three equal parts, a washroom, a staffroom and a store. In between the rooms ran a passageway that led to the back door and to a space where I kept several larger items that I had no real use for but that my mean streak wouldn't let me throw out, a few old roller trolleys, a couple of worn out chairs, and a large red wheelie-bin.

I knew what I had to do.

After moving the chairs out of the way and carefully propping them outside the back door, I eased the wheelie-bin along the passageway and into the salon. Unusually, Marjorie Warton was being very quiet and hadn't moved at all. Laying the bin on its side, I pushed it along the wall closest to the fig tree, between the Mirror and the chair where I had sat Mrs Warton, and then I started to lower both the chair and Mrs Warton to the floor. Although she was a hefty woman, and I never have been a particularly muscular man, it was actually quite easy and I got her to ground without any bumps at all. That was when my problems began.

Even as I was preparing to shove one of my wealthier clients into a battered old wheelie-bin, I was conscious of her

23

comfort and safety. I wanted her to travel upright at the very least. I hoped that by lifting her legs I'd be able to slide the wheelie-bin under her, reckoning that by applying the same method - in neat and tidy succession - the bin would eventually swallow her hips, chest, arms and head. Alas not... I managed to deal with her legs easily enough, but when confronted with Marjorie Warton's nether regions, the wheelie-bin simply would not move. I twisted and shoved but she wouldn't go in. The bits of her that weren't too heavy were just too floppy, and the bits that stayed put seemed to weigh a ton.

For over thirty years, I'd done my utmost to make sure that all of my clients received a good and considerate service, even the horrible ones. I found it incredibly frustrating that during this one single appointment so many things had gone so dreadfully wrong.

Having decided that for the sake of practical packing, dignity would have to be sacrificed, I lifted Mrs Warton's legs out of the bin and rolled her back into the tilted chair. However, now raising the chair was not so straightforward. Each time I took the strain Mrs Warton sagged sideways, twisting the base of the chair in towards my legs, almost tipping her out. Eventually I resorted to tying her to the chair with bandages from the first aid kit. Then I spun the chair around and using my own weight as a counter balance I pulled both of them upright. Back where I'd started, I dragged the wheelie-bin away from the wall, turned it on its end and then dropped it over Marjorie Warton's head. It seems terribly callous now, but then what else could I do.

Righting the Wheelie-bin was less of a struggle. Once it started to move and Marjorie Warton slid further to the bottom, like a giant wobbling Weeble, the bin almost righted itself. I peered inside and reached to untie the bandages and to retrieve the chair, Marjorie Warton looked smaller, and crumpled, and well... upside down. After apologising for the inconvenience, I swung the lid shut, and using three rolls of gaffer tape, I sealed her inside.

It only took me a few minutes to tidy the salon. I popped all the towels and gowns into the washing machine on a good hot wash. I wiped down all the work surfaces and mopped the floor. I rinsed the curlers and cleaned my tools and by half past four, with the battered red wheelie-bin ready to roll, I put my jacket on and made for the door.

'Hallooee.' Tristan the Christian's husky voice sang tunefully from outside. I'd completely forgotten that I had asked him to come back.

'Yoohoo-oo.' He called; he was at the back door. 'I thought I might have missed you.'

'*Oh I wish you had*' I thought and shook my head.

'I saw you through the window, I saw you shoving that bloody great bin around, it looked seriously heavy... it looked like you could do with a hand.' It was so typically *new* Tristan, always full of nosey well-meaning interference.

'I'm fine, really I'm fine... I can manage.' I said trying to convince him, but even through my own ears, all I heard was a strangulated croak.

'That's okay Matey, you sound knackered... don't worry, I got the afternoon off work today so I'm happy to lend a hand.'

'Honestly Tristan', I said, putting my mouth close to the door and softening my voice. 'Honestly... I can manage'

I prayed that he'd get fed up and just go away.

'What yer got in the bin then?'

I should have guessed that the question was coming, that it was only a matter of time before Tristan's 'prying head' would need to know what his cousin had been doing with a battered old wheelie-bin.

'Just rubbish that's all,' I fibbed, gathering my thoughts quickly. 'Some old stock, I've been having a bit of a clear out.'

'Well there you are then Matey, that's sorted it for definite. I've my pick-up truck round the corner. I can run you to the tip... you see? I knew I could help.'

There comes a time in any crisis when it is probably best to stop struggling and instead pay some attention to what it is that you're are actually struggling against. Although I had successfully sealed Marjorie Warton into the wheelie-bin, I hadn't a clue what I was going to do with her. My scant plan ended just outside the back door of my salon. Not terribly clever or inventive I grant you, but I was still in a daze, I just wanted the whole fiasco over. However, Tristan's suggestion set my mind buzzing. Maybe his pick-up truck was the answer, maybe, if I were careful, with a spot creative management Tristan would be able to help me after all.

I opened the door.

'The thing is Tristan,' I leaned out through the gap and beckoned him closer. 'The trouble is that I've filled the bin with all my old chemicals and stuff, the kind of stuff that you're supposed to pay to tip.' Tristan nodded knowingly. 'It's not dangerous.' I continued. 'It's an environmental thing. I'm supposed to get *green* and buy a licence from the council, but I know they just chuck it in with the rest of the rubbish and then they'll bury it in a great big hole. I don't see why I should have to pay them any extra.'

'Aha... I knew you were up to something crafty,' Tristan tapped the side of his nose and closed one eye, 'and I don't blame you Matey... bloody council, bloody *greenies*. But you didn't need to hide it from me.' He said shaking his head. 'We're family... and I can help'. Then he leaned in closer and whispered, 'I have a friend up at the tip.' He made a peculiar face and waited for me to show some sign of approval, I duly nodded. 'Nothing illegal of course,' he frowned, 'but for the price of a pint he'll make sure that whatever you take up there stays up there and is properly disposed off... nothing left over and no questions asked'.

The County councils household and industrial waste recycling and reclamation centre was a spectacular and contradictory monument to environmental salvage. Set on the side of a three cornered valley and proudly visible from miles around the site came straight from the set of a sci-fi movie. A moonscape corrupted by pen pushers, environmentalists and engineers who presumably lived on the other side of town. Dozens of concrete silos and heavy high tech machines spread in perfect order over God knows how many acres and surrounded by more chain link and barbed wire than Alcatraz ever saw. And below it all were mountains, not beautiful crags of rock and snow, but ugly slag heaps of tyres, and asphalt, and of glass, and squashed beer cans, nothing remotely green at all. Naively, and given what I was proposing to do, probably quite unreasonably, I was shocked.

'We'll have to drive up to the weigh bridge.' Tristan said pointing vaguely towards a separate enclosure fronted by a large pair of gates further up the hill. 'Ripper works the scales see, no one gets in or out of the industrial tip without his okay… but no worries,' he nodded, 'Ripper's cool.'

I used every ounce of self-control to make my face to smile.

'Ripper,' I said. 'He's your Pal?'

'I met him at a prayer meeting a few years ago, he's gentle as a lamb these days.'

'And before?' I asked.

'Come on Matey… Ripper's not his real name.'

I swallowed hard and hoped for the best.

At 4.58pm, two minutes before Francis 'Ripper' Dobson clocked off for the day, Tristan pulled his pick-up truck between the gates and onto the weighbridge. A moment later, a few yards to the right, the door to a yellow painted hut swung open, and an enormous hairy man, bigger and hairier even than Tristan, stepped out.

'Rriipperrrr!' Tristan bellowed, and then my second cousin opened the door and jumped from the truck and ran towards the bigger, hairier man. The noise of his bellow alone knocked me sideways.

Watching the two huge men greet each other was like viewing a scene from Wild life TV, an up-close and unpleasantly personal documentary on animal habits, perhaps. It was like watching male buffalo rut. First, the foreheads met, smacking hard with an audible thud. Then came the chests, proudly thrust forward they bounced together two, three, four times. I'd have been flattened by the first bump. Finally, they hugged, if I hadn't been so painfully wound up, and the two brutes hadn't been… well… so brutal, it might have been touching. When they'd finished their display I heard Tristan mumble something to his friend, I heard my name, and then saw him point to the wheelie-bin that we'd strapped into the back of his truck. Ripper looked first at me and then at the bin, he closed one eye, and then scratched at his bristly chin while apparently thinking. An image of Blutto from Popeye sprang to mind. A moment later, the big man nodded to Tristan and held up his hands splaying all ten fingers. At first Tristan didn't appear to be too impressed, but after saying something that made Ripper laugh he threw back his head and with an unusually camp gesture, he ran his hands through his hair. Then both men laughed and then Tristan came back to the truck motioning to me to open the window.

'No prob's Matey,' he called, and then added with a grin. 'But you're going to have sort his missus' with a haircut… is that okay?'

He seemed to be so pleased with himself and I was so relieved that I grinned back, and while bobbing my head up and down like a nodding dog, and wondering what the heck a woman who would hitch herself to a man called Ripper might look like, I babbled, 'Lovely yes… that would be great, smashing, I'd love to cut Mrs Ripper's hair, I really would.'

Tristan climbed back into the cab and slapped my thigh quite hard. He didn't say anything, but I guessed that in his eyes our little adventure was becoming something of a bonding exercise; we were spending quality time together doing stuff… I reckoned that a blessing probably wouldn't be far off.

We drove further up the hill followed by Ripper who was now riding a noisy quad bike. He passed us as we rounded a left hand bend and took a narrow ramp that led up to the wheels of an enormous mechanical something-or-other. Tristan stopped the truck in front of, but well below, the machine.

'So… um, what do we do now?' I asked. I liked to ask succinct, pertinent, and well thought out questions.

'We'd better untie the bin I reckon.' Tristan shrugged an eyebrow. 'Otherwise you, and me, and the truck will all get hoisted into the *Masher* too.'

'The *Masher*.' I mouthed into empty space. Although I didn't know which machine the *Masher* actually was, the name gave me a good idea of what it did.

When Tristan first mentioned taking the bin to the tip, I suppose that I thought, or hoped, that Marjorie Warton was going to be buried. Okay, I'd accepted that the coffin and graveyard would be a touch unconventional, but at least she would be underground.

'Oh my God!' I remember thinking as I looked up at the colossal machine, then, 'Does it really matter?' I asked myself. I screwed my eyes tightly shut.

'You okay Matey? Come on, let's get on with it.' Tristan gave me a playful punch on the arm, and then opened the door, reached behind the cab to grab the ladder bar, and then swung himself round into the back of the truck.

While we were untying the wheelie-bin, I noticed that some of the gaffer tape had peeled away from the lid. I'd no doubt that the remaining tape would have held perfectly well under normal circumstances. However, the machine that I had seen Ripper climb into was truly scary, a gigantic orange lobster with claws of steel that hung from enormous hydraulic arms. One smallest false move and I knew that the powerful claw could easily burst the wheelie-bin open, sending Mrs Warton crashing to the ground for everyone to see. I suddenly realised that I was about to entrust my liberty and perhaps even my life to one hairy man's control of a monstrous machine.

When I think back to that day, and I often do, I wonder at the many ways what happened with Marjorie Warton changed my life. I learned that when the chips are down, I can do almost anything, is probably the most obvious example. However, I also discovered that a good dose of stress helps to shed unwanted pounds more quickly than any fad diet ever can, and that I can hold my breath for a very long time. Today, David Blaine holds the World record for holding his breath, with a ridiculous and soggy seventeen and a half minute effort spent underwater on the Oprah Winfrey show. I cannot pretend to be able to do anything like that, but I know that on that peculiar day there were several occasions when I stopped breathing for minutes on end, and that when I did start breathing again, I sucked in such great rasping lungfuls of air that I thought my chest might explode.

This was one of those moments.

When I recovered my senses, Tristan lifted me from the back of the truck and then hauled me up the fifteen-foot shale slope between the pick-up and the orange lobster. The Masher was behind the lobster. Ripper started the engines; there were sirens and flashing lights.

'Course we're s'posed to wear hard hats and hi-viz vests.' Tristan shouted to me, I could barely hear him over the din.

'Health and safety, Matey, but seeing as we're not really here… nobody's gonna know.'

'No one cares.' I muttered, and attempted a smile.

Ahead of us, the engines roared even louder as the lobster's claw started to move. Ripper waved to us, beckoning us up to the cab where he was sitting. Tristan led the way up the steel ladder then turned to offer me his hand. In that second, I caught his eye and for a fleeting moment, I glimpsed my father. I'd never noticed the resemblance before. My father had been a tall man – apart from me we are a tall family - but nowhere near the size of Tristan. I reached and took his hand.

'Wanna 'ave a go?' Ripper asked me as I eased my way into the lobster's cab.

'I'd probably break something.' I shouted back shaking my head and trying my hardest to smile. I noticed Tristan look at Ripper with a sappy hopeful grin, like a kid who wants to play with his best friend's new toy. I was already terrified that at any moment Marjorie Warton would be dangling out of a squished wheelie-bin. The last thing I needed was for a novice to take control of the machine. I pushed myself between them and yelled 'Maybe you could show me how it's done Mr Ripper; it looks awfully complicated to me. Driving this beast must take years of practice.'

I'm a clever sausage sometimes, he bit straight away.

'Well guv'nor,' he said 'yer not wrong, it does take a bit of getting used to, that's for sure. Especially when we're s'posed to be being a bit fly like. I'll show yer how it's done.'

The engines roared again and Ripper started work. It was like watching the ad for Renault or Toyota, the one with the precision robots all whirring and bleeping. A flip of a button here and a careful roll of the wrist there and the lobster's claw moved gracefully over Tristan's pick-up truck. It was all so quick. Within a few seconds, my old wheelie-bin was high in the air whisking its way towards the *Masher*. As the hydraulic arm neared its goal, a series of lights began to flash below and two long horizontal doors opened revealing the *Masher's* belly, a cavernous pit of churning metal. And it was then that Ripper turned the dial or pulled the leaver or hit the switch that released the wheelie-bin. Down it fell in painful slow motion. My whole body started leaking. Slower and slower, and frame-by-frame it fell, and then to my horror, my battered old red wheelie-bin hit the side of the *Masher*. It hit the side and then bounced off one of the doors and split open, somersaulting Marjorie Warton deep inside the grinding metalwork of the awful machine.

'Did you see that?' Ripper shouted. My pounding heart sank to my feet, my scalp tingled, and my bladder almost burst.

'Yes I bloody did.' Tristan replied. I slumped to floor, my head was swimming and I think I may have started to sob.

'Can you believe that anyone would use a Ferrari 355 GTS to bring their old crap to the tip?' Ripper sighed, shaking his head in disbelief. I looked up and followed my second cousins eyes.

'It's a 360 Modena.' He said gazing off somewhere distant.'

'Bollocks it is… I know my Italians.'

I stretched from the floor to peek out through the lobster's window. Twenty feet below me the *Masher's* doors were closing on Marjorie Warton. Tristan and Ripper continued to squabble, while on the far side of the tip, its paintwork gleaming in the sinking sun, I saw a brand new red Ferrari pulling away.

At three O'clock in the morning, I gave up on the idea of sleeping and made myself a cup of tea.

The world outside my kitchen window seemed a different place, changed somehow, the air heavier and the night darker, as if some of the colours had seeped away.

I wasn't surprised that I couldn't sleep. I'd expected to be wracked by guilt, or by remorse, or fear. I had a feeling that I might never sleep properly again. What I hadn't expected, was to spend those restless hours thinking about my family, my mother and my father, my cousins, and my aunts and uncles. Marjorie Warton's untimely end had dominated so much of the day that it wasn't until Tristan dropped me back at Gillycote Road that I remembered my uncle's telephone call. My mother had died and now, because of me, and my glib thoughtless act, so had someone else's.

In an odd way, Mrs Warton reminded me of my Grandmother, my mother's mother. Although separated by a generation they seemed to share a common nasty streak. My grandmother was a mean woman, even as a child I knew she didn't deserve my love. I grew up dreading every visit and loathing every kiss. Then one day she had a stroke, I was thirteen years old when it happened. My father told me that half of her had died. To keep him happy I went to see her in hospital. He was right. Half of her had died. One arm, one leg and half of her face, it turned out that it was the nasty half. From that day on, my Grandmother and I were fine. The rest of the old love hung on until I was thirty-five. She spent twenty-two years smiling from a wheelchair. The sad thing is that she only became a happy person when she had a miserable life. Mrs Warton had a mean streak just like my grandmother. She seemed to have everything, but I doubted that she'd ever been happy, and now I'd probably ruined her chances.

My mother, on the other hand, was always happy.

I finished my tea and took the empty cup over to the dishwasher. As I bent to pull the door open, a beam of light flashed across the kitchen followed quickly by another. I heard a gentle squeal of breaks and then an engine idle and die. I waited, I heard footsteps, and I looked out of the window. Two uniformed policemen were walking up my garden path.

CHAPTER THREE

They say that you know you're getting older when policemen start to look as if they should still be at school.

The two police officers outside my house looked very young and I was certainly feeling older. I remember feeling pretty awful when they knocked at my door. I remember pulling my dressing gown close and curling my toes into my slippers.

I was once invited to a passing out ceremony at the Metropolitan police college in Hendon, North London. A younger cousin on my father's side, who because of our age difference I'd always thought of and referred to as a niece, had completed the six months' basic training and was about to be released onto the streets of our capital. A lively cheerful girl, she had invited me to her passing out, not because our knot of the clan was particularly close, but because as a good and upstanding member of the community I'd once written her a reference. I don't think my niece or her immediate family expected me to accept the invitation, but 'what the heck', I thought, the event coincided with a day off and it might've been fun. As it happened, the head-honchos at the Police Training College made certain that any hint of fun was sucked clear of the place well before anyone arrived for the ceremony. Nevertheless, early on a warm July morning, with my hopes of an interesting day-out still reasonably high, I travelled from my home to London, and took the Northern line to Colindale for Hendon.

On the site of an old aerodrome, the college campus dominated a large area east of the M1 and west of the North-circular Road. I arrived later than I'd hoped, and after skirting what felt like miles of the tightly fenced perimeter, I was hot and sticky. Although I'd hurried, by the time I found a seat in at least partial shade, the passing out parade had already begun. A band was playing, flags were waving and the fresh faced recruits were... well... I'd like to say that they were marching. However, with one or two exceptions, most notably my niece, the procession around the parade ground more resembled a junior school sponsored walk. One hundred or more expensively trained officers, and most of them couldn't even walk to a beat let alone police one.

After half an hour of parading came the ceremony, a chance for the big wigs to pontificate and for the better trainees to shine. Those assembled were ushered from the parade ground into a sports hall where plastic chairs had been lined, and despite the afternoon sunshine, it felt like the heating turned up. I took my seat at the end of a row near to the front of the hall where an open window offered me the hope of some fresh air. Again, apart from my niece's sensibly laconic three-word speech when presented with her best student award - 'Thanks very much' - the occasion was a fiasco. Of the seven senior officers seated on the podium, two fell asleep, two couldn't stop scratching themselves, and the most senior, a chief superintendant who looked like a bulldog and was supposed to be holding the event together, fell of his chair.

The experience left me with the firm conviction that a great many of our wonderful police officers probably *should* still be at school.

I tried to keep that thought in mind as I opened my front door.

In fact, it turned out that I'd been worrying in the wrong direction. The boys in blue hadn't come to arrest me for bumping off nasty Mrs Warton after all, they'd come to tell me that earlier that night some drunken thug had smashed the front window of my salon. Obviously, I was pissed off, but considering what I thought they'd come for, what should have been bad news actually came as such a relief that I had to struggle to hide my joy.

Despite my misgivings, the police officers were actually very helpful. Once I'd pulled myself together and dressed, I grabbed my mobile phone, a grubby old macintosh, a hat and some gloves and followed them to their car. From then on, the machine took over, the police officers ran me into town, they gave me the telephone number of a twenty-four hour glazing firm, and after helping me to clear away the worst of the broken glass from my salon floor, the taller of the two even made me a cup of tea.

We sat in my salon's reception area with the hot drinks and some Gingernut biscuits that I kept in an old first aid tin for emergencies.

'When the glazier turns up get him to order you laminated glass, it is a bit more expensive but it's much better.' The shorter cop told me earnestly. 'Laminated glass hangs together when it's smashed, so next time there won't be such a mess.' While I appreciated the suggestion, I was disappointed that he expected there to be a next time. To illustrate his point, the policeman then leaned over the side of the reception settee and reached for a shard of glass that we'd missed lodged in the foliage of my fig tree. As he moved a branch something beneath the tree caught his eye, he leaned in further and pulled out Marjorie Warton's Birkin handbag. How could I have forgotten it?

'Yours?' He asked ingenuously.

I gulped and my throat was instantly dry.

I should have laughed an airy chuckle and simply taken the bag from him. I've been accused of far worse things than owning a handbag (especially a Birkin), but instead, in my panic I heard myself stutter, 'No… It's my mother's… She died yesterday… watching Richard and Judy… it was a birthday present.'

Why I told him all that, I really don't know.

'Oh dear, I'm sorry,' he said kindly. 'Did she live locally?' he asked. I am sure that he was just being polite and that I could have just nodded and smiled, and he'd have accepted whatever I told him, but for some daft reason I said 'No,' and then followed up by telling him that my mother had lived in Winchester all her life. I could see the cogs whirring straightaway. 'If my mother had just died in Winchester, what was her handbag doing here?' he didn't have to say it. It was all I could do not to snatch the wretched bag from him. Thankfully, the emergency glazier chose that moment to arrive at my salon door and was the perfect distraction.

'Hello boys.' He called through the broken window. 'Either of you two got a crime number for me?' He grinned at the cops far too cheerfully for my liking.

I reckon that the level of a workman's humour correlates directly to the size of his call out fee, and at four o'clock in the morning, it was a fair bet that this chap's fee was going to be large. Without realising what he was doing, the shorter cop stood up, tucked Marjorie Warton's very posh handbag under his arm, and then reached for the paperwork that he'd left on my reception desk. The grinning glazier raised a quizzical eyebrow at the bag catching the cop somewhere between embarrassment and irritation, again the moment worked in my favour. The cop handed me the bag quick as a flash.

'I'm sorry about your mother.' He said, the question that I'd seen in his eyes fading instantly. I didn't trust myself to say anything else. I just took the handbag from him and shoved it roughly under the reception desk.

An hour or so later the glazier had finished. He'd patched the window with plywood promising to return with glass by the end of the week. The two cops didn't have much more to say, they'd review the town centre CCTV, and might ask a few questions around town, but unless the assumed drunken thug gave himself up, they thought it unlikely that the culprit would be caught. Neither of the policemen seemed bothered, and hey, wasn't I the lucky one, thanks to the thug and my Aviva insurance policy I was going to get a shiny new window. Maybe they thought I'd be grateful, but when I was a kid if I'd have broken a window it would've mattered, I would have been caught and punished, and I wouldn't have done it again. There seemed to be a new level of acceptance in my town, maybe in the world. Not so much zero tolerance as total tolerance. Do what you like, but just don't get caught. I wondered if what had happened to me the day before might secretly be viewed in the same way, swept under the carpet, too many badly parked cars to deal with. What the eye don't see, the heart don't grieve, and the arm don't have to do the paperwork. Was I the only person left who gave a stuff about anything?

When everyone had gone and the salon was once more my own, I locked the door and went back to the reception desk, and pulled out Marjorie Warton's handbag. Hidden from view by the glazier's sheet of plywood, I undid the catch on the bag and emptied its contents onto the desk. Marjorie Warton was a far tidier woman than my mother was. My mother's handbag would've contained all sorts of knick-knacks and rubbish. Tattered bags of mint imperials, perished elastic bands, tissues... dozens of scrunched up half used tissues, and probably more stolen sugar sachets than her local tearoom would use in a week. The Wart hog's handbag was far more orderly and fragrant. Her purse, key fob and credit card wallet were all made from matching soft leather. There were two photographs in a similarly manufactured travel frame, one of Mrs Warton and the other of her late husband Barry. I reckoned that they'd both be late now. Among the other pristine items that I shook from the handbag was a lipstick (sheathed in an eighteen-carat gold case), a magnifying glass, a pair of pearl earrings, a watch (Seiko, but nothing particularly special), several receipts from Marks and Sparks and an insignificant grey velvet pouch that contained a small .22 calibre silver gun.

I was shocked, although I remembered that some months before Mrs Warton told me that she wanted to get something for her personal protection, I thought she meant to install a burglar alarm. I never imagined that she'd carry a gun. Not used to handling firearms, I lifted the weapon gingerly between my finger and thumb, and after making certain the safety catch was on, I checked to see whether it was loaded. Finding the clip release at the bottom of the mother-of-pearl clad grip, I clicked it open. The clip held five small bullets, and it was full.

When I'd finished being nosey, I put everything except the key fob and the gun back into the handbag. Keeping the keys handy, I returned the gun to its velvet pouch and then slipped it into the pocket of my grubby old macintosh. I tucked the handbag under my arm, and then looked for my hat and gloves.

From the opposite side of the street my salon looked old. It was an architectural con. My salon was one of five similar but individual business units that fronted the ground floor of a large and smart residential development built on the northern side of the High Street between Boots Pharmacy and Marks and Spencer. The shops were all leased independently from a property company based in Bristol. Between recessions in the 1980s, the company's architect had the foresight to design a building for the town centre that not only blended with its surroundings, but also wouldn't quickly go out of date, an idea that has become unfashionable more recently. When I took on the lease of my salon, I saw the residential element of the development as a huge bonus, a captive mass of potential punters. Over the years clients moved in and out, some stayed with me, some moved away, and others died. I guess that an ageing population will gravitate towards the convenience of a town-centre and my client base was certainly ageing.

Mrs Warton's penthouse apartment spanned the fifth floor of Pelham House, the more imposing and taller of the two main blocks in the development. Marjorie had lived there since I'd known her, if a straight line could be drawn, probably less than a hundred feet from my salon. So long and so close, and yet I'd never seen her front door. However, I was familiar with the buildings, their stairways and their landings, their elevators and their halls. I'd helped carry shopping bags and I'd pushed wheelchairs, I'd even 'house called' the odd poorly old dear who couldn't make the stairs. So when it came to finding my way the top I had no trouble.

Just as the handbag had been orderly so was the key fob, from left to right seven keys, from largest to smallest and each one marked with a coloured dot. The largest key was obviously to the front door. I knew this partly because all of the apartments and even my salon had a similar type of lock, but also because the key had 'FRONT DOOR' written on it.

The front door itself was a jarring piece of furniture and something that I would have dropped a few quid on to gamble that Marjorie Warton had chosen herself. It sort of

38

looked like her. It was big and heavy and like something from Wonderland, it was in the wrong place. Other than as a tasteless display of wealth both the door and its redundant portico belonged more outside on the street, on the front of a bank or some minor government building, than it did at the end of a hallway on the fifth floor of 1980's apartment block.

Sliding the key into the lock, I held my breath as the door inched open. I could hear music, radio two, it didn't worry me, and I didn't feel nervous at all. I knew the place would be empty. People like Marjorie Warton don't share their homes.

I'm not entirely certain why I climbed the stairs to the fifth floor, not to burgle, that's for sure. I didn't intend to steal anything. Perhaps I just needed to be nosey or lay a ghost to rest.

I pushed the door wider and stepped inside.

The carpets were thick and sumptuous and the air smelled of Parma Violets. An inner hallway, maybe ten feet by twenty, ran away from the front door. The decor was far less extravagant than I had expected; soft painted Lincrusta mouldings pinched with gold and topped with oriental silk panelling, a tad ostentatious but there was taste used here… and loads of dosh. Five closed doors lined the hallway, two to the left and three to the right and at the far end, a pair of glazed oak doors opened into what an estate agents brochure would probably describe as a magnificent drawing room.

'A *well proportioned and beautifully styled triple aspect room with fine views over town and the surrounding countryside. The room boasts an Adam style feature fireplace, solid oak joinery and fine decorative mouldings to the ceiling and walls, door to…*'

A darned serious kitchen.

The Wart Hog certainly didn't scrimp when it came to her personal comforts. The kitchen came straight from the pages of Home and Gardens, and in my book, it was almost perfect. The ridiculous front door aside, I was beginning to doubt my judgement of the woman, maybe she wasn't the spendthrift style-free zone that I'd always thought. I had a fairly thorough rummage around the kitchen, opening the cupboards and pulling the drawers. The opulence left me feeling envious but apart from the glossy luxury, I didn't find much to satisfy my nosey bone. While I was looking around, I decided that the Kitchen would be a good place to leave Marjorie Warton's Birkin handbag. So, careful not to disturb anything unnecessarily, I emptied the contents of the handbag onto a tea-towel; I took a cloth from a drawer and wiped everything that I had touched clean of any marks. When I was done, I put everything back inside, tucked the cloth into my pocket and placed the handbag in the cupboard beneath the work surface closest to the hallway door.

On the far side of the kitchen, a third door opened into a formal dining room. The room was grand but cold with a navy blue carpet and a walnut dining suite that was set for ten; as far as I knew Marjorie Warton had no close family and only a few friends. I wondered when she'd last used the room, not recently I guessed. My mind flitted to the Dickens scene at Satis House and Miss Haversham, wasting away in her vast and evermore unused dining room. Had Marjorie Warton become a Miss Haversham, left alone in the world to fester? The clocks were working but her apartment seemed oddly impersonal. I'd seen no photographs, no ornaments or souvenirs, no sign that anybody cared.

I closed the door quietly and made my way back to the hall.

To the left of the Drawing room I found the source of the music that I'd heard earlier – a radio alarm clock that hadn't yet switched off - and the entrance to a fluffy palace that even the real Miss piggy would have been comfortable in, the Wart hog's bedroom. Pink, pink and even more pink. The bedroom restored my faith in my original judgement of the woman. I began to realise that at least two minds must have worked to create this place. In contrast to the stylish simplicity of the kitchen and the opulent splendour of the drawing room, the bedroom was a garish box of girly frills. The room seemed so at variance with what I knew of its owner's hardened exterior that I found it too creepy to go in. I turned instead to the bathroom next door, another contrasting magazine spread of gloss and contemporary chic… I wished it were mine.

There's something strange about other people's bathrooms that invites nosiness. Perhaps it's the act of locking oneself in. Perhaps it's all the interesting bits and pieces that people fill their bathrooms with, the face wash, the deodorant, the corn plasters, and the shampoos. We all have the same basic needs but we worry that other people may know something that we don't, that they may have discovered a deodorant that really works for twenty-four hours, or an ointment that will actually cure piles. Whatever the reasons, this bathroom, Marjorie Warton's bathroom, might have been designed to be snooped.

I closed the door, turned the lock, and tried to decide where best to start. Between, above, and around, the more traditional porcelain fixtures, mirror faced drawers and hidden cupboards had been fitted so that no clear space went to waste. I started my snoop with the drawers. Most were neatly filled with the finest odds and ends, cotton buds from the Ritz hotel, a face cloth marked Cunard, soaps from Claridges, and a dozen ball point pens from Coutts & Co bank. I suppose the pens should have twanged my string straight away, but it wasn't until I started on the cupboards and found one full of expensive hair care products from my hairdressing salon that I realised Minging Marjorie Truffle-snuffler Wart hog Warton had been stocking her shelves with goodies that she had stolen from her favourite haunts, and worst of all… from me.

'How dare she!' I hissed to myself. I was amazed, shocked, and quite frankly, properly cheesed off.

I slammed the cupboard door and in its mirror caught sight of my own reflection. I looked pink and puffy, as if tainted by the horrible bedroom. I turned away and then for some reason looked back again and stared at myself for a long moment almost daring my reflection to wink. It didn't. I didn't.

Back in the drawing room, my curiosity satisfied although still feeling niggled, I saw that the sun was at last rising. I'd never seen my town from this perspective or under such a delicate light. Its sepia boundaries seemed to stretch further than I'd imagined they would. The view was oddly calming, hypnotic. I felt compelled to set myself within it and to find familiar places. Although my house was out of sight, I traced my way almost home along a fading dot-to-dot of street

41

lamps, and when the street lamps finally blinked out, I felt the new day begin, and tomorrow at last.

I left Marjorie Warton's key fob on a small marble topped console table close to the front door. As I was about to leave the apartment I glanced back to check that I'd had left the place in order and I noticed a short length of gold chain caught under the door opposite the kitchen. The door was wider and more solid than the other four doors in the hallway, and one of two that I hadn't been able to open. I would have left the chain on the floor but there was something familiar about the unusual shape of the links; something that I recognised. I bent down to pull it out.

When I first moved to town, I had a very good friend who'd had a very good friend who died. The friend of my friend was a jeweller, a goldsmith, and when he died, he left my friend an unusual gold chain. The chain was his apprentice piece, a handmade testament to hard work and learning and a gift that was deeply treasured. On the day I opened my salon, my friend asked me for a haircut. I was happy to oblige, I only had few clients at the time. Unfortunately, after I'd shampooed my friend's hair, I caught a towel in the links of the precious chain and the precious gift fell to the floor. I picked it up and put on a shelf close to the reception area for safekeeping. That was the last time either of us saw the chain... it simply disappeared. The next day I had a two hundred pound lottery win. It was marvellous luck I was thrilled and couldn't wait to spread the news. Suddenly my friend's usually soft hazel eyes didn't look so happy. A great many things in my life went wrong after that.

I cupped my hands around the carefully crafted pieces of gold and I swore a lot. I'd vowed to myself not to take anything from Marjorie Warton's apartment, not to steal from the dead, even if the wretched Truffle-snuffler was a thief herself. I put the chain into my jacket pocket and walked out through the door.

Three days later one of my more agreeable local ladies arrived for her regular blow wave appointment. I could see that she had something to tell me as soon as she came through the door.

'You will never guess what.' She started before she'd even sat down, and I knew I never would so I kept quiet and let her run with the cookies.

'Well… you know that dreadful Warton woman? Yes of course you do; the brassy trout with the fake fur coats.' (I don't think they were fakes actually.) 'Well she's had a burglarer. The police were up on the top floor all day yesterday and again this morning. They caught him. Nasty piece of work by all accounts, drugs I reckon. Silly blighter got himself locked in her lift. I went to the doctors yesterday - Mrs Warton and me both see Doctor Carmen - and the receptionist at the surgery told me that the burglarer had to phone the police himself to come and let him out. You'd never believe it would you?'

She took a breath and then started again.

'Well… apparently, he was in such a state that the police had to call Doctor Carmen in to calm him down. The receptionist told me that the burglarer had gone straight for the jewellery. That Marjorie Warton might be a common sort but she does wear some nice pieces. It seems that he didn't bother with anything else. Diamonds and gold, that's what these drugs barons want, I've seen it on telly. My cleaner's son has a friend who works for the Chief Constables mother and she told her that our town has a drugs time-bomb just waiting to explode… But do you know the worst of it?'

I shook my head because I didn't, and then I mouthed 'No'.

'Well…' She said. 'Marjorie Warton doesn't even know that she's been robbed. She's away somewhere; probably on one of her cruises… nobody can find her.'

CHAPTER FOUR

Prozac, was marvellous.

When I was a teenager I played around with cannabis for a while, we called it wacky-baccy. My friends told me it was great, that it would 'Chill me out' but the first time I tried it I was sick over my shoes. I got used to it (the wacky-baccy not the sick), but after a while I got bored with the secrecy and the potheads. Prozac, on the other hand, was recently stigma free, available on prescription, and even my accountant took Prozac. Prozac always 'Chilled me out' and never made me sick.

It was my doctor's suggestion. I'd been to see her a few times that year with one problem or another, but after my mother's funeral I was in a terrible state. I couldn't stop crying, I wasn't eating properly, my work was suffering, and I was losing clients fast. My doctor glibly dubbed it 'Reactive Depression'. Obviously well used to seeing patients with similar symptoms, she quickly arranged for me to attend an anxiety management workshop, prescribed me, what she referred to as, 'magic pills' (*not yet Prozac*), and promised me that time was great healer. Other than fending off panic attacks and stopping the constant tears, the pills didn't help much, I still felt rotten. However, after reading a pamphlet that I'd picked up when leaving the surgery I was optimistic about the workshops.

I arrived early for the first session. It was a cold and soggy Monday morning with a heavy grey sky. Close to the town centre, and tucked between the library and the bus station, the entrance to the Psychiatric day care centre was a short walk from my salon. I'd called in at Starbucks on my way along the High Street. Country boy barista Colin, recently my favourite grinder, served me with my usual. I tucked the slice of lemon cake into my pocket, pulled my coat up around my ears, and braved my way forward sipping at my skinny latté. It was a strange morning and a difficult walk. I came close to turning back several times. While I knew that I wasn't firing on all cylinders, I found it hard to accept that I needed psychiatric help.

Three people were waiting outside the day care centre when I arrived, and from the look on their hollow faces, I guessed instantly that they might be my classmates. Inside I was quickly proved right when the four of us were welcomed by the woman who we were told would be running the course and assessing our needs.

Imelda Smith, a tall and not unattractive Jamaican psychiatric nurse, led us to a room that overlooked the bus station. Six chairs had been arranged in a broad circle around a coffee table.

'Please find yourself a seat in the circle,' Imelda said softly, and then she smiled and added, 'wherever you feel most comfortable.'

I knew the tone of voice from my childhood, it was my mother's 'Now go to sleep' voice, saved to comfort me if I'd woken during the night. I grabbed a seat with my back to the only clear wall and tucked my coffee under the chair.

'We're just waiting for another friend to join us and then we'll begin.' Imelda smiled again. We all nodded and smiled back.

It was all terribly reassuring and warm. From the soft green paintwork to the water lily prints hanging on the wall, a scene set to sooth. We sat there quietly, smiling anxiously at each other, for something over five minutes before the door flew open, and a woman dressed entirely in orange burst in.

'Don't look out of the window,' she implored us, 'or they'll know where I am.'

We all sat very still as the woman circled the edge of the room like a manic giant spider. Glancing at my classmates, I reckoned that we were all wearing the same expression... a 'what the hell am I doing here' face, with an inane grin, and Lily Tomlin eyebrows. Just getting through the front door of the centre had been a struggle for me. Was this how I'd end up?

'Becky, why don't sit down next to me.' Imelda said calmly, and then she patted the cushion on chair to her left. 'Let me introduce you to everyone.'

In fact, the spider woman's contribution to the group session didn't last very long, just enough to put us all on edge. She sat down for a moment or two, but she was obviously dreadfully distressed and as soon as anyone moved, she clutched at her ears and started to sing. Sensibly, Imelda didn't let her suffer too long before calling in help.

When the woman had gone and the group had settled as much as it would, Imelda encouraged us to introduce ourselves and to explain why we thought we were there. A woman sitting to my right started the ball rolling.

'Hi… I'm Cynthia.' She said, and then she sucked enough air through her teeth to inflate a small bouncy castle. 'Why am I here? Well… I'm here because.' She sucked in again; it was a very irritating noise. 'I suppose I've been having a few problems recently, trouble getting out of the house, nerves, that sort of thing.' Cynthia sat back and folded her arms protectively across her chest.

'Thank you Cynthia.' Imelda smiled her warm ingratiating smile and then nodded slowly to the chap fidgeting on a chair to Cynthia's right.

'Ah, me… well, my name is Peter, Peter Marshall, I'm fifty five years old and I'm recently unemployed.' Peter nodded, then he smiled at Cynthia, and then he twitched. 'I've had a bad time of it too actually, really rather dreadful. You know, anything that can go wrong bloody well has. I feel terrible all the time, I can't swallow properly, I can't eat, and sometimes I can't even catch my breath. Everything seems so…' Peter couldn't finish the sentence and clasped his hands across his face, 'I'm sorry, just give me a moment.' He said stifling a sob, and then he started to rock in his chair.

If Imelda had hoped to say anything consoling or sympathetic, then the interruption from the young chap sitting to Peter's right stole her chance.

'I'm Brian, Brian Gobby.' He blurted through a tight smile, and if his name wasn't burdening enough Brian's voice came straight from Walt Disney, Mickey Mouse meets Tarzan. He went on to explain how his stresses and anxieties were far worse than either Peter's or Cynthia's. Cynthia looked heartbroken and the speed of Peter's twitching increased. We heard about Brian's terrible childhood, his irritable bowel, his post-nasal-drip, the pustules in his armpit, and his compulsion to scratch. A competitive fruit-loop, he was just what we needed. When Brian had finished I knew more about the human body's physical response to mental buggered-up-ness than any sane person should.

By the time my turn to speak came I was feeling quite good about myself. After listening to the others, my anxiety attacks, and alternating loads of guilt and grief, seemed trivial. I suppose I should have played the game. I should have added to Brian's list of woes and revolting symptoms - I can be creative - but instead I decided to tell them what really I thought.

'You're all barking mad.' I said flatly. As an opening line, I'll agree that it was probably a touch insensitive. I should have guessed that in any place even vaguely psychiatric the word 'mad' would definitely be taboo.

Cynthia looked at me as if I'd slapped her across the face and then she started to shout.

'I am not mad. I am not mad. I am not mad.'

Brian pretended that I wasn't there, and Peter headed straight for the door.

'Whoops,' I thought. I crossed my legs tightly, took a long sip from my cold skinny latté, and felt for the slice of lemon cake in my pocket.

I visited the psychiatric day care centre three more times before Imelda sent me back to my doctor with a note. Colin let me steam the envelope open under the Starbucks Gaggia on my way to the surgery. Imelda had written.

Dear Dr Marshall,

Following your telephone call and referral.

I contacted your patient and arranged for him to attend a number of our anxiety management group sessions. As you know, we hope that these sessions will allow patients to meet others with similar problems, to share their experiences, and to begin to understand that they are not suffering alone. Although your patient attended only four of the usual twelve sessions his contributions were such that I believe he, and more particularly, the other members of the group would be better served if he were treated elsewhere.

Yours faithfully...
Imelda Sombodyorother.

I had been dumped.

My doctor knew that I had read Imelda's note, I didn't bother to disguise the damp and wrinkled envelope, and she didn't pretend that she hadn't noticed it. Our conversation was brief.

'How are you feeling now?' she asked frostily.

'Pretty crap.' I answered... (probably the rejection)

'We'll try Prozac.' She said.

It was as simple as that. She picked up a pen and started scribbling on a pad. When she finished writing she tore off the prescription, waved it at me and said, 'keep in touch.'

CHAPTER FIVE

I got through Christmas and New Year more or less in one piece, vodka helped... Vodka with a spoonful of sugar and a dash of water, I like vodka and sugar.

I spent Christmas Day and Boxing Day with Tristan the Christian, his mother, and two of his sisters, both of whom had recently divorced. Tristan's sisters were nearer my age than his, yet despite their age, and over forty years of marriage between them, neither of the women had children. My thoughts on the matter were simple. They had seen what their brother had done to their mother. Tristan, the immaculate contraceptive.

So Christmas Day was an adult affair, we ate turkey and cake, and pulled crackers, but none of us laughed too much. I had to watch the Queen's speech twice, once with the three women and then again later, after Tristan returned from the pub. The beer had told him to pray for the Royal Family. His prayer was going well until he asked God to bless Princess Diana, then he started to cry. Tristan was still at school when Diana died, I doubted that his memories of her were his own, more likely a product of too much beer and years of media hype. When he finished the prayer, he slumped onto the settee and fell to sleep. I heard his mother breathe a sigh of relief.

'Fancy a turkey sandwich?' she asked with a wink and a grin.

I didn't, I was still fit to burst from Christmas lunch, but my mouth said yes anyway, and when she brought me the sandwiches, it munched its way through a plateful. She watched me swallow every mouthful. I reckoned that my cousin was a secret 'feeder', no wonder Tristan had grown so big.

I slept badly that night, rich food and the best part of a bottle of vodka curdled with an upsetting mix of memories and fretful dreams to wake me a dozen times before dawn. My cousin brought me a steaming mug of coffee just after eight o'clock.

'It's going to be a beautiful day.' She told me.

I took the mug in both hands and inhaled its vapours, my nose sniffing out any stray molecules of caffeine, if only it could. The coffee smelled okay but it tasted ghastly, I longed for Colin and his frothing Gaggia.

'I heard you last night,' she said quietly, 'I wanted to come in to you, but I thought…'

'Oh dear was I talking again? I do that sometimes, I'm sorry.'

'I thought you were upset, I thought you might be crying.'

'I don't think so… I don't know.' I said too quickly. I knew that I had been crying in my sleep, I'd always been a bit of a crybaby and my eyes felt sticky, and the pillow was damp, I just didn't want talk about it. 'I often make funny noises at night. Mum used to tell me I'd wake the dead.'

My cousin looked at me wistfully and said simply. 'I miss your Mum.' It was lovely to hear somebody say it.

Boxing Day came and went as it always did. We took a walk, we chatted about old times, we didn't expect too much from the day and we weren't disappointed. Tristan dropped me home after tea. His mother had packed me off with two knapsacks (actually Tesco's carrier bags) full of what she called 'Crimbo goodies', leftovers to the rest of the world. She and I both knew that most of it would end up in a bin, but our small family Christmas was all about pretence, so I kissed her on the cheek and said 'Yummy', and she told me not to get fat.

'Fatter' I thought.

I spent New Year's Eve on my own with an old Anthony Worrall-Thompson cookbook, a pound of fillet steak, and a new favourite dessert from Marks and Sparks. I'd had invitations to go out, naturally, but none that I fancied and as it turned out, spending such a significant evening at home alone with my thoughts did me good. I wonder now, whether it was then, at the beginning of a new year, that I first recognised that I didn't mind being on my own. Perhaps when I finally understood, that aloneness need not mean loneliness.

I didn't open the salon until the first Monday after New Year's Day, and it was a struggle to do that. I always found the first few weeks of any new year hard work. The days are dull and short and people seem despondent. When I opened the door, it felt like I hadn't been there for a month or more. I took a deep breath and stepped inside, the place felt cold and lifeless, even the smells had faded. Across the salon, a pile of letters waited for me on the floor by the front door, and on the reception desk, the answering machine flashed angrily. 'Just another day…' I sighed. Three years before, I would have been unlocking the front door to let my staff in, a half dozen giggling girlies who, fresh from the Christmas break, would keep me on my toes. Alas no longer. I stamped my finger on the flashing play button and shook the sour thought away.

The first three messages were cancellations, clients who had gone down with the usual post-Christmas bugs and blues. Next came a recording telling me that I'd won a sunshine holiday in Florida, and that all I had to do to collect my prize was dial a magic number. 'And I'm Donald Duck.' I muttered at the taunt. Finally, came the usual stream of messages from people who'd either forgotten when their appointment was, or who wanted to change their booking to another time or day. They were all dreadfully annoying. However, after I'd turned the heating up and switched the lights on, I sat down at the desk and started to wade through the numbers.

By nine forty-five, I'd finished the return phone calls and had started on the pile of letters. The first two clients of my day had been among the cancellation messages, and so I was surprised when as I ripped open the first envelope I heard a knock at the front door. I looked up to see a tall woman with longish blondish hair smiling at me through the upturned collar of a white fox fur coat. She leaned her head slightly to one side, and then reached towards me tapping at her watch face while mouthing, 'What time do you open?' It was only then that I realised that I was still wearing my hat and coat. I jumped up quickly and rummaged in my pockets to find the salon keys.

'I'm sorry,' I called, 'first day back.'

I shoved the key in lock, gave it a good hard twist, and then yanked the door open.

'I'm so sorry,' I said again, while taking my hat off, 'we are open, please come in.' I ushered the woman towards the reception desk, and then I closed the door behind her. As she let the fur collar drop away from her face, I could see that my caller was an attractive woman whom I guessed to be in her mid thirties.

'How can I help?' I asked. A new client was a rarity at that time of year, I should have been delighted to see her, but I suddenly felt terribly awkward.

'I'm Cindy Dobson.' She replied with another smile. 'I think you met my husband Francis. I think he helped you with something.'

'Oh.' Was the best I could manage and I could feel the expression on my face dissolve to match the complexity of the word. I didn't have a clue who she was, or her helpful husband.

'Francis Dobson, 'Ripper' Dobson,' her eyes narrowed and she put her left hand on her hip, 'he's a manager at the recycling centre.'

Suddenly it all became perfectly clear. I was talking to Mrs Ripper, the wife of the guy who had disposed of my red wheelie-bin at the local tip, the woman whose hair I had promised to cut.

'Of course,' I dragged the word out long and slow to hide my astonishment, 'How very stupid of me.' I couldn't believe that the lovely woman that I was talking to could possibly be married to Tristan's rough and hairy friend.

'That's okay.' She said, her smile returning, but I could tell that she'd noticed the surprise in my eyes. 'I should have come to see you earlier, but I'm afraid that Francis only remembered to tell me about your little deal when he picked me up from my usual hairdresser in December. I couldn't see the point having it cut any sooner…'

'It's no problem, I assure you,' I said, and it wasn't, she was lovely and had the kind of beautiful thick hair that I quite fancied getting stuck into. 'The question is; when would you like to come in?' I asked, and I found myself grinning at the prospect.

Twenty minutes later, and I was glad that Mrs Cooper had gone down with 'flu and had cancelled her morning appointment. Cindy Dobson was a breath of spring air on my wintery morning. I shampooed her hair and we agreed on a gentle trim. She laughed and chatted easily as I snipped, reminding me that I had once enjoyed every working day. That there had been a time in my career when every client was new and that I'd approached each one with enthusiasm rather than apprehension.

'So how did you meet Mr Rip… Francis?' I asked, trying to disguise my mistake with a cough. I needn't have bothered Cindy just chuckled. It was a nice sound.

'My Aunt Cecile,' she said. 'It's a bit of a tale. Francis served in the Gulf with her second husband Derek. They were both Navy. It was terribly sad actually. Derek was a thoroughly nice chap, I'm not sure that my Aunt Cecile deserved him. He was a chaplain, you'd have thought that alone would have kept him safe, but he got caught up in a freak helicopter accident. He was only fifty-four, ten years younger than Aunt Cecile was. When Francis came home, he took Cecile a few of Derek's personal bits and pieces that the Navy had failed to ship home. I suppose Cecile felt grateful, so when she heard that Francis was struggling to adapt to civilian life she helped him by wangling him a job with the local council. To be honest I think she only did it to make her feel better. She married again within a few months of Derek's funeral. Aunt Cecile's not usually one for sentiment.' Cindy put a finger to her lips and added wistfully, 'I was living with her at the time and somewhere along the line she introduced me to Francis.' Then she giggled, 'She wasn't so happy when we got together… and although sometimes I wonder if she was right, overall I think she did me a favour.' In spite of the careful choice of words, Cindy Dobson didn't sound too certain and I had to wonder if the reassurance was more for her own benefit than for mine.

'Aunt Cecile,' I said, ignoring the uncertainty, 'should I know her? The name seems familiar?'

'You should,' Cindy answered quickly, 'you've been her hairdresser for the last fifteen years.'

Although maths was never my strongest subject, I could manage two plus two and now all the names were falling into place. Cecile Ablitt, formerly Truscott, formerly Lloyd and probably formerly something else, an ex-1950s fashion model and possibly the unluckiest widow of all time was among my longest serving clients and a proper madam to boot. Of course I knew Cindy's story, Cecile told me when it all happened. Cindy was right, her aunt had been furious when she and Mr Ripper ran off together. I hadn't twigged the connection simply because the dull face that my imagination had created for Cindy didn't match the glamorous reality at all.

'Ah, Cecile Ablitt, of course, she's one of my favourite clients.' I said. It was a lie, but as I'd only just met Cindy I could hardly tell her that I thought her aunt was a stuck up old trout.

'Really?' She said, and she looked genuinely astonished. 'I don't have much to do with her these days, I'm afraid. Not since, she married that dreadful Ablitt fellow. The only thing he ever did that was good for Aunt Cecile was to change his will. I should build some bridges and get in touch with her now that she's on her own again.'

I finished Cindy Dobson's haircut just before eleven. It had been a treat and she'd cheered me up. Although I found it hard to believe that such a lovely woman could be married to Tristan's hairy friend Ripper, I hoped she'd come back, and as I showed her to the front desk she brightened my day still further by booking a follow-up appointment towards the end of February.

When she left the salon, I followed her to the door and waved her goodbye from the pavement outside. I watched her walk away along the High Street, flicking her hair from side to side and glancing at her reflection in shop windows. Her movements were light and carefree and as I watched her, I knew that my world should have been a better place.

CHAPTER SIX

As January had been cold and gloomy, February breezed in bright, and I was at last feeling the benefits of Prozac. Looking back, I am sure that as each winter's day passed the drug had lifted my mood a little more, but I remember that there seemed to be a moment, one wintery morning, when some unseen hand drew an oily fog from my head. The difference was remarkable and more than welcome. I felt better in almost every way, and not just improved from my recent malaise, but also relieved from what felt like a lifetime of angst and unrest. I was still me deep inside, but when I looked at myself I felt happier about what I saw, more comfortable in my own skin. I guess there was a down side to my drug-induced contentment. There were side effects; a loose tummy, a dry mouth, a limp cock, I'd put on a few pounds, and I swear it made my hair thinner, but nothing that I wasn't prepared to get used to.

The weeks between New Year and Valentine's Day had been unusually quiet. Although my business year was cyclical and the winter months were always among the worst, that year's dip in trade was deeper than ever. I knew that my business had been in a gentle decline for several years. At first, I'd blamed my staff, my silly girlies who didn't understand the needs of the older client. Then there was a recession; an almost perfect excuse. However, while those around me would battle through the tough times to emerge bigger and brighter than before, I trudged complacently sideways.

Now I didn't need excuses, with happy pills safely popped, it simply didn't seem to matter. When a regular client complained that I'd kept her waiting too long, I told her that she was a clockwatching neurotic and that she should sit her bony arse down and wait her turn. When one of my larger ladies asked for a gamine Audrey Hepburn style hair cut, I answered by puffing my cheeks out and telling her that she'd look like a fat man in drag. Whilst my comments may have been accurate, such unfettered honesty was a sure way of losing further paying customers.

On one Monday morning late in January, a police car, or rather, a car with a couple of policemen in it, pulled up outside my salon. Long and white, its engine rattled and buzzed all the time it was there like a London taxi waiting for a fare. The officer driving stayed with the car, but the other got out and came to the salon door. A swarthy chap with bushy eyebrows and enormous hands, he introduced himself as Detective Sergeant Dennis Sapsead. We sat on the reception settee. After softening me up with a few pleasantries, 'nice shop', and 'been here long?' he asked me brusquely when I'd last seen Marjorie Warton. I could tell he didn't like me from the off, his eyes sort of squinted and sneered. I didn't much care. His questions, that caught me on the hop and that I should have found awkward, and were certainly asked in a very pointed manner, hardly worried me at all. Although I answered him carefully, in fact, I spent an easy half hour casually spinning the kind of tale that would ordinarily have left me a babbling wreck. When Detective Sapsead left my salon, despite the fact that he seemed a tad cheesed off, I thought I'd handled him rather well.

Of course, at the time, I didn't realise that anything was going wrong. Overall people seemed to like the new me, I liked the new me, and most of the time most of my clients liked the new me. If there were occasions in the salon when my new relaxed approach worked against the perfect business model and allowed my usual professionalism to slip… well so what? If sometimes, I was a jot too ready to accept second best… big deal. Maybe that was the point. With the aid of my happy pills, I felt much better; no longer the neurotic clock-watcher, far more relaxed, far more accepting of life's little whoopsies.

With one small exception, the third Tuesday in February of that year was a marvellous day. I got up early, not because I was expecting the day to be particularly marvellous, but because thanks to the pills I was able to hope that it might be. I showered, dressed, and ambled down the stairs. Even early, the late winter sun was nudging at my kitchen window; I breakfasted looking across my garden, anticipating its warmth.

I left home about half an hour earlier than usual, I wasn't wearing a hat or gloves, and for once in my life, even though the air was chilly I didn't give a stuff. On my way down my garden path I picked a daffodil, I clipped its stem with my fingernails, and then I slipped it into the lapel of my overcoat. At the bottom of the path, I stopped to pick up a three quarters full garden waste sack, and then I turned around and paused to look back at my house.

When I bought the property on Gillycote Road, I thought that I was more than just a man with dreams and ambitions; I thought that I was a doer, a player. Owning my own home was an important step, a base from which I would propel myself into a high-flying world. I had plans. Fate changed those plans. The things that I'd hoped to do, the people that I'd hoped to love, and the person that I'd hoped to be. When I looked back at my house on that marvellous February morning, I understood that I'd lived the last several years of my life in a state of lazy resentment, that I'd passively blamed fate for all my woes.

Although the chilled veil of Prozac tainted my view of the world rosy and pink, on that marvellous February morning my house looked wonderful, and I promised myself that from that day on fate could go hang.

From my garden gate, I turned right instead of left and carried the green waste sack to the bottom of my next-door neighbour's driveway. The sack was heavy and full of rotting hedge clippings and weeds that my lovely neighbour had sneakily been dropping over our party wall since the end of the summer. Unlike my neighbours on the other side, a charming couple who I think worked at the local hospital, I'd never liked the guy. Short and sweaty, like a blubbery seal, his skin looked too tight to hold him all in. As I passed his driveway, I stepped in and emptied the contents of the sack onto the bonnet of his car. I made my defiant gesture with a satisfying flourish and a swish of the empty sack, and I hoped that somebody had seen me do it.

The walk into town was lovely. The air was fresh and my mind was clear. I walked with a smile on my face, and took the long route through Saint Michael's Churchyard and then followed the millstream footpath until it passed behind the library. The fence between the footpath and the library car park had been broken down for some time. I scrambled over it easily enough and crossed the car park towards the bottom of the High Street.

Arriving at Starbucks early, I found the coffee shop much quieter than usual, so quiet in fact, that for the first time ever, while Colin my favourite barista frothed my skinny latté, very bravely, I decided to sit down and drink it with him. A quick point to note here - I didn't ask for a slice of sharp lemon cake; I didn't dare. Already late in February, and I was still having to disguise my Christmas bulge. After I'd made myself comfortable on the crumpled leather settee closest to the window, Colin brought my coffee over to me.

'The sun usually brings people out.' He said thoughtfully, gazing through the window, his country accent more noticeable than usual. 'Not today though… looks like we're in for another easy one.' He put my steaming latté on the table in front of me and smiled. 'I expect you're always busy.'

'Usually.' I said, bluffing, unwilling to admit to anyone other myself that my business was struggling.

'I watch people,' Colin shrugged and nodded towards the window, 'out there, when I've nothing much else to do, I'm a people watcher.'

I'd heard the phrase before and I remembered the sitcom on TV in the 90s 'Watching' about a neurotic couple who exchanged notes on anyone who caught their eye, but I never realised that it could be so much fun. Under Colin's tutelage with occasional helpful pointers from one or two of his colleagues, I spent the next half hour before going to work, sipping my latté, and quietly learning the ropes.

At about quarter to nine, when Starbucks' queue was bigger than I could comfortably ignore, and Colin and the others were too busy to play, I remembered that I needed to open my salon. I buttoned my coat, checked my mobile phone, and took my mug and saucer back to the counter.

'Well that's a first.' Colin said with a smile as he reached for the tray.

'I was early.' I smiled back. 'But I have to say that the coffee tastes better from a proper mug, and I enjoyed the lesson, I'll be back.'

'I hope so.' Colin's smile flicked on and off for an instant and then he looked away.

The salon telephone started to ring as I was unlocking the door. I didn't rush to the desk but the caller was patient, and so I still picked up in time. I gave my usual greeting and then listened for a few seconds until I heard a weak voice reply.

'Oh, hello dear.' I knew the tones immediately. Enid Fulton. I'd neither seen nor heard from Enid in quite some time. She was one of my golden girls, a happy band of widowed ladies who might've still lunched or played Bridge if some of their marbles hadn't rolled away. When I first met Enid she was a formidable witty sixty year old, freshly launched into a retirement where the days weren't long enough, and with good luck and a fair wind, the nights might still be fun. However, health can be unkind. Three years after Enid retired, she had her first stroke, it wasn't a biggie, just enough to confuse her and soften her up, but from then on it had all been downhill, made worse recently when Enid fell from a bus and broke a hip and a wrist.

'Hello Enid.' I said with a smile. I read somewhere that if you smile when you speak on the telephone it makes your voice sound more cheerful. 'How are you, old thing?'

'Not so good dear.' She replied in not much more than a croaky whisper. 'Not too good at all. The hip's been so bloody uncomfortable and now Doctor Carmen has just told me that I have breast cancer... God.' Enid breathed a rasping sigh. 'Cancer in my saggy old tits, can you believe it?'

'Oh dear, I'm so sorry Enid, can I help?' Now I have to tell you that whenever I ask that question I feel a bit of a fraud. First, because the list of possible answers terrifies me, and second, and probably more importantly, because caring for, or even about, the old and sick doesn't come naturally to me.

'Well, actually dear, yes you can' came the answer that I most dreaded.

'Oh.' I tried to hide my dismay under a sympathetic tone but the single syllable didn't give me much scope.

'Would you be a sweetie and come and do my hair?' Enid continued, 'I feel an absolute wreck. It's enough to be told that you're falling to bits, I'd rather not have to look the part too.' Then she started coughing.

What could I say?

I waited for the church clock to strike five before I closed the salon. Although it hadn't been especially busy, apart from Enid Fulton's bad news, it had been a great day, the first full day that I had honestly enjoyed for years. I felt quite tearful when I locked the front door. Whether I was scared that it might never happen again or simply relieved that it had happened at all, I don't know. However, the overriding feeling that I most remember from that moment was that of joy.

I tidied my way back through the salon feeling good, with my face screwed into a wide grin, and I even started to sing.

I know I stand in line, until you think you have the time to spend an evening with me.' Robbie and Nicole tried hard but... *'And if we go someplace to dance, I know that there's a chance you won't be leaving with me.'* Frank and Nancy's version was best. *'And afterwards we drop into a quiet little place and have a drink or two.'* Everything was just so... cool, *'and then I went and spoiled it all by doing something stupid like...'* looking into the mirror.

When my reflection winked at me, as it had done all those weeks before, it dragged my high spirits crashing to the floor. I'd felt sure that the stupid figment had been a symptom of my anxieties and something that thanks to my happy pills, I'd left behind. I turned away hoping that I'd been mistaken, but when I turned back to the mirror it happened again and then again and then again. I grabbed my face, placing my fingers firmly around my eyes - desperate to hold everything perfectly still - just to make sure - but when I looked in the mirror and caught my own gaze, my reflection winked again.

I sat in the chair next to the fig tree with my head in my hands and my eyes tightly shut. I felt a peculiar floating sensation and although what I had seen had shocked me, from my relative high the sudden low didn't seem quite as bad as I'd expected it would. I started to think my predicament through. I'd had a good day. In fact, I'd had a good week or so, and there was no reason to suppose that the trend wouldn't continue. So what, if my reflection was a tad unpredictable, people live quite happily with all sorts of weird symptoms. Surely, I could cope with the odd wink. I'd have other good days, perhaps in time every day would be a good day.

I opened my eyes and took a long deep breath. The bounce of emotions left me feeling drained and taut. A twinge of anger tightened my forehead, I ran my hands through my hair and then rubbed at my neck, it was thick with tension. Rolling my head from side to side, I stood up. I needed to pull myself together. I'd promised Enid Fulton that I'd call on her after I closed the salon and I wasn't prepared to let the old sweetheart down just because of a stupid wink.

To the east of the town centre, between the ring road and the appalling 1970's Parkway housing estate, was an area known locally as Little Amsterdam. Personally, I always felt that it should've been known as Very Little Amsterdam, or even Teeny-weenie Amsterdam. You might think that the area got its name because of its remarkable similarity to the capital city of Holland, and you could very well be right. However, the differences were fairly major. Amsterdam, the jewel in the Netherlands' crown, boasts hundreds if not thousands of beautifully gabled canalside townhouses. It has fifteen hundred bridges and over sixty-five miles of ancient canals. Teeny-weenie Amsterdam didn't boast about anything much at all. Only two of its eight Victorian townhouses were built with Dutch gables, and its half mile of the recently restored Brewery Canal looked like a long thin murky pond. Indeed, there were one or two more cynical locals who suggested that there might've been other reasons why the area to the east of the town centre got its name, but I never saw a red light bulb whenever I passed by.

Enid Fulton lived at the far end of the Brewery canal in a house that her late husband, property developer and local councillor, Jack Fulton, built for her just before he was supposed to retire. What Jack Fulton hadn't been able to tell his wife was that their new home was all he had left. On the day they moved in, Jack declared himself bankrupt, and a week later, on his sixty-fifth birthday, and before Enid found out, he drove to a local wood and shot himself in the head. I never met Jack Fulton, but several years later, when Enid became a client of mine, a friend of hers told me that despite the magnificent front she put on, Enid had never recovered from the shock. How could I be surprised?... bloody men.

As I stepped onto the towpath, a solitary streetlamp a few yards ahead blinked into life, its light bouncing across the breeze-rippled surface of the canal like a shoal of silver minnows tracking flies. I walked the length of the path, and at the far end of the not so *Dutch* terrace, I turned into a short cul-de-sac. Enid Fulton's home was dead ahead.

The crunch of my footsteps on the driveway worked better than an automatic doorbell, and before I'd reached the front porch, an upstairs window shuddered open.

'Oh, hello dear, what a lovely surprise.' Enid called down; her voice was weak and breathy. 'Have you come to see me?' She asked, I smiled and said yes, it didn't surprise me that she'd forgotten that I was coming. 'Be a love and let yourself in, it will save me the stairs.' She dropped a set of keys from the window that I caught easily. 'It's the one with the yellow top.' She added, pre-empting the obvious question.

I found the key and unlocked the front door. Although, as a guest at a few charity garden parties, I'd visited the house several times, I'd never been invited inside. At first glance, Enid's home appeared exactly as I'd imagined it would be, neat, tidy and uncluttered, and very much to the point, until fairly recently, just like the woman who lived in it. The front door opened into a square hall from the back of which a wide staircase rose and split left and right to form a galleried landing. The lights upstairs were on. There were four other doors leading from the hall and each of them was open. The first door led to a dimly lit kitchen, from what I could see it was nothing particularly inspiring. Simple, but dated, utilitarian units on a vinyl lay floor. The rest of the rooms were in relative darkness, but from the shadows I guessed, a lacklustre lounge, a dull dining room, and sad study, and awful lot of magnolia paint.

Now this is not a snipe at Enid, just something that I'd seen happen many times before. You get old, and tired, and lonely, you want to hold onto your past, but your past becomes hard work. Your house is too big, your car is too fast, and if you are lucky enough to have family, then they are often too busy to help. And then you get sick, like Enid.

As my eyes grew accustomed to the gloom I was surprised and upset to see that the beneath the neat facade the place was actually filthy. Not the fluff and dust of a few missed days with a vacuum cleaner, but months of grimy neglect. When I closed the front door, I noticed a smell too, wafting down from upstairs, an unpleasant blend of stale fish, cleaning fluid, and urine.

'Shall I come up?' I called, knowing that I had to, but hoping that she'd say no, and would send me away.

No such luck.

'Do.' She replied, and then she started to cough.

With each step the smell got stronger, it was almost overwhelming. I held my breath wondering if I'd be able to stand it long enough to style Enid's hair. When I reached the landing, I found the cause of the smell. A jumbled pile of badly soiled bed linen, unwashed plates, and a large grubby washing up bowl full of bright green liquid that had been pushed into a corner. The liquid appeared to have something soaking in it, underwear I guessed. The thought made me shudder.

'Enid?' I called.

'In here dear.' She croaked.

I don't need to tell you how dreadful she looked. It was shocking. I tried to remember when I'd last seen her in the salon. It was certainly before she broke her hip, well before Christmas, and probably even before my mother died. I remembered that while I was doing her hair then we'd laughed about something I'd read that Prince Charles had come out with, something to do with the press or Camilla no doubt.

Enid laughed so hard that she started to cry and had to cross her legs. When she recovered herself, she'd forgotten what we were laughing about and so I had to tell her the story again. I was used to that sort of thing with my golden girls. Nevertheless, apart from the confusion and her usual lop-sided gait, Enid looked fine that day.

Perhaps I should've called to see how she was before.

The bedroom light was glaring and harsh from a single filament light bulb that was hanging shade-less in the centre of the room. Enid was sitting in her bed, her face thin and contorted; I reckoned that she was trying to smile.

'Hi' I said, in not much more than a whisper. I tried to keep the horror from my face. As I got nearer, it became obvious that Enid had lost an awful lot of weight, probably two or three stone, and she never had been a big woman. She looked emaciated.

'How are you?' I asked the question because it's what we all do in situations like that, but as soon as I'd asked I felt stupid.

'Not so good dear.' She replied. 'Not to good at all. The hip's been so bloody uncomfortable these last few days, and now Doctor Carmen has told me that I have breast cancer... God.' she wheezed. 'Cancer in my saggy old tits, can you believe it?' Enid used the exact words that she'd spoken on the telephone earlier. I guessed that she was reading from a sad script that pain and fear had etched into her mind, tragic words that she could never forget.

'I'm so sorry.' I said, feeling utterly hopeless.

'Never mind dear,' she tried to make the weird smile again, 'it's very nice of you to pop in and see me. I don't get many visitors these days.'

That I could see all too clearly, whoever was supposed to be caring for the old bird ought to have been shot. The neglect was appalling, I decided there and then, that I'd try to find out who was responsible for Enid's terrible decline and make them answer a few questions.

'It's no trouble,' I said, 'I'm just happy to see you.'

Okay, so I know that it was a bit of a lie. I know that I was wishing that I were somewhere else, anywhere else in fact, but Enid looked so tired and frail, and she was so pleased to see me that I just wanted to say something kind.

'But are you sure that you feel up to having your hair done?' I asked.

'Ooh! That would be lovely dear,' her eyes brightened, 'I was going to telephone you and see if you could manage… but I didn't want to put you out, I know that you're such a busy boy.' Her voice still sounded strained but was suddenly more cheerful. I didn't bother trying to remind her that she called me that morning, and I didn't kick myself for believing that she might have actually remembered; neither mattered. Instead, I reached for my kit bag and took out a brush.

Enid's hair was sparse and oily; it smelled of old lady and stale talcum powder. I perched myself on her bedside cabinet and started to brush it - long soothing brush strokes. I wasn't sure that I could do much else for her. Shampooing would be difficult, she looked far too frail to start hanging over the edge of a bath and regardless of how charitable I may have felt I certainly wasn't prepared to bathe her. I resigned myself to the hope that if nothing else, some company and pampering might leave her feeling at least a little better. After a moment, Enid closed her eyes and her weird smile relaxed into a look of easy contentment, like a cat enjoying a good stroke. I half expected her to start purring.

Then suddenly she lurched forward and let out a blood-curdling wail.

'Oh no, oh no!… I cannot do this any more! Please, I want to die, oh please let me die.'

I'd never heard anything like it; I dropped the brush and leapt off the bedside cabinet. Then Enid sucked in a gulp of breath that sounded like the beginnings of an air-raid siren and started again.

'Oh god please let me die, please. I know I'm going mad; it's not fair I can't stand it. I just want to die, please. Please God… please let me die!'

Enid's face screwed into an expression that was somewhere between anger and desperation. She wasn't looking at me when she cried and I don't think she was speaking to me either, I think that she was pleading with God. I didn't know what to do.

Then something peculiar happened.

While I stood frozen on one side of the bed, I caught a glimpse of my reflection in Enid's dressing table mirror on the other side. However, unlike me, my reflection wasn't rooted to the spot. As Enid wailed and groaned, and rocked back and forth, my reflection and her reflection were together. My reflection seemed to be holding Enid, comforting Enid, but while looking directly at me. I gasped and felt my knees weaken. Then something changed in my reflection's face. Its eyes began to darken and its mouth began to shape words, and while I watched, it looked away from me towards the head of Enid's bed. I followed its gaze to a cluster of pillows and then my reflection spoke to me.

'Help her, help her.' it said. I don't know if I actually heard a voice or if I read its lips and imagined the sound, but at that moment it didn't matter, I felt the crushing weight of understanding bear down on my head and I knew what I was being told to do.

CHAPTER SEVEN

The first time Enid Fulton stopped breathing I couldn't believe my luck. I'd barely picked up a pillow, before in a sudden fit of what appeared to be final despair she howled like a banshee and flung herself backwards, crashing into the heavy wooden headboard behind her. Her head took a heck of a whack. An instant later, she slumped down onto the bed shrivelled like a burst balloon. I just stood there with my mouth open and the pillow in my hands, waiting to see what would happen next, but nothing did, she just lay there, crumpled. I was certain that she was dead and felt quietly relieved that I'd been saved from a terrible job. After a few moments, I let the pillow fall to the floor, and for some reason began to look for the brush that I'd dropped earlier. I found it on the far side of the bed partly hidden under a fold of blanket close to Enid's feet. I leaned over to reach it. It was an old brush, maybe twenty-five years old. I'd bought it at a trade show when I was training in London. It was a limited edition, vulcanite nine-line Denman... very special. I picked the brush up and looked at it closely. Woven between its bristles, fine strands of Enid's silvery hair trembled with the shake of my hand. I teased the hairs out and decided that in respect to Enid Fulton I would never use it again.

Sitting on the edge of the bed, I looked around Enid's bedroom, from the door to the window, from the window to the dressing table, and from the dressing table to the mirror. I saw myself clearly, there was no hallucination, just me, and Enid, and a messy bed. Had I chosen that moment to leave, had I stood up and walked downstairs, I might never have spoken to Enid again, and I might never have learned what an incredibly tough woman she was.

However, I didn't leave. Instead, I reached for my kit-bag and took out a comb and a pair of scissors. I couldn't help that Enid would be found unwashed and in a filthy house, but at least I could make her presentable. I put the comb and scissors in my pocket and then climbed on the bed. Kneeling beside her and careful not to be heavy handed, I reached under Enid's shoulders to lift her back against the headboard. As soon as I took her weight, I felt something change around me. Enid's body stiffened, her arms clamped down against her sides, and my hands became trapped under her armpits pulling my face close to hers. Just as I was about to scream, in that instant of terror when I thought things couldn't get any worse, Enid's mouth opened and let out an almighty stomach churning belch. Wrenching my hands free, I almost jumped off the bed. The burp seemed to go on forever, a diminishing spiral of gassy hisses and pops, that when it stopped left me in no doubt that Enid had eaten fish for dinner. It was among the most disgusting moments of my life. I suppose I should have expected something like it to happen. I'd read books and I've seen some graphic documentaries on TV. However, what I could never have expected or prepared for was what happened next. When Enid straightened up, looked me in the eye and croaked, 'Pardon me.'

I could list a dozen thoughts that flashed through my head at that moment and most of them began with the letter 'F', but in the forefront of my mind was the conviction that poor dear Enid was supposed to be dead, that she needed to be dead.

Glancing around the bedroom in a state approaching hysteria, I quickly realised that the options available to me were limited, pillow one on the floor, or pillow two on the bed. However, before I had the chance to pick either of them up Enid spoke again.

'Am I dead yet?' She asked hopefully. Her voice clearer and stronger than it had been before.

'Not quite.' I answered.

'Will it be long?'

'I'll do my best.' I said, and honestly, I wanted to, Enid deserved my best.

'You are a good boy.' She patted my trembling arm. Her eyes open and twinkling under the stark glare of the single light bulb, and then she lay back.

I took a long swallow and a deep breath and then slowly, and very gently, I grasped pillow two in both hands, and eased my weight forward pressing it down firmly over

Enid's face. I used no real force and she didn't struggle, she simply escaped, a moment or two later I felt her go.

Was I a hero or a heel?

When I lifted the pillow Enid was smiling, I took that as my answer.

I couldn't bring myself to change Enid's nightclothes; wrinkles are just not my thing, but I did find her clean bed linen and I did my best with her hair. When I left her, the bedroom was clean and tidy and Enid looked quite presentable.

While I'd been searching for the linen, I had come across an open safe tucked behind what should have been a secret panel inside the airing cupboard. From what I could see, I thought it likely that Enid had been trying to find something and had simply forgotten to lock it up. Nothing suspicious - just a batty old dear.

As I was leaving, I stopped at the top of the stairs, my curiosity gene twitching and dragging me back to the airing cupboard. I simply had to peek. I opened the door and peered inside. Most of the safe's contents were dull. There was some cash, a few hundred pounds, no more, a large wad of papers and a few legal documents. I found Enid's passport and one or two other personal bits and pieces, and then I pulled out a jewellery wrap.

The wrap itself was unremarkable, about eighteen inches long and ten inches wide, covered in a deep red brushed satin, cheap but functional. However, when I opened the wrap I quickly realised that the contents did not match their cover. Three separate padded wallets unfolded equally, and at the bottom of each wallet, a further fold revealed a line of nine pockets where rings and brooches could be stored. Inside the first wallet were half a dozen masculine heavy gold chains and couple of identity bracelets. It seemed that Enid's late husband, Jack, had been a bit of a medallion man. In the second wallet, a similar weight of gold trinkets, but this time much finer and more feminine, hung well ordered from a large and complicated silver clip. The jewellery was already an impressive haul. However, on opening final wallet my heart thumped. When I untied the ribbon and revealed a hard lizard skin case embossed with the names Asprey & Garrard. The case was obviously old and somewhat tattered but inside it, I found the most fabulous emerald and diamond necklace that I'd ever seen.

I sat on the landing floor outside the airing cupboard staring at the necklace for several long minutes. The artistry was wonderful and even with my limited knowledge I was sure that the stones were real. A single octagonal emerald supported centrally by two large diamonds and set amongst a floral cluster with similar clusters repeated in a falling pattern as the necklace narrowed to its ornate clasp. Pursing my lips, I blew a silent whistle, and I decided that I'd let Enid wear the beautiful jewel one last time.

Before I took the necklace into bedroom, I returned the would-be 'loot' to the safe and shut the door, I heard something whir and then click inside. I replaced the *not so* secret panel and then closed the airing cupboard door. Stuck half way up the front of the door was a small piece of paper that I hadn't noticed earlier. It seemed that Enid had written herself a note, it read: *Don't forget to cook the fish before Saturday.* As it was already Tuesday, I began to realise why the house and Enid's burps smelled so bad. I reckoned that she'd had meant to stick the note on the fridge. I might have smiled if it weren't so sad. I turned out the landing light and carried Enid's necklace back to the bedroom.

Thankfully, Enid was exactly where I'd left her. I'd propped her head on a pillow and draped one arm over the covers, and the rested the other against her chin, hoping that she would look as if she'd simply dropped off to sleep. The 'Baby Jayne' pose would have fooled me. I took the emerald necklace from its case and carefully slipped it around Enid's neck. The clasp tried to be awkward for a moment, and a tiny gold claw hooked on the collar of Enid's nightgown, but I soon had everything back in place, and by the time I'd finished I was pleased with my work. Enid looked lovelier than I'd seen her in a while. Before I left, I pushed a stray curl of hair from her forehead and then bent and whispered, 'Goodbye'.

The towpath was dark, the lone streetlamp seeming to shed its light only into the canal. A wafting mist rose a foot or so from the water and then melted into the stillness of evening. I walked slowly. It seemed fitting. Ahead of me, a man stepped out of the gloom, a big man wearing a long overcoat. I moved to one side to let him by.

'Good evening.' He said curtly, his voice seemed somehow familiar.

'It certainly is.' I replied. I glanced at his face as we nodded to each other but I can't say that I recognised him.

The man's footsteps quickened as he walked away from me, and a few seconds after we'd passed, I heard their tone change as he stepped from the path to the road. A few steps later, the sound changed again, to the trudging crunch that came from Enid Fulton's drive. I slowed and looked over my shoulder, wondering who the man could be, a friend, a lawyer, a doctor, I couldn't guess, but whoever he was, he probably should have done more for Enid. I'd remember his face. As I neared the end of the towpath, I stopped and peered back into the gloom. Among the distant shadows, a murky silhouette approached Enid's front door, and then, on that the quietest of evenings, I heard a noise that made me laugh. When the man pressed Enid's doorbell, a very naff, and loud electronic version of Colonel Bogey struck up. The silliness was an example of the Enid Fulton that I would choose to remember.

On my way home, I dropped my kit bag into the salon and took a short cut through to the High Street. I was feeling quite buoyed. Although the shops were closed for the day, the town centre felt alive and welcoming, and I fancied a drink. The nearest pub was The Wheatsheaf, only five minutes walk away, a half a mile north of Marks & Sparks and the library. I'd lived in town for over twenty years, but until that evening, I'd never been inside The Wheatsheaf. The public bar was one of my second cousin Tristan the Christian's, favourite haunts. As I hadn't seen him since Christmas, I thought it might be good to catch up.

The door hissed like an ancient airlock when I pushed it open, as if the reek of spilled beer cheered on by the sound of tired rock and roll, was trying to bust out. Inside, a dozen weary looking punters were slouched along the length of a heavily polished Victorian bar, and behind them, a dozen more lolled around small tables on hard wooden chairs. A committee of soap opera producers might well have designed the place. Apart from a lack of horse brasses and smoke, The Wheatsheaf was the archetypal dull downtown English pub, not at all what I'd hoped to find. As I suspected, my favourite God-botherer stood at the far end of the bar, a half pint of Guinness in his hand. Tristan was chatting to big chap who, although he had his back turned to me, looked uncomfortably like Mr Ripper. I was beginning to have second thoughts, when before I could sneak away, Tristan spotted me in the doorway and in a loud voice called over to me.

'Well the Lord bless us all,' he bellowed, then he opened his arms wide in my direction. 'Hello Matey, what a sight for sore eyes.'

Although my face smiled, inside I winced.

Actually, once I settled myself, within a few minutes of sitting down at the bar, I began to feel like a local. The easy uncomplicated company was just what I needed, calming and fun; a total distraction. In all, I spent a jolly hour and a half or so sipping at a long vodkas with sugared water, while chatting about all sorts of nonsense with a viciously camp barman, and two of the biggest (physically at least) Bible bashers in town.

The barman, Marcus (Cus to his colleagues behind the bar, and if you asked me the name suited him remarkably well, although, despite his camp appearance, the young man's voice carried far less drama than I'd expected, his language was certainly fruity) turned out to be Mr Ripper's stepson. They were a contradiction of men that only fate's fickle digits could possibly have thrown together. Tristan told me during a quiet moment, when Ripper had nipped off to 'wring his rattler' as he put it, and Marcus was serving further along the bar, that Mrs Ripper, the lovely Cindy Dobson, had fallen for her son when she was just fifteen years old.

'Well I never!' I said, and I felt just like Mavis Riley from Coronation Street, sitting on a barstool listening to gossip in the Rovers' Return.

'And...' Tristan whispered, now obviously enjoying a gossip too, 'Nobody knows who his dad is... Cindy has kept it secret all this time. If you ask me, I reckon it's because he's somebody famous. You know, if you stuck some big glasses on Marcus I reckon he'd look just like a younger and maybe hairier Elton John, and Elton John used to live round these parts back then...' Tristan gave me a knowing look, tapped the side of his nose, and then took long a slurp from his beer.

'You are joking Tris? You must be'. I chuckled, incredulous. 'Elton John...'

'Don't you scoff,' my second cousin frowned at me, 'Cindy may have got herself knocked up a tad young, but the woman that you keep calling 'Mrs Ripper' is the daughter of the Right Honourable Martin Hendy-Coombs, a Home Office Minister in charge of something or other to do with prisons. Imagine it, hey, Marcus over there, his granddad a Member of Parliament, and his stepdad more or less a dustbin man. Huh! I know which one of 'em I'd rather be related to. But anyway... despite appearances, our Cindy is a proper posh bird see, all jolly rounders bats and croquet hoops.'

'Yes, but Tristan,' I said, and although I was surprised and suitably impressed that Marcus's grandfather was an MP, regardless of Tristan's wild conclusions, I didn't smile or laugh. 'Just because Marcus is 'testosteronially' challenged and a bit chubby in the face, and his mother used to live near to Elton John, it doesn't mean that the world's favourite Rocketman is his dad. For goodness' sake, I doubt if Cindy Dobson ever met Elton John, let alone shagged the poor chap.' I said, and I then slapped my hands on the bar to emphasise my point. I suppose that it was a bit of a rant but it didn't seem to deter Tristan.

'Aha, that's where you're wrong.' He said triumphantly. 'You see, Elton John didn't just live near Cindy, he lived next door. Sure as eggs is eggs, Cindy and her friends would have been in and out of his place all the time... pop stars... groupies you know.'

'Alright, look... Tris... Elton John is gay... he is married to a man.' I said and then I sighed in exasperation.

'Nah... You see, that's exactly what the bloomin' tabloids want you to think. Ever since Elton dumped the German woman, they all hate him. Look, there are loads of men that are a bit girlie, bless'em, men that are... well... in touch with their female parts, it doesn't mean they're all woolly woofters, does it? I mean look at you.'

'What do you mean? *Look at me*.' I said. I couldn't believe what I was hearing. Fortunately, before Tristan had the chance to dig himself any deeper into the metamorphic graveyard of non-pc-ness Mr Ripper returned from the bathroom.

'Anyone fancy some grub?' he asked, slapping my second cousin on the back.

The mention of food was like a magic charm, Tristan's eyes glazed over and I reckon that if he'd been a dog, he'd have started drooling.

'Kebab or pizza?' he asked

'I was thinking of fish and chips.' Ripper suggested.

'Maccy D's?' Tristan shrugged, obviously unimpressed with his friend's suggestion, but still hopeful that he might get his way.

While the two big men were discussing their higher gastronomic alternatives, a group of five grimly clad walkers entered the pub and moved to a table a few yards away from the bar. Four of the group sat down while the fifth took a note of what each of them wanted to drink and then turned towards me.

When our eyes met we both froze, the chill of frosty recognition that passed between us was palpable. It had been nineteen years since we'd last spoken, yet from the first instant of that icy stare, I could tell that the animosity remained strong. This had been my very good friend, the person who I'd loved and trusted, but who had turned their back on me because of a stupid misunderstanding. Although we lived in the same town, since that dreadful day when Marjorie Warton stole my friend's gold necklace, somehow we'd managed to avoid each other very well. Surely, we'd glimpsed each other from time to time, on the street or across a crowded room, but we'd never been caught like this, never face to face.

I reached into my jacket pocket and my fingertips found the gold chain that I'd carried with me since I picked it up from the floor in the Wart Hog's apartment. Since the day that I discovered what had really happened in my salon on July 17th nineteen years ago. I cupped the chain in my hand and shook it gently, it rattled like a pair of dice, the six numbers on each gambling together in my palm. If I'd thrown an odd number, I might have held the gaze for a second longer and given the chain back with nothing more than a wry smile. However, my imagined throw came out evens and the hurt still burned my fingers, and so I turned away.

Tristan grabbed my shoulder and pulled me back to the bar.

'It's a Mega Family Bucket from Kentucky Fried Chicken then,' He said, 'is that okay with you?'

'Yeh… anything… no…' I stuttered, trying to clear my thoughts. 'Actually Tris I think I'm going to head on home now. I've had a long day, thanks though.'

'That's okay Matey, all the more for me. It's been good to see you though. God bless.' Tristan rubbed his stomach and grinned.

I patted my second cousin's arm, nodded at Mr Ripper, and after smiling and waving goodbye to Marcus at the bar, I turned for the door.

The night air nibbled at my earlobes. I turned my collar and bunched my shoulders against the random draughts gusting between the taller buildings on the Upper High Street. Although my feet weighed heavy against the pavement, I walked quickly, sifting my thoughts into their proper compartments with each step. I reckoned that overall I'd had a good day, a marvellous day in fact. I felt more alive and in control than I could remember. I had dealt with conflict that I would have normally avoided. My working day had been fun, and I had done something of which I felt I could be truly proud. If there was a blot on my otherwise spirit-raising horizon, it was that I hadn't returned the gold chain when I had the chance. I wondered if the chance would ever come again.

Towards the top of the High Street, I passed a man wearing an insipid green trilby hat and a three quarter length cream macintosh who reminded me of my father. A fleeting daydream had him stop and talk to me.

'Hello Sonny-Jim,' he might have said, looking me in the eye, 'what have you been up to?' My father always knew when I was keeping secrets.

When I was sure that the man had walked far enough by I allowed myself to answer.

'Not much.' I said timidly. I imagined my father smoothing his chin and cocking his head to one side, giving me the sort of look that made me hunch my shoulders and shove my hands deep into my pockets when I was a child.

'Have you been a good boy?' He would've asked.

'I think so.' I said aloud. My ears caught a metallic echo from the otherwise empty street. The answer wouldn't have satisfied my father, but I was happy enough with it.

When I arrived home at Gillycote Road, my naive contentment was quickly dented. I found my front door in a terrible state; spattered with slimy clumps of rotting garden waste. A green sack shoved partway through the letterbox and on it, someone had written in large black letters a single word, 'Prat'. It took me a few seconds to realise what had happened. I yanked the sack free and screwed it into a ball. My fat pig-faced neighbour's revenge had been brutal. I silently declared war. Although I was livid, and leaving my front door in such a state was hard to bear, I was tired and I couldn't face cleaning up muck at that time of night. And so instead of wading through the mire of rotting filth, I followed the garden path around the house to the kitchen door.

After fixing myself a light supper of a tuna melt and salad, I poured myself a large shot of vodka with big spoonful of sugar, and crashed on the settee in front of a re-run of Sex and the City. It was an old show that I'd seen before and had only put on to wind down from the excitement of the day. I managed to watch about five minutes of banter between Carrie and Big before I drifted off to sleep. I woke up with a start just after midnight with a stiff neck, a blocked nose and pins and needles running down my left arm. I'd been dreaming of Enid Fulton and Marjorie Warton. I uncurled myself slowly and rolled on to my feet. I felt exhausted… physically and emotionally drained.

The dream was ridiculous, quite frightening and still vivid in my mind. It centred round an outrageous circus on the High Street just outside my salon. A Wurlitzer organ was playing Elton John songs throughout, and a full tally of dazzling circus folk, led by a deep pink serpentine creature that looked uncannily like Marjorie Warton, were parading by. As the procession passed, several other clients appeared, all in brilliant costume, including a young Enid Fulton creepily attired as a drag queen ringmaster complete with bondage gear, eight-inch heels, and a long black whip. She threw the whip to me. Suddenly, I was in charge of my own personal Rocky Horror Show. Disappointingly, my unconscious mind had garbed me in a navy blue chequered dressing gown that I remembered from my early childhood, a birthday present from an aged aunt I think, that became something of a comforting blanket. Even more disappointing was that beneath the dressing gown, at the collar and cuffs, I could see traces of pink satin. Now here comes a minor confession. I'm afraid that I did own a pair of pink satin pyjamas once. They'd also been a gift, this time a jokey 'Secret Santa' present from a close colleague. Obviously, being bright and shiny they weren't particularly practical, so slippery in bed in fact, that I hardly ever wore them because whenever I did, and rolled over in my sleep, I woke up afraid that my momentum might flip me out of bed. Actually, in my dream the pyjamas weren't quite the same as they'd been in real life. Although, in my dream, I couldn't see them clearly under the dressing gown, somehow, I knew that for some reason my mind had chosen to embroider the pink satin with neat rows of little black arrows. I wouldn't have minded the disappointment, but as it was my dream, you might have thought I'd have given me a more dynamic costume.

As the show went on, the imagery grew darker, and like an obscene corruption of a Beryl Cook sketch, Enid Fulton began to bloat. From my vantage point, somewhere high above my salon I watched as her body grew tightly engorged with a roiling purplish fluid. It was then that the pink serpent creature that was Marjorie Warton reappeared. Now more resembling a giant slug, she didn't look happy. The creature slid alongside Enid's swollen body and together, like huge twin blobs of yuck they opened two gaping maws, howled hot spittle, and foul breath in my direction.

Whoah!

Surprisingly, it wasn't that that woke me up. While the Grisly Goo Sisters were yelling, a group of a dozen of my favourite clients had gathered round them and were starting to throw stones. I could see the danger straight away. Marjorie and Enid were not so exclusively interested in me, that they'd ignore having lumps of rock hurled at them. I had to do something.

With a flick of my wrist, I unfurled the whip that Enid had thrown to me, twenty, maybe thirty feet of harsh leather quivered in my hand. Of course, I aimed the whip at the Goo Girls, but I was never much of a shot. The first strike hit one of my clients, Silvia Cokeley, a member of my salon's bridge club and the wife of John Cokeley, the vicar of St Michael's Church. Silvia took the blow full in the face and promptly burst like a party balloon. My second strike hit Helen Kenyon, Baroness Hels, as posh as you like with a seat in the Lords. My whip caught Helen with an upward crack straight between the legs... Puff! she was gone... and so it went on. Once I'd started I simply couldn't stop, no matter that I kept missing my target, ten more hopeless lashes, until I'd got the lot.

Finally, it was just me, the whip and the Sisters Goo. For some strange reason (this was a dream remember), I knew that my next lash, the thirteenth, wouldn't miss. I swung my arm back, as I did I seemed to grow an extra forty or fifty feet taller, and whirled the black leather whip in the air until it sizzled and then crashed towards Enid and Marjorie. A split second before the point of impact the women's form changed back to my last memory of them, Marjorie, hair frazzled in my salon chair, and Enid, small and frail in her dirty bed. When at last the lash struck it seemed to wrap itself around both of the women as if drawing them together. There was a moment, an instant, when they both looked at me, when perhaps one of them smiled.

And then, like a shock of hair scorched in a candle flame, they shrivelled, burning into the dusty ground. I closed my eyes.

It was the thought of the dreadful smell that woke me up.

I thanked God for vodka and sugar, and stumbled off to bed.

CHAPTER EIGHT

Alas, the second half of the third week in February in my rather special year failed to live up to my hopes. It was a shame, because the Wednesday started out quite well. Tristan turned up quite out of the blue, and woke me by whistling outside my bedroom window. When I opened the window, he called up to me. He'd come early because he knew that I would be seeing Cindy Dobson that morning and he wanted to make sure that I didn't repeat anything that he'd said about her or her son Marcus the evening before. I promised him I wouldn't and invited him in for breakfast. As Tristan ducked under the porch, he raised an eyebrow and asked me about the state of the front door. I'd quite forgotten the mess that I'd come home to on the Tuesday evening. I told him what had happened with my neighbour, over breakfast. I had my usual, a small bowl of granola and cup of strong coffee. I made the coffee especially potent, as my head was still thick from the extra slug of vodka that I'd downed to get off to sleep. Tristan munched his way through the best part of a large loaf of multi-grained bread, a quarter pound of butter and most of a new jar of Robertson Golden Shred. He made himself three cups of tea, and drank a carton and a half of pineapple juice, which drained my supplies completely, and pineapple juice was my favourite. And the man wondered why I didn't invite him round often.

When I'd finished my story about the conflict with my neighbour, I put my hands flat on the table and muttered something terribly brave about getting my own back. At first Tristan laughed, but after a moment his expression changed to one of indignation, he steepled his fingers in thought.

'This…' He said seriously, 'is a family thing.' and then he stood up, he put on his coat, and ducked back out through the front door. Fifteen minutes later, - after I'd showered and dressed - I heard noises outside and opened my front door to find my neighbour on his hands and knees scrubbing my front step. He didn't say anything he just glanced at me and shook his head.

Tristan gave me a lift to work that morning. It was a dull drizzly day, the kind of day that confuses windscreen wipers.

'You didn't hit him did you?' I asked.

'No I didn't.' Tristan eyes flashed at me. I guessed that he was surprised and probably hurt that I'd even thought to ask.

'It's just that I have to live next door to him.' I said defensively.

'That's okay, don't worry, I just pointed out where he was going wrong, that's all. Then I read him something from the bible. Matthew 22 verse 36 to 40, the first bit goes something like - *Love the Lord your God with all your heart and with all your soul and with all your mind. This is the first and greatest commandment.* And then the second bit goes: *'Love your neighbour as yourself. All the Law and the Prophets hang on these two commandments.'*

'Bloody hell.' I said weakly.

'Your language maybe a tad inappropriate Matey, but I understand the sentiment.' He said piously.

'Yes, sorry and… Thanks Tris.'

'No prob's, he's coming to church on Sunday too.' Tristan looked at me solemnly for a moment and then grinned, I wasn't sure if he was telling me the truth but I wouldn't have put it past him.

Tristan dropped me on the pavement outside Starbucks and as I waved him off, I saw him fiddling with his mobile phone. A second later, my mobile chirped to tell me that I had a new text message. After hitting a button, I squinted to read the latest little gem my lovely second cousin had chosen to send me. *'Remember… Today is national Hug-a-Looney day, so if a stranger gives you a cuddle don't get upset like you did last year'.*

I smiled.

Inside Starbucks, I was disappointed to find that Colin had called in sick. A girl called Julie who I'd never seen before, but who had terrible acne and smelled of patchouli oil, told me that he had the mumps. All those swollen glands, I winced at

81

the thought. Julie mistook my squeamish concern for irritation and was quick to reassure me that Colin had given her a list of his regular customers' requirements. She proceeded to make me a tall skinny latté and then cut me a generous slice of sharp lemon cake. I tried to protest and patted my tummy, but Julie suggested that as Lent began the following week it would be sensible to start my diet then. She was a nice girl. I liked Julie.

Cindy Dobson was my only client that morning. She was late. She arrived at twenty past ten in something of a tizzy. I didn't mind too much. I didn't think that she was going to turn up at all. When I sat her down, she told me that she'd just had a terrible row with her husband, Tristan's friend, Ripper. She gave me the impression, that although her marriage tended toward the fiery, this morning's quarrel had been a real humdinger. I oohed and ahhed in all the right places, good old professional empathy and all that, but from what she told me, disappointingly I found that I was on her husband's side. She had done her man wrong. The gist of the tale hinged around an evening out that Cindy had told Ripper she'd spent with some girlfriends. They'd started with dinner in a local Bistro, and had then headed off to a club. In my experience the combination of alcohol, loud music, and short skirts, always seems to get girls and boys into trouble, and it sounded as though Cindy had found plenty. Although she didn't say as much, I guessed that she'd been naughty with someone that she'd met at the club. She just told me that she didn't get home until very late.

Apparently, Ripper had been furious, but that after a couple of days, tempers calmed, and things had settled down. Then the text messages started, *'It was great, when can we do it again?'* that sort of thing. Cindy left the messages saved on her phone, the silly thing. When Ripper couldn't find his phone and used Cindy's to make a call he came across them. Cindy tried to persuade him that they were from a girl friend, but then he found one that read, *'I'm aching for you, baby. I want you now.'* When he read message aloud, Cindy ran out of the house. That was why she had been late into the salon.

I spent most of Cindy's cut and blow dry appointment trying to convince her that Ripper probably wouldn't actually kill her. I hardly got my scissors to work at all. Where I'd found her first, surprise appointment, an uplifting experience and fun, this was hard going. As I put the finishing touches to her haircut, she looked in the mirror, flicked at her fringe and asked me if she needed highlights.

'I feel dull.' She said, with a pout.

To be perfectly frank, since Christmas, business had been appalling, and while by then Cindy's nervous prattle was like an irritating fly buzzing in my ear, and in truth, I thought her hair already looked quite good, I needed the money. Mercenary, I know.

'Highlights would look gorgeous.' I said. I'm afraid I'd become a shade too comfortable in the company of deceit over the years, three decades in the trade and all that jazz… blah, blah, blah.

When St Michael's Church clock struck two, Cindy, with her hair neatly wrapped in dozens of tiny tin foil packages, was still sitting in my salon. One of my two afternoon appointments had already cancelled, and when the phone rang again, I was afraid that the caller would polish off my day completely. I was wrong.

I didn't even know that Enid Fulton had a daughter. Enid had never spoken of her. I could only assume that they weren't particularly close. Her name was Elizabeth, she pronounced it precisely, not Liz, Lizzie, or Beth. She told me quite simply that her mother had died and that she would no longer require her regular Friday afternoon slot. I didn't tell her that Enid hadn't visited the salon in several months or that I'd already taken her regular bookings out. Elizabeth asked me if her mother owed me any monies. I told her no. Then she asked me if I'd be able to attend the funeral at St Michael's Church, at two o'clock on Friday. Her invitation caught me by surprise.

Friday… I thought… *so soon…* I said I'd go.

Finally, Elizabeth Fulton thanked me for all I'd done to help her mother and wished me a good day. While I was glad that she thanked me, I couldn't help wondering where she'd been those last few months. Certainly not looking after her mother.

I have to say that when I finished Cindy's hair, it looked great. I was right; with my highlights, she looked gorgeous. It was one of those, sadly all too few, cathartic moments in my life, an ego confirmation, '*I can still turn it on,*' I thought, and I slapped myself a mental high five. Cindy was delighted. She twirled round the salon shaking her hair and posing in the mirrors in a nifty and shameless skit of Twiggy in the 1960s, and for that moment, all her worries seemed to disappear.

Unfortunately, our good cheer lasted only as far as the credit card machine. We pried four cards from Cindy's wallet in all. In fairness, the first was simply out of date, but according to Cindy, the other three should have been fine.

'The rotten bastard.' She spat, and she looked angry. I guessed that she was referring to Mr Ripper. 'It's my bloody money.' She continued. 'Well my father's actually, but how dare Francis stop the cards!'

...And that was it, without another word, Cindy grabbed her coat from the rack, snatched up her handbag, and ran out of my salon.

I wouldn't have minded but I could have done with the eighty-five quid. I'd already had a call from my bank manager that week, suggesting that I pop in to see him for a chat about my overdraft. Not that I needed to pop in for a chat anywhere, I didn't need the bank manager, I could've handled the chat all by myself.

The bank: 'Give us the money.'

Me: 'I can't.'

The bank: 'We want it back.'

Me: 'I haven't got it.'

The bank: 'Where is it?'

Me: 'Starbucks, Marks and Spencer, Tesco's wine shop... quite a lot in Tesco's wine shop actually.' The list could've gone on.

I slumped into the chair behind the reception desk and sighed.

The week went downhill from then on really. My only other appointment on that Wednesday, Agnes Carmen, failed to turn up. She didn't even bother to call me, bloody cheek. A year or so before and I probably wouldn't have given a stuff. Agnes Carmen wasn't even a regular, and any unexpected gap in my schedule allowed an extra cup of tea, but the recent trend was worrying.

Thursday was hardly any better; two blow waves, two dry haircuts and two shampoo and sets. At least they all paid in cash. I bought another bottle of vodka on my way home.

I'd never liked Fridays, although since the happy pills kicked in, they no longer got me down. The trouble with Friday in a hairdressing salon is simple. Friday is the day when all the old dears want their hair done to look good for the weekend. It's not as if they're likely to do anything particularly special. Most of them will sit in watching Strictly Come Dancing and Songs of Praise. The problem is that they all book their appointments months ahead. For me, the average Friday comprised twenty half hour slots filled with the same person, at the same time, every week, year in year out - riveting.

However, this particular Friday was different. In order to get to Enid Fulton's funeral I needed to take the afternoon off and therefore had to telephone several of my regular clients to reschedule their appointments. Most understood my dilemma and simply swapped to another day. There were one or two miserable blighters who were obviously miffed and cancelled their appointments altogether; and then there was Cecile Ablitt, Cindy Dobson's aunt. Usually a moderate example of womankind, Cecile reacted to my telephone call to change her appointment by screaming profanities and threatening to sue me. I was stunned. The tirade lasted for well over a minute and only stopped because her hysterics brought on a coughing fit. When she recovered and I managed to get a few words of sense, I quickly discovered that Cecile was upset because she needed her hair to be 'absolutely perfect' for a special charity engagement that weekend. On Sunday afternoon, at a quarter past five, Cecile, Cindy Dobson's aged aunt, and a three time military widow, was to be presented to Her Majesty Queen Elizabeth II during a dedication ceremony at the Army and Navy Club in Pall Mall. What was I to do but give in? I found myself promising to call at Cecile's home with my box of tricks on Sunday morning.

Considering the shortness of the notice St Michael's Church looked splendid.

I'd finished my last client, Carolyn Croucher, a creepy little woman with slathery lips and a permanently runny nose, a few minutes earlier than I'd expected to and so arrived at the church almost half an hour before the service was due to begin. To save myself a walk through the graveyard, I entered through the south transept door. I probably shouldn't have. I'd noticed, when passing before, that the particular entrance to the church seemed to be used mainly by newlyweds and dead people. When I pushed the heavy door open - probably more quickly that was sensible I'll admit - I almost flattened the verger. The poor chap had been standing behind the door sneaking a crafty smoke. I don't think the door caught him particularly hard, just enough to knock him off balance and topple him to the floor. He didn't make much noise. I'm not sure which of us was more embarrassed, me for being where I shouldn't have been, or him for... well considering what he was doing... probably ditto. Whatever, before I could blink, the old fellow was scrabbling back to his feet, and stubbing his cigarette out under his shoe, while muttering something about 'bloody coffin nails'. Perhaps not the most appropriate choice of words at a funeral I'll grant you, but in the event, the unintentional irony made both of us chuckle, and probably helped to diffuse what might have been an awkward situation. However, happy that the old chap was obviously okay, I was about to apologise and continue past him to make my way inside, when a man's voice called from behind the curtain covering the entrance to the church.

'Are you okay Mick?'

'I'm fine… I'm fine' The verger replied anxiously while brushing himself down and fanning a hand in front of his mouth.

A second later, a fold in the curtain drew back and a swarthy face that I recognised immediately peered through.

'It was just a bump, an accident.' I said reflexively to Detective Dennis Sapsead who was now staring at me through the gap in the curtains. For some reason I felt instantly defensive. 'It was the door… I just pushed it too firmly, that's all.'

What exactly the detective who'd come to see me after Marjorie Warton disappeared was doing in St Michael's Church right then and why his appearance bothered me so much when all I'd done was inadvertently bump into an old man, I didn't know, but thankfully, as if to confirm what I'd said the verger started nodding.

'That's right Dennis.' He said. 'I thought the wind had blown it in… it knocked me clean off my feet.' Then, turning his back to the detective and discretely pointing to his cigarette end on the floor, the verger put a finger to his lips and mouthed. 'Ssshh.'

Fortunately, understanding his dilemma quickly, I nodded back equally discretely and then tried to help by fibbing to the policeman.

'I was just having a quiet smoke outside before the funeral began and when I leaned on the door it fell open.' I said, and then I added, reaching for the stub on the floor, and looking back at the verger. 'I'm most dreadfully sorry.'

'No trouble… no trouble at all.' The verger said, while silently thanking me with a wink.

'Well that's okay then.' DC Dennis Sapsead said to both of us but while looking only at me, and I could see from something in the furrow of his bushy eyebrows that despite what he'd said he knew that I'd lied. However, after holding my eye for only a moment longer than felt comfortable, he turned to the verger, and added. 'I've got the bell ringing rota, so if you're okay, I'll be off now Mick. I'll see you on Sunday.'

Finally, Detective Sapsead pulled the curtain back fully, opening the way into the church, and I think, with both the verger and I breathing a sigh of relief, we were all about to head off in our separate ways when quite abruptly the tall policeman asked.

'Who died?'

'Enid Fulton.' The verger said, and his face dropped and he shook his head as he spoke her name.

'Oh no.' Detective Sapsead said.

'I'm afraid so, quite suddenly on Tuesday.'

'Heart?'

'Stroke, I think.'

'Such a lovely woman.' The detective said, and then he looked back to me. 'A customer of yours?' He asked, his eyebrows again furrowing.

'Yes…' I replied, almost flinching from his stare. '…and a jolly good'un… one of my favourites actually.' I found myself saying, once again feeling suddenly defensive.

'Another one bites the dust then.' He said, and what could I do, but nod?

The main body of the eighteenth century parish church ran from east to west and had been decorated for the funeral with tall candelabra arrangements of cream calla lilies and red gladioli. A soft ethereal midday glow from the circular stained glass window in the nave lit the flowers perfectly. I've often thought it a pity that lilies are so closely associated with funerals and sadness; they are such a beautiful flower.

Beyond the nave, close to the main door, a cluster of people had gathered and some were chatting with the vicar, John Cokeley, a pasty balding man with a 'Dick Emery' smile. I recognised one or two of the group as clients. John's wife Sylvia, who although she was wearing a veiled hat, looked much better than she had in my dream on Tuesday night, Hilary Sidebottom was there too. A lifelong friend of Enid's, Hilary was an unfortunately ugly woman who I'd never taken to, but as she liked to keep her expensive hair colour touched up fortnightly I always smiled and made her welcome in the salon. Among the others talking with the vicar was a woman who I reckoned to be in her late forties and guessed was Enid's daughter Elizabeth. My assumption wasn't from any family resemblance or from any obvious offspring grief, but simply that the others in the group, and even the vicar, appeared to defer to her sympathetically. To the woman's left, the only other man in the group, a tall, solidly built chap with a shock of silver grey hair whose face I recognised from somewhere but couldn't place, stood close to the door and seemed to be looking back in my direction. When I caught his eye, instead of turning away the man simply shrugged his shoulders and carried on staring. I wondered why, but at the time, I can't say that the attention worried me.

After politely, and I felt thoughtfully, switching my mobile phone off, I took a seat towards the back of the nave, and with time to pass, engaged in my newly learned game of people watching. I thought of it as doodling in the mind. I was respectful naturally, no licentiousness; I was in a church after all. I started with the vicar's group by the door and by 01:55, I'd followed the entire mourning congregation to their pews and had given most of them a new film star name and a pertinent story. Actually, it wasn't particularly testing. To be frank, there weren't many people there. Somehow, I'd expected the church to be packed, full of the friends and relatives, and former colleagues of a woman who I'd always known to be bright and gregarious... but sadly not. Of twenty rows of pews, only the first three had no spaces. It seemed to me that people had given up on Enid all round. It made me wonder if that's what happens when a life fades badly. Stuck on my own towards the back of the church, when the organ struck up with some miserable Wagner dirge, I felt bound to move forward and quietly sneaked to a seat at the end of the fourth pew, behind the tall man who I'd thought I recognised.

As John Cokeley took his place at the lectern, I thought of my mother. Her funeral had been a simple affair. No flowers, only one hymn, 'Great is Thy Faithfulness'. I'm not a religious person but that particular hymn always raises goose bumps.

Enid's service on the other hand, I'm afraid began with that most silly of hymns, 'All Things Bright and Beautiful'. It seems to me that whenever a person is stuck for something to sing in a church, at a wedding, a christening, or even at a funeral, then that wretched song is first to be dragged out. Perhaps I'm a cynic. I have heard it sung well. Five hundred Welsh schoolchildren did the lyricist, someone-or-other Alexander, proud on the BBC's 'Songs of Praise' during a 'Children in Need' special. In my experience however, apart from the chorus, the hymn's soppy sentiment is most likely heard as a half-mumbled, self-conscious chant. The few assembled for Enid's last bash didn't let me down either. An elderly woman, sitting close to the front next to Hilary Sidebottom, warbled somewhat ahead of everybody else. The chap in front of me groaned his way through every verse, but most of the rest of us, yes - including me, opened and closed our mouths like lines of guppies, rhythmically gasping for breath, only pretending to sing. Even the organist played to my rule, an adagio rendition of each verse that made Beethoven's Fifth Symphony seem nifty.

Unfortunately, when at last the congregation sat down, John Cokeley followed the mood by leading us into a funeral service that was so dull and uninspiring that I found it hard to keep awake.

I suppose it wasn't entirely his fault. Apart from choosing three very naff hymns and a two-line reading from Lao Tzu that went something like:

'*Death is at once*
the   end   of   the   body's   old   journey
and the beginning of the soul's new journey.'

Enid's daughter didn't give him much scope. I have to confess that rather than listening to the vicar I spent a deal of time watching his mouth and wondering why it was that the clergy so often had protruding teeth. I'd never noticed it before but as he stood there solemnly reciting the traditional funereal text, with his piously nodding head and goofy chops, John Cokeley looked a splendid caricature mix of a bald Billy Graham and Bugs Bunny - the archetypal comedy priest.

Towards the end of the service, after we'd *sung* the third hymn, and when the pallbearers were preparing to remove Enid's coffin, I began to realise that nobody was going to stand up and speak. There would be no eulogy. Not even from Enid's daughter. I was horrified. At my mother's funeral, we had a job to keep people down. Almost everybody wanted to say something. It was true that quite a few of us struggled to blub much more than to say that we'd miss her, but my Uncle Bert, and my mother's cousin Ruth, both did her proud. Uncle Bert was up for almost ten minutes, telling us stories of my mother's childhood. Apparently, she was a terror... I remember promising myself that I'd call on Bert one day and get him to tell me some more.

As I watched the pallbearers carry Enid away, I looked around at the miserable faces and I was tempted to get up to the lectern and say something myself. I suppose that considering the circumstances and my part in her passing, it might not seem entirely appropriate, but at the time, it felt to me that whatever I'd said would have been better than the nothing her family were offering. I could have told the congregation that the poor old girl had wanted to die, that I'd helped her along, and that she'd been glad to get away from them. I could have told Enid's daughter that her mother had died in dirty sheets on a dirty bed and that I'd had to clean her up... but I didn't. Instead, at the end of the service, I sat down, and like everybody else, I bowed my head and I said a prayer.

The organist played us out to the music from the Hamlet cigar advert, Bach's Air on a G-string. I've always liked the tune. It reminded me of cups of tea and chocolate cakes, and warm settees and Sunday afternoon naps. When I'd said my prayer, I raised my head to look around and I found that the chap sitting in front of me, the man who I'd seen talking to Enid's daughter before the funeral began, had turned to face me. The instant our eyes met I realised that I did recognise him after all, that he was the man I'd passed on the towpath the night that Enid died. The chap fixed me with a stare that he held for several long seconds, and then he leaned forward, and said.

'I know what you did for Enid.' A moment later, he was up and gone.

CHAPTER NINE

I was stunned.

I took a long deep breath and leaned back against the church pew, the hard wood pushing my spine straight; a sharp and uncomfortable distraction. I sat there for several minutes, trying to draw a thousand strands of chaotic thought into one clear ribbon. My mind raced and a tingle of anxiety rose through my body as adrenaline beat its way past my happy pills' defences. 'Who was this man?' I wondered. 'Had I heard him correctly?' I knew that he'd seen me by the canal, but why would he think that I'd even been to Enid's house let alone done anything for her?

Before I could fully gather myself, I became aware that someone was standing close by. I glanced up to see Hilary Sidebottom. She was looking directly at me and wearing a sickly smile that made her look even more unattractive than usual.

'I'm surprised to see *you* here.' She said it sweetly enough, but there was a catch in her tone. 'I didn't realise that you knew dear Enid so well, it was such a shame and she'd been doing so well, but still, God's will.' Then Hilary stepped closer and, before I had a chance to say anything about Enid's health, she added in not much more than a whisper. 'I don't suppose you're expecting to come to the crematorium or to the hotel afterwards, but in case you are, maybe I should tell you that Elizabeth would prefer to keep both strictly to friends and family.'

'I understand.' I said meekly.

I understood all right, in fact I knew my place in her sort's scheme of things all too well. I was trade, maybe one jump above service, but still half a dozen below the professional.

'Well dear, I must fly.' She said, straightening up and renewing her smile. 'We must give poor Enid a good send-off, mustn't we'?

I nodded my head but I didn't bother answering. I was afraid that if I'd opened my mouth at all, it might have bitten her head off.

A blackbird was singing in the churchyard. I saw it perched on a toppled headstone as I left the church. When it saw me, it flew away. The grave gave me pause. It belonged to a man called Frederick William Jarvis.

My father was a Frederick William. Red-Fred, they'd called him at school. I don't think he was a kindergarten communist or anything sinister, just a bit gingery on top. My father had a tremendous sense of fun and was the most nicknamed person I've ever come across. It seemed to me, that everyone that knew him gave him a pet name. As a teenager, he'd sported drainpipe trousers, and brothel creeper shoes, and his best friend had called him 'Ted-Fred' for the rest of his life. When it came to National Service, in the army catering corps, my father put on so much weight that a sergeant dubbed him 'Shed-Fred', and so it went on, his friends and the family alike. If he was sick, they called him Bed-Fred, when he bought a scooter he became Moped-Fred, and thanks to Bernard Cribbins, when people saw him, they'd whistle the tune to 'Right Said Fred'. My favourite was my mother's name for him, Swinger. It caught everybody out because it didn't rhyme. However, put aside the more obvious naughtier thoughts, my parents were churchgoers. No, nothing vulgar, the nickname came about because my father took a few days off around the 1966 World Cup. I'd barely been born. My mother asked him, apparently quite innocently, 'are you swinging the lead, Fred?' Swinger stuck.

Years later, only a few months before he retired, and by then quite the local comic character, my father earned his most tragic nickname, the local newspaper even used it in the headline to the report of his death.

In order to battle an ever-increasing waistline, my father took up power walking; it became a serious hobby. One summer Saturday, he led a group of walkers on a £10,000 charity fundraiser to, in my father's words, 'Yomp the crags of Mount Snowden'. It all went terribly well, until they reached the top. In the spirit of all 'proper' mountaineers, my father had taken along a Union flag to claim the peak for Queen and

Country. As the group approached the summit, he broke ranks and marched ahead at full speed. Unfortunately, before he could plant the pennant, my father suffered a massive heart attack. The doctors told us that he would have been dead before he hit the ground.

Knowing my father's sense of humour, the editor of the local paper called my mother before they published the report of his death, she laughed when he told her what they wanted to print, she said that my father would have loved it, the headline read, 'Drop Dead Fred peaks at £10,000'.

The only pity was that my father, so wrapped up in being larger than life, that he never really took to the one name that mattered to me... Dad.

I gazed at the blackbirds wonky perch. *Frederick William Jarvis. Who departed this life on June 1st 1925. Son, Father and Husband.* That was it. I wondered how this Dead Fred's tale might have read. Maybe headstones should tell us more.

I'd planned to visit Starbucks on the way back to the salon, to treat myself to a latté and a small slice of cake, but as I left the churchyard and I noticed the time, I realised that I needed something more substantial to eat. I could've dropped in to Marks and Sparks, found a healthy salad and some fruit and eaten it in the salon with a bottle of fizzy camomile water. I could've called at Charlotte's Tearooms and ordered a slice of wholemeal quiche with boiled potatoes and long green beans. I could have, but as I passed McDonalds first, I pulled up my collar and snuck inside.

A cheese quarter pounder with medium fries, a banana milkshake and a thermo nuclear apple pie later, I wiped my mouth and was about to sneak back onto the High Street when Marcus Hendy-Coombs, the rotund barman from the Wheatsheaf and Cindy Dobson's son, tapped me on the shoulder. On that Friday afternoon, he looked pale, pudgy and uninteresting, not as I'd remembered him from the pub and nothing like his mother at all.

'Well now, fancy seeing you here.' Marcus smiled coolly, his dark eyes firmly fixed on mine. He was carrying a takeaway bag and obviously on his way out of the restaurant. 'I wouldn't have thought eating at the big 'M' was your style.' He leaned against my table as he spoke.

'Ordinarily, you'd be right,' I replied far too quickly, 'but I've just been to a funeral and I'm due back at the salon. I'm very short of time.' I tried to excuse myself by suggesting that I'd just dropped in for a quick snack, but the pile of debris on the table told a different story. 'Anyway,' I added 'I'm sure I could say the same for you.' but as I said it, I looked at the size of his middle and realised that he probably lived in the place.

'Mmmm.' He answered slowly, following my eyes, a hint of a frown flickered across his face and the tone of his voice confirming my guess. 'Well, whatever you like to eat.' He added, his smile slowly returning, 'you're looking good on it. I don't usually find older men attractive, but…'

'Oh!' I said, and despite the negative inflection, it seemed to be a reasonable response at the time. 'Thanks, I think.'

'I wanted to tell you the other night, but those two brutes were always in the way.'

'Ah, Tris and Ripper,' I said, 'yes they were, weren't they?' I wasn't quite sure how I was going to handle this new development. Marcus may have been interested in me, but I was certainly not interested in him. 'Tristan's my cousin,' I blurted, trying to think of something to defuse the situation. 'We do lots of stuff together… blokey things mainly, football, fishing, a bit of rock climbing.' I haven't fished or watched a game of football since I was at school and as for rock climbing, I'd have sooner cut my own ears off.

'Oh, but Tristan told me that you were…' Marcus stopped mid-sentence looking confused for a moment and then, his expression hardening, he added 'Never mind… I am surprised though.' Now he sounded disappointed and for an instant, I thought my ruse had done the trick, but then after thinking for a second or two he said coolly 'Tristan's always off doing something or other with my stepfather; I'm amazed he has time to play with you too.' Marcus fixed his eyes on mine, and I could tell from his stare that he no longer believed a word that I'd said. 'Well never mind, if you ever fancy some company just give me a call. You know where I am.'

After making certain that Marcus and I left Mcdonalds in opposite directions, I headed back to my salon. Although it was only half past three, I had no more appointments; I'd cancelled them all, and I wasn't expecting to be back so soon. Contrary to what I'd allowed pug-faced Hilary Sidebottom to think, I had expected to attend the burial and, if I'm honest, I think I'd hoped that I'd be invited to the wake as well. Ridiculously inappropriate perhaps, but I felt that as it was me who had helped Enid most, and even if I couldn't tell anyone what I'd done, well, the least they could do was give me a ham sandwich and a glass of wine.

Walking along the High Street, irritated, my mind wandered back to the funeral, and to the last few words that I'd heard before Hilary Sidebottom so unceremoniously put me in my place. The man had spoken slowly and deliberately. I had the feeling that he had chosen his words with great care. 'I know' he had begun with certainty in his voice, but what, I wondered, could he possibly 'know'? So he had been first person into Enid's house after I'd left her, but I'd been cautious, what could he have found to make him so sure about anything? I realised that it was important for me to find out who he was as soon as possible. It wouldn't be hard, both Hilary and Sylvia Cokeley would know, and I was sure that Sylvia was due to see me soon.

When I arrived at my salon, I locked myself in, pulled the blinds, and checked the appointment book straightaway. I quickly found that I was right; Sylvia Cokeley had a booking first thing on Monday morning. Although I knew that I wouldn't need reminding, I tugged a post-it note from a pad on the reception desk and stuck it to the page alongside her name. As I pressed the yellow scrap of self-adhesive paper firm and marked it with a large question mark, I noticed a telephone number written on the fresh post-it now revealed at the top of the pad. Ordinarily I would have ignored it, but the note seemed odd on two counts, firstly it wasn't in my handwriting, and secondly I recognised the number very well.

CHAPTER TEN

If I'd had the sense to leave the telephone alone, I'd never have preened myself in the mirror, and would have left the salon straight away and headed home.

If I'd had the sense to kiss Deborah Clifford, my childhood sweetheart, properly on her eleventh birthday, I might have grown up to marry her, inherited a share of her father's vast fortune, and retired to the Caribbean at thirty-five. As it was, Deborah dumped me because I bit her tongue... and I didn't leave the phone alone.

I picked up the handset and dialled the number exactly as I'd seen it written on the pad.

When the ring tone began, I wandered from the reception desk into the salon. Perching against the back of the chair closest to the fig tree, I stared into the big floor-to-ceiling mirror. I was wearing a dark grey pinstriped suit, a white shirt with a tall collar and a bold, if not strictly funereal, black and white tie. I thought I looked rather good. The ring tone went on. I pushed my hands through my hair; it was a tad longer than I usually wore it – cobbler's kids' shoes and all that - but it still fell nicely. I remember thinking that the flecks of grey were at last suiting my skin tone. After seven beeps, I decided that I'd hang up at ten. It was a pointless exercise anyway; the telephone number written on the post-it pad was my home phone. After eight beeps, I stood up, stretched my left arm forward and yawned. Nine beeps, and I turned to the reception desk and brushed at the front of my jacket, and as the telephone beeped ten, I was about to put the handset back in its cradle when my call was picked up.

Why I dialled the number, I'll never know, but it came as quite a surprise when my call home was answered. I slumped into the chair that I'd been leaning against and spun it back towards the mirror.

'Hello?' I said. I watched myself as I spoke. There was no reply. 'Hello.' I said again, this time louder, still no reply. 'What the f...' I started to shout, but as soon as I raised my voice, my reflection stood up.

'We need to talk.' I saw my lips move in the mirror but heard the words in my own voice through the telephone earpiece. I yanked the handset away from my ear and jumped to my feet. My reflection didn't move at all. I stepped away from the mirror, clutching the telephone to my chest.

There were six mirrors in my salon, two pairs of back-to-backs, a landscape mirror above the basins and the large floor-to-ceiling mirror that filled the wall between the reception desk and the staff room door.

I moved into the centre of the salon. I could see myself in four places at once, four reflections that apart from perspective should have looked exactly the same. They didn't. From the mirror above the basins, I grinned back at myself like a psychotic clown. In the first back-to-back I was crying like a fool, and in the second I looked a nervous wreck. It was only in the floor-to-ceiling mirror that I recognised myself as I thought I should have looked. In that mirror, I stood tall and held the telephone handset confidently to my ear.

'Don't pay any attention to them.' I heard my voice say. 'They'll soon go away.' My reflection waved a dismissive hand across the salon and then beckoned me to his mirror.

'I don't understand.' I said. It was all I could think to say. I stepped forward and began to tremble.

'Don't worry.' The expression on my reflection's face softened. 'I can help; I'll always be here… just for you'.

Then the phone went dead, I blinked, and my reflection blinked too.

Surprisingly, I slept extremely well that night. I don't know why, I'd had enough stimulation to fuel a thousand restless nights. Perhaps the cumulative effect of the happy pills helped. That, and running out of vodka. Whatever the reasons I didn't dream at all and I woke feeling refreshed and, surprisingly, reasonably happy.

Bucking the recent trend, Saturday turned out to be a good day (the bank would've been delighted if I'd told them.) I dealt with most of the re-bookings from the time I'd taken off to go to Enid's funeral, I cut three new clients' hair – a recent record – and Cindy Dobson popped in to clear her bill. Cindy was profusely apologetic and even kissed me on the cheek. She smelled delicious, Jean Paul Gaultier, I think. When I tallied the till at the end of the day, I felt quite buoyant and for the first time in weeks, I actually had spare cash.

On my way home, I called in at a smart new bistro that had opened on the corner of the High Street and Brewery Lane just before Christmas. Le Petit Paris looked great, replacing two run-down units, one a betting shop, and the other an old-fashioned jeweller, the new occupants had gutted the building and dropped a tiny piece of France inside, ambience and all. They'd done it tastefully too, simple chic, no onion ropes, no blue and white awning. Every time I'd passed the place I promised myself that I'd give it a try, and on that Saturday evening I had two reasons to celebrate: I had money in my pocket, which seemed to be becoming a rarity, and I'd managed to avoid looking in mirrors all day.

It took me a few minutes to persuade the grumpy maître d' to let me in. I find that single diners are never particularly welcome in better restaurants, so I fibbed to him and said that I wanted a table for two and that my 'partner' would be joining me later on. The miserable guy only bought into the fib after I waved to a woman who was parking her car across the road, when she waved back – as I find people invariably do if they think that you've recognised them - he showed me to a table straight away… what a twit.

According to the menu, the English chef specialised in what it described as 'franglaise fusion cuisine'. A disappointment that I reckoned really meant that the restaurant had hired a Limey cook who couldn't do proper French food. As I read on, I quickly realised that the menu might as well have been written in Swahili, that in an act of misguided cleverness the bistro's owner had tried to fuse the languages too; it hadn't worked. I'm not a food heathen but nothing was familiar, so I chose to eat safe with an entrecote steak in a mild mustard sauce, and topped my order off with a half-decent bottle of my favourite Cabernet. The wine arrived almost half an hour before my food showed up. I reckoned that someone on the staff was waiting to see if my 'partner' would appear.

Two people served me, the lad who had taken my order and a girl with neat mid-length sandy hair and bright blue eyes, who I thought to be in her early twenties and quickly recognised as one of the new clients whose hair I had cut that morning. Then she'd told me that she'd just finished training as a teacher so I was surprised to see her in the bistro only a few hours later. However, I'd felt that we got on quite well while I was cutting her hair. It made a change to have a younger customer to talk to, and I'd encouraged her to come back. I tried to remember her name but the grey cells failed me. After the lad presented me with a wonderful looking steak, the girl followed up with an impressive array of vegetables.

'Hello,' I said, and I smiled and then pointed to the boiled potatoes and the sautéed broccoli. I could see that she recognised me too. 'I didn't know you worked here.' It was a silly throwaway remark; I didn't know anybody who worked there, and I was sure that she knew I'd never eaten in the place before.

'Actually I don't.' She shook her head and smiled in return. 'The restaurant belongs to my brother. Three of the staff called in sick today. I didn't have much on this evening so I said I'd help him out for an hour or so.'

'Ah.' I said. I wanted to say more but at that moment, my mouth and brain didn't seem to want to coordinate properly. The 'single syllable stump' had been happening quite a bit, and I know now, that it probably should have worried me more than it did.

The steak was delicious and I polished off the bottle of wine with no trouble at all. When I'd finished and paid the bill, I left a five-pound tip on the table, and feeling comfortably fed and a tad squiffy, I made for the door. As I reached for the door-handle, a flibbertigibbet or somebody or something breezed past me and beat me to it, I glanced up to see the smiling face of my beautifully coiffed server, whose name I still couldn't remember.

'Allow me.' She said politely, and then she opened the door with a flourish.

'Thanks.' I said, and noticing that she was wearing her coat and gloves, I asked. 'Finished for the evening?'

'Thank goodness.' She smiled and then raising her eyebrows, she added 'I need to get home to feed my cat; she'll be starving by now, the poor old thing.'

As we left the bistro, we turned in the same direction along the High Street. It was a cold evening, colder than it had been for some time, a light wind had picked up from the east, and I could smell smoke from a distant bonfire in the air.

'Do you live nearby?' I asked as we started to walk together. The question was more a clumsy effort to escape the embarrassment of walking in silence than an attempt to strike up conversation.

'Gillycote Road.' She answered with a nod and a shiver, and then pulled her coat round her ears against the wind.

'Really?' I said in surprise. 'I live on Gillycote Road.'

'I know.' She turned to me and wriggled her chin out from behind her collar. 'I see you most mornings.'

'Good Lord.'

'I've lived on Gillycote for years,' she smiled at me again, 'apart from when I was away at college. I see you quite often actually. You live in the pretty, white house, with the trellising and the huge buddleia in the front garden. Lots of butterflies in the summer, I like butterflies'.

'Yes I do… and so do I… like butterflies' I said.

'Actually, I've said good morning to you a couple of times recently, but I don't think you noticed me, you seem to be busy with your thoughts in the mornings.'

'Do I? I'm very sorry.' I frowned, and I was sorry, she seemed perfectly sweet, I hated to think that she thought me rude. I despise ignorance in people and it comes hard to have it pointed out in oneself.

'Don't worry.' She said, and this time she shone me the full pearly grin, she had a pretty smile.

'Why didn't you say anything this morning in the salon?' I said. 'I feel silly now.'

'Oh please don't, I didn't say anything because, well, because I didn't want to embarrass you. I just wanted a good haircut, that's all. I knew you didn't recognise me, but it hardly matters does it?'

101

'Well it does matter, and I'm very sorry.' I said. 'I didn't mean to ignore you and I promise that I will always say good morning in future.' It bothered me that I hadn't noticed her, as a professional hairdresser I felt disappointed with myself. She was an attractive girl. She had good hair and the type of strong, almost masculine, bone structure that looks great in headshots; I should have noticed her straight away.

'Apology accepted.' She nodded. 'And I promise to stop calling you Johnny.'

'Johnny? Why do you call me Johnny?'

'Johnny head-in-air, from 'Struwwelpeter'.'

'Oh my god, you're kidding me?' I laughed, I was amazed, I knew all about Struwwelpeter, it was an old book from my childhood, and maybe from everybody's childhood, and probably the most politically incorrect children's book ever written. From a nineteenth century German author. Johnny Head-in-Air was a silly lad who walked everywhere without looking where he was going, eventually he walked off a cliff into the sea. There were half a dozen or more other characters in the book, each of whom had an equally gruesome moralistic story to tell.

'I'm sorry.' She grinned again. 'I'll never do it again.'

'Do you remember Conrad Suck-a-Thumb?' I laughed, asking about another of my favourite characters.

'And the Red-legged Scissor Man who ran to cut his thumbs off.' She nodded.

We were both laughing hard when suddenly a shrill and studiedly camp voice called from behind us.

'I'm glad to see that you're having such a wonderful evening.'

It was Marcus from the Wheatsheaf Pub.

'I thought you might be out gallivanting with Tristan and my stepfather, maybe training for full contact Ludo, or some other such 'blokey' game.' He sounded very pissed off and was glaring at both of us as if we'd done something dreadful. I reckoned that my dismissal of his advances on Friday afternoon hadn't gone down too well.

'Hello Marcus.' I said and then I did something that obviously annoyed him, I smiled at him. In my defence, I was a little sloshed and I'd been having a nice time, but as soon as my face creased, I should have realised that if I'd have been him the sight of my soft soppy grin would have riled me too.

And so there I was, standing on the High Street on a cold late February evening, a man at the more serious end of his forties with two twenty and a bit year-olds vying for his attentions. It should have felt great, I should have been flattered, but it didn't and I wasn't. I just wanted to be home.

'Ah.' I said, quickly regaining command of the astute single syllable stump. An instant of stress and the power of connective speech had deserted me altogether.

'Ah.' Said Marcus, mimicking my voice unkindly and screwing his face into what I guessed to be a grimace of frustration. 'People like you need to sort themselves out, you know?' Then he scowled at me, harrumphed at whatever-her-name-was, and then turned round and stomped back down the High Street in the direction of the Wheatsheaf public house.

We walked most of the rest of the way home to Gillycote Road in silence. I think we both felt embarrassed. Although I apologised for Marcus's outburst I didn't bother with explanations. What could I say? There was no point in me pretending that I didn't know why Marcus was angry with me. Of course I did. He felt rejected. Marcus had made a typically crass, and I suppose, a sexist assumption that because I was a hairdresser I must be gay, and that I would therefore be interested in him. In his defence, he'd probably been encouraged by his stepfather and my stupid cousin Tristan. It had happened before and I had no doubt that it would happen again. Whichever way I swung on that particular day, I wasn't afraid of my sexuality, but I resented the fact that Marcus, or anybody else for that matter, felt that it was their right to make hasty assumptions about me.

When I was young, maybe six or seven years old, I used to collect keys. I used to clip them to my belt. It didn't matter where they came from or what they unlocked, just having them on my belt made me feel important. It was probably my grandfather's fault, my father's father. He had been a jailer in the army and he'd told me stories about all the bad men that he'd had to lock up. He carried his keys on his belt too, on a fancy key ring that was so big and so shiny, that as a lad I knew that my grandfather must have been the most important jailer to the most important jail in the whole world.

When I first moved to London, to Harlesden, in the 1980s, my family warned me to be careful of drugs, of thieves, and of dark alleyways and darker people, and I was careful. Mostly, I stayed away from drugs. I kept my money locked up in a bank, and my keys on a strong key ring that like my grandfather, I attached to my belt. I never walked a path not lit by a bright street lamp, and if I saw a darker person, then I never looked them in the eye.

What caught me out went something like this...

'Hey..! You..! Faggot..!' The smartly dressed lily-white sixth form schoolboy from a nice North London school shouted at me from across the street. I ignored him; I'd just finished work and wanted to get home, the last thing I needed to do was encourage the idiot.

'I'm talking to you!' He shouted louder.

My 'watch-it' bump itched; I glanced over my shoulder. Now there were two of them and several more were only yards behind. The second boy wore the same uniform as the first but was much larger and not so scrubbed with dirty trainers and a face like Pizza Huts finest Margherita.

'You. Poofter... Arse bandit.'

Although I didn't dare look again, the voices sounded much closer and from their footsteps, I guessed that the 'oh-so-clever' schoolboys were crossing the street.

'Shirt-lifter!'

A new voice sneered, and this time from right behind me. I turned round. Now there were five of them. All in uniform, all white, all nasty, I knew the type.

The lad who shouted at me first leaned forward and flipped the key ring on my belt. I glanced down instinctively and as my head dropped the lad's hand flashed back up and caught me squarely on the nose. The crack of cartilage sounded worse than it hurt, but the real pain came when I saw my blood splash from my nose onto the Bruce Oldfield shirt I was wearing, almost two weeks' wages almost certainly laid to waste.

'Queer boy…!' The lad spat.

'Why do you keep saying that?' I yelped. It was a stupid and in hindsight, I'm sure, a provocative question. At the time, I was training as a hairdresser in a top London salon. I worked with twenty-three boys and girls and more than half of them were gay. The most important thing in our lives right then, was image, the way our customers looked, the way we looked. That day, I had biggish, longish, highlighted auburn hair. I was wearing burgundy platforms, shiny black leather high-waisted peg trousers, and a pale lemon frilly shirt. It was the 1980s remember, Glam-rock the dawn of the New Romantic era. However, the ultimate confirmation of the sixth form thug's assumption came from the bunch of shiny keys hanging from my patent leather belt. Of course, the homophobic bigoted bastard assumed I was bloody gay, why wouldn't he? the keys clipped to my belt were the badge of the day.

A second later, I was on the floor, kicks and punches raining in from all angles. Oddly enough, although I was taking quite a beating, I'm fairly sure that it was only a couple of the group who were putting any venom into the assault. Even while curled on the ground, I was aware that although when the biggies hit home they hurt like hell, the majority of the blows were half-hearted. I guessed that at least half of the kids were just there to prove their place in the gang.

The attack went on for what seemed like several minutes, but in fact was probably only a few seconds, when quite unexpectedly, after one particularly nasty kick caught me in the back of my head, everything stopped. For a moment, I wondered if I'd blacked out and was dreaming, but then I heard a new voice, raised but not shouting, an authoritative tone. I eased my head from between my arms and while peering through a crowd of legs saw a rough looking black African man remonstrating with my assailants. More than that, he was telling them quite firmly that if they didn't stop he'd, 'rip their damned hide'.

The sixth formers didn't seem particularly fazed and started to circle the black guy like a pack of hungry dogs. He just shook his head and grinned.

'You're in trouble now boys.' He said, then he stepped back a pace and reached into his coat, pulling out what looked to be a roll of brightly coloured gift-wrapping paper.

'What yer gonna do? Pack us up and send us home.' The Margherita faced thug sneered, and then he laughed and turned to the others, and they laughed too.

'I warned you man.' The black guy said abruptly, and then he hoisted the wrapping paper to his shoulder like he was presenting arms at a military parade. He held the pose for a moment, then took a breath, and swung the roll of gift-wrap in a wide arc, from right to left, directly at the kid's head. As soon as I saw the shape of the black guy's body, and the effort that he needed to put into the swing, I realised that there was more to the roll of glittery gift wrap than either I or any of my attackers had guessed. I didn't actually see what happened, I closed my eyes, but I heard the sounds, three crunching swipes, three screams of pain, a lot of swearing, and a bundle of footsteps scurrying away.

When it was over, there was a brief quiet moment until a strong pair of hands gripped my shoulders, and pulled me to my feet. It was only when I tried to stand on my own that I realised how much of a beating I'd taken.

'You okay boy?' The black guy said, he smiled at me and then winked. The smile softened his face and made him look much nicer, not half so ugly; not half so rough.

'I think so.' I said.

'Do you live nearby?' He asked.

I nodded.

His name was Phillip Johnston. He looked like Will Smith, the Fresh Prince of Bel-air, the same kind eyes, but just a whole lot tougher. He told me that he grew up in Peckham. He walked me home. It wasn't far. On the way he told me that he carried the disguised Iron bar because sometimes he mugged people, just a matter of fact, like he was telling me that he enjoyed basketball or cricket. When we got to my place, he smiled at me again and then took my arm more gently and asked if he could come inside. 'Just for a coffee or a beer, no funny business, I promise.' I thanked him for his help but I pulled away, and after rubbing at the growing bruise on my face, I said no.

I'd had enough people and their assumptions for one day.

I said goodbye to my beautifully coiffed server about fifty yards before my garden gate, she also asked me if I was okay.

I said 'I think so.' to her too.

While I'm telling you this, I am aware that I haven't yet mentioned my reaction to the telephone conversation that I'd had with myself in my salon on Friday afternoon. This is because I don't remember having a specific reaction and I think, perhaps, that I'm wondering why not. I'm sure that I should have. I do remember that when I hung up I felt at odds with myself, a sort of trembling inner conflict between reality and disbelief. However, I knew that, unless somebody had sneaked me a blast of 'Crack' cocaine, while I knew what I'd seen and heard was intrinsically wrong, it had felt quite real. I'm sure that I must have asked myself a few questions, 'Am I going mad?' should probably have been the loudest, but if I did, then I didn't ask it seriously, and I certainly didn't answer myself or think I was. My only real concern remained the 'I know...' comment from the tall chap at Enid's funeral.

When I left the salon on Friday evening, I didn't go straight home. I considered popping into Marks and Sparks to pick up some groceries, but I struggled with the thought of the crowds inside and so instead settled on a quick trip to Starbucks. Julie, the new girl, Colin's temporary replacement, was on duty, and unusually for Starbucks staff she didn't smile when I opened the door.

'You look like you need more than a latté' she said sternly.

I think I feigned a chuckle, I don't think I said anything in reply, but Julie started working on the Gaggia, and a minute or so later handed me a small cup with a double espresso in it.

'That'll get you home.' She said, and she was right, the stronger coffee perked me up nicely.

CHAPTER ELEVEN

Sunday morning started very badly indeed, not only did I have to wake indecently early and got out of bed to find it raining hard, but in my hurry to get ready, I kicked the heel off my favourite Gucci loafers. Okay, so the shoes were getting old, but that was why I liked them so much. Made from the softest brown leather, the hand stitching was perfect. I bought them from Harvey Nicks in the 'Grand' millennium sale. A fantastic reduction, from over £500 to £250, I'd never have been able to afford them otherwise. They were a perfect fit and had aged jolly well, nicely wrinkled but without losing their shape. Only the best quality shoes mature properly. The disaster happened, when putting out some rubbish, I caught my foot on the weather bar to the back door sending the heel in one direction and the rest of the shoe in the other. Apart from getting a wet sock, I found both easily enough, but that wasn't the point. I was dressed and ready to set off to fix Cecile Ablitt's hair for her special do with good-ol' Lizzie Windsor, and I wanted to wear my favourite shoes.

With time pressing, good fortune resolved my dilemma when, while searching for an umbrella and a coat in the cupboard under the stairs, I found a forgotten pair of brown Chelsea boots buried beneath an old macintosh that I hadn't seen in ages. I blessed my luck on two counts; I pulled on the boots quickly, and threw the grubby old mac and my kitbag over my shoulder and dashed out of the door.

For once, on its rubbish schedule, the number 17 bus arrived precisely to time. Being the only passenger on the wet Sunday morning, after I'd paid my fare I took my favourite seat directly opposite the central door. While making myself comfortable for the twenty-minute journey through town, I came across something hard and heavy in the pocket of the macintosh. I reached inside and pulled out a grey velvet pouch that immediately seemed familiar and was about to open it when I suddenly remembered - all those months ago, and probably the last time I'd worn the coat - Marjorie Warton's handbag and the small silver gun that I'd found inside. How could I possibly have forgotten it? I could only blame the upset of the moment. My heart skipped a beat. I glanced anxiously at the bus driver, a thin guy with grey stubble and a ponytail who'd smiled at me when I got on, and then, not having a clue what I would do with a gun, I shoved the pouch back deep into the pocket.

As it happened, on that wet Sunday morning, the journey to the south of town took only fifteen minutes and I arrived on Marlborough Avenue well ahead of time. The address that I'd been given was simple, Marlborough Lodge, No.1, Marlborough Avenue. Although not so much a lodge-house as a smart 'Gentleman's Residence', I found Cecile's imposing double fronted Victorian home easily. While not what I'd expected, it was indeed an impressive house. Surrounded by neatly trimmed gardens, and fronted by a long and perfectly cut privet hedge, the building towered above its neighbours. Set centrally in the hedge, between a pair of tall brick pillars, a wrought-iron gate opened onto a broad gravel footpath that led directly to the front door. After pulling on the latch, the heavy gate squealed open and I stepped in from the pavement.

No sooner had I pressed Cecile's doorbell than Dolly Parton and Kenny Rogers struck up with 'Islands in the Stream' on my mobile phone. I bought the ring-tone accidentally a few months before, when I replied to a spurious text message that kept popping up once or twice a month. The tune had cost me over twenty quid before I realized it was a con. I was furious and I complained to my phone company vehemently. They didn't care a fig. They told me that I should've been more careful. So, as I'd always liked Dolly 'P', I kept the ring-tone on my phone and sought revenge by pushing a gift-wrapped dog-poo through their showroom letterbox. I'm sure the messy-present went to the wrong person; some poor unsuspecting lackey who didn't deserve it at all, but in my experience it's always the innocent who suffer most in guerrilla warfare, and I did feel better for a day or two.

Reaching into the wrong pocket, my hand missed my phone and once again found the velvet pouch and Marjorie Warton's gun. Having hidden away for all that time, the wretched thing suddenly seemed magnetic. I dropped it back

110

quickly and tried with my other hand in the opposite pocket. Thankfully, I found my mobile before Dolly and Kenny hit the first 'Aha' and rejected the call.

'Hello'. I said, simple and to the point.

'Thank God, why didn't you answer before? I've been trying to get hold of you. Where are you? Have you left home yet?'

I recognized Cecile Ablitt's voice above her neurotic whine. I'd no idea that she'd been trying to call me. I guessed that something on the number 17 bus must have blocked the signal. Uncertain which question to answer first, I settled for; 'I'm standing outside your house.' and hoped that it would calm her down. I was wrong.

'Well I'm still at the blessed church.' She screeched. 'My car won't start and I'll never get anyone to fix it on a Sunday, I just don't know what I'm going to do.'

I knew how she felt; I was still pissed off at kicking the heel off my lovely Gucci shoe.

'Can't you leave the car there and get someone to give you a lift home?' I asked' and it seemed like a perfectly reasonable question at the time.

'No… stupid.' she snapped. 'I need my car to get to London.'

Obviously, I was wrong again.

'AA or RAC?' I said, and even as I asked that question I knew that I was tempting fate. The eruption that blasted into my ear almost immediately left me in no doubt that Cecile was a member of neither.

Eventually, Cecile's shouting subsided and although by then I was holding my mobile phone well away from my ear, I became aware of another voice speaking in the background. While I couldn't make out what was being said, from Cecile's softened tone, I gathered that the situation was suddenly looking more hopeful. A few seconds later, while I was still holding on her call, Cecile spoke to me again and confirmed my guess.

'I'm so sorry about that.' she started, and now her voice was as thick and sweet as Tate & Lyles Golden Syrup. 'I

111

have a terribly nice man here who thinks he might be able to help me after all. You stay there and I'll keep you informed.'

...and then she hung up.

I called her back straightaway. I had no intention of standing outside her house in the drizzling rain while she tried to get her car fixed. I understood her predicament, and I felt for her naturally, but I might have been there all day, I might have been drenched through.

'Yes,' she snapped, after a couple of rings.

I didn't mess about, I told her quite bluntly that I wasn't prepared to hang around indefinitely, and suggested that she meet me at my salon. The church wasn't far from the town centre, and if she managed to get the car sorted out, she could pick it up after she'd had her hair done. I would call a taxi and make my way back as quickly as I could. I'd have billed her of course.

'Oh, for God's sake,' she snorted, obviously the *nice man* who'd offered to fix Cecile's car had moved out of earshot, 'do you honestly think I want to come to your horrible little shop today of all days? No, you stay where you are. Let yourself in if you must, you can make yourself a cup of tea or something. There's a key hidden under the red flowerpot, below the kitchen window.' Then she hung up again.

COW!

The key wasn't under the red flowerpot anyway; it was under a blue one with white flowers that had 'The World's Greatest Aunt' written on it. I raised my eyebrows at the sentiment and wondered if it had been a sarcastic gift from Cindy or even Marcus. I doubted it. Although I was sure that both Cindy and her son would have enjoyed the not-so-subtle acidic humour that I saw in the motto, from what I knew of their relationship, I reckoned Cecile would have seen through it straightaway and would probably have thrown the pot out. I wondered how many nieces and nephews the rotten woman had.

With the door unlocked and the kettle found, filled, and plugged in, never one to turn down an opportunity of a good nose around, once I made myself a cup of tea and dug up a biscuit, a yummy chocolate Hobnob, I wandered. Cecile

Ablitt's home was an odd mix of styles. Her various husbands' military influences were obvious, brass and polished wood everywhere. However, there was a surprisingly feminine aspect about the house too. Not knowing precisely how soon Cecile might arrive home, although initially I fought the temptation to open cupboards and pull drawers, I still managed to glean quite a bit about my irascible client from the pictures and ornamentals and other bits and pieces that she'd chosen to leave on view.

That Cecile was a tarter was widely known, that she'd been married and widowed three or four times, she'd never made much of a secret, but that in her youth, as a model, she had been at the forefront of British fashion and one of the most striking women of her generation, came as something of a surprise.

While I knew that she'd tramped the odd catwalk in her time - I'd heard stories and rumours - I'd no idea that her career had reached the dizzying heights that her mementos revealed.

What appeared, at first glance at least, to be random groups of simply displayed photographs gave the game away. Each room that I entered boasted its own mini exhibition. In the kitchen, a cleverly haphazard collage hung between two north-facing windows. Perhaps taken from editions of Vogue or Tatler published sometime during the 1950s, the dozens of pasted clippings summarized Cecile's working life. In the drawing room, pride of place went to three iconic monochrome plates – maybe eighteen by thirty inches apiece – of a young, and without any doubt, a beautiful Cecile, dressed in a cinch-waisted black taffeta number. Each of the plates was signed simply,' Henry'. *Clarke*? I wondered. However, my favourites, and possibly the most impressive evidence of the glittering career were the two clusters of photographs that I found in the stairwell. A hotchpotch of out-take pictures full of fun and irreverence. Both clusters featured Cecile with celebrities of the day. I didn't recognize all of the faces, but enough to be convinced of her former stature.

Seeing Cecile's memories presented so proudly, I couldn't help wondering if there was a correlation between her glamorous past and her present spiteful disposition, if maybe, like many similar miserable buggers, she now lived her life in a state of permanent disappointment. I could've understood it. It seemed to me that the life portrayed in her photographs, a life that must have promised her so much, had ultimately delivered little more than a few dead husbands and an anonymous dotage on the outskirts of a one-horse-town in Southern England... big deal. I could almost have felt sorry for her... but then I remembered her appointment with Her Maj' that afternoon, and the way that she'd spoken to me on the telephone, and quickly decided that Cecile was just a crusty old mare after all.

The piece-de-résistance of my unguided tour, I discovered when opening the second door to the left at the top of the stairs. Immediately above the kitchen and fitted from floor to ceiling with rails and open shelving, I guessed that it was Cecile's dressing room. While at first glance, the room beyond the door seemed ordinary enough, when I stepped inside and pried within its many closets, my breath caught in my chest. Carefully wrapped and in tissue and cellophane, and hung in pristine order, filling every conceivable space, I found a wonderful collection of vintage 1950s and early 60s haute couture.

It was fabulous.

There would be no point in me trying to defend what I did next, because I couldn't help myself. I've since blamed Coco Chanel. If she'd never designed that wretched classic box suit I'd never have tried it on. I don't know what possessed me. I knew that Cecile might be home at any time. Perhaps it was seeing the snapshots in the kitchen, of Cecile wearing it while laughing with Dirk Bogarde. Perhaps it was the thrill from the risk of being caught. I don't know. It certainly wasn't a sexual thing. Sure, I'd dressed in women's clothes before, for the odd party, for a fun night out when I was younger, priests and hookers, that sort of thing - I made a good hooker actually - but I'd never felt a need to cross-dress, it had never turned me on.

I'd been rummaging through the rails and had found several glorious 'one-offs' that I'd hung to one side to take a closer look at, before I found the suit. Simple and black, and beautifully tailored with thick pillar-box red piping to the collar and cuffs, as soon as I pulled it out, I knew I'd struck gold. Most remarkable of all, was the size, although Cecile was a tall woman and not slight, and I liked to keep trim, I'd never have imagined that any of her clothes would actually fit me, but the Chanel suit did fit... beautifully.

In for a penny, in for a pound... third in from the right on the second row of a long shoe rack, I found the perfect pair of black patented leather Prada stilettos that I thought would just about take my foot. I lifted them down, they were gorgeous; virtually unworn. Unable to bring myself to put a naked foot into such distinguished footwear, I placed the shoes on the floor in front of a tall A-frame mirror and began to search for a pair of stockings. On the wall opposite the dressing room door, a modern whitewood chest filled the space below the only window. I tried several drawers before noticing a triple pack of Dior Ultra-sheer 8-denier pantyhose on the sill above the chest, one pair in tan, one in coffee and one in black. I chose the black hoping that the colour would help disguise my unshaven legs. After carefully opening the packet and unravelling its silky contents, I leaned against the chest of drawers and carefully eased them on.

Whilst I recognized there was something slightly peculiar and quite definitely chancy about what I was doing, quite strangely, my main concern wasn't that Cecile might come back and catch me, but that I might not do the Chanel suit justice. As I drew the pantyhose up around my waist, I caught a glimpse of my nylon-encased bottom in the mirror, and for a moment, I felt as though I was peeping on someone else. A warm flush of embarrassment rose in my face. I pulled the skirt down quickly and after straightening the seams, stepped back to the shoes. My composure quickly regained, thanks to the silky tights, my feet slipped into the beautifully crafted footwear easily. I turned to face the mirror, although the image I saw made me smile, and I filled the suit out quite well, I knew immediately that I needed to do more.

Across the landing, Cecile's bedroom reminded me of a scene from a Pino Daeni painting; faded European antiques, scrubbed wood washstands, and frilly white linen, shabby chic I suppose, tired even then, but otherwise okay. A large well-lit Joliette dressing table with a resplendent array of feminine goodies stood adjacent to the door. I sat myself down and started to rummage. Mostly from the better houses, Cecile's selection of cosmetics was broad if not adventurous. Pots, tubes and packets from Lancôme, Arden and Yves St Laurent, I found what I needed quickly, and thanks to the hints and tips that I'd garnered from my salon girlies over the years, I'd soon painted a face that I thought suited the suit very well.

Through the mirror, looking behind me, above Cecile's bed, a narrow cupboard linked two small wardrobes and on a shelf between the ceiling and the cupboard, I spotted several hatboxes and two polystyrene wig-stand heads. Kicking off the Prada shoes, I climbed onto Cecile's bed and pulled down a couple of the boxes and one of the heads. When I opened the hatboxes, the hats inside were flouncy and floral and wholly inappropriate, but under a polythene cover, pinned to the polystyrene head, a dark auburn 'bob-cut' wig looked almost perfect.

And do you know what?

When I stood in front of the mirror back in Cecile's dressing room, wearing the wig and the make-up, and the gorgeous Chanel suit, and those lovely Prada heels, I knew that I looked fantastic. I even winked at myself… deliberately.

While listening to my boast it's important to remember that interpreting the image of femaleness, strong, soft, or however, was my business at the time, and it had been for over thirty years. I knew very well when it worked. Looking into the mirror on that rainy Sunday Morning, I saw no cheap drag act.

It was fortunate that I'd taken the trouble to shave closely that morning. Cecile's foundation and powder had smoothed over my skin nicely. I suppose I could have plucked my eyebrows and painted my nails, but apart from that and the odd stray hair that might have squirmed its way through the knit of Mr. Dior's pantyhose, there wasn't much man in my reflection. I reckoned that even the fickle Coco Chanel would have been happy enough.

While I was preening, and posing, and generally feeling pleased with myself, I didn't hear Cecile Ablitt's new Venetian silver Toyota Yaris pull into the driveway, I didn't hear its engine die or its door slam. While I was daydreaming of choosing a new name and of whom I might fool, I didn't hear the sounds of keys in locks and footsteps on the stairs. I didn't hear anything much at all, until the dressing room door burst open, and Cecile stormed in, and with a look of anger and surprised puzzlement on her face, she yelled:

'Who the hell are you?'

While I knew there was always a chance of being caught, I hadn't considered that she might not recognise me, but she didn't seem to. The force of her voice hit me like a slap across my face. I backed away. Strangely, the immediate shock of her bursting in lasted only a split second and before she could launch herself again, as the prickles of anxiety started to push through my skin, I felt an unpleasantly familiar cracking sensation from somewhere between my ears. Shuddering and squinting my eyes, in that briefest of instants, my view of the room seemed to shift. Where I had been facing Cecile from the window with the mirror between us, suddenly, although I knew that I'd stayed perfectly still, it was as if I'd moved and was now standing behind the mirror itself.

'What the hell are you doing in my house?' she shrieked 'and where's the bloody hairdresser?' Cecile's scowling expression demanded an answer but she wasn't looking at me, she was looking towards the window where I'd been.

'Who are you?' She yelled again.

I tried to respond, to say sorry. I tried to tell her that I didn't mean to do any harm, but although my mind fought hard, my mouth simply wouldn't form the words.

'I'm going to call the police.' Cecile snapped finally, and then she turned to the door.

When I look deep inside, I understand now that I must have been in control of what happened next, but I've never been sure why it happened, or even of the precise sequence of the events. There was a point, immediately after Cecile turned away from the window when she caught my eye, and when she did, a fleeting hint of recognition seemed to pass between us. I knew her then and I think that suddenly she knew me. Although nothing physically changed, it was as though a hidden voice whispered through her eyes, 'Oh my God!' Maybe it was just that she'd recognised me through the make-up, maybe she saw something more sinister, I don't know.

I felt cold then. Not from a draught, but I think from the overwhelming combination of adrenaline and fear. I followed Cecile out of the door onto the landing to the top of the stairs, the relentless stab of pins and needles now coursing through my entire body. I think that she tried to turn to face me, but I didn't let her. Instead, without any conscious thought, I felt myself push her... very hard and very fast.

I didn't see her fall.

I heard the noise from my place by her dressing room window. Bumpety bump, badump, bump, bump, and probably a few more bumps besides, she made a heck of a racket. I dashed to the landing to see if I could help her, but in my panic turned an ankle dodging the mirror and was too late - bloody Prada heels! Cecile was lying at the foot of the stairs, wedged in a gruesome contorted position, with her neck bent at an unnatural angle, and her head resting against the front door. Alas, most of the wonderful photographs from the stairwell wall smashed on the floor around her.

Just when I needed a moment to compose myself, the bloody doorbell rang.

CHAPTER TWELVE

My ankle was dreadfully sore, and stepping over Cecile without turning it further was jolly awkward. Even more of a nuisance was that Cecile had fallen in such a way that her nastily bashed head had landed between the front door and the bottom stair. Consequently, opening the door, even an inch or two, without squishing Cecile's head would have been tricky. I solved the problem by pushing my right foot under the doormat and then wedging my left knee against the doorframe. When I turned the latch and pulled, the door caught on the mat and levered Cecile's head up, straightening her neck and clearing the step. Fortunately, despite the clatter and the scattered photographs, she'd fallen quite neatly and well out of any possible view from the porch. Once I was certain that nothing looked amiss in the hall, and that my wig was straight and my disguise still intact, although my heart was pounding, I eased the door further open and peered through the gap.

Cecile's caller was an extraordinarily dumpy, bottle-dyed redhead – much too bright for a Sunday morning - whom I guessed to be in her early sixties. Wearing beige woolly tights with a beige woolly skirt and cardigan topped off with a white woolly scarf, at first glance, under the bright red hair, she looked like a furry iced bun with a cherry on top. I was sure that I'd seen her somewhere before, maybe in the library or a supermarket. After engaging my most ladylike voice and adopting the mannerisms and tone that I hoped said "female, middle-class, middle-England", I greeted her with a cheery 'Hello' and the kind of smile that I usually saved for especially good tippers. I think she was surprised not to see Cecile and so cautiously stepped back from the porch.

'Oh good morning,' she said in a clipped nasal tone, 'it's only me, Pru, Prudence Percival... Mrs. I'm a neighbour. I was hoping to catch Cecile before... well... you-know-what... this afternoon.' Then she leaned forward, and putting a finger to her lips, she sprayed me with a shushing sound while furtively glancing over her shoulder. Less than ten seconds on the clock and already the woman was annoying me. I knew what she was talking about of course, and after a brief tussle with a childish thought to play games with the silly woman, my sensible head prevailed and instead I quickly proved my allegiance to her apparent secret by whispering, 'I know. We mustn't do anything to upset Her Majesty must we?' Pru Perci… Poppy-Mop was immediately my best friend.

'Oh my dear.' She said, grinning at me. 'It's all so exciting isn't it? Cecile and I are both actively involved with the Veterans' Charity of course; our late husbands were both military men. I'd hoped I might be invited myself but, well, just Cecile this time… never mind.' She frowned, shook her head, and then started smiling again. 'Just to think that the president of our little branch, and a resident of Marlborough Avenue, will soon be chatting with Her Majesty the Queen, I only wish I could be there to witness the event.' …and I swear her eyes were misting as she spoke.

'Oh yes indeed.' I said enthusiastically. Unfortunately, in feigning excitement, my voice squeaked and then dropped a tone. I don't think she noticed but to the cover the hiccup I quickly coughed as if clearing my throat. 'Excuse me…' I stuttered, 'but we're all terribly thrilled here too.'

Then, while I should have been concentrating on getting rid of the woman as quickly as possible, I made a silly mistake that quite flustered me. I glanced to the floor behind the front door to check on Cecile. In that brief horrifying glimpse, I saw that she had rolled to one side so that her head was no longer on the bottom stair but once again resting against the back of the door. It wouldn't have been a problem - I'd wedged the door with my knee and hadn't even noticed the extra weight - but unfortunately, a trickle of blood had started to leak from somewhere near Cecile's right ear, and since she'd moved it was pooling just behind the door and slowly working its way towards the threshold. Even though my eye movement had been small, Poppy-Mop had followed the glance and was looking curiously towards the bottom of the front door. While she couldn't yet see the growing pool of blood, it wouldn't long before the incriminating mess oozed under the door. Fighting a wave of squeamish alarm, I needed to act quickly, and after a flash of what I admit was probably a 50/50 mix of desperation and inspiration, I turned away from the gap in the front door, and after pretending to listen for a second or two, I called upstairs in a loud voice.

'Yes dear, I shan't be a moment.' I said, then, peering back at Poppy-Mop, I said to her as calmly as I could. 'Cecile's in the bath, I promised that I'd scrub her back, can I take her a message?'

'Oh! Yes, it's just that… well, I've brought her the flowers, the corsage. I made it especially you see. I don't make up so many these days. My eyes you know, blasted cataracts. I can't do the close work. I'd have them seen to, but the quack tells me they're not 'ripe' yet, whatever that means…'

While Poppy-Mop was babbling, she drew a blue and white striped Tesco carrier bag from beneath her cardigan, and after rustling inside, she proudly produced a beautiful pink orchid shoulder-spray.

'I'd hoped to pin it to her frock myself.' She said with a weak smile.

'Oh my dear, it will look lovely.' I said, and then, my panic almost reaching breaking point, I reached out and fairly snatched the corsage from her hand. 'I'll ask Cecile to call you as soon as she's ready.'

I pushed the front door closed just as the leading edge of the pool of Cecile's blood met the edge of the wooden threshold. With the comforting click of the latch I leaned breathless against the door listening as a small stuttering voice called from outside.

'Oh… j… jolly good then… I… I'll be off… give her my love, won't you… Cecile that is, not the Queen… aha ha ha.'

The glistening crimson slick shrouded my thoughts as a sepia tint on black and white film. I didn't dare try to see if the flower woman had gone. My knees gave out and I sank to the floor across the hall from Cecile. She didn't look good. I couldn't believe what I'd done. I sat on the floor, my knuckles white and my knees tucked, trembling, trying not to look at her, the trauma of the moment biting hard as the reality of my situation bore home.

Another death, how on earth had it happened?

After several long and lonely minutes, the distant sounds of life broke my reverie; an aircraft on its approach to London, a motor scooter bubbling through town, a child laughing, a bird singing - the here and now. I pushed my head against the wall behind me and sighed.

Realising that I daren't stay where I was much longer and determined not to fall apart under the weight of panic, I struggled to my feet. I'd no idea if anybody had seen me arrive at Cecile's house or indeed, if anybody knew that I was supposed to be there. I'd no reason to assume that Cecile had told anyone that she'd arranged for me to call, but then again, why wouldn't she? If nothing else, Cecile was a show off. The idea of having her hairdresser running around at her beck-and-call would certainly have appealed to her sense of self-importance. But then again, even if she had, did it matter? Perhaps I'd come and gone. Time can be vague on a Sunday morning, and the only person who I knew had seen me, hadn't seen me at all.

Standing motionless in the hallway, considering what I should do, I became aware of a narrow gilt-framed mirror hanging on the wall beneath the staircase. Beyond the glass, I faced the woman I'd created. There and then, my reflection was somehow clearer and more authentic even than it had been in Cecile's dressing room. Watching closely, beneath the fringe of the bob-cut wig, I sucked on my cheeks and pouted, turning slowly from side to side: 'Was this really me?' I asked.

I held my curious gaze for several moments before my reflection breathed the answer aloud.

'No…!' It said, it was the only possible answer, and in hearing it, I knew that I had one more act to play.

CHAPTER THIRTEEN

I thanked God that it had stopped raining.

Although I walked as quickly as I could, the four-inch heels on Prada shoes and the heavy bag that I'd borrowed from Cecile to carry both my clothes and, I'm ashamed to admit, one or two of the more spectacular pieces that I found in her wardrobe, slowed me dreadfully. It took me almost three quarters of an hour to reach my salon.

I found traversing town dressed as a woman an odd experience. I was on edge naturally, but despite the nerves and having to concentrate on my tottering gait, the disguise and the anonymity it gave me felt eerily liberating. Together with the obvious necessity to maintain a visual pretence, as an actor strutting across a real-time stage, the combination of freedom and restraint compelled me to perform, and for those few moments, even to live the part of a woman.

Holding my head high, the further I walked, the more feminine and natural I sensed that my movements became. My path crossed with three people before I reached my salon, two women and a man. Although all three bade me 'Good morning', none of them looked at me for more than a split second nor took a second glance. If asked, I'm quite certain that their only recollection would have been of a tallish - and hopefully stylish - but otherwise unremarkable woman, carrying a large brown leather holdall.

My confidence growing and my dry throat in need of coffee, as I crossed from Boxalls Lane into the town centre, I even considered calling in at Starbucks. I knew it would have meant walking the length of the lower High Street and speaking to people who knew me, but all of a sudden, the challenge seemed quite exciting. Was I good enough? Could I get away with it? Thankfully, before either question tempted me to push my luck too far, it started to rain. Opting for a dry wig and a cup of instant in the staff room, I turned from the High Street and cut behind the Wheatsheaf pub. Fiddling my way through the backstreets of town, between the Brewery Canal and the one-way system, I let myself in discreetly through the back door of my salon.

Cold, although quiet and wonderfully familiar, the calm of my little haven soothed any remaining agitation immediately. Letting the heavy holdall drop to the floor, I breathed long sigh, allowed my shoulders to drop, and kicked Cecile's Prada shoes from my feet. My need for coffee now approaching desperation, I made straight for the staff room. After filling a kettle and rustling up a packet of gingernut biscuits, I was about to spoon a heap of Marks & Sparks finest dark roast into a favourite mug, when my mobile phone startled me by chirping the arrival of the first of three successive text messages. Guessing that they'd be a weekly update of rubbish jokes from Tristan, I didn't bother reading the messages straight away. Instead, I took off Cecile's auburn bob-cut wig, threw it onto a shelf above the microwave, scratched my head for almost a minute, and finished making the coffee. When I finally checked my mobile phone, I discovered that I was right; my second cousin had sent a trio of his latest text gems.

The first message surprised me, a crass one line racist gag that I wouldn't have expected Tristan the Christian to approve of, I certainly didn't. The second was better; it read simply, *'I'd kill for a Nobel Peace Prize.'* I quite liked that one... at least it made me smile. However, it was the third message that made me sit up and take notice. *'Why did the transvestite enjoy a night out with the girls? Because he could eat, drink, and be MARY!'* Tristan's jokes might not have improved over the years, but glancing in the mirror at my still made-up face, I reckoned his psychic abilities must have. I sent back the most appropriate reply I could think of under the circumstances, *'Ha-oh very-hahaha,'* Tristan wouldn't have expected any better.

A few minutes later, while I was at last enjoying my well-deserved coffee and confident that my ribs had safely survived their weekly Tristan tickle, a fourth chirp came from my mobile phone. I'd flopped into an old chair in the corner of the staffroom and had left the phone on top of Cecile's holdall. Tired, comfy and reluctant to move, I sighed, then reached forward and without picking the phone up, poked at the necessary buttons. The screen lit up, as I'd expected it would, with another message from Tristan. *'Glad to see you're out of bed,*' I squinted to read, the cheeky bugger, '*Mum's doing a roast and you're invited. I'll pick you up at 12:00pm.*' There was no question that I might not accept the invitation. Tristan knew my fondness for his mother's, all too infrequent in my opinion, Sunday roast, and I guessed that he simply didn't see the need to ask.

Actually, I was delighted. Although avoiding social occasions had become something of a habit around then, Tristan's bad jokes and his mother's invitation arrived with perfect timing. Not only did they lift my mood, but also, the prospect of munching one of my cousin's wonderful roast dinners felt like chicken soup for my addled brain. The time was 11:35 and my reply brief; '*Pick me up from the salon.*'

With a need to get a move on and to step back into real life, I unzipped the large brown leather holdall that I'd borrowed from Cecile, and took my clothes into the Ladies room at the back of the salon. While, as I am being honest, I'd quite enjoyed the time I spent pretending to be a woman, it wasn't something that I felt I needed to make part of my daily routine; just getting out of tights without snagging them was a pain in the bum... literally.

After folding the Chanel suit with the wig and the shoes and the pantyhose into the holdall, I set about removing the face. Make-up removal is never as easy as it should be. I've always sympathised with women, the agonies they have to suffer and the fuss they have to contend with. Forget pregnancy and childbirth. Hair, make-up, exfoliation, cleansing, toning, moisturising, that's the real chore. Trannies might think it fun, but ask anyone with a real female chromosome, and she'll tell you the truth.

I was okay until it came to removing the lipstick. Stupidly, while Cecile's dressing table offered a marvellous choice, Muggins picked a deep cherry two-stage lip-coat that promised not to bleed, smudge or fade. I guess the wretched product was actually jolly good, because despite my best efforts, the stuff would not come off. I'm exaggerating, in fact after resorting to pouring surgical spirit onto an old dry towel and then scrubbing hard, I did manage to shift the worst of it - obvious really. I reckoned that having to spend the rest of the day with sore lips and looking as if I were in dire need of coronary care was just the price I'd have to pay for what after all had been an unnecessary vanity.

Tooting less than tunefully on his car's horn, eager to announce his arrival, quite unusually Tristan pulled up on the High Street outside my salon bang on time. Although I was ready, after waving from the window, I nipped back to the staffroom and took a moment to decide what to do with Cecile's holdall and whether I need bother taking my old macintosh. Before I'd come to a decision on either, Tristan started banging on the front door.

'We've got to get going, Matey.' He called urgently. 'Mum wants me to pick up some veggies from Sainsbury's on the way and she'll have our guts for garters if we're late.'

Although I knew that my second cousin's anxieties were born more from the chance of being denied his Sunday lunch than from the fear of his mother's wrath, his impatience flustered me. I grabbed both bag and coat, and dashed for the door.

Using the motorway and common sense, the twenty mile journey north to my cousin's home should have taken no longer than thirty minutes. However, having decided that on a Sunday-lunchtime in February, the back roads would be quieter and quicker, Tristan used neither. I tried pointing out that his route would pass half a dozen popular pubs, two large garden centres and a plethora of roundabouts and traffic lights, but he wouldn't have it. In fairness, the first ten miles passed more or less as he'd suggested they would. A straight run from the east of town, we took the ring road behind the Parkway housing estate and then joined the Old London Road, hardly any traffic; no problem at all.

Our troubles began - as did the first hints of a 'sinusy' headache I seem to remember - when we caught the tail of a line of cars held up by road works between the railway crossing at the end of the London Road and 'The Dairyman's Daughter'. A nice enough place with an interesting name and not a bad pub if you're happy in the company of uncouth farmer types, and enjoy the unrelenting smell of cow poo.

When we met the traffic jam, a mile or so south of the pub, things didn't look too bad. The queue kept moving and although Tristan growled at the delay, it took only a few minutes longer than usual before we'd passed the cause of the holdup, a set of temporary traffic lights and two gas maintenance trucks.

What we didn't know was that less than a mile ahead, trapping us between it and the traffic lights that we'd just negotiated, a lorry delivering sacks of compost to a garden centre had shed its load. Following a tight line of cars along a winding road, we caught the second traffic jam within two minutes of clearing the first. Alas, this time all hope of our cheerful, family, Sunday lunch, died behind the grim glow of dozens of brake lights.

Tristan and I sat trapped in his tired, navy blue and rust-inhibitor red, patchwork style, Ford Pick-up, for over two hours before the services finally cleared the road ahead. To this day, when I think of it, I can still smell the weird mix of warm engine oil and Tristan's feet. After five minutes, frustrated and probably already hungry, Tristan got out of the car, walked to the front of the jam and offered to lend a hand. He came back almost immediately, hunkering his giant frame into the car, his tail between his legs and his eyes cast down. He mumbled something about a police officer, a fire fighter and an ambulance driver. It might have been the beginnings of a joke, except that Tristan wasn't smiling. From the little he said, I guessed that good-ol' health and safety had turned his offer down. With both Tristan's mood and my head tightening, we didn't chat much after that.

In moments of reflection - and there have been many these last years - I look back at those two long hours in the traffic jam and wonder whether it was then that I first began to question the benefits of my happy pills. When I now consider what occurred earlier that morning in the house on Marlborough Avenue and my feelings while stuck in the queue of cars, I realise that even then I understood that the contrast between the shallow horror of Cecile's demise, and the sheer delight I felt at receiving the simple invitation to lunch, were entirely without balance. More than that, I wonder now if I'd already begun to recognise, that bolstered by my happy pills even the smallest joy completely undermined my conscience. While never accepting full complicity in any death, it would be fair to expect that under normal circumstances - with a clear and drug-free head - even admitting to the slightest involvement would have left me feeling at least a tad guilty. However, as I recall, sadly, I did not.

As soon as I saw the face of the policewoman who waved us through, I understood why Tristan had been so glum when he'd returned to the truck after his offer to help clear the road met rejection. While I'd heard that she'd transferred from London, I had no idea that she'd moved so close to home. The officer controlling the traffic around the scene of the accident was my niece. I guessed Tristan felt that if only for the family connection, whatever they actually were to each other, she should have let him help with something. I'm sad to say, that as Tristan squeezed his tatty old Pick-up through the gap between the toppled lorry and the large pile of compost sacks, we passed each other with no more than a nod of recognition. It was hardly the time for family reunions, but the chirpy girl who'd once invited me to her passing out parade at the beginning of her career, hardly even bothered to smile. I made a mental note to write to her mother.

Back on the open road, if Tristan had pushed his poor truck any harder I'm sure its wheels would have fallen off. The vibration through my buttocks was awful. We hurtled towards his home village at a terrible lick, bouncing kerbs and cutting corners. Other than as an exercise to vent frustration, I couldn't see the point. It was already 2:15pm; we were so late that stealing a few minutes from the Highway Code could hardly help. As we neared the end of our luckless journey, on the edge of the village, as if fate needed to add insult to our injuries any more, matters leapt from bad to worse. Hidden from view, behind the open door of a white Transit van, and exposed only through its own brilliant flash, a cop with a speed-gun shot Tristan.

For a fair-thinking, good-hearted Christian, the strength of the language that poured from my second cousin's mouth was wonderful. I felt a perverse swell of pride as three whole sentences constructed almost entirely of foul invective singed my ears. Fortunately, despite making a valiant if somewhat naive stab at the brakes, Tristan was driving too fast to be able to stop the truck in time to berate our sneaky photographer. From more than a hundred yards further along the road, I turned to glimpse a darkly uniformed figure step from behind the white van, I guessed he'd seen it all before and hearing the squeal of the brakes expected trouble. Thankfully, the damage done, Tristan made his first sensible decision of the day and put the Pick-up back into gear and slowly pulled away.

Turning into Cedar Crescent, my sinusy head now truly thumping, the sense of relief I felt at finally arriving at my cousin's house was as real as a taste in my mouth. I heaved a tremendous sigh and pushed the truck's passenger door open.

'I'm sorry.' Tristan muttered sheepishly.

I turned to him and smiled, and shaking my head, I said quietly.

'It wasn't your fault Tris, don't worry.'

'Maybe, maybe not,' he said, sounding unconvinced, then looking me in the eye, he added 'do me a favour though, Matey, don't tell Mum about the speeding ticket… and hey…!' then looking more closely at my face, he said, 'what happened to your lips?'

I didn't bother trying to blag an answer.

Sunday lunch never actually happened.

Although my cousin was remarkably forgiving, even sympathetic, and had pot-roasted a fabulous rib of beef, in all the kerfuffle, Tristan and I forgot to call in at Sainsbury's. While I felt awkward and was disappointed, and Tristan looked crestfallen, the 'make-do' option wasn't so bad. My cousin, magically producing a wonderful loaf of home baked crusty bread, and quickly prepared an ad-hoc kitchen-picnic of thickly cut, hot roast beef sandwiches with horseradish mayonnaise. When she'd done, like a spoof on the three bears, at the time normally reserved for afternoon tea, we sat at her round kitchen table and prepared to munch according to our size. Despite my thick headache, I was so hungry that in the time it took my cousin to nibble her way through one of the enormous sandwiches, I'd scoffed two. Ordinarily I would have felt embarrassed, guilty maybe, that by eating them so quickly I was inferring that her culinary hospitality was somehow lacking, and if Tristan hadn't been there, I probably would have been. However, Tristan was there, and like the biggest and most grizzly father bear of all time, he saved all my blushes by out-scoffing me easily three to one, and by giving his mother and me a nastily up-close lesson in gross carnivorous gluttony. The sight and sounds of his gastronomic demolition of his own huge pile of roast beef sandwiches were disgusting.

'Do you see what I mean?' my cousin asked, shaking her head ruefully. 'Just like his bloomin' father.'

My mind went back to her desperate telephone calls, all those years before, when she was pleading for my help when Tristan was a lad, and although I only knew his father by reputation, even if he was half so bad I had to feel sorry for the poor girl.

While I've never thought of that particular Sunday as a 'good day', by the time Tristan and I were heading home, I felt a great deal less bad about both it and myself than I could ever have hope I might. My cousin, as had become usual, proved a particular fillip. Although she was only five years older than me, and we didn't see each other or even speak on the telephone often, I think, that after my mother died, she saw herself as some kind of maternal surrogate, perhaps even as the new matriarch of our small and scattered family. Certainly, she'd taken to speaking to me as if I were Tristan's older and more sensitive and sensible brother. I think Tristan noticed it too, and I think he liked it. I wondered if a big brother was what he'd always needed.

As we pulled away from my cousin's house on Cedar Crescent, a smudge of grey crept over a hole in the clouds closing out the last of the day's meagre sunlight. Having eaten most of her food, instead of handing us her customary knapsacks (carrier bags full of leftovers), my cousin packed us off with a kiss on the cheek, a pat on the head, and the words of advice, *'You can't grow new family'*. Then we all smiled and waved goodbye and Tristan called from the window:

'Love you Mum… See you soon... God bless.'

She blew us another kiss in reply, then waved again and called something that I didn't hear.

'You're a lucky chap.' I said to Tristan.

'Yeh! She's a good cook alright.' He replied, patting his stomach, not so much missing my point as being oblivious to why I'd even made it. There are some things that you just can't explain to Tristan.

Cussed to the last and still needing to prove himself right, Tristan once again refused to take the motorway and insisted on reversing our earlier dreadful journey. My head still pounding, I couldn't be bothered to argue with him and so instead, as he turned from the main drag, I slid down in the seat as far as the seatbelt would allow and closed my eyes. A full tummy and the steady drum of the tyres on the road quickly blended to form a potent sedative. While not actually sending me to sleep, I soon found that half-land between the real and dream.

My father was driving the car and we were travelling to visit my very sick grandmother. The smell of Tristan's feet and his worn out engine, replaced by the scent of my mother's Eau De Cologne and a curl of smoke from the single 'Guards' coffin-nail that my father would puff on to mark the halfway point of any journey. When I was a child, the odd mix smelled good to me, like a familiar blanket, or a favourite Teddy bear.

Low, but above the rhythmic thrum of the engine, softened Voices spoke in urgent tones.

> *Father.* 'She could die you know?'
>
> *Mother.* 'I know, but if you don't slow down so could we.'
>
> *Father.* 'You drive then.'
>
> *Mother.* 'Don't be ridiculous.'
>
> *Father.* 'If she doesn't die we'll have to put her in a home.

131

Mother. 'We'll cross that bridge if we have to.'
Father. 'She can't afford it… we can't afford it.'
Mother. 'We'll manage, don't worry.'
Father. 'I'm not worried, but… well… maybe I could help her along a bit. There are ways you know.'

I snapped back to the moment as Tristan squealed the brakes and pulled his truck into a space alongside the pavement on the road opposite my house.

'There we are Matey.' He said, slapping his hands on the steering wheel.

'Oh, right, thanks.' I yawned my reply.

'It's cool, Cuz', no probs at all, I'm just glad you've stopped snoring.'

'I don't snore.'

'Oh yes you bloody do.' He said.

Too tired to argue and in need of painkillers for my head and sinuses, I stretched to the back seat to retrieve my macintosh and Cecile's leather holdall. Scooping both over the back of my chair, I reached for the door handle. As I pushed the door open and turned to slide from my seat, something hard and metallic clattered from the folds of my macintosh. My pulse instantly racing, I spun back to see Marjorie Warton's small silver gun nestling comfortably behind the gearshift, in a coin well only inches from Tristan's hand.

'Blimey heck, Matey!' He cried. 'Is that thing for real?'

Like a miniature spark of illumination, the happy doubt in my second cousin's voice when asking his innocent question lit my escape route.

'No no.' I said, quickly feigning a chuckle and without a moment's thought or hesitation, I added. 'No… it's just one of those novelty cigarette lighters, a client left it in the salon the other day. I stuffed it into my pocket in the hurry when you picked me up this morning.' I grabbed the gun and fiddled with it as if trying to get it to light. 'Wretched thing, it's useless.' I scolded when it apparently wouldn't.

Before Tristan could take any more interest in the gun, luck behaving well for a change, a young woman, who was crossing the road a few yards ahead of the truck, caught his eye. Peering through the gap between the door and the car, I recognised her quickly as the girl I'd walked home with from the new French-*ish* restaurant whose hair I'd cut on Saturday morning. Judging from the soppy look on Tristan's face, I reckoned that he thought she was hot stuff. After wrapping the gun in my coat, and folding the coat carefully between the straps on the holdall, I eased myself out of Tristan's truck, slammed the door, and forcing my widest smile, I called:

'Good evening...' Unfortunately, while I'd at last acknowledged the girl, I still couldn't remember her name.

'Oh Hi,' she replied, and then, I reckoned referring to Marcus Hendy-Coombs outburst the evening before, she added, 'how are you? I've been worrying about last night; I'd feel awful if I'd caused you any trouble.'

'Please don't worry, I'm fine.' I said with a shrug, and then I shook my head as if to brush aside any hint of concern.

While we were speaking, from the corner of my eye I could see Tristan looking at me through his car's open window. My second cousin's eager but confused twitchy expression told me that to avoid driving his curious nose completely mad I'd soon have to introduce him to the girl and would probably have to explain how I knew her. Although my wicked streak wanted to string the intrigue out for as long as possible, and to that end I did my best to ignore him completely, I was quickly disappointed when any chance of teasing him properly was ruined when quite unusually, especially when it came to women, Tristan took matters into his own hands.

'Hi indeedee, the names Blandy, Tristan Blandy.' He began, with a broad smile and a raised eyebrow. Unfortunately, he looked and sounded more like a monkey from Brooke-Bond rather than James Bond. 'And who may I ask are you?'

Poor old Tris, if his attempt at a chat up line wasn't bad enough then the girls reply smashed the credibility of his pulling power through the floor.

'Shut up Tristan, it's me, Samantha Gough,' she said, shoving her hands firmly on her hips and narrowing her eyes, 'I helped you out at the St Michael's Sunday school every Sunday for two years you Oaf, before I left for college, remember… dummy.'

'Sammie…?' He stuttered, his eyes flicking between the girls face and her very well formed chest. 'Oh my goodness Sammie Gough… you've… well… you've grown up.'

'Oh bugger off Tris.' She snarled, folding her arms quickly across her front.

Wonderfully to the point, it seemed that Sammie my occasional waitress was a woman after my own heart.

I have to say that Tristan took his curt dismissal in a grown-up manner and squarely on the chin, while his apology was weak, he didn't hang around to wheedle, but then neither did he storm off. Watching his decrepit Ford Pick-up rattle away, I almost felt sorry for him.

Sammie stood close to me on the pavement, quite close actually, perhaps too close.

'How do you know Big Tris?' She asked, looking up at me.

'He's my cousin's son.'

'Oh!' She said, raising her eyebrows, I found her easy use of my *single syllable stump* pleasantly reassuring.

'He's okay when you get to know him.' I smiled, feeling that I should at least try to defend family.

'Yes… I'm sure… it's just that… well… he's so big,' and then Sammie smiled and added, 'do you fancy coming in for a coffee?'

I don't suppose there was any reason why I shouldn't have; a cup of coffee is a cup of coffee after all, but somehow, the invitation coming from such a young woman, made me feel like I'd be doing something wrong.

'Not this evening thanks, it's been a long day and I've a headache that just won't shift.'

'I understand,' she said, 'but, before you go… Your lips, they look terribly sore… would you like to try some of

134

this.' and then she scrabbled in her bag and pulled out a small tube of lip-salve.

Reaching for the tube, I smiled and said,
'Thank you' and 'good night.'

CHAPTER FOURTEEN

Pulling up three yards short of the Starbucks bus stop, very cleverly, the driver of the number eight bus made sure that the passenger door aligned perfectly with a large and grimy puddle. Although the thoughtless stupidity thoroughly cheesed me off, after a restless night and waking horribly early with the same thick head and stuffy sinuses that I'd gone to bed with, I couldn't be bothered to start a fight and so meekly followed the rest of the passengers in their hop, skip, and jump to the kerb. Feeling disappointed with myself – ordinarily I'd have enjoyed a good Barney with a bus driver on a Monday morning – I made straight for the coffee shop, where looking through the window, the sight of a whole, uncut, sharp lemon cake sitting, irresistibly, in the centre of the curved glass counter, immediately lifted my mood.

'Good morning.' I called as cheerfully as I could manage, after opening the door. Julie, Colin's temp', was sitting on a stool behind the counter and looking sheepish. 'And how are we today? I asked.

'Oh Hi there,' she said, her mouth barely breaking a smile, 'I'm fine thanks… and how are you?'

'I've been better,' I shrugged, and then nodding towards the cake added, 'but nothing that one of your best frothy lattés and a nice slice of my favourite wouldn't help cure.'

'Oh my goodness… I'm really sorry,' she said, sliding off the stool, her expression suddenly changing to one of guilt, 'but I can't cut you a slice. I'm afraid I was just about to box it up. A lady called in first thing this morning. A Mrs Carmen I think. You haven't been in much these last few days, so I didn't think… well… I'm afraid I sold her the whole cake. For a coffee morning at the Conservative club, I think. She said that she usually buys the coffee and walnut, and that she'd never tried the sharp lemon cake. She said it would make a change. I'm really sorry. I know it's your favourite, but would you like to try something else? The Victoria sponge is delicious…'

I couldn't believe it. For ten years I'd been a regular customer at the Starbucks on my High Street, ever since the wretched place opened - ten years! Spotty Julie had barely been working there for ten minutes, how dare she sell my cake!

'Who did you say bought it?' I growled.

'A lady from the Conservative Club. Mrs Carmen. I'm sure that was her name. She seemed very nice. Apparently they have a coffee morning in the hall every Monday, for the pensioners I think, but I'm sure anyone can go, maybe you could...'

'The Conservative Club? A coffee morning for 'old' people?' I said, although I'd meant my questions as a rhetorical sneer, silly Spotty Julie chose to ignore the scorn in my voice and answered me anyway.

'Yes, yes,' came the annoying breathy whimper, 'I'm sure if you asked her, Mrs Carmen would...'

I didn't give her the chance to finish the sentence, I'd heard enough. I was sure that I knew who she was talking about. Agnes Carmen, a twig of a woman with candyfloss hair and the bandiest legs I'd ever seen. A newish, casual client, she'd first come to see me just before Christmas following a recommendation from ugly Hilary Sidebottom. I'd had to cut and set her wispy locks several times in recent weeks, not that my efforts made much difference, curled or not her hair usually looked dreadful. She told me that she'd moved to town when her son took up a senior medical post at a local health centre. I'd heard his name from several clients although as yet I'd never met him. I suppose that being new to the area the twig Agnes, or Twaggy, was trying to ingratiate herself locally with a spot of do-gooding. Why couldn't the lazy cow bake her own cakes? Why did she have to steal mine? While, until then, other than because she had rubbish hair I'd no particular reason to dislike the woman, I saw her early morning raid on my Starbucks and subsequently depriving me of my favourite treat as objectionable at the very least.

I didn't exactly stamp my foot as I turned for the door, but I was certainly angry and I probably stomped a bit on my way out. Of course, the trouble with throwing public 'huffs', is that they almost always backfire. From the child who hurts his throat when he screams too loudly, to the man whose dinner is spat on by an unfairly berated waiter, at one time or another, whether by life or by revenge and whether we know it or not, we are likely to be paid back. I'd only taken half a dozen steps when my left foot slithered from under me. I hate dogs that crap on the pavement almost as much as I hate their selfish owners. The sickening pile of doggy-doo that I skidded on must have been enormous. Perhaps if I hadn't been so pissed off with stupid Julie and twiggy Agnes 'the cake-thief' Carmen, I would have spotted it quickly and dodged.

Fortunately, crammed tightly into a red and white plastic charity bag, the roughly folded bundle of my old macintosh broke my fall. After the incident in Tristan's car, knowing that I'd pushed my luck far enough, I'd taken Marjorie Warton's gun from the coat pocket and hidden it in a more sensible place, under the floor of my garden shed. I planned to drop the tatty raincoat into the Oxfam shop on my way to work. Despite the cushioned landing and having actually avoided the worst of the dog-poo, the humiliation and dent to my ego, fraying my temper like a dull blade slashing at silk, only added to my rage.

At 8.47am, late, in pain, and by now convinced that I was under attack from some kind of supernatural conspiracy, as I approached my salon from the High Street I saw Sylvia Cokeley, the vicar's wife, waiting for me on the doorstep. Certain that her appointment wasn't until 9.15, and afraid that my sanity preserving 'start-the-day-right' routine was under threat, already seriously pissed off and still with dog-poo on my shoe, I marched straight up to her, ready for a fight. Being five minutes early is one thing, positive punctuality if you like, but arriving almost half an hour before the allotted time just smacked of pushy impatience to me. Even on good days, I hated it when clients did that.

'Good morning.' I said curtly, rubbing my throbbing head and distantly conscious that I probably smelled of the dog-poo. 'It's nice to see you up so bright and early, but you do realise that your appointment isn't until quarter past nine? I make that twenty-six and a half minutes from now. I won't be opening the salon till then I'm afraid.'

'Oh... oh... Of course, that's fine.' She stuttered her reply, and then she looked at me as if I'd hit her. 'I didn't mean to be so early, I'm sorry, but I had some bad news this morning and... well... I just needed to be doing something.' Then Sylvia's face crumpled and she started to cry. 'It's been a bad few days actually, two friends gone and neither of them ready.'

Always a soft touch when it comes to tears, although I wasn't sure what she was talking about, she looked so sad that I quickly forgot my irritation with her and just felt rotten for being so horrid.

'Don't worry,' I said, 'come inside, 'I'll put the kettle on.

Actually, I'd always liked Sylvia Cokeley. The not unattractive, late forty something, clergy bride, was a loyal client and at times had been quite a friend. She and her husband moved to town in the same year that I did. John came to St Michael's as curate to the old vicar - Father Peter something-or-other - a man I didn't know, but whose reputation as a blood and thunder preacher long survived him. To the dismay of many stalwart locals who branded John a happy clapper, when Father Peter died, the bishop and diocesan bigwigs handed John the reigns as Priest in charge, a post he probably still holds.

I met Sylvia long before I met her husband, not as a client but as a reader in the library. Both of us thinking that we'd joined a literary circle, and flattered when told that our voices carried the necessary timbre for recordings, we were duped into volunteering to read for a local audio book scheme. Sylvia became a client only after our last recording. We shared a series of marathon sessions in the millennium year reading Louise Doughty's 'Fires in the dark', quite an epic recounting a history of European Romany folk. Sylvia turned up for our final session upset after visiting a 'Madam Beryl' type salon on the edge of town. The owner, a brassy woman with big orange hair and even bigger orange breasts, had promised a total restyle and boy had she kept to her word. From Rapunzel to a botched Mia Farrow in ten brutal snips. Keen to console, I salvaged what style I could with an old comb and a pair of scissors that I found in a drawer at the makeshift studios above the library. A few days later, Sylvia came to my salon, and with the aid of some nifty lowlights and a cutthroat razor, I completed what turned out to be a pretty neat job. The vicar's wife became a regular client from then on.

Sometimes relief comes from the simple things in life and in my opinion among the most reliable is coffee. After hanging our coats and kicking off my smelly shoes, I settled Sylvia onto the reception settee and headed for the staffroom. Reaching for mugs rather than cups, I knocked up two coffees, grabbed the remains of a packet of Gingernut biscuits from the old first-aid tin, and took them back into the salon.

'I'm sorry I spoke to you like that,' I said, with a small shrug and a half smile to cover my embarrassment, 'My morning hasn't been so great either.'

'Mondays, hey!' She smiled through drying tears. 'It seems to me that they are often a challenge.'

Taking a moment as we sipped at our warming drinks, I glanced at my day in the appointment book hoping to find a gap between clients large enough to nip out to see my doctor. Although I'd been popping Ibuprofen like Fruity Skittles, the pressure from my 'sinusy' headache was becoming unbearable. Unfortunately, while the day ahead wasn't busy, I was disappointed to find that the few bookings I had were too evenly spread for me to get the necessary break.

'Blast.' I sighed aloud.

'Oh dear, not more trouble I hope?' Sylvia asked.

'No, not really… just a bit of a headache.'

'Physical or emotional?'

'Uh! Both.' I chuckled and took a longer sip from my coffee.

Sylvia smiled and then casually changing the subject said: 'Actually, I meant to catch you at Enid's Funeral. It was good of you to come along. I saw you sitting behind Dr Carmen.'

'Oh yes,' I swallowed hard, 'the tall chap, I wondered who he was.'

While inadvertently she'd saved me asking the question directly, Sylvia's easy remark sent my thoughts reeling. Dr Carmen, of course, 'I know what you did for Enid', that was what he'd told me. Forget any coincidence with his miserable thieving mother. Suddenly I no longer cared who'd stolen my cake. Now, at last, I understood why he'd spoken to me. I guessed that as Enid's doctor, after he'd seen me by the canal, he'd carried on to her house, let himself in and found Enid dead in her bed. Although I'd been careful, I wondered if he had found something else, maybe something I'd left behind?

Distracted from my thoughts by a hair clipping caught in a draught on the floor, I was suddenly aware that Sylvia was still talking to me: '…and it was such a lovely day, just a shame you couldn't come along to the hotel after the service.' She finished, shaking her head.

'Well…' I said, letting out a long breath and struggling to think straight. 'I didn't know many people there, and I had to get back to work.' Then, remembering what pug-faced Hilary Sidebottom had said to me just before I left the church, I added. 'Besides, occasions like that are generally only for the closest friends and family.'

'I know,' Sylvia sighed, 'but of course the trouble was, to fit in with the crematorium's calendar the funeral arrangements had to be made so quickly that there weren't actually very many of us there. Elizabeth, Enid's daughter, was the only family member to turn up, and I could've counted the friends on one hand, it was a relief that the Doctor and some of the church folk came along.'

'Oh dear,' I said, 'and Enid was such a sweetie, she deserved better.'

'Yes of course she did, especially after dying so suddenly, it was such a shock for us all.'

'Really?' I asked, surprised at her choice of words. 'I thought Enid had been ill for some time, she hadn't been into the salon for ages, and I'm sure I heard somebody say that she had cancer.'

141

'No… no… hypochondria maybe, but not cancer… at least I don't think so. I know that she'd been struggling to get around, and I suppose her nuts and bolts loosened somewhat after the hip operation, but according to Dr Carmen, there was nothing wrong that would've polished her off. He reckoned that somebody had…'

'What?' I cut in quickly, snapping back from a drifting notion and half anticipating that Sylvia would finish her sentence with the words - killed her - but she didn't of course, instead she continued:

'…given her some dodgy fish.' And then she added, in a loudish whisper 'I probably shouldn't tell you this, but Doctor Carmen told me - in the strictest confidence - that although to save Enid's dignity he cited 'natural causes' on the death certificate, her kitchen was so dirty that his first diagnosis had been food poisoning.' Then as an afterthought and with a soppy expression on her face, she said. 'He's such a nice man, Dr Carmen.'

'Goodness!' I said, speaking more to myself than to Sylvia and while trying to put everything she'd told me into some kind of order – not so ill after all - no cancer - just bonkers – and such nice man - I began to wonder what else I might have got wrong.

'And now we'll have to go through it all again for poor dear Cecile.' Sylvia sighed. 'Such a tragedy and she didn't even get to see the Queen.'

'Yes, such a pity.' I said without a second thought.

CHAPTER FIFTEEN

A year or so before my mother died, when I was visiting her while she was recovering from a particularly nasty bout of flu, I spent an interesting twenty minutes in the company of our elderly family GP, Dr Kenneth Challon. I remember that during our lively conversation the rotund and heavily whiskered Welshman surprised me by revealing that his favourite general practice procedure was syringing the wax from dirty ears. I was dumbfounded. It seemed ridiculous to me that anybody so highly trained could enjoy such a gruesome task. However, Dr Challon told me that he'd followed his father and grandfather into medicine with the express ambition to make sick people well. He went on to explain that for Doctors like him, who'd chosen to work in general practice, actually curing the sick was a rarity. Most people visit their local doctor's surgery presenting symptoms of illness that either need longer-term medicinal treatment or referral to a specialist, only a very few patients present conditions that can be cured on the spot. After he'd recited a list of some of the more disgusting curable disorders that a general practitioner might be confronted with during a working day, mainly warts, sores, and pustules, I thought I was beginning to understand. However, he further explained, that it wasn't just curing the physical ailment that was important to him, but also the satisfaction he got from seeing a happy patient on their way.

'And after all, a man who can suddenly hear again is likely to be far more appreciative that a teenager with a lanced but still painful boil on his bum.'

With time to think on the journey home, after my chat with the ageing doctor, I began to wonder if perhaps I should feel more fortunate with my lot as a hairdresser. Every day, and maybe ten times a day, the average hairdresser will see customers who are ripe to be 'cured'. Unlike most professionals, tradesmen, and service workers, who strive to produce the perfect piece to fit their own particular corporate jigsaw puzzle, every day, and maybe ten times a day, a good hairdresser will complete - and may even be personally thanked by the end consumer for - a fully finished piece of work.

Job satisfaction guaranteed.

Unfortunately, sitting waiting to see my own doctor on that the last Monday in February with my head thick and now even my face throbbing, I doubted if either of us, the physician or me, actually gave too much of a stuff whether we cured anyone or not.

Disgruntled at having to wait so long, when the number on the irritating gizmo above the door to the consulting rooms flipped '18', I rolled my corresponding ticket into ball and flicked it across the waiting room floor.

I'd been relieved when whichever it was of the Clarke twins, Marie I think, had telephoned the salon to cancel her appointment. Not that I didn't like her, if it was Marie, I did like her, she was okay, the good twin, it was Jayne the pain, the Dragon, her not entirely identical twin sister, that I wasn't so keen on. Whichever of them cancelled, the forty-five minute space in my diary should have given me plenty of time to get to see my doctor. What I hadn't bargained on was the fifty-minute wait at the surgery.

I'd checked in with the receptionist just before noon and, content to flick through the pages of a winter House and Gardens and a Christmas edition of Cosmo', the first twenty minutes passed quite quickly. Understanding that in turning up at the surgery without calling first I'd been given an unscheduled emergency appointment, I expected to have to wait my turn, but at twenty past twelve, I thought I'd better check that they hadn't forgotten me. It was only then that the pasty-faced receptionist told me about the new numbered ticketing system. The snotty woman pointed to a dispenser beside the desk as if I should have known it was there. I didn't bother commenting on her stupidity, I just snatched a ticket and stalked back to my seat. Before I had a chance to sit down, the opening bars of Dolly and Kenny's 'Islands' from my mobile phone signalled the first of two calls that would change the course of my day.

'I'm really sorry.' I heard Marcus's voice the instant I put the phone to my ear. 'I don't know what came over me. I really value your friendship. It's just that… well… sometimes I just can't help myself. Can we meet for a drink maybe? Please let me make it up to you.'

Talk about put on the spot. Standing in my doctor's hushed waiting room, surrounded by bored inquisitive eyes and ears, and hardly in a position to deal with an awkward conversation, all of a sudden felt terribly uncomfortable. Friendship? What Friendship?

'Okay.' I found myself saying.

'Great, shall I pick you up from the salon? What time? Would six o'clock be okay?

'Yes Marcus that would be fine.'

Why on earth I agreed to meet him, I don't know, I think that I just wanted to get him off the line. I had to assume that Marcus was apologizing for accosting me while I was walking home with Sammie the server from the restaurant. Although I hadn't thought about it, Marcus's odd behaviour was worrying. He seemed to think that somewhere along the line we'd made a connection. It was news to me. I'd only met him three times, first in the Wheatsheaf with Tristan and Ripper when although he was fun we hardly really spoke. Then there was his strange attempt to chat me up in McDonalds, and most recently the dreadful episode on Saturday evening.

Before I'd even closed my mobile phone, the jangly tones of Dolly and Kenny struck up again. This time, wishing that I'd left the damned thing at my salon, I answered it quickly, and to my surprise my ear was met by the lah-de-dah tones of Elaine Hennessey, an occasional customer, a sort of friend, and also my terribly posh 'Roedean-belle' solicitor. Once finished with the usual pleasantries Elaine asked me if I was sitting down.

'Actually I'm standing in Dr Marshall's waiting room.' I said quietly.

'That may be prophetic actually.' she chuckled. 'I probably shouldn't be calling you, but I thought you might be interested to learn of something to your advantage.'

'Intriguing,' I said, 'it sounds almost Dickensian.'

'Yes indeed.' Elaine took an exaggerated breath and then continued. 'I've spent most of this morning reviewing the last will and testament and affairs of a late client of this firm. Although, only recently deceased, at the behest of her family, her daughter actually, I am to expedite matters and in my capacity as executor, clear the estate as quickly as possible.'

'Jolly good.' I said, while I didn't have a clue what she was talking about, I liked Elaine's voice, and when she paused for another of her overly long breaths, somehow it seemed like the right thing to say.

'Well, my dear chap... much to our late clients daughters chagrin, it seems from the paperwork that you are a named and quite significant beneficiary of the will.'

'Good lord.' I said, still confused but also now quite excited. 'Who?' I asked.

'Well... it just goes to show you that perhaps being nice to your loyal elderly customers is worthwhile after all...' Elaine replied, with more than a twang of sarcasm in her voice, and then she added simply, 'Enid Fulton.'

I was flabbergasted.

After listening to a few more details and promising to drop some ID in to Elaine's office later in the afternoon, I closed the cover on my telephone and finally sat down. Lost in the moment's thought, I couldn't help wondering, despite my earlier doubts, if my selfless act of mercy for dear Enid was now somehow being rewarded.

I eventually got in to see Dr Marshall just before one o'clock. My god the woman was a cow. I think she'd decided what was wrong with me before I even got through the door. After waiting for the best part of an hour to see her, it took less than a minute for her to glance down my throat, grimace, write me a prescription for good ol' antibiotics, and then grunt something about steam; not a breath of compassion in her body. I turned to leave my doctor's consulting room to the rattling chorus of polished acrylic nails on computer keypad feeling somewhat short-changed. Just as I reached for the door handle, though without looking up from her VDU, she surprised me by asking:

'How are you getting on with the Prozac?'

'Fine... I think.' I said.

'Good, any problems - call me.' She said, and then she did something that I'd never seen her do before... she tried to smile, alas, somehow it didn't really do it for me.

The rest of the day didn't pan out quite as I had hoped.

When I got back to the salon, albeit a few minutes behind time, I found a note pushed under the front door telling me that the client I was late for had already come and gone, and that fed up with what she described as my 'recent laissez-faire attitude', she would not be coming back; *another one bites the dust*. It was a shame actually. Val Yarwood had been among my first clients when I'd opened the salon and was generally an okay sort. The trouble was I found it hard to disagree with her, but while understanding that losing another regular customer was a bad thing, with my head still in the clouds with fairy dust, after the turmoil of the day so far and following the phone call from my solicitor, well... let's just say that I wasn't as concerned as I should've been.

Boredom and autopilot carried me - and my headache - through the rest of my working afternoon. In the gap between my two remaining appointments, a Mrs. Deidre Foot for a cut and blow dry and a Kathleen Legg for a shampoo and set (a coincidence of names that I found more amusing than either of the dear ladies) I managed to both fill my prescription at the chemist and call in at Elaine Hennessey's office.

Although Elaine was busy and I needed to hurry back to the salon, after her secretary had photocopied my ID, and I'd signed all the necessary pieces of paper in all the necessary places, I couldn't help but ask the obvious question. While Elaine either wouldn't or couldn't put an exact figure to Enid's bequest - apparently, the old sweetheart had left me a share of some government bonds – she did eventually give me a rough indication.

'...I doubt that it will be much more than fifty thousand.' She concluded, with an almost apologetic shrug.

I nearly fell over.

I don't know what I'd expected, maybe a few hundred quid, or knowing my recent fortunes, more likely, the keys to the padlock on her bike, but definitely not fifty thousand pounds. Quite simply, I couldn't believe my luck.

Walking back to the salon, even with the painful tension in my head, I couldn't stop grinning. I'd no Idea why Enid had decided to give me the money, or come to that when I'd actually get it, but with the way my business had been failing in recent months, I really didn't care, it was all just a tremendous relief.

Mrs. Legg left the salon with her long, shining, auburn (courtesy of L'Oreal Paris) hair, sleekly, swirling around her bony, emaciated face - she needed cake far more than I did – just before five o'clock. I locked the doors as soon as she'd gone. Alone in the salon, with over an hour to wait until my awkward outing with Marcus, still uncomfortable but feeling wonderfully elated, I should have known what might happen.

After making coffee, I picked up a copy of Hello or OK from the mag-rack, and dropped into my favourite chair next to the variegated fig. As usual, I'd left my mobile phone on the reception desk. When Kenny and Dolly piped up for the third time that day, although a part of me hoped that the caller would be Marcus cancelling our outing, I think I knew who it would more likely be.

I didn't run to pick it up and nor did I flinch when I heard my own voice.

'What have you learned today?' I heard myself ask.

I didn't answer straight away. Instead, I took the phone back to my seat by the fig tree, and I looked closely into the mirror. My reflection was bright and sharp, like a 1960s American TV ad with the contrast and colour turned up slightly too high. We stared at each other for a long moment before I saw and then heard myself ask the question again.

'What have you learned today?'

There was so much… what a day… where should I begin.

CHAPTER SIXTEEN

The distinctive popping exhaust of the Lambretta engine began to rattle in my ears a full minute before I saw the baby-blue Paul Smith endorsed scooter pull up on the pavement outside my salon. The swiftly rising noise was all the distraction my subconscious needed to break away from my reflections grip. From my vantage point looking backwards through the mirror, I watched the rider swing his leg behind the seat and in one deft movement, drop his foot to the kick bar and heave the trendy and pristine machine up onto its stand. His pudgy face squeezed into a canary yellow helmet and partly hidden behind a pair of cool dark sunglasses, I didn't recognise Marcus straight away. I didn't know Cindy's son rode a motor scooter. I'd assumed that when he said he'd pick me up from the salon, that at least he'd be driving a car.

I pushed myself up from the chair and went to unlock the front door. Marcus was standing directly outside and was carrying a brown leather holdall similar to the one I'd borrowed from Cecile. He had taken the sunglasses off, but left the helmet in place, still squishing his chubby cheeks. I'd like to say that he'd reminded me of a cute bumblebee, and wearing the yellow helmet and dark shades some people might have. However, sadly, when I looked at Marcus now, grinning and I reckoned, just desperate to be loved, the creature that first sprang to mind was a bullfrog. Trying to smile through tired and aching eyes, I turned the key in the lock and pulled the door open.

'Hi Marcus,' I said, and then pointing to the scooter, I asked 'are you expecting me to get on that thing?'

'I've brought you a helmet and jacket,' he said lifting the holdall and unzipping it for me to see inside, 'it'll be fine we're not going far, you needn't worry.'

'It's still February Marcus… only just I'll grant you, but last night it was minus two.'

'I've brought gloves for you as well; so let's not argue, it'll be fun.'

'I must be mad to even consider it,' I said, shaking my head and rolling my eyes, which with my head still sore wasn't a good idea, 'I'm already feeling grim, this will probably finish me off.' I added with a sigh.

Daylight was fading fast as we pulled away. As Chance would have it, after instructing me to hold on to him tightly, Marcus started along the same route that Tristan had taken when driving me to see his mother on the previous afternoon. While the breeze in my face was skin-tingling cold, and although Marcus took it easy, regardless of my misgivings, I found the fifteen-minute ride exhilarating. I'd guessed where he was taking me after only a few miles and at the time I reckoned that it was quite good choice. Although I'd made a habit of regularly disparaging the Dairyman's Daughter as being a favourite boozer for oiks and tractor drivers, in reality, as I remembered it anyway, for an early evening drink or even a reasonable priced meal, the old country pub had always been okay.

Marcus steered the scooter into a bay close to the saloon bar door and cut the engine.

'Was that so bad?' He called over his shoulder.

With my lips almost completely numbed from the cold, I didn't bother trying to reply, but instead, patted him on the shoulder and gave him a blokey thumbs-up.

I don't know when I last visited the Dairyman's Daughter, but when I followed Marcus inside, I quickly realised that it must have been some time, and since whenever it was, the pub had undergone a complete makeover. I barely recognised the place at all. Unlike The Wheatsheaf in town where Marcus worked, which I reckoned embraced the phrase 'The Traditional English Pub' as a banner to hide behind should anyone dare criticise its sticky carpets or smoke stained windows. Since my last visit to The Dairyman's Daughter, the owners appeared to have conceptualised our national drinking heritage Disneyland style. I'd never seen so much lacquer and tat in my life. I'm not sure which of the two I disliked most.

Although I didn't examine every corner, I knew immediately what was on offer. From our place at the bar, I could see three individual areas. To my left, themed as a milking parlour in fibreglass cream and cornflower blue, complete with pool tables and soft-play ball-pit and cut down milk churns for chairs, was a large family games-room. Beyond the bar to my right, on the opposite side of the building, through a pair of wide faux barn doors, using similar colours but with softer lighting and plastic flowers, a restaurant boasted fifty or more (empty) tables. And between the two, where Marcus and I sat perched uncomfortably on saddle shaped barstools, maybe twice the size of my salon and apparently set out to celebrate 'A day at the races' was a bar area where I reckoned the designer must have finally gone mad spending the owners cash.

'Do you know what this reminds me of?' I said to Marcus, pointing to the bunting, the gauche race-day memorabilia and the dozens of fancy hats that festooned the bar.

'Mary Poppins.' I said, answering my own question before giving him a chance to speak. 'The scene where Dick Van-dyke as Bert, drags Mary and the Banks' kids through his pavement painting and they pinch the horses from a merry-go-round and end up singing supercalifragilisticexpialidocious.'

'Wow!' he said, raising his eyebrows, 'I'm sure you're right'.

Alas, I could see instantly that he hadn't the remotest idea of what I was talking about.

'You must know the song surely?' I asked.

'Yellow brick road?' Marcus shrugged uncertainly.

'No, that was The Wizard of Oz. Julie Andrews wasn't even in that film.'

Quickly realising that I was in danger of exposing myself as a daft old fart, I did the only sensible thing and caught the eye of the barman.

After a couple of glasses of wine and despite our best efforts, with twenty or more years between us and a couple of vintage children's films to testify to the depth of the gap, by seven O'clock, Marcus and I had more-or-less exhausted all our common ground. I knew we'd hit trouble a few minutes earlier, when Marcus nipped to the bathroom; the silence was such a relief. When he came back, I popped a handful of pills at the bar, flushing them down dramatically with a gulp of Chardonnay and a long sigh. I did it more to prove my ongoing fragility than because I needed the medication. Although not a particularly subtle ploy, I knew that it had been effective when Marcus looked at me with an odd mixture of irritation and sympathy and asked if I'd rather be at home.

'It's been fun...' I started.

It was just a small lie and it rolled off my tongue as easily as speaking my name, but as soon as I said it, I saw something change in Marcus's eye that told me that he knew I wasn't being entirely truthful.

'...but you're right,' I continued quickly, trying to bluff over the tricky moment. 'I need to give in to this sinus thing and get a good night's rest.'

'Well at least you came out with me.' He shrugged and tightened the corner of his mouth, his tone changing, dropping decidedly downward. 'I didn't expect you to, not after catching you with that tart from the crappy French restaurant, but then, when I saw you yesterday morning, I thought that maybe I had a chance after all.'

'Yesterday morning?' I asked abruptly, suddenly concerned, I didn't remember seeing Marcus at any time on Sunday.

'Yeh, late yesterday morning, you looked fabulous actually darling,' Marcus sneered. 'I saw you sneaking through the back way in to your salon.'

'Ah!' I said silently, my voice lost in shock and my mind flashing up images of me, fully cross-dressed, and boldly walking through town wearing Marcus's great Aunt Cecile's classic Chanel suit. Suddenly I felt incredibly stupid.

'I'd no idea.' Marcus said, his sneer rising to meet a grin. 'Does Tristan know about your little hobby?'

'It's not a hobby, I was just...' I started to say defensively, but then almost immediately I stopped myself, realising quickly that lacking any other plausible excuse, although not ideal, admitting to having a transvestite 'hobby' might be not be such a bad idea.

'Look Marcus... nobody knows.' I said, swiftly changing tack and even daring to feel quite clever. 'It's just my little secret.' We looked at each other for a moment, and I thought that I'd got away with it, but then Marcus's eyes narrowed and hardened.

'No...' He said coldly in reply. 'Now it's <u>our</u> little secret.' His tone put me firmly in my place and left me in no doubt that neither of us misunderstood the potential power behind the words.

'Could you take me home now please?' I asked.

CHAPTER SEVENTEEN

'What have you learned today?'

There was so much... what a day... where should I begin.

Lying in the palest chink of moonlight blue, with my eyes wide open, and my feather duvet snuggled under my chin, like the softened wax in a Lava-lamp, the answers to the question roiled inside my head.

Marcus dropped me outside my house soon after half past seven. The ride home was one of the creepiest experiences of my life. Being stuck with the slime-ball was bad enough, but having to ride behind him on the scooter with my arms wrapped around his waist felt disgusting. I swear there were moments when, charged with his new and ill-judged self-confidence, the Fat-Brat pushed his bottom back into me.

My head still thick and heavy, when we turned onto the town by-pass the brightness from the streetlamps hurt my eyes. With a mile of straight dual carriageway ahead of us, despite my earlier protests, Marcus couldn't resist the temptation to open the throttle. Squinting against the wind and the light, I tried to peer over his shoulder to see how fast we were going, but Marcus shrugged me back and shouted at me to 'Keep Still'. For that moment, I did exactly as I was told.

About a quarter of a mile further on, I looked up again to see that we were fast approaching a stationary lorry. Marcus didn't slow, but eased the scooter into the outside lane to pass the vehicle. I tucked my head down and closed my eyes, and for an instant, I imagined dragging his helmet back over my left shoulder, choking him and throwing us both underneath the giant wheels; a problem shared is a problem halved...? On another day, I might have done it, but although at that moment I felt that Marcus deserved to die, I had other plans for me.

When I got off the scooter, I was an angry bundle of nerves. I screwed the jacket that Marcus had lent me into the helmet, shoved the gloves on top, and all but threw them at him. Marcus grinned, his smug self-satisfied expression made me feel sick. I said good night curtly and walked to my front door without looking back.

An hour or two later, still feeling lousy, out of vodka and unable to eat, after chilling a while on the settee listening to soporific music, I decided to give up on that particular Monday and took myself to bed. Alas, although I was worn-out after what seemed to have been the single most irritating day of my life, the relentless churn of discomfort and agitation kept sleep firmly away. A minute lying this way, ten laying that, an hour steadily getting hotter and more bothered, if it wasn't pain from my infected sinuses keeping me awake, it was the frustrations of the day. Determined not to get up, I rolled onto my back and stared at the softly moonlit ceiling. Beyond and between those roving darknesses in the corners of my bedroom, in the places that would've been shadows, vague patterns and rolling images sucked on my eyes.

When I'd been listening to my reflection in the salon, before Marcus picked me up on his scooter, the one question that I'd made a point to ask myself seemed too obvious and crass to bother answering. I'd mistakenly thought that I expected myself to recite a simple list of the lessons of my day; don't trust bus drivers, I like Colin better than stupid Julie, Mrs Carmen is a greedy cow, dog poo still stinks, and so on. However now, while quietly concentrating on nothing but the swirls of blackness in a fidgety night, I began to realise that the question I'd asked of myself should not have been 'what have you learned today?' but rather 'what have you learned *from* today?' To answer the former had been all too easy, and in reality, I'd not learned much that I didn't already know. However, although perhaps asked too early in the day, the later question was a far more complex matter.

Lying still and awake in my bed, I allowed my thoughts to wander back over the real issues that I'd faced that day; when Sylvia Cokeley told me about Dr Carmen, the telephone call from my solicitor, discovering that Enid had rewarded my compassion, and Marcus's thinly veiled threats of blackmail. In not answering the obvious, I thought I was being clever, a step ahead of myself, I had been wrong and I wondered if my reflection already knew.

What had I learned?

Piecing the jigsaw together, I could see the beginnings of a broader answer to the question. 'I know what you did for Enid', Dr Carmen had said. I wondered if despite what the doctor had told Silvia Cokeley, he knew that Enid would have suffered unreasonably and, unable to act himself, he was actually grateful that someone – an angel of mercy… me - had the courage to lend a helping-hand. Maybe Marjorie Warton and Cecile Ablitt had needed my helping-hand too. With this thought as a mental signpost, pointing in all directions across my life, I drifted to the simple conclusion that what I'd learned most from the frustrations of the day was that I needed to be more careful.

CHAPTER EIGHTEEN

For the first time in over fifteen years, on Tuesday the twenty-*somethingth* of February, I took a day off sick. It wasn't that I felt any more poorly than I had on occasions in the past, but that with only two appointments in my book and my face now puffy and my head still sore, I simply couldn't be bothered to go in. Waking at disgusting-o'clock after only an hour or so sleep, not even properly dressed, I took a taxi into town early and left a note for my two customers taped to the salon door. On the way back home, I asked the taxi driver to avoid the traffic lights at the top of the High Street; the last thing I needed was for anyone I knew to spot me looking like a hamster. The taxi driver did as I asked and drove the long way back to my house, down the Lower High Street, onto the town by-pass and eventually back to Gillycote from the north. As the taxi pulled on to my road from what I usually considered to be the wrong direction, I looked ahead to see a tatty navy blue and rust-inhibitor red Ford Pick-up being driven slowly along the side of the road in front of us.

At the time, I'd no idea what Tristan was doing kerb crawling on Gillycote Road. It was only several weeks later that I found out that he'd been hoping to see Sammie from the restaurant on the off chance that he could give her a lift into work. I ducked my head as we drove past him, but alas, his eyes scanning the area for Sammie, he spotted me straight away. Less than thirty seconds later, as I was paying the taxi driver, my mobile phone chimed in his text message.

'*Yo Bro*', it started, '*whatsup?*' I wasn't intending to reply but as I was reading the message, my phone announced an update '*How many heterosexual male hairdressers does it take to change a light bulb…*' it read; the answer came a moment later under a separate message… '*Both of them,*' then Tristan had added a postscript… '*I'm still hoping you are one of them.*' …Oh dear, I thought.

Out of the taxi, as it drove away, I sat myself on the step to my garden path, keyed Tristan's name into my phone, hit the dial button, and waited for him to answer.

'Ah… Matey!' his loud voice crackled in my ear. 'You're up early… on your way home?' He asked, with a side tone in his voice.

'Yes…' I said, 'but not the way you're thinking…' I went on to explain what I'd been doing in the taxi and why I was taking the day off work.

'I'm sorry to hear that,' Tristan said sympathetically, and he sounded as if he meant it, 'I just thought that… well… Ripper told me that you had a date with Marcus and I was afraid…'

'It wasn't that kind of a date Tris.' I said quickly, cutting him short. 'We went for a drink, that's all, and if you must know, if I was intending to stay out for an all-nighter, Marcus *bloody* Hendy-Coombs would be the last person I'd choose to do it with.'

The conversation pretty much ended there. Tristan apologised, but as only Tristan could, in a way that made me even crosser and eventually I hung up on him. I received three more text messages in quick succession after that. The first read, *'I'm sorry'* the second, *'God bless you Matey'* and the third *'I don't suppose you can lend me fifty quid.'* The expletive I sent to my second cousin as a reply put a halt to any further communications for quite some while.

While the sun was mostly hidden behind a mottled haze of beige and pale grey, the morning was brighter and warmer than had been forecast. I ate a breakfast of granola and yoghurt standing on the path outside my back door. The fresh air soothed my head. Breathing as deeply as my sinuses would allow, I decided that as far as I could I'd spend the rest of day outside, maybe walking in the hills on the edge of town.

For the second time in three days, I caught the number 17 bus and although this time it pulled away from my house in the opposite direction, I recognised the driver as the thin guy with grey stubble and a ponytail who'd driven me to Marlborough Avenue on Sunday morning. While he didn't pay me any more attention than he did the other passengers boarding, from something in his face I got the feeling that he remembered me too.

The journey out of town to Cattleford copse, took no more than fifteen minutes. I was the only person who got off the bus. Cattleford and the open countryside that surrounded it had been a favourite walking area of mine several years ago when I was on a fitness kick but I hadn't been there in quite some time. Nothing much seemed to have changed. The bus dropped me at a T-junction on the main road a half mile or so from the old 'cattle ford'. Across the road from the bus stop, a footpath led down the side of a shallow valley in the trough of which a winterbourne stream crossed a farmer's lane - the ford – the first dot on my mental map.

The ground beneath my feet was soft but not wet, and above my head, the trees were beginning to show the first hints of new life. Although I might've walked the path a hundred times before, that day, under that particular sky, could have been the first. As a gap in the woodland allowed me a view across the valley I paused a moment and breathed a long slow sigh. I've often thought that while for speed 'Ten-League Boots' might be handy, when it comes walking the English countryside what a hiker needs is a pair of stilts. *Elevation my dear Watson, elevation.* Our green and pleasant land may be beautiful, but unless one is standing at the top of a hill or on the side of a valley, the average height person on foot rarely gets the best view.

Towards the end of the path, near the bottom of the valley, the trees thinned and gave way to a gravelled lane that was bounded by open grassland. The air smelled different here and was cooler. Certain that the freshness was doing me good I inhaled another long deep breath. At last, my head seemed clearer and less painful, less stuffed up. Stepping from the path on to the gravel, a pair of wood pigeon, startled by my crunching footsteps, flustered into the sky from undergrowth ahead of me, followed a moment later by another and then another. When I'd walked ten paces more an old looking black and white cat slunk from the same spot and gave me a baleful stare, I reckoned I'd cost him an early lunch.

Fifty yards before reaching the ford, while standing in the centre of the footpath looking up and to my left between two groups of fir trees, set on a small hill above the southern ridge of the valley, for the first time in maybe ten years I glimpsed Broughton castle; the second dot on my map.

I crossed the stream at the bottom of the valley via a wooden footbridge that hadn't been there the last time I'd passed that way. It must have been at about ten a.m., and although low in the sky and still watery, when I reached the far side of the stream, the sun eased its way through a misty tear in the clouds. I doubt if the temperature actually changed much at all, but when the sun's rays first lit my face, I felt warmed.

Beyond the bridge, the lane widened and then split in two, the right hand fork following the course of the stream while the left meandered its way up towards the castle. I took the left and picked up my pace against the steepening climb. Less than a mile on from the ford the lane split again. I'd never taken the path to the east. However, from what I could see, it led back down to the stream and then on to a group of farm buildings that poked through the trees some distance farther along the valley. I was tempted to follow it just out of curiosity, but in the few seconds it took me to consider the option, I remembered the view from the Broughton castle and turned south.

Unfit, still feeling unwell, and carrying a few pounds more than would look good in a Versace dressing room mirror, the effort of the final climb told sharply on my pulse, lungs, knees, and head. By the time I reached the castle my face probably looked as if it was about to explode. A tuft of long grass growing thickly against a large chunk of stone beneath the castle walls suddenly looked terribly comfortable... it wasn't, and under the weak late winter sun, it wasn't particularly dry either. Still, I sat there regardless, twenty feet or so below the ancient castle for about half an hour. The view was spectacular, a full vista from east to west, marred only by a row of electricity pylons that ran from somewhere distant behind the hill to way beyond the horizon. '*Central Southern Middle England at its best*', I'd seen written somewhere, probably on a tourist office wall, I couldn't argue with it.

As I was about to get up and continue my walk, I heard a scrabbling of sliding feet on gravel up towards the castle behind me. I turned sharply to see a figure dressed in long waxed coat, clambering awkwardly up a particularly steep section of the path. I was about to wave a greeting when something in the set of the figures head and shoulders and the way it moved sent a chill running up my spine. Watching until the disturber of my peace and quiet had moved out of sight, I stood up and thrust my hands into my pockets, immediately my fingers found the gold chain that I'd picked up from Marjorie Warton's hallway floor. Tucking my head down into my collar, I would have quietly walked away, but before I could move, I heard another sound, a rush of falling stones, then a scuff of shoe-leather, and then a shout of pain. I recognised the voice.

A week ago to the day, in the Wheatsheaf pub, after almost twenty years, now this… incredible.

Above the silence of the otherwise deserted hill, I heard a moan and instantly I knew there would be no escaping this time, no excuse to run away, no easy way out.

'Are you okay?' I called.

No reply.

Climbing up to the castle wall, I called again and this time louder.

'Are you okay?'

Still no reply.

From the higher position, I could see beyond the sloping gravel path, and down towards the stile in the hedge that I'd climbed through earlier. To the right of stile, a yard or so off the path, a hump of green cloth rose up from the flattened winter grasses and then fell over. Hurrying with a lopsided gait along the contour of the hill, I made my way round to the path.

'Are you okay?' I tried again. This time the hump of green cloth twisted round and a white face peered from beneath a shock of chestnut hair, the usually bright hazel eyes looked dazed and at that moment didn't seem to know me.

'Do you need a hand?' I asked.

'Please.' The voice sounded shaken.

161

I leaned into the hill and allowed my feet to slide sideways from the edge of the gravel path and a few feet down the grassy bank.

'Give me your hand.' I said, reaching out while holding onto a tuft of longer grass. As our fingertips touched, our eyes met again and this time, I was recognised.

'You!' Was all I heard, and the hand was instantly withdrawn.

'Don't be silly,' I said, 'you're hurt... let me help you.'

'I'll be fine, thank you very much.' The chestnut hair flicked away defiantly, and the white face disappeared, back into the green cloth hump.

It seemed so ridiculous. I'd felt terrible after we'd almost bumped into each other in the Wheatsheaf pub when I was with Tristan and Ripper. Disappointed that I'd not tried to make amends then, I'd convinced myself that if I had I would have at least been met halfway, obviously I'd been wrong.

I didn't hang around for any further rejection, and pulling myself up back on to the path, I started towards the stile. As I put my foot onto the first rung of the weathered timber steps, I paused and reaching into my pocket took hold of the gold chain.

'Here.' I said.

Turning and stepping down from the path, I cuffed the back of my hand against a defensively hunched shoulder. The white face appeared again. I looked once more into the hazel eyes; the colour seemed weaker than I remembered.

'I came across this the other day.' I said coolly, swinging the chain from my fingers. 'It's yours. I know how much it meant to you. You should take it. I've never wanted it.'

From beneath the folds of the green-waxed coat, an open hand reached out. I dropped the chain into the palm.

A moment later, I was leaping the stile, and running back along the path the way I'd come. I'm not sure if it was my sinuses or the upset, but by the time I reached the fork in the lane my face was wet and my eyes stung like I'd been sniffing ammonia. Wiping my eyes on the sleeve of my jacket, I looked in both directions and then for no particular reason, at least none that I can remember now, instead of heading back to the ford, I turned and ran east and followed the track down towards the farm buildings that I'd noticed earlier. At the bottom of the valley, the narrowing path met and turned sharply to follow the eastern stretch of Cattleford stream back roughly in the direction of town. I slowed my pace here and wiped my eyes again and took time to breathe.

As the fresh chill of the cooler streamside air filled my lungs, and the soft sounds of the lapping water murmured in my ears, at last I began to feel calmer. I stopped for a minute or two to watch the glossy silver grey ribbon pass me by. An early crow shouted a warning to someone from the sky, and a sheep somewhere not so far away bleated a reply. I shrugged and then shivered. Shoving my hands roughly into my jacket pockets and bunching my shoulders against the world and my headache, although only partly recovered, I stepped out again.

A mile or so along the path I came to the farm that I'd seen from the hill sitting so prettily amongst the trees in the valley. Alas, rather than discovering the haven of rustic tranquillity that I hoped I might find, when I turned the final corner on the path I was greeted by a noisy shaggy black and white dog that came charging and at me from a muddy yard. Set between an old barn and pair of white stuccoed cottages and boasting a large Bed and Breakfast 'We have Vacancies' sign with the spookily coincidental telephone number 28-08-64 which apart from one year - in the wrong direction I'm afraid - matched my birth date exactly, much as I'd guessed from the view from the valley, the farmhouse and farmyard were indeed picturesque. Under other circumstances, I'm sure that I would have stopped and been nosey. However, catching me so unprepared, and barking and growling as it did, the wretched dog terrified me, not only testing my already shredded nerves, but ruining the moment altogether. Thankfully, a stout rope fixed to a post close to the corner of the barn pulled the beast up a few feet short of the path. Although dogs don't usually bother me, faced with the snarling brute, for a moment I'd frozen in my tracks. However, after the dog stopped and once confident that I was safe, I let out a nervous laugh and hurried on my way. A few hundred yards past the farm, when the dog finally stopped barking and my pulse had begun to slow, I rounded another bend in the track found my path blocked by a tractor and trailer. A youngish, thickset lad, a farm hand I thought likely, was standing on the trailer, and was looking down at me.

'Excuse me,' I called up to him. Still shaken from my encounter with the dog, I rested my hands on my knees to catch my breath, 'but exactly where does this lane finish up?' I asked.

'Church.' He said, and although he only spoke one word, from his accent and by the way he said it, I didn't expect to get too much more out of him, but ever hopeful I pressed on.

'Which one? I asked.

'Saint Michael the Archangel Parish Church,' he started, and then he surprised me and proved my hasty assessment wrong by continuing. 'The one on the edge of town with the church yard where my Gran and Grandar is buried and where they have bells what ring on Thursday evenings and Sunday mornings except when people die and they don't.'

'Wow!' I said, barely able to conceal my astonishment. 'Any idea how far?'

'Could be three miles, could be a four. It took us over an hour and a half to take Gran's coffin and my Dad reckons that he couldn't have walked any faster even if the hearse had been nudging him along, I reckon he's right too because his knees aren't what they used to be...' Then he took a breath, paused for a second or two and said thoughtfully, 'Wait up... Don't I know you?'

'I don't think so.' I said, straightening myself under his renewed and closer stare.

'You're the hairdresser aren't you?'

'Well... yes... I am.' I said cautiously, wondering why a farm hand would know me.

'I thought so.' He said, and put his hands on his hips and nodded to himself triumphantly. 'My brother is Colin; he works at the Coffee shop on the High Street.'

Of course, I thought, recalling that at some time while we'd been chatting my favourite barista had told me that he lived on the outskirts of town on his parents' farm.

'How is he?' I asked quickly, remembering that he'd been off sick suffering from a bout of Mumps.

'He looks like a bloody hamster, to tell the truth… do you want to see him? It's quite funny.'

'Him and me both.' I muttered to myself under my breath thinking of my own puffy features in the mirror that morning, and then I added more loudly, 'No, no, don't bother the poor chap; I've got to get on my way, but please, give him my best.'

I reckon that the path back into town was actually closer to five miles than the three or four that Colin's brother had promised. Even walking at a reasonable pace it actually took me the best part of two hours to get home. The farm lane wound through the valley following the course of Cattleford stream until it ran into a few acres of water meadow a half mile or so to the west of St Michael's Church. There the stream disappeared into fields, but the lane continued on, eventually meeting with another that I was more familiar with, and which I knew as a short cut back to the western end of Gillycote Road. Reinvigorated at the thought of a nice cup of tea, my pace quickened. A hundred yards short of the main road, I pushed from the path through a low hedge onto a lay-by at the end of a cul-de-sac where three large cars had been parked facing into the small road and were obviously for sale. A red Corvette, a smart Mercedes Benz, and a large navy blue Audi estate. I remember wondering why anyone would think that such an out-of-the-way spot would be a good place to market a car. Shaking my head, although still mulling over the apparent absurdity, I followed the cul-de-sac to another lane and then at last onto Gillycote.

At one o'clock precisely, my legs tired but otherwise feeling physically refreshed, having negotiated my way around another large car, this time parked close to the kerb outside my house, I stepped from the pavement through my garden gate to find a man in a dark grey suit and a uniformed police officer waiting on my doorstep.

'Good afternoon Sir.' The less obvious of the two Bobbies said, turning towards me. My heart dropped. I recognised the man immediately as Detective Sergeant Dennis Sapsead; the creepy bushy eyebrowed chap, with the big hands, who had called at my salon after Marjorie Warton disappeared, and had scowled at me at St Michael's Church before Enid Fulton's funeral. As before, I could see from the thinly disguised sneer on his face that he didn't like me.

'How very nice to see you again.' He said, not even attempting to hide his sarcastic tone, and I bet he thought he was being terrible droll. 'Another of your customers dead I'm afraid, I wonder if you'd mind helping me out again with just a few more questions.'

As if I could refuse.

CHAPTER NINETEEN

The few questions actually went on for well over an hour. Detective Sapsead was thoroughly unpleasant, another presumptuous homophobe I reckoned, and he left me in no doubt that I needed to be wary of him. I tried to be helpful, but as I told the snide pig, as I never actually made it into Cecile Ablitt's house on Marlborough Avenue on Sunday morning, I didn't know very much. I couldn't tell them who the tall smart woman with the neatly cut hair was, nor did I know where she'd gone. I did my best to help him with everything else. I explained how Cecile had asked me to do her hair for her 'big day' with the Queen. How I'd set off bright and early in the morning. How I'd caught the bus. How Cecile had telephoned me and told me about the disaster with her car, and how we'd arranged for her to meet me in the salon when and if she managed to get the car fixed. I told them that when Cecile didn't show up I'd assumed that she'd simply run out of time… I'd felt so sorry for her… having to meet the queen with her hair so dreadfully undone… and 'Oh! I was so shocked when Sylvia Cokeley told me that she'd fallen down the stairs… such a tragedy'

After the policemen had gone, I made myself a very strong and very hot cup of tea, and took an extra dose of Prozac just for good measure. While sipping at the drink looking across the back garden through my kitchen window, the one thing that kept coming to mind was what Marcus had told me the evening before. 'You looked fabulous actually darling.' He'd scoffed. The Fat-Brat was definitely a problem. I pulled my mobile phone from my jacket pocket and checked in the contacts list to see if I had his number, although I didn't remember taking it, I found him listed Under H for Hendy-Coombs. As it was lunchtime and I knew Marcus would probably be working behind the bar at the Wheatsheaf, so I didn't bother calling just then, instead, I sent him a text message.

Hi M, Thanx 4 the drink, sorry I got so shitty, speak soon to explain… and then I signed off with an '*xxx*', Self-preservation all very well, but I still felt a terrible fraud. I pressed the send button, put the phone back into my pocket, and then finished my tea.

Later that afternoon, my head feeling better than it had for several days, although my knees were tired and the skies had clouded over to a heavy grey, I decided to walk into town. I needed to pick up a few things from Marks and Sparks, non-essential groceries mainly, but I was also low on toothpaste and loo roll, items that I simply couldn't do without, and so I had to go in. The shopping didn't take me long at all, but by the time I'd finished and done my usual trick of buying twice as much as I needed, I quickly realised that my legs didn't fancy the walk home.

Crossing the quiet late afternoon High Street diagonally from Marks and Sparks towards Starbucks, I glanced in through the coffee-shop window surreptitiously to see what cakes they had left on the stand. While after the ups and downs of the last twenty-four hours, I felt that I fully deserved a treat, I was concerned that after my paddy with Julie, my custom at Starbucks might no longer be welcomed. I needn't have worried, as sitting neatly placed one above the other in the centre of the curved glass counter, with a hand written flag stuck in the higher reading '*SORRY*', was not one of my favourite sharp lemon cakes but two.

Julie rushed up to me as soon as I opened the door.

'I'm so glad to see you,' she started, 'I was afraid that you might not come in any more. Look…' She said pointing to the glass counter. 'I ordered you a whole cake specially to make amends, I'm so sorry about what happened yesterday.'

I didn't know what to say. Naturally, I thanked her. It was thoughtful. I'd always liked Julie… apart from the smell of Patchouli oil… and the fact that she didn't brush her hair very often… and the spots.

Balancing the cake and carrying the two heavy Marks and Sparks bags to my salon wasn't so easy. With every step I took, I could feel the cake sliding in its box. Eventually I resorted to struggling with the two bags in one hand, it made my right arm ache terribly, but at least the cake was okay. Once safely across the road, the few steps to the relief of the salon was easier. I unlocked the High Street door, dumped the bags under the desk, and took the cake out to the staff room.

The kettle seemed to take ages to boil. While I waited, I checked through the calls on my answer phone. Four had come in while I'd been off, two from numbers that I recognised and two that I didn't. I played the messages in order. All of them were cancellations for later in the week. I sighed and I wished I hadn't bothered checking. The two numbers that I knew were regular clients, former head-teacher Miss Eileen Browell, who usually came in on Wednesday mornings, and Sue Boniface, a cashier at Marks & Sparks, my first appointment after lunch on most Thursday afternoons; both said they were poorly. The other numbers turned out to belong to a husband and wife who were trying to cancel the same single appointment for highlights and a cut and blow dry; they didn't give a reason. I didn't recognise their name or either of the voices but their crying-off ruined my Wednesday completely. I hung up the telephone receiver and penciled a line through the next day's page. The trend was bothersome, but I consoled myself with the thought that another day of light duties wouldn't do my sinuses any harm.

Walking back through the salon to the staffroom feeling glum, I noticed my reflection in the floor to ceiling mirror standing with its hands on its hips staring at me. I stopped and I guess sarcastically, perhaps even defiantly, adopted the same pose while winking and poking my tongue out at it.

'Oh very clever.' My reflection said immediately, through tight slightly pursed lips.

I was quite surprised; it hadn't spoken to me directly for quite some time. I dropped my hands from my waist and stuck them in my pockets.

'Well what did you expect?' I grumbled, and I think I intended to end the conversation and carry on to the staffroom and munch into a huge slice of the sharp lemon cake. However, before I could move away, my reflection stepped forward, reached out from the mirror, and I think it slapped me hard across the face.

My mouth dropped open and my eyes screwed up in pain.

'What did you expect?' My reflection said back to me.

I stood there for several long seconds, my cheek stinging and my eyes watering, too stunned to do or say anything. I didn't understand what had happened. Had I really just hit me?

'Let us get something straight.' My reflection continued before I was able to react properly. 'This isn't a game we're playing here,' it said, 'this is the way forward to the rest of your life.' ...and ridiculously, no, incredibly, suddenly, without any further explanation, no words, no signs, no pictures, I knew exactly what I meant.

CHAPTER TWENTY

Easter was early that year, almost as early as it can be. March came in with its usual bluster and the radio weatherman threatened a miserable spring, but after only a few days of what felt like pestilence and plague, the rest of the month had been lovely. I was feeling well. My sinuses had at last cleared. Business, while not booming had at least picked up enough so that for two weeks in a row, I actually paid sensible amounts of money into my bank. Oh… and best of all, Colin was back at Starbucks.

Marcus responded quickly to the text message I'd sent him the day after our falling-out at the Dairyman's Daughter. However, in the three weeks since I'd met him for our fate determining drink, I hadn't seen him at all. Although we'd spoken on the phone several times and he'd tried to set up other outings, either he'd been busy working shifts in the pub, or I'd managed to convince him that I had prior and conflicting arrangements. I knew my time was running out though, and on Maundy Thursday afternoon, shortly after three O'clock, I took a call from Marcus at the salon while I was trimming his mother's fringe. It was a crafty move on his part and it worked perfectly. I tried hiding the call from Cindy, but Marcus must have known that she'd be in the salon because halfway through our call he asked to speak to her. Reluctantly, I handed the phone over. Although they only spoke for a few minutes, and I only heard a part of half the conversation, I quickly realised that whatever the Fat-Brat was saying to his mother, he was leading her to think that he and I would be seeing each other over the holiday weekend. Although she smiled at me as she spoke, something in her expression made me think that she wasn't too impressed. I remember naively thinking that our age difference probably bothered her. I didn't even consider the Gay thing. However, for quite different reasons I wasn't too impressed either, and not just because I didn't think I fancied her son. I was more concerned that if I needed to help him out of my way, I didn't want people thinking that there was anything between us.

When Cindy had finished talking to Marcus, she handed the phone back to me; she still didn't look happy but she muttered something about seeing me on Sunday. I shrugged a shoulder and put the phone to my ear.

'Mum's invited us for Easter lunch.' Marcus said immediately. I knew she hadn't, but I couldn't tell him that I'd been listening in so I let him carry on. 'Don't tell me… you've promised to perm some old dear's hair on Easter Sunday.' He jibed feigning a sigh. While it was a bluff that I might've tried, even over the telephone line we both knew that he had me cold, and from somewhere up in the fairyland space inside my head, I heard myself saying;

'Okay. That would be lovely.'

When I'd finished Cindy's hair, as she was leaving the salon, she paused in the doorway for a moment before turning and fixing me with cheerless stare.

'Do you remember when I first came in to see you, just after Christmas?' She said, arching a perfectly penciled eyebrow.

I nodded.

'I was so miserable that day and you really cheered me up.' She continued. 'Actually, I thought you were trying to chat me up, I found it quite flattering. To tell you the truth, with things as they'd been with Ripper, if you'd tried just a little harder you might have been successful.' Then she pouted, turned on her heels and walked out onto the High Street without looking back.

'Shit.' I said aloud, and I wished somebody had been in my salon to hear me say it. I was beginning to wonder what was going on, after almost twenty years of what felt like enforced celibacy all of a sudden, I seemed to be flavour of the month with every Tom, Dick, and Harry.

While watching Cindy float out of my day, beyond Marks and Sparks and into the distance, I caught sight of my next two cut and blow dry clients waiting to cross the road opposite Boots Pharmacy. Although they were ten minutes late, and despite my frustrations, it was actually a relief to see the Clark twins. One or other of them had cancelled a booking a few weeks earlier and I'd begun to worry that I might not see either of them again. Marie had the first appointment. The pleasanter of the spinster sisters, Marie sometimes brought me in cupcakes or chocolate. Unfortunately, when she opened the door and let her sister Jayne walk into the salon first, although she smiled and said 'Hello' cheerfully enough, I could tell that there was trouble between the women and any chance of a sweet treat for me was totally out.

'How's it going?' I said to either or both of them.

'Fine thanks.' Marie replied, closing the door.

Jayne the Dragon ignored me completely, and striding past the desk, threw her raincoat at the hat-stand, and then plonked her bony and obviously peeved bottom on the reception settee. Like a spoilt child showing off her anger, she immediately started flicking roughly through the magazines on the coffee table. She and I had crossed swords before and I wasn't about to tempt fate by speaking to her any more than I had to. Instead, after muttering something along the lines of 'Make yourself comfortable', I took her sister straight through to the salon and sat her down in my favourite chair.

Three quarters of an hour and a natty feathery graduation later, I was putting the finishing touches to the more attractive, and in my opinion the younger looking, of the not quite so *identical* twins hair, when Jayne shouted from reception.

'Are you two going to be all bloody day?'

Marie looked at me and shook her head then beckoned me to come closer; I leaned in.

'She's been like this all day… all year actually.' She said with a scowl, and then she covered her mouth with her hand and added in a whisper. 'She's just been dumped. A chap from the bridge club, he was a hopeless partner, and he had the most dreadful bad breath, but nobody dumps Jayney.'

Understanding that the rest of my afternoon wasn't likely to be easy; I was further dismayed when, as I showed Marie Clarke the back of her hair, instead of paying attention to her hair she called to her sister.

'I'm fed up with you.' She said, without actually looking round. 'I've had enough of your moods for today. In fact, I've had enough of your moods for the rest of my life. You can do what you like from now on, because I don't care... after I'm done here I'm going home on my own.'

'*Marvellous,*' I thought... '*bloody marvellous. Wind her up more why don't you.*'

From that point on the sisters might as well have been on different planets, they didn't look at each other, they didn't speak, they barely acknowledged each other's existence. I'd seen them fight before, usually petty squabbles about who spent the most on groceries or who was the better bridge player, but it was rare for Marie to be the more assertive. When I'd fully finished her hair, I left her in front of the mirror and she spent several minutes fiddling and faffing, first with lipstick them with mascara, all obviously just to keep her sister waiting. Sadly, for me, the provocation worked well. When I eventually got Jayne to my chair, she was seething.

'A trim?' I asked, nothing too time-consuming or controversial I hoped.

'I need a complete restyle.' She replied sharply, 'I hate it as it is.' Her bony fingers flicked at the greying fringe that I'd only cut a few weeks before. My heart sank; I knew it wouldn't take her long to throw the blame fully in my face and get spiteful.

It started quickly.

'These chairs are so uncomfortable.' Jayne grumbled as soon as I sat her at a basin. 'It's about time you updated this place and thought of your customers for a change. It's all very well charging us a fortune for a haircut, but when you don't deliver a top notch service it's no wonder so many of us are voting with our feet.'

Although she was just being a grumpy old bat, it was hard to argue with the woman. Just glancing from my place behind the basin, I could see that it was obvious to anyone who looked even a hairs-breadth beneath the surface that my salon was no longer doing so well. However, while there may have been a deal of truth in what she said, hearing it so nastily and at that particular stage of my life was more than just annoying.

Our bad start plummeted to a career-time low with almost the first snip of my scissors. After I'd shampooed the Dragons hair, I moved her to the chair in front of the tall floor to ceiling mirror. I'm sure that only to emphasise her point about the comfort of the seat by the basin, as soon as she sat down, she started fidgeting. First, she leaned this way, then she leaned that, getting her level was impossible. In an effort to keep her head still, I put my hand on her forehead and ran my comb through her hair without letting go. When I reached the back of her head, I divided the hair into two equal sections. As I exposed her scrawny neck, a familiar and knobbly friend popped out to see me. The mole on the edge of Jayne Clarke's hairline was a particularly gruesome and awkward little blighter. Speckled brown and protruding a full centimetre like the Wicked Witch of the West's wart, the thing had a habit of getting in my way.

'Mind *Moley*.' She'd say reflexively whenever I got near it.

'Of course.' I'd reply, struggling with a shudder. As if I needed warning.

Alas, with one hand on her forehead, and with her shoulders twitching, my confidence turned out to be premature and foolish.

The moles demise wasn't deliberate… I swear. I pushed one piece of hair to the left, and another to the right, and then I aligned my scissors a full finger width below the wretched beast, but when I closed the blades together, everything went haywire.

My God it bled… my stomach churned.

Gathering my thoughts… and my stomach, as soon as I saw that 'Moley' had gone I shoved the towel that I'd wrapped around Jayne's neck over the wound. I had a sudden moment of déjà-vu and a vision of a skewered Marjorie Warton flashed across the back of my eyelids. I shook the image away quickly and peeked under the towel. Thankfully, of the initial spurt of blood, only a small scarlet circle remained. Regardless, I pushed the towel back over it and glanced around for the mole. I looked on the floor immediately beneath my feet, on the back of the chair, in the towel, I couldn't see it anywhere, and eventually I gave up.

'What's the matter?' Jayne Clarke's shrill voice suddenly piped up making me jump.

It was only when she spoke that I realized that she hadn't seemed to notice what had happened. Apparently, the quick clean cut hadn't actually hurt.

'Nothing.' I said swiftly, gulping at air to hide the lie. 'I just dropped a clip that's all.'

'*Amazing*', I thought, happily stunned that I seemed to have gotten away with it. I pulled the towel down lower and picked up a section of hair between my fingers well above the point of impact. I was about to snip again when as I opened the scissors my eyes met a revolting horror... Jayne Clarke's mole was stuck to the edge of the top blade.

'Bloody hell!' I shrieked, leaping backwards and shaking my scissors as hard as I could. Alas, despite the good flick when I glanced at my scissors the mole hadn't budged. I shook them again, and then again, and finally, on the third flick of my wrist, the wretched thing shot from the blade, flew over Jayne Clarke's head, and landed with a small but audible splat on the mirror directly in front of her.

'What on earth are you doing, you stupid man?' She snapped ...and then she saw 'Moley'.

Like an over-fed maggot, wriggling its greeting from the shiniest apple, from where I was standing, reflected in the mirror the thing looked like it was growing out of her nose.

'I seem to have had a bit of an accident.' I said, suddenly feeling the craziest urge to grin. 'I'll just get you a Band-Aid.'

When I came back from the staffroom a minute or so later, with a small circular sticking plaster ready to dress Jayne Clarke's wound, although still not sure whether to laugh or cry, but thank god, at least more in control of my face, I found the abominable twin in what seemed to be a state of shock. Her eyes glazed and frozen into a hard stare, she reached her hand to the back of her neck, and then mouthed in a hoarse whisper -

'What the hell have you done?'

I'm not one for using bad language, but I know that in moments of extreme stress, for some people nothing else will do. In the past I'd found Jayne Clarke to be such a person and quite profane, and so naturally, knowing that I was in trouble and that she was bleeding and minus her mole, I braced myself for the onslaught.

When she opened her mouth, I turned my head to one side, screwed my face and made ready to wince.

'Can you get on with my hair now please?' Was all that she said - I couldn't believe my ears. 'I'd like to get to my solicitors office before he closes for the day.' She finished.

I understood.

We didn't talk much after that.

Despite the Dragons hair being thick and curly, her cut and blow dry took me under forty minutes. I was quite pleased with my creation, neat and to the point, it was just what she'd asked for and I'd been quicker than I had with her sister. I thought the turn of speed alone would have pleased her, even made up for my accident with 'Moley'. Alas, I was wrong.

'I suppose you think that's good enough.' She said, turning up the corner of her mouth and then flicking at her hair with the backs of her fingers. 'I could have done better with it myself.'

I didn't get too many complaints about the quality of my hairdressing in those days; my temper perhaps, but not my work. So when Jayne Clarke opened up, although I knew she was just after a free haircut, it felt like a stab in the back.

'What?' I said, feeling the flush of anger rising in my cheeks, the words 'silk purse' and 'sow's ear' leaping swiftly to mind.

'I don't like it... do it again... and not so puffy this time.' She demanded with a sneer.

I blow dried Jayne Clarkes hair three times in all that afternoon and still she wasn't happy. By the time I'd finished my third attempt at crusty-customer satisfaction, Jayne's hair was behaving like a Dandelion in a breeze, and I was hot and sticky, and feeling very very bothered.

'Straightening irons.' She snapped at me just when I thought I'd finished at last, and then she added sarcastically to herself as an aside under her breath. 'I doubt if he even knows what they are?'

I didn't answer her, but went straight to the small cupboard beside the nearest basin and took out a pair of one and three quarter inch GHDs. The irons were heavy and tactile; they felt good in my hand. I ran my fingers over the smooth organic contours of the moulding and stepped back to the mirror.

'Oh my god!' She said, sneering at me again. 'You did make it into the twenty first century after all. Now tell me… do you know how to use them?' Then her face curled itself around her pointy nose, her eyes sank, and a slither of a sarcastic smile escaped her lips.

I gripped the heavy straightening irons firmly as if holding a squash racket and then I wacked Jayne bloody Clarke as hard as I could across the back of her head.

The Dragon went down like a sack of spuds.

One-nil, Saint George…

Whoops.

Unlike after my little accident with Marjorie Warton, when I stopped Jayne Clarke whingeing, although the ferocity of my actions shocked me a bit, I understood exactly what I'd done. I know that in the time between the two events something had changed within me, a mental adjustment maybe, something that released me from conventional constraints. It might have been the drugs. It could've been the influence of my reflection. I don't pretend to know. What I do know, is that at the time, helping Jayne Clark find her way to a happier existence felt far more dangerous and unnervingly exhilarating than anything else I'd ever done.

'Bravo, bravo.' My reflection called, suddenly coming into view like a spectral entity from the wrong side of the large mirror.

'It's about damned time you stood up for yourself.'

Looking into the mirror, my reflection was standing in the opposite corner to me, with Jayne slouched in the chair between us, as if our images were no longer reversed. Spatially the shift in our relative positions was disorientating, and even when I moved behind Jayne, even though I could see myself take the step, my reflection didn't budge, instead the salon moved around it. Watching it happen made me feel dizzy.

'Have you checked her hand bag?' I asked me, I think sensing my confusion and somehow enjoying it. 'It might be worth it, she was quite a wealthy woman.'

'I'm not a thief.' I said, both surprised and annoyed that my own reflection would even suggest it.

'Oh don't be so trite.' I snapped back. 'If you're going to be the new Robin Hood of miserable souls, then somebody has to get the booty, it might as well be you.'

'Robin Hood?' I said.

'Well… whoever you're going to be, and whatever you're going, to do from now on, there's no point served in wasting opportunity.'

Suddenly angry at everything, I cut the conversation short with a wave of my hand, and regained my balance by stepping away from the mirror. I wasn't feeling good or proud of myself right then, but oddly I felt much stronger than I had before on similar occasions. Crossing to the reception area, I dumped the straightening irons on the desk, locked the front door and pulled the blinds. While I'd no particular plan, I quickly realised that I had to keep cool and do something with Jayne quickly, and through my anger a couple of ideas sprang to mind.

CHAPTER TWENTY-ONE

The taxi dropped me on Gillycote Road at five fifty five and I tipped the driver five pounds. On the way home, I told him my favourite of Tristan's Easter jokes, a short tickle about Jesus instructing his disciples not to touch his Easter-eggs over the weekend because he'd be back for them on Monday. The driver sighed then forced a weak chuckle and shook his head, he might not have found my cousin's joke particularly funny but I reckoned he'd remember me.

After slamming the taxi door as noisily as I could, I bumped my way through my garden gate and shouted goodbye to the driver from the top of the steps at the top of my voice. Halfway along my path, while watching the bemused driver pull away, I spotted my chubby neighbour peering at me through his living room window.

Perfect.

'Hi.' I called, waving furiously and making absolutely certain that I had his full attention. 'I'm a bit later than usual this evening.' I continued calling unnecessarily loudly, while over emphasising each syllable and mouthing out each word and pointing at my watch. 'It's almost Six O'clock'.

Eventually, after what seemed like an eternity, the guy acknowledged me with a nod, but then he quickly disappeared into the shadows behind a curtain. The chubby chap looked frightened. I wondered why for a moment and then remembered that the last time we'd had dealings, after the incident with his garden rubbish, Tristan had paid him a visit. I'd meant to ask my cousin if the blubbery blob had ever turned up at church like he promised, I doubted it somehow, he had the look of a heathen to me.

Once inside my home, for a moment, the kettle took priority. I plumped for tea over coffee, nothing to do with the caffeine levels, but simply because after my stressful afternoon I was thirsty and for me tea is more refreshing. At about a quarter past six, with a second hot mug and a third Gingernut biscuit in hand, I pulled the curtains in my lounge and settled on my settee to listen to some music. I'd decided what I was going to listen to on my way home in the taxi, I'd even told the driver. A Mike Oldfield collection of Tubular Bells, Hergest Ridge and Ommadawn, I hadn't played them in years. After stacking all three albums into the CD player, I set the volume at six on the scale of ten – just loud enough I reckoned – then pushed the button marked play and let the music begin. Unfortunately, while I was enjoying the hypnotic melodies, after only a relatively few minutes, before Mike could even announce his 'Two slightly distorted guitars', the sun dipped enough from the sky for me to start thinking about heading back to my salon.

Leaving the music playing, I went to my bedroom and changed into an old charcoal grey jogging suit that I usually only wore when gardening. My immediate plan was simple. Dressed in the shabby dark suit with a dark hat and gloves and wearing an old pair of trainers, I intended to sneak out of my house, through my back garden and make my way back into town unseen. Alas, while the plan itself seemed straightforward enough, actually following it through properly didn't prove quite as easy as I'd hoped. The first hiccup, although handy as it turned out, caught me before I'd even left the house. While rummaging through the cupboard under the stairs, hunting for my training shoes, I came across Cecile Ablitt's big leather holdall. I knew it was there, so finding it and being reminded of Cecile didn't come as a particular surprise. However, when I pulled the bag out of the cupboard, a subtle waft of familiar perfume came with it. I recognised the scent immediately. Nina Ricci's L`air du Temps, Cecile's favourite perfume. The evocative smell instantly reminded me of my adventure escaping the house on Marlborough Road dressed as a woman, and suddenly, the memory of what had happened to Cecile threw a spanner in the works, and an addendum to my plan began to form in my mind.

Hoisting the heavy leather holdall, one handle over each shoulder, after donning hat and gloves, I pushed my feet into my old trainers and made for the back door. Outside the air was cool and still. A hint of mist glistened close in on the halo-glow of a distant streetlamp. As I closed the door behind me, above the quiet of the evening, strains from the second phase of Tubular Bells began to play. Pausing for a moment, I listened as Mike Oldfield switched seamlessly between musical instruments. I'd forgotten how much I liked the album and promised myself that I'd make the time to play it again soon.

Towards the bottom of my back garden, the dusk deepened under shadows from my overgrown boundary hedge. I followed the path leading from the back door to my garden shed. Hidden nicely in the darkness, my shed backed onto a narrow lane that ran in a hollow behind my chubby neighbour's house and then between the gardens on the north side of Gillycote Road and a strip of community allotments owned by the council. Feeling my way through the darkness behind the garden shed, I eased myself between two bushes and slid apparently effortlessly down a short bank onto what I thought was the narrow path. Forgetting the holdall slung across my back, before I was quite clear of the bushes and had made certain of my footing, I made the mistake of trying to stand up.

Hiccup number two.

As soon as I moved, three things happened in rapid succession. First, my feet slid from under me, then the weight of the holdall toppled me backwards, and finally, the holdall itself caught on what was probably the most solid branch for hundred yards around. Before I knew what was happening, I felt a rush of wind in my face, and found myself hanging askew swinging in the darkest mid-air with my arms wrenched backwards through, although slowly sliding out of, the handles of the holdall. Knowing that I was about to fall, but not having a clue how far, forgetting my need for stealth, I yelled.

When I hit the ground, thankfully it was with a gentle featherbed tumble rather than the cataclysmic crunch that I'd feared. As luck would have it, the drop from the branch couldn't have been more than a couple of feet and I landed on what felt like a pile of leaves. The only thing that hurt was when, now freed from the branch, the holdall flicked into the air and landed on my head. Something hard and pointed hit me just above my right ear, the heel of a lovely Prada stiletto, I guessed. I lay on the ground for a minute or two, recovering my composure and counting my fingers and toes, certain that at any moment someone would come running to see what all the shouting was about. I needn't have worried about either. My fingers and toes were just fine and it seemed that nobody had heard me yelling at all.

Although perversely disappointed that our local neighbourhood watch scheme was so completely ineffective, once sure that I was safe and unhurt, I clambered to my feet and scrabbled in the dark for the holdall. I found the bag quickly enough, and from the little I could see, my inadvertently using the handles as a trapeze, hadn't damaged it at all. Silently thanking Cecile for buying such a tough bag, I threw it over my shoulder and hurried west along the path.

Perhaps three quarters of the way along the path, maybe fifty yards or so before the route curved south to cross Gillycote Road and met with the lane to St Michael's Church, it started to rain... heavily.

Hiccup number three.

While I hadn't actually checked the weather forecast, when the taxi had dropped me home earlier the skies had been relatively clear. Okay, so it was March and this was England, but as I felt the cold droplets soaking through my towelling jogging suit, I still felt short-changed. Beginning to wonder if the day and now nature were conspiring against me and my mission, exasperated, I cursed under my breath that if one more rotten chunk of either held me up I'd turn back home and face the consequences in the morning.

'Don't be stupid.' I heard a voice say. I glanced around in all directions but despite not being able to see in the darkness, I knew I was alone. Then I noticed the puddle. A few feet ahead of me, caught in the only shard of light for yards around, its surface glimmered through the raindrops just enough for me to see my distorted reflection. Naturally, I didn't answer myself, it wasn't the time for conversation, but the jolt to reality reminded me that I needed to press on.

Hiccup number four came by way of coincidence, and so even if my reflection in the puddle hadn't brought me up short, I doubt that I would have turned back. It happened when I was trying to cross Gillycote Road.

Walking along the path behind the gardens, I hardly heard an engine or saw a headlight, but as soon as I reached the main road, playing at being action man, crouched and ready to scamper across, it was as if somebody had tipped a multi-storey car park on its end. Cars seemed to be coming at me from all directions.

I'd tucked myself behind a low wall. By now, the rain was falling in stair-rods and every time a car whizzed past it sent a jet of spray straight at me. My jogging suit was soaked through. I clutched Cecile's holdall tight to my chest hoping that at least its contents would stay dry. After a few minutes, when I'd counted twenty-two cars pass by, and the traffic had begun to ease, keeping my head down, I listened for road-crossable gaps. Four seconds, five seconds, six. When my count reached seven, I raised my crouch. At eight, I took a peep and made ready to dash. However, just as I was about to bolt, above the thrumming rain, at nine seconds, I heard a soft rattling motor coming towards me from out of town. I ducked down again quickly. The engine sounded like it was from a van or a small lorry. I didn't watch the rattler pass me, but when the glow of the headlights wasn't far by, the engine slowed and the vehicle pulled into the side of the road.

I waited in my place, crouched behind the wall with nothing coming or going in either direction for a full minute before I dared take another peep, but when I did, what I saw made me wish I hadn't. Up ahead, parked on the northerly pavement only a few yards from my home, with its cab-light on, and the head and shoulders of its large driver clearly visible, was a navy blue and rust inhibitor red Ford pick-up truck.

'Bugger.' I scowled.

Peering through the rain, even so far ahead, thanks to the bright cab-light, I could see Tristan holding a mobile phone to his ear. I'd deliberately left my own phone at home, switched off in a drawer in the kitchen. I could only hope that if Tristan had come to see me and was bothering to call me first when his call went straight to my voice mail he'd think that I was either out or had gone to bed and would give up and go away. Alas, dashing my hopes quickly, the cab-light blinked out and the offside pick-up truck door swung open. Stepping out into the middle of the road, Tristan paused before slamming the door then looked over to my house. I swallowed hard suddenly remembering Mike Oldfield still playing his Tubular Bells at volume level six. However, as I watched, instead of heading towards my house, Tristan turned and crossed the road and quickly disappeared through the gate of a house few yards up on the opposite pavement.

'Sammie?' I thought, suddenly realising what my cousin was up to. The occasional waitress from the nearly French restaurant, of course, and a few cogs clicked into place. I heaved a huge sigh of relief and dashed across Gillycote Road.

I finally made it back to my salon shortly before half past seven. Although the rain turned out to be quite helpful in concealing me creeping through town, it didn't let up until after I was inside and by then I was soaked through and very cold. I let myself in through the back door and grabbed a towel from the shelf behind the staff room door. Everywhere was dark. I didn't switch the lights on but relied on the glow from the street outside. Rubbing at my hair and face with the towel, I left Cecile's leather holdall by the staffroom and then stepped into the salon. Jayne Clarke was sitting just as I'd left her; a tad slouched perhaps, with her head flopped to one side, but otherwise she looked comfy enough.

On the walk down, I'd begun to worry about the poor unfortunate woman. Had the blow from the straighteners actually polished her off or was she just stunned? If so, I was afraid that she'd have had a terrible headache when she came round. Moving closer, I quickly saw that the murky shadow on the floor to one side of her chair wasn't a shadow at all. Slick and dark, I needn't have doubted that the straighteners had failed. Walking around the chair, I gently lifted Jayne's head. The wound wasn't as bad as I'd imagined it might be and not particularly messy either. Not much more than a small dent behind her ear really, with a small split at the bottom where some of her blood had leaked out… actually… quite a lot. I hadn't noticed the blood when it happened. Letting Jayne's head fall back softly to the opposite shoulder, I used the damp towel to wipe her face. Although her eyes were closed, as I moved her head, Jayne's mouth dropped open and a small gold denture fell out and landed on her lap.

'Booty!' A voice behind me said promptly. 'I told you there'd be rich pickings from this one.'

Not even bothering to shake my head, I picked the peculiar trinket up with my fingertips, popped it in my pocket, and then went back to staffroom to find Cecile's holdall.

I hadn't opened the large brown leather bag since I packed it with the clothes and make-up that I'd borrowed from Cecile Ablitt on that fateful Sunday morning three weeks before. Unpacking it carefully, I laid the fragrant contents out on the work surface in the staffroom, relieved to find everything dry. All I needed was there, the shoes, the tights, the make-up, the wig, and despite having been packed tightly for several weeks, they all looked fine. Even the Chanel jacket and skirt unfolded with barely a crease, a testament to the quality of the fabric I reckoned. With no time to waste, I pulled the empty holdall open, put it on the floor in front of me, and started to get undressed.

Wearing the Chanel suit for the second time was quite a different experience from the first. In the dressing room in the house on Marlborough Avenue my motive had been a curious mix of excitement and devilment, today it was simply need. Buttoning the jacket over a large bosom made from two small towels stuffed into a plastic bag, I breathed in and glanced in the long floor to ceiling mirror. The full bust looked genuine enough and with the wig freshly brushed and a slightly more restrained make-up than I'd managed last time out, although I say it myself, once again I cut a pretty good figure.

Since I'd been in the salon I'd been trying to work out exactly how I was going to move Jayne Clarke, when while making myself a calming mug of Marks and Sparks finest instant, my eyes fell on a roll of hairdressing clingfilm and the large salon broom. Although the mug of coffee was probably the worst I'd ever made, the impromptu broomstick and clingfilm idea turned out to be a corker.

Leaving my soggy clothes in the holdall pushed under the sink in the staffroom, I took a few rolls of clingfilm from the stock cupboard and the long salon broom back to where

Jayne Clarke was sitting. Binding us together like an elaborate entry into a geriatric three-legged race took no time at all. After laying Jayne on the floor, I shoved the broom handle down the back of her neck, through her jumper and bra and eventually between the cleft of her bony buttocks into her knickers. With a few lengths of clingfilm wrapped around it and her neck, as a support for her head the broom handle worked perfectly. Lying down next to her following a similar principle and glad that Jayne was only a small woman, I used the clingfilm to wrap an arm and leg from each of us together. For an ad-hoc plan, with an extra long length of clingfilm wrapped a dozen times around our waists it all worked out terribly well, even standing us up wasn't as difficult as I thought it might be.

After spending a few moments in front of the mirror tidying our appearance and covering as much of the clingfilm as possible with our clothes, I pulled Jayne's raincoat from the hat-stand and drew it around our combined shoulders. A few minutes later Jayne Clarke and I left the salon.

Marching at a slow clockwork pace tucked well under the largest umbrella my cloakroom could offer, I hoped, looking no worse than two elderly ladies who might have had a tipple or two and were now taking the damp evening air, as St Michael's Church bells chimed eight o'clock, I led our way onto Lower High Street. Unfortunately, regardless of her small size, after walking Jayne no more than a few hundred paces, the clingfilm began to stretch and the evil twin became awkward to handle. In an effort to ease what was becoming an obvious carry, instead of relying entirely on the clingfilm, hidden by the raincoat, I hooked my bound arm behind her and grabbed the back of her pants. The move worked well not only taking the strain off the binding around our arms but it also meant that I could swing her free leg to match our stride. Looking at our reflection in a shop window as we passed, I reckoned our strolling looked almost normal.

With very few people about on such a miserable evening, after another few hundred paces or so, just before we turned into Brewery Lane, although still managing to make reasonable progress, I abandoned the umbrella in a shop doorway. The rain had eased to a drizzle and the damn contraption kept catching in the breeze almost pulling me off balance, and twice causing our tied legs to spin a full pirouette. The second time it happened we almost spun into the path of an oncoming bus. God knows what the driver thought when he saw us madly spiralling towards him. Thankfully, if untypical of bus drivers, he swerved out of the way otherwise I'm sure he would have squashed us. As we turned in towards the canal, above the exertion of heaving Jayne around like a giant ragdoll, I found myself writing mental headlines for the local newspaper. *Spinning spinster and shrink-wrapped transvestite squished on route number 7* – or - *Dancing drag queen and done-in twin unravelled by the last bus home.* Neither quite told the story, but by the time I'd stop grinning to myself, we were only a few yards from my goal.

The last time I'd walked by the brewery canal it was along the towpath on the other side of the water. I was heading for Enid Fulton's house and only one streetlamp was working. Tonight, although I was getting used to the dark, even that lamp was out.

Huffing and puffing, and despite being cold, sweating from my efforts, I swung Jayne Clarke onto West Bank lane less than ten minutes after we'd left my salon. Ahead of me and to my left, a row of cars parked close to the canalside quickly disappeared into the murky distance. I focused my eyes fifty yards into the gloom, to a white or grey Transit type van that I reckoned marked the halfway point along the narrow street. The van would be a perfect cover. Heaving Jayne one more time into my exhausted arms, I stepped from the pavement, and began the final trudge.

Apart from a few minor distractions, from the odd dog barking or a flickering light from the canalside cottages, nothing interrupted our stride. As we approached the van, an unexpected glimmer of weak moonlight dancing on the rippling canal a few feet ahead of us suddenly lit our way. Stepping into the dim light a sparkle from the polished grill of a dark Five series BMW caught my eye, and when I looked up at the car, parked only a few feet ahead of the van, it seemed to smile at me. Easing Jayne Clarke into the gap between the two vehicles, sheltered by the van and close to the canals edge, I wanted to smile back, but something to do with propriety, and conscience probably, and maybe even the mood of the moment, stopped me. Instead, I put my hand into the pocket of the classic Chanel suit, pulled out a pair of small but sharp scissors, and then proceeded to cut the abominable Dragon twin free.

Gathering the remnants of the clingfilm even as Jayne Clarke was falling into the inky water, I struggled to let go of her without following on in. Considering the effort I'd been to, the splash was surprisingly small, almost disappointing. Screwing the clingfilm into a tight ball, and throwing it in after her, I was just about to turn away and hurry back to my salon when suddenly, from out of the darkness ahead, the world exploded into light.

Instead of smiling at me, beyond its dazzling headlights, the grille of the dark five series BMW now seemed to snarl. I shielded my eyes against the glare while trying to peer into the car to see who was inside. I needn't have bothered. A second later, the driver's door burst open and tall man leaped onto the edge of the canal. I saw instantly that it was Dr Carmen. I couldn't believe my eyes, not again, in almost the same place, and at almost the same time of day. Caught in a moment of horror, my feet stuck to the ground and my mouth dropped open.

'Aren't you going to help her?' He shouted at me, slamming the car door. 'For God's sake woman, it's freezing in there. She'll drown in an instant.'

Suddenly the good doctor was tearing at his collar and tie and kicking off his shoes. I took a step back towards the van and made ready to run, but before I could move, as quick as a flash, the doctor grabbed my arm.

'What the hell?' He screamed into my face. 'She didn't fall... you pushed her didn't you?'

I didn't waste a second. I sucked in a quick breath and then punched him as hard as I could straight on the nose.

'You bitch!' He cried, releasing my arm to grab his face. Then, for once in my life, noticing when opportunity came knocking, I pushed him backwards into the canal.

This time the splash was much larger, far more satisfying. I didn't hang around to see if he was okay, I just ran like hell.

CHAPTER TWENTY-TWO

The sight of Marcus's baby-blue motor scooter parked behind my salon made me slither on the Prada heels. Dashing round a corner and suddenly trying to stop, I slid into a pile of cardboard boxes that somebody had left on the kerbside. The tumble scratched the lovely patented shoes and ruined Cecile Ablitt's Dior tights.

'Bugger!' I said panting, rubbing my knee, and pulling some of the longer hairs from the wig out of my mouth. I tried to stand up.

'What on earth do you think you're doing?'

I followed the voice to see Marcus step from the shadows close to his scooter. As soon as I saw him, I wanted to scream. Having the creep catching me dressed up for a second time was all I needed, especially after what had just happened. I wondered who else might turn up, Tristan perhaps. I could've done with a quick blessing. Maybe his mother, she could have made us all a nice pot of tea. I scowled into the ground then turning my face back to the Fat-Brat, I forced a pathetic smile.

'I'm so glad you're here.' I said, fibbing for all I was worth. 'It's been awful; he grabbed me and tried to throw me into the canal.'

'What?' Marcus said, his expression quickly changing from scorn to concern. Then he ran the few steps between us and started to help me up. 'Who... when?' he asked furiously.

'Just now...' I said, 'I ran away, I didn't see his face.' While I was speaking, I suddenly realised that my lie was far too near the truth, I should never have mentioned the canal. Annoyed with my haste and stupidity, I tried to limit the damage by changing tack quickly.

'Can you help me into the salon, please, I need to sit down.'

'Yes of course I can.' Marcus said now looking a touch confused. He put his arm through mine and helped me hobble over to the back door. 'We ought to call the police.' He said.

'No!' I said, probably too quickly, but a nice chat with a friendly policeman was the last thing I needed. 'I don't want anybody seeing me like this. It's just… It's just something I have to do sometimes… something private Marcus… and now it's all gone wrong… I don't want anyone else to know.'

Whether Marcus bought into my story, I don't know, but after I'd finished, he never mentioned calling the police again. I guessed that somewhere deep and dark within his psyche he took my - *anyone else* – remark to mean - *other than him* – and that in his eyes I'd just confirmed our special bond, but you know, right then I really didn't care, I just wanted to be somewhere else… anywhere else.

I made Marcus wait in the staff room while I changed into my soggy jogging suit in the ladies' loo. Neither of us went into the salon. The puddle of blood on the floor beneath my favourite chair would have to wait until morning. Regardless of Marcus's presence, I had neither the nerve nor stomach to deal with it then.

Clambering onto the pillion of Marcus' Lambretta, cold and soaking wet, was not pleasant. I hooked the holdall across my back as I had when I'd left home earlier and tapped him on the shoulder. He pulled away quickly and I held on tight.

CHAPTER TWENTY-THREE

Easter always used to be my favourite time of the year, brighter warmer days, new shoots in the garden, birds singing, lambs gambolling; all the usual reasons. Sometimes, when I look back from my present circumstance, I wonder where England's sunny days have gone. When I was a child, it seemed to me that in spring, and summer, and most of autumn, every school holiday or half term and most weekends were warm and bright. These days, from what I hear, it never seems to happen. Maybe it's because I'm away. Perhaps I just miss all the good days. I don't know, but what I do know is that during the Easter holiday weekend of my rather special year, the weather was so bad that I began to wonder if what my town needed, even more than a new shopping mall or eco-tram system to bring it up to date, was a roof.

I had to rap the highly polished oversized brass knocker twice before anyone bothered to open the door at number 23 Ocelot Close on Easter Sunday lunchtime. I was standing with my back to the weather, sheltering half under the small tiled porch, and half under a SpongeBob squarepants umbrella. I wasn't complaining. If it hadn't been for the bus driver lending me some poor child's forgotten SpongeBob brolly, I'd have been soaked for the third or fourth time that weekend.

While I'd dashed from the bus stop in something of a hurry, even through the lashing rain and from under the umbrella, it was hard to miss Cindy and Mr Ripper's house. The medium sized detached estate des-res itself looked okay, it was in a pleasant enough setting, and architecturally it wasn't an ugly house. However, I quickly decided that whoever had done the paint job needed their eyes testing. It was such a disappointment. When I first met Cindy, she seemed a classy bird with good taste and panache and from what Tristan had told me about her father being an MP, and from what I knew of her late Aunt Cecile, her pedigree should have been impeccable. I'd expected so much better. In fairness, Marcus had warned me about his stepfather's dodgy eye for colour, but I don't think anything could have prepared me for what fronted poor Ocelot Close.

As it was Francis 'Ripper' Dobson himself who answered my knock, when the huge hairy man peered at me through the crack in the front door and growled 'Yes', for some stupid reason, abject fear probably, before even saying 'Hello' I found myself feeling an insane need to pass comment.

'Nice house.' I said with a smile that very nearly grew itself into a giggle. Instantly I wished that the sodden ground beneath my feet would rise up and swallow me whole.

'What?' The big man snapped back, looking at me as if I'd just kicked his dog and then shouted at it for yelping.

'Your house...' I said shakily, glancing up at the orangey bricks, the blue tiles, and the lime green paintwork. 'It looks very nice... jolly... good walls... good paint... great colours.'

'Oh it's you.' He said disdainfully. 'I didn't recognise you under the girlie toy...' and then opening the door wider and filling the space with menace, he frowned and added with a low growl, 'You're not taking the piss are you?'

I didn't dare reply. I just grinned at him like an idiot, quickly gathering from his obvious hostility that he, like Cindy, wasn't so keen on the idea of my friendship with Marcus. I wanted to yell at him that I wasn't so keen on the idea either but before I could say anything, thankfully (I think), the Fat-Brat opened a window above the door and called 'Hi!'

'Hi Marcus.' I called back in the cheeriest voice that I could muster.

'I'll be down straight away.' He said.

After a nasty glowering stare and a pause, before Marcus made the stairs, Mr Ripper moved to one side and begrudgingly ushered me in. I had to squeeze close to the hall wall to avoid brushing against him. It wasn't an easy manoeuvre, but I was scared that if even the smallest part of my anatomy dared to touch him, the big hairy lummox might have sat on me there and then.

I have to say that once inside the house things did improve. The interior paintwork wasn't as disgustingly brash as outside for a start, Mr Ripper stopped frowning at me directly and only growled under his breath, and Marcus took my soggy coat and the umbrella and brought me a towel. SpongeBob made him laugh. He twirled the umbrella round his head a few times like a camp Gene Kelly and then started singing 'Bigger, squarer, spongier,' the tiny yellow chappy's TV tag-line song. I didn't mind his playful tease until he told me that he thought my carrying the thing was sweet. Ripper Dobson was standing right behind him. From the expression on the big man's face, I thought he might vomit. The frown quickly returned, the growling grew louder, and the hairy monster shuffled past me shaking his head.

'Sweet!' Indeed. For a moment, I was afraid that even I might throw up. I am not now, nor have I ever been, sweet.

After making me listen to a second chorus of the daft SpongeBob theme song, Marcus finally finished playing with the umbrella and stood it on the doormat by the front door. Then to my horror, and creepily, he took my hand and led me after his stepfather from the hall into the kitchen.

Much larger than I'd anticipated and almost perfectly square, the kitchen was surprisingly pleasantly fitted with quality hardwood units and had a long refectory style table running down the middle. The smell of roasting meat and steaming vegetables teased my nostrils as soon as Marcus opened the door. Stepping into the room, I was both shocked and yet somehow relieved to find his mother Cindy sitting at the table holding a copy of this week's local newspaper with my second cousin Tristan looking over her shoulder. I pushed Marcus's hand away immediately. The Fat-Brat hadn't bothered to mention that Tristan would be lunching with us too.

'Cindy… Tris…' I nodded trying to hide my surprise.

'Yo bro, my Matey. What are you doing here?' Tristan said smiling at me sideways, then he pushed the newspaper away and straightened up. He was obviously as surprised to see me, as I was to see him.

'Marcus invited him for lunch.' Cindy said coolly, before I had a chance to answer.

'Oh, I see.' Tristan replied, the smile falling from his face instantly.

'Just for lunch, that's all.' I said quickly, and eager to reassure my cousin, probably a touch too defensively. Tristan nodded slowly and then sat back at the table. Alas, while my second cousin seemed happier, from somewhere a few inches behind me, I felt Marcus shoot me an angry glance. I couldn't win. I cringed inside and moved further into the kitchen.

'Anything interesting this week?' I asked with an edgy chuckle, pointing at the newspaper, desperately hoping that a change of subject might help prevent the sudden drop in the temperature from reaching freezing point.

Big mistake.

'We were just reading through my Aunt Cecile's obituary.' Cindy said. My hopes for a casual cheery uncomplicated lunch immediately plummeted through the floor.

'...and the report on the police inquiry.' Tristan added. 'They still haven't found the woman.'

'What woman?' Marcus asked abruptly. Apparently concerned that he might have missed something important, the Fat-Brat marched past me towards the table. Reaching over his mother, his face reddened, he turned the newspaper towards him. My heart rate soared. I'd not spoken to either Cindy or Marcus about their Aunt Cecile's tragic accident but as Marcus hadn't mentioned anything to me, I'd guessed that at least he hadn't been particularly bothered. However, judging from the Fat-Brat's reaction to Tristan's remark about the mysterious woman not yet being identified, I began to wonder if my guess had been wrong. Although I knew from Detective Sapsead that the police weren't entirely happy with circumstances surrounding Cecile's death, I hadn't realised that the local rag had gotten hold of the story. As I watched Marcus lean over the table peering hard at the newspaper, I just hoped that the report didn't include a description.

Sometimes heaven sends little angels to help the helpful get along, my own Easter Sunday angel turned up in the pretty form of - sometime teacher sometime waitress - Samantha Gough.

When the oversized doorknocker rattled the arrival of a new visitor to the colourful house on Ocelot Close, as if the room itself had been waiting for a monumental event, everything in the kitchen stood still.

'She's here.' Tristan said in a loud and excited whisper while slapping his hands on the table. Then thankfully, before Marcus had been able to properly start reading the report, my lovely second cousin grabbed the newspaper from under his nose and roughly folded it up. 'She's here, she's here' He said again, ignoring the Fat-Brat's moans.

'Don't worry Tris, calm down.' Cindy said. 'Take a breath, swallow or something, you look nervous, you're sweating, it's not attractive… Marcus, please go and answer the door.'

'Do I have to?' Marcus grumbled. 'I don't even like the girl.'

'Don't be a brat.' Cindy chided. (I knew I was right.)

'It's okay I'll let her in.' Tristan said, and then he headed towards the door.

'I'll come with you.' Mr Ripper piped up from his place in the corner opposite the door. He was propped against a large stainless steel waste bin. While his post seemed somehow appropriate, despite his size, I'd almost forgotten he was there.

'Oh no you won't Francis…' Cindy snapped. 'You'll both stay just where you are. Marcus, we have guests, you will behave properly and you will do as you are told.' She said sternly.

A few seconds later apart from me, the kitchen was empty. In the end, still bickering, all four of them had gone to answer the door.

Choosing the seat next to where Cindy had been sitting, hoping to take advantage of the moment alone, I sat down and picked up the crumpled local newspaper and was considering sneaking it into the waste bin, when to add to my already bothersome troubles, I noticed a photograph of a face that I recognised. Printed in an advertising block at the bottom left hand corner of the folded back page, half hidden under a crease and next to an article praising the town council for its marvellous recycling record, under the heading 'HAVE YOU

197

SEEN THIS WOMAN?' was a snapshot of a smiling Marjorie Warton.

If I wasn't already wishing that I were somewhere else right then, seeing the picture of the Minging Marjorie's ugly mug certainly made me start. I dashed from the table, and stuffed the wretched newspaper deep into Mr Ripper's shiny kitchen waste-bin seat and then shifted some of the other rubbish inside to cover it up. A moment later, just as I was taking my seat back at the table, Tristan led Sammie into the kitchen.

...and so there we were, the jolly six of us.

As awkward social events go, considering the start, my mood, and the odd mix of personalities, that Sunday lunch at Cindy and Ripper's should have been a humdinger. In fact, although probably thanks only to Messrs Chardonnay and Shiraz, it turned out to be quite fun.

Although Marcus made a Valliant stab at getting the table placements to his liking, his mother and stepfather's ultimate insistence on sitting at opposite ends of the long refectory table restricted his options. I knew what he was trying to do. If he'd had his way, I reckon he and I would have sat at one end of the table with Tristan and Sammie at the other leaving Cindy and Ripper to cover the neutral territory in between. It was never going to happen though. I saw Mr Ripper's hackles rise the minute Marcus started to try and organise things.

'I shall sit at the head of my own table.' He said flatly from his perch on the bin.

Already safely in my seat, I found myself thinking that to save any arguments, if I'd been the big hairy brute I would have sat down and bagsied the head of the table straightaway, but then I reckoned if I had been Mr Ripper, I wouldn't have had to. I would probably have done exactly what he did, stayed right where he was, picked his nose and dared anyone to defy him.

As it turned out, Marcus needn't have bothered trying to keep Sammie and me apart anyway. After our rather embarrassed 'Hallo', and a few double take glances at me, and

198

then at Marcus, and then at me again, we hardly managed to speak to each other at all. Tristan was so overbearingly attentive to the girl, that even sitting opposite her, whenever I tried to chat I didn't stand a chance. For a while early on, it felt like Marcus and my second cousin were singing from the same hymn sheet only with different targets for their attentions. A constant barrage of facile questions, forever topping up an empty wine glass and an instant giggle whenever either Sammie or I said anything even remotely funny, it was all a bit cringey. However, unlike good ol' Tristan, whose brain once fogged by a pretty face couldn't think again until morning, after a few sharp remarks from his mother, at least Marcus stopped trying so hard and eventually we began to relax.

Although Cindy served lunch at around one o'clock, no one left the table much before five. The food was great and plentiful. A traditional English roast surrounded by every conceivable vegetable, far too much for me. I had to assume that Cindy was used to catering for much bigger appetites than mine.

'You eat like a girl.' Ripper said to me shortly after we'd started to munch, bumping me down to reality just as the halfway decent red wine was lifting me above it. I looked at his plate and then at mine. I guessed that from his point of view he was quite right; the comparison was ridiculous, maybe three or four to one.

'Leave him alone Rip.' Tristan said, his attention briefly slipping from Sammie. 'Crikey mate, you were in the Navy; you should know it takes all sorts to make a world.'

'I was just talking about his dinner, that's all.'

'Well that'll do it for today then, Yeh?' My cousin said with a note of finality in his voice. I reckoned that despite Tristan's daft idea that Ripper's few years in the Navy should've made him a more tolerant person, supporting me was quite brave of him, daring even. Ripper didn't come across as the type of guy who even a friend should mess with, and especially not in the hairy giants own home. Fortunately, Ripper just harrumphed, then nodded and carried on eating. Although I was grateful to Tristan, his big friends petty bigotry was no more than experience of his type had taught me to expect. I suppose I should have thanked my second cousin, but instead I said nothing, and like Ripper, quietly returned to munching my jolly good lunch. When, after a moment, I looked up to reach for another sip of wine, I caught Cindy smiling at me.

'I'm sorry.' She mouthed silently and I think without anyone else noticing.

Somehow, from that moment on, number 23 Ocelot Close became a much pleasanter place.

Ripper was the first to leave the table. 'Fit to burst and fed up with sitting down.' he told us, but I reckoned that he was drunk. Although he used carrying crockery to the dishwasher as an excuse, I reckon that really he left the table just to wake himself up and get back to the comfort of his bin. For a very brief moment, I felt quietly smug, I had survived, but then I tried to stand up and had to sit back down again quickly. I only realised that I was smashed too, when I looked around the table and saw that nobody else was. They were all looking at me and smiling... even Sammie. I wondered where I'd gone wrong... too much Prozac perhaps... surely not too much red wine?

'Am I my age in here, or is hot just me?' I asked, concentrating too hard on getting the words out in the right order and failing miserably. Then, as if to confirm what everyone all ready knew, I blotted my likely very red face with a gravy soaked napkin. Everybody laughed.

'I reckon you've had enough Matey.' Tristan said, reaching across the table with his clean napkin and wiping my face. 'Come on, I've promised to run Sammie home, I'll drop you off too.'

...and so, with those words of wisdom, the ordeal of Easter Sunday lunch with Marcus at Cindy and Mr Ripper's was over.

Or so I thought.

After paying a visit to the little boys' room, while the others were in the kitchen making ready to leave, I found Cindy waiting for me in the hallway holding my coat and the

SpongeBob Squarepants umbrella. She had a soft but slightly pained look in her eye.

'This is all new to me and Francis.' She said to me quietly. 'Marcus has never brought anyone home before. I'm sure we'll get used to the idea, but please, take things slowly.'

I just wished that I hadn't been so sloshed. Unable to trust my brain and mouth coordinate reliably, instead of trying to answer her with a clever non-committal parry, I just nodded and slurred, 'Of course, but I'm not who you think.' I wanted to tell her the truth. I wanted to tell her that, right then, I thought her son was a creep and that if the world had been fair, and alcohol, genetics, and death, hadn't been in the mix, it would have been someone like her that I'd have taken home to visit my poor old Mum. Although my drunken slurring had probably confused Cindy, before either of us could say anything else, Marcus, Tristan, Sammie, and Ripper filed out from the Kitchen. Marcus frowned at me as he passed and for a moment, I wondered if he'd heard what I said to his mother. I shook my head and he shrugged. Then, I think in an effort to cement some actually un-agreed agreement, as her husband and son moved towards the front door, Cindy reached for my hand, squeezed it and smiled at me.

'Thanks.' She said.

I turned away quickly and headed for the door.

Outside, Tristan was shaking giant hands with Mr Ripper while Sammie climbed into the cab of his pick-up truck. Marcus was waiting for me in the porch. As I tried to ease past him, he grabbed my arm and pulled me back to the door. For a dreadful moment, I thought he was going to kiss me goodbye, right there in front of everyone, but as if reading my thoughts he shook his head and then leaned in close to my ear.

'Don't worry, not here, not now.' He said. 'You're perfectly safe.' Then his grip tightened. 'You know, I read most of that newspaper report this morning before you arrived. I know I'll inherit well from the old trout, but did you have to kill her?'

A sobering chill shivered up my spine. I turned to look at him but his eyes were suddenly blank.

'I don't know what you're talking about.' I said.

'Oh come on dear… Tell that to the woman in the canal.' He replied.

CHAPTER TWENTY-FOUR

I woke wrapped in my duvet on the settee in my living room just after midnight. Although I didn't actually remember much about getting home – my system reacts badly to fresh air sometimes, especially after the odd glass of red wine - I guessed that Tristan had tucked me in. My head throbbed and my throat felt like I'd been sucking on a sandpaper lolly. The air in the room smelled like Cindy's gravy. The stuff might have been great on my lunch but the stale aroma wasn't so good to wake up to. Too hot under the duvet but cold as soon as I flung it off, I tossed and turned for ten minutes or more before reluctantly giving in to my bladder and getting up use the bathroom.

My timing was close.

Sighing with relief and blinking into the pastel blue neon lit mirror above the toilet pan, once the pressure on my nether regions had eased, I noticed a nasty brown crust of greasy sludge smeared across my top lip under my nostrils. Through the fog of residual sloshedness, I remembered wiping my face with the gravy soaked napkin. No wonder Marcus hadn't tried to kiss me goodbye. A sudden and unbidden vision of Marcus's pursed lips lunging toward me made me feel ill, and instantly reminded me of my dreadful predicament. A handful of cold water and a shiver later, the stale smell of gravy was gone. I turned out the light and made straight for the kitchen.

Initially, and I am quite sure very foolishly, opting for a numbing hair of the dog over a nice cup of tea, I began searching for bottle of vodka in the cupboard under the sink. Bending down was not a good idea either. I was quickly disappointed when the bottle I found came out of the cupboard empty. It was only then I remembered the 'Blooms not booze' promise that I'd made to myself in the supermarket the day before. I'd heard something about 'units' on breakfast television and had been shocked to discover that my forty plus a week was considered by doctors to be a tad high. I glanced at the windowsill, the forced chrysanthemums that I'd purchased instead of vodka looked lovely, but at the time, after Marcus's revelation, I was sure that a slug of almost anything spirituous would have done me better.

Although sulking, eventually I settled for a strong double bagger of Twinings Breakfast Blend, a chocolate covered marshmallow, and half a dozen gingernut biscuits. After putting everything onto a tray to guard against spillages, I wobbled my way back to the living room. As I opened the door, through bleary eyes, I noticed the red 'message-in' light flashing on my telephone answering machine. After putting the tray down next to the settee, I casually hit the necessary button.

'*You have two new messages…*' The metallic voice began.

'*Message number one – Sunday at 11.26am…*'

'Oh hi, it's me. I thought I might catch you in this morning, it being Easter and all that… but never mind. I don't know what to say. I should have phoned sooner, but… well… Oh, I don't know. Look, I really appreciate you letting me have the chain back. I can't believe that you found it after all these years… or found me on the hill by the castle for that matter. I should apologise… say sorry for being so horrible… maybe sorry is not enough… Look, I'll call you again… I'm not good with these machines.'

'*Message ends.*'

'*Message number two – Sunday at 12.00pm…*'

'Twice by the canal, such a coincidence… We need to talk don't you think… I'm sure you know who I am and where you can find me… Call me… soon.'

'*Message ends.*'

'*There are no more messages – press 1 to delete… press 2 to save… press 3 to hear the message again*'

I listened to both recordings three times over and then checked for caller ID. Only the second call to my answer-phone showed a number. Obviously, it had to be the bad one… I cursed my luck. First, the Fat-Brat and now Dr Carmen, soon everyone in town would know that I'd been cross-dressing and bumping people off.

Flopping onto my makeshift bed, I reached for my tea. Wonderfully potent although it had cooled more than I preferred, the strong brew scoured my mouth and restored at least some of my senses. I stared into the mug watching two small bubbles circle each other and eventually collide, quite calmly pondering on what I should do. While Marcus was a threat, I had the feeling that if push came to shove I'd be able to control him. Promise this, promise that. Although I reckoned that he was naturally as sly as a fox and greedy as hell, he wasn't an overly bright chap, ultimately so long as I was careful he'd go where he was pushed.

Dr Carmen, on the other hand, was a different matter altogether. As I'd never even properly met the man he was an unknown quantity. However, when I thought about him and what he'd said, I had to ask myself the question, what exactly had he seen? Me obviously, I know, but the first time at least, all I was doing was walking along the canal towpath. Sure, I'd been coming from the direction of Enid Fulton's house, but that didn't mean I'd even been to see her let alone done anything to help her. I could have been walking the quiet cut back towards town from half a dozen places for goodness sake. My favourite '8-till-Late' shop - the nearest newsagent to my salon, or maybe my optician, 'The Spectacle Man' by the roundabout on the one-way system, who cares that he was closed, so I'd made a mistake. I'd meant to call him the morning after to make an appointment, but you know what it's like, you get busy, you forget.

The second time Dr Carmen saw me, I'll admit, was trickier to explain… but then, had he seen me at all? Was the tall woman with auburn hair and large boobs really the diminutive wimpy hairdresser? Not my view of myself, but I know what people think. When I hit him he called me a bitch, he obviously thought I was a woman at the time. So when and why did he decide that the murderous woman was me? And surely, even if it had been me who'd pushed Jayne Clarke into the canal, I'd have been mad to do it dressed as I was, with the hindrance of a skirt and the high heels. No, without corroboration – okay so I needed to keep Carmen and Marcus apart - I reckoned a straightforward denial that I'd even been near the canal on that Thursday evening would take some disproving. Instead of panicking, I sipped at my tea and decided to try to get some sleep. I would call both Dr Carmen and Marcus later in the morning. With any luck, once I'd heard what they had to say, I'd have at least some idea what I needed to do.

Settling down underneath the duvet on my settee, thanks to the alcohol in my system probably more satisfied with my reasoning than I should've been, while trying to drift off to sleep, my thoughts turned to the first message on my answer-phone. In some respects the call had come as more of a surprise than Dr Carmen's did. Although hoping against hope itself, while after what he'd said at Enid's funeral, I was sure that the doctor wouldn't let his suspicions lay, I'd been equally certain that after the ridiculous episode at Broughton Castle, I'd never hear from my friend again.

There was a time, when, for the couple of years before I opened my salon, my very good friend and I were rarely apart.

We met on the London underground while travelling the Northern line between Waterloo and Camden Town. I spent the journey, as I often did when riding the Tube, watching the flickering bouncing reflections of my fellow passengers in the grimy windows. I didn't realise that I was being watched back until sometime afterwards when I literally bumped into my watcher as we disembarked the train at the same station. After we collided, I fell onto the platform. I'm sure it looked far worse than it actually was, but my dramatic tumble caused quite a kerfuffle. A few people started to gather round me. It was then, through the crowd of faces, that I first spotted the hazel eyes.

'Are you okay?' The soft voice behind the pretty eyes asked.

'I think so.' I answered, hearing the words clearly above the usual din of the underground station.

'I'm terribly sorry.' Hazel eyes said. 'I was distracted.'

It was several weeks before I discovered that I'd been the distraction. I expect I laughed, I was probably flattered; the owner of the hazel eyes was good when it came to flattery.

After the incident on the station, when my newly met friend had helped me to my feet and the crowd had grown bored and moved on, to steady my nerves, we went for Coffee at the Starbucks on the junction of Camden High Street and Parkway. It was my first time in a Starbucks, my first skinny latté and my first slice of sharp lemon cake. That tube ride has a lot to answer for.

On that particular morning, I was supposed to be going to a job interview at a new salon on one of the trendy lanes off Camden Market. Unfamiliar with the Northern line and the Camden area, I'd left home far earlier than I needed to and so passing a half hour in a coffee shop with pleasant company and a nice slice of cake should have been a fine way to fill the time, and it was. However, I never made it to the salon for the interview. Instead, after only a few minutes of animated, mind clicking, small talk, I rashly decided to content myself with the job I already had, and spent the rest of the warm early spring day getting to know my new friend while strolling the myriad of paths in Regent's Park.

...And that's where it all began... my downfall probably. Within a matter of days - despite us both carrying recent emotional scars, my friend from the loss of a long-term partner, and me from the shock of my father's collapse on Mount Snowden - we became a couple. Although dating was new to me – I'd never been involved in a serious relationship before – I quickly found that coupledom suited me surprisingly well. Together our social life in London became fuller and more exciting than I think either of us had experienced before. We gelled perfectly. We did interesting things, went to interesting places, and introduced each other to our most interesting friends. Okay, a minor moment of truthfulness here, I didn't really have many interesting friends when I lived in the city. In fact, apart from a couple of sappy colleagues and the druggy girl with the remarkably fit tattooed boyfriend who lived in the bedsit above mine in Fulham, I didn't have many friends at all. However, my very good friend's plentiful acquaintances seemed to take to me kindly, and for a while at least, I, and I hope we, were happy enough and probably in love.

Then it all started to go wrong. Experience now tells me that this is quite usual, a good splosh of encouraged over familiarity, a pinch of complacency, and a dash of petty jealousy, all simple stuff, but at the time – as a novice in matters of the heart and never a fan of weepy cinema - I was heartbroken. I don't know why, how, where, or when it started to fall apart but looking back I do remember lying in bed on my own one rainy birthday night feeling suddenly rotten. We'd had an argument... not a particular biggy, just the first of too many. It went on like that for several months. A good day followed by a bad day. We both hated it I'm sure, but neither of us could bear the thought of running away. Thank goodness, we never moved in together. I wanted to, but the timing was never right. I would be committed to this; my friend would be committed to that...

...and then, one day out of the blue, maybe eighteen months after we met – possibly at the point of make or break when we should have broken - I had the opportunity to open my own salon. The excitement was overwhelming, and to my surprise, it carried us both in its wake. My friend turned out to be wonderfully supportive. The arguments stopped. It seemed that we became closer than ever. We moved out of London taking neighbouring flats in the same block in the centre of town. My friend got a job with the local newspaper and on July 17th, nineteen years before my fateful visit to Marjorie Warton's luxury apartment, after a month or more of cheerfully shared hard labour in DIY shop fitting, I opened the doors to my salon.

So sad the song... Minging Marjorie Warton... thief... dead-un'.

Of course, we might have broken up anyway.

I've never liked speaking on the telephone. When I hung up after my conversation with Dr Carmen, I wished I could have rewound my tongue.

His voice was calm and measured with a hint of Hannibal Lecter in the drawn inflection and, as I'm sure he'd calculated, the tone completely threw me off my stride. I reckon he knew that it was me calling before he even picked up. I know if I'd been him and had been expecting my call I'd have been checking the caller ID every time the phone rang.

Of course, I could have withheld my number, but I didn't see the point and it might have seemed suspicious. However, something about the way he said the long slow 'Aah hallo' was just too well prepared... creepy. Naturally, I tried to stay cool and collected. 'Oh hi, I'm just returning your call.' I think I said, and as casually as I could manage, but before he'd even answered me, maybe just from the sound of his breath, I could tell that he knew my knees were knocking. I don't know why I was so nervous. Before I dialled the wretched number, I felt fine.

'You took your time...' He said, 'considering your precarious position.'

'Who am I speaking to?' I asked. I thought I might as well start from the ignorant innocent position and see where it led. Unfortunately he just laughed.

'My dear fellow,' he chuckled at me condescendingly. 'You don't really think me so stupid do you? No... of course you don't. I'm sure you're much too clever to do that. So clever in fact, that you have almost everybody chasing shadows, uncertain if a crime has even been committed... but I know better.'

'I really don't know what you're talking about.' I said in reply, and I tried to say it flatly with a note of derision hidden in a half laugh, but somewhere along the line my voice cracked and I'm sure it sounded just as I was feeling... suddenly terrified.

'Then I'll tell you exactly what I'm talking about.' Dr Carmen said, now speaking very slowly indeed. 'Fresh hair clippings on Enid Fulton's saliva soaked pillow and more scattered on her nightclothes... I was with Enid when she telephoned you on the afternoon of the day she died. I know that she asked you to call and I know what you did when you were with her. Oh, I expect Enid gave you some loopy story about her being terminally ill. She wasn't of course. The poor creature had simply had enough; she'd convinced herself that she wanted to die...'

'She begged me...' I found myself saying before I could help myself. I couldn't believe that I'd come out with such a stupid admission. Despite being out of sight at the end of a telephone line, I slapped my hand over my mouth to prevent the blessed thing from blurting out anything else.

'It is still murder.' Dr Carmen replied. '…and then there's poor Cicily Ablitt, I was the first medic at the scene you know… called in for a pronouncement by the police. You'd been there too hadn't you? All dressed up in your Sunday finest and high heels. I didn't realise until I saw you struggling with Jayne Clarke by the canal, but it all fits together so neatly… maybe too neatly.'

'This is wild.' I said. 'You're just guessing, guessing and making up stories.' I tried desperately, but Dr Carmen ignored me.

'…and then there's my broken nose.' He went on. 'I should be angry of course, but I understand your dilemma and I have to say that, for a hairdresser, it was a jolly good shot. I wouldn't try it again though. I promise you that if there's a next time I'll bite back.' He left the thought hanging for a moment, but before I could speak, he added, using a sharper more clipped tone. 'We need to meet, I think. I have a proposition for you. Lunchtime, at my home, I know I can trust you to be discrete, bring a bottle of wine, a red perhaps, something bloody.'

I pondered what to do for most of the Easter bank holiday Monday morning before eventually deciding to do as I'd been told. I knew that accepting Dr Carmen's invitation was tantamount to admitting guilt, but after agonising between what he wanted, and what he might do if I didn't turn up, I didn't see that I had much choice.

I never called Marcus as I'd planned, but instead, probably hiding my head in the sand and trying to delay the doubling of my crisis for as long as possible, as I left home to walk to meet with Dr Carmen, I sent the Fat-Brat a text message.

'Hi M. I'm feeling terrible this morning. Bad head etc. I can't believe what you said yesterday. I can see that I have stuff to explain… but please don't assume the worst. I'll call you ASAP.'

After I pushed the 'send' button, I opened the 'Write new' folder for a second time and started a message to Tristan.

210

'Thanks for tucking me in Cuz.' I began. *'Sorry if I embarrassed you yesterday. But please, don't tell your Mum.'*

I hadn't reached the end of Gillycote Road before my second cousin's reply chirped in.

'I didn't tuck you in...' It started. *'...Sammie did, and you're the one who should be embarrassed not me, be very embarrassed... you had an erection!'*

CHAPTER TWENTY-FIVE

The house on Princess Grove was not unlike Cecile Ablitt's home on Marlborough Avenue, tall and imposing with deep bay windows and a central porch sheltering a grand front door. To the left of the house, parked behind a low juniper hedge on a broad red tar-macadam drive I could see Dr Carmen's dark BMW smiling at me once more.

Carrying a bottle of Cabernet/Syrah given to me by a client at Christmas and still, I confess surprisingly un-drunk, I edged my way quickly along the pavement. My legs quaked as I approached the house. A dog howled. A ball of newspaper tumbled in the breeze ahead of me. High noon on the easterly fringes of my little town and the image of drawing Marjorie Warton's tiny gun from a velvet holster flashed through my mind. I reckoned it might have been handy if I could ever have raised the courage to fire it. I shook the thought away, held the bottle of wine in front of me and pressed on towards the front door.

The doorbell chimed like a country church on Sunday morning, two ups and downs followed by short peel. For some reason the naffness made me smile. I reckon Dr Carmen must have been waiting close by inside because like something from the Addams Family TV show, the door creaked open almost immediately the bells stopped ringing. I took a reflexive step back but kept the smile firmly fixed in place.

'...and to think I doubted your good sense.' The doctor began before our eyes had even met. 'Come in dear boy, come in.' He said, slowly opening the door wider.

The front step turned out to be where any similarity between Dr Carmen's house and Cecile Ablitt's stylish home ended. Inside was an austere place. Recently moved into, sparsely furnished and minimally decorated, it reminded me of a cheap seaside hotel where the owners had stretched their family's unwanted belongings to make their penny pinching business feel homely. It was a horrible mix-up.

'Go through to the end of the hall and turn right.' The doctor said. He closed the front door behind me; still our eyes hadn't met.

'I see you did as I suggested, is that a Chenet?' He asked, I guessed referring to the bottle of wine I was carrying – I hadn't noticed the name on the label - I didn't turn or answer.

'By the lean of the neck, I believe it is.' He added 'Unsophisticated and inexpensive, but I am sure it will do the job well enough. I've prepared us a light lunch; I hope you enjoy Foie Gras.'

To be honest, I'd never tried the stuff; just reading about the meanness of its preparation had always been enough to put me off, however, I didn't comment and carried on along the hall. Dr Carmen was certainly a cool customer, although unlike when we'd spoken on the telephone, when his tone made me nervous, this time, in the flesh I found his calm smooth voice almost soothing. I began to wonder what he was doing. My wine, his food, all jolly convivial, but the accusations that he'd thrown at me on the telephone were hardly a cause for a lunch party.

While at the end of the hall, as instructed, I turned right through a pair of double doors and entered a bright conservatory, the doctor carried straight past me into a room that I could see through a crack in the door was the kitchen. I paused, wondering if I should wait for him or follow.

'Make yourself comfortable.' He called either noticing my hesitation or reading my mind, I wasn't sure which. 'I expect you'd like to sit with your back to the garden. This time of year at this time of the day any sun we have shines straight in through the glass, a touch warm sometimes, and the glare might make you feel as if you're under interrogation.'

Once again, although the doctor's politeness and consideration seemed oddly out of place, I found myself doing exactly as I was told.

The conservatory was not large. Perhaps twelve feet by nine, I reckoned it squared an empty corner in the house between the kitchen and the first room off the entrance hall, probably a dining room or a lounge. There were only four chairs and a small coffee table in the room. All made from an ageing and yellowing white Rattan, the chairs were set in a rough circle, so that two faced into the room, and two enjoyed a view through four full height Georgian windows over a swimming pool and the doctor's walled and well-tended garden. The small glass topped coffee table sat in the centre of the circle. Hung on the wall opposite the windows and adjacent to the doorway where I stood, a large and similarly faded Rattan framed mirror reflected yet more light in from outside. Always keen to be the good boy, as suggested I took the seat furthest from the doors and with my back to the garden.

A minute or so later, just as I'd begun to allow myself to feel comfy in the chair, Dr Carmen came into the room carrying a large wooden tray. As he put the tray down, balancing it on the small circular table, he glanced in my direction. For the first time since I'd been in the house, indeed, since I'd punched him on the nose by the canal, I met his eye. I suddenly realised that I was still smiling and almost immediately two things struck me, Dr Carmen's eyes were weaker and uglier than I remembered from either of our previous encounters, and his nose looked dreadfully sore.

Following my gaze to his bruised beak and I think also finding my manic grin somewhat disquieting, the doctor surprised me for a moment by turning quickly away. 'Maybe not such a tough cookie after all?' I dared wonder. Alas, my optimism was quickly dashed when an instant later, very obviously confident that he was in control of the situation, Dr Carmen stood tall above me, jabbed his hands into his Chino pockets and looked down and said:- 'I expect you are wondering why I've asked you here and not simply taken my deductions to the authorities.'

I didn't answer him and neither could I hold his stare. Instead, my gaze fell to the floor and my own fidgeting feet. I watched them squabble over which would rest on the other's ankle. Neither of them won and eventually I gave in and looked up. From my sitting position, the doctor looked to be quite a big chap, long legs, a thickish waist, broad shoulders. Facially, he took after his mother, the same square features and heavy brow as the cake thief, but actually more attractive on the man than on the woman. His hair, salt and pepper, cut short and brushed casually back, reminded me of Bill Clinton.

In fact, in the right suit and tie and under the right lighting Dr Carmen might have made a reasonable, if somewhat slimy, presidential double.

'Well… I'll come to that later.' He said coolly, snapping my thoughts back to the moment. 'First, let's open that bottle of wine.'

It was only then I realised that I was still clutching the bottle of bloody red wine that I'd been instructed to bring. Dr Carmen reached out to take it from me. I passed the bottle over without too much thought, but a few days later, while trying to unravel an awkward mental knot in the middle of the night, I found myself wondering if that simple act, the symbolic passing of blood between us, had been more prophetic than the doctor could ever have guessed.

'Thank you.' He said, returning to his slow, overly studied enunciation. At last my smile dropped.

We ate lunch and each drank a glass of the wine in almost complete silence. After twenty minutes or so, when most of the Foie Gras and mustard salad had been eaten and our plates were completely cleared, Dr Carmen leaned back in his creaking Rattan chair and steepled his fingers.

'I'm not a 'nice' man.' He said, looking at me thoughtfully. 'So I'm not going to dress up what I'm about to tell you with any fancy excuses just so you'll think well of me… the thing is… I want you to kill my mother.'

I want you to come and see me at lunchtime. I want you to bring a bottle of red wine. I want you to sit in my conservatory and wait for me patiently while I prepare you some smelly hot goose liver pâté and silly bits of almost burned toast. Oh… and by the way… I want you to kill my mother. All simple enough requests, but somehow the later made me sit up and listen most.

'It shouldn't be too difficult. I've come up with an array of suggestions, I'd jot them down for you, but I'm sure that a man of your obvious talents wouldn't need my advice.'

'I'll be travelling for most of April. I'll be away for three weeks. That should give you ample time to get the job done. I've prepared a small fact sheet for you. Where the old love goes, what she does, you know the score… *Your mission*

215

should you choose to accept it is… Except that unlike Ethan Hunt in Mission Impossible, you don't actually have a choice.'

'When I return from my sojourn, perhaps after my mother is securely in her box underground, we can discuss payment and guarantees… your safety… my silence… etcetera. Until then I don't see any need for you to contact me… oh… I should mention that I shall be lodging details of my suspicions with a suitably reliable person, just in case you have any clever ideas.'

Then Dr Carmen stood up. He smiled at me and before I had any chance to answer him or even comment on what he'd just said, he added flatly: 'Well, it's been good to meet you. I'll have to ask you to leave now. I have important things to be getting on with. Thank you for bringing the wine. Not quite bloody enough for the Foie Gras somehow, but a reasonable choice nonetheless.'

Then he led me to the front door. A moment later, I was standing outside on the doctor's porch clutching a cream coloured A5 manila envelope, feeling dazed and confused with the door closing behind me.

You know, I'm getting fed up with using the phrase, 'I didn't know what to do.' but here's the thing, at that moment, at about 1.30pm on that Easter Monday afternoon, I really didn't know what to do.

I'd expected Starbucks to be empty, a bank holiday afternoon, the skies dull and grey, and so far as I knew, nothing much going on in town. However, I was soon proved wrong. When I pushed on the door handle, my ears met a rattle of multi lingual chatter from a motley group of teenagers – students from the local language school I thought likely – who had taken all but one of the seats in the coffee-shop window. The expression on my face must have given my thoughts on the invasion of my space away far too clearly, because before I could either get properly inside, or turn round to walk out, a voice called to me from behind the counter.

'One tall skinny latté and a slice of your very most favourite, coming up.'

I looked over smartly to see Colin grinning at me through the chromium spaghetti pipe-work of the Gaggia geyser. Although my favourite grinder had returned to work after his bout of mumps a few days before, it was the first time he'd served me since his illness. I smiled back.

'Don't worry, they'll soon be off.' He said quietly as I approached the counter.

'What's going on?' I asked.

'An Easter egg hunt, would you believe it?' He replied. 'After the wash out in yesterday's rain, the organisers are trying to hold it today. This lot are all helping.' He said raising a sceptical eyebrow in the direction of the students. 'It's due to kick off in the park at 3.o'clock.'

'I think I'll pass on it myself…' I said with a shrug. '…love chocolate, just highly allergic to eggs and… well… most kids.'

'I expect there will be hundreds of both.' Colin chuckled. 'I'd stay here and drink coffee if I were you.'

'That sounds good to me.' I said. 'It's good to see you back.' I added.' You're looking well… your hair has grown and I think you've lost some weight.'

'Thanks.' Colin said, smiling coyly. 'It was rotten actually, jolly painful, losing a few pounds was about the only consolation… anyway, I feel much better now.'

As Colin turned up the steam to heat and froth the milk for my latté, almost as if prompted by the awful noise, the group of students began to stir from the settees.

'See.' Colin mouthed the word almost drowned out by the hissing steam. 'I knew they wouldn't be long.'

A few minutes later, the students had gone and I was sitting comfortably in my favourite - it was the third time that I'd sat there after all – seat, sipping my favourite coffee and nibbling at a large slice of my favourite sharp lemon cake. With so many favourites in the same place and at the same time, I should have felt fine.

I'd gone to Starbucks because I was cold and feeling very alone and I couldn't think of where else to go. After what Dr Carmen had said to me, I didn't want to go home. For some reason I felt that I needed to keep moving. I'd walked into town via the top end of Brewery lane. I avoided the canal. When I got to the High Street, I made straight for my salon. I don't know why. I had nothing to do there. I didn't go in. Actually, I couldn't have gone in even if I'd wanted to, quite unusually, I didn't have a key. Standing outside looking in on my working world through a dirty window, suddenly the place seemed changed. For so many years, those walls and all that they held mattered more to me I think than anything else in my life, but right then, it meant nothing. Fighting tears and trying to get a handle on my feelings, I was wishing that the place would burst into flames, when Dolly Parton and Kenny Rogers started singing from my trouser pocket. I took a long deep breath reached inside and pulled out my mobile phone.

'Hullo.' I said, while staring at my blurred reflection in the salon window.

'I know I stand in line, until you think you have the time to spend an evening with me.' My own voice started singing to me...

'And if we go someplace to dance, I know that there's a chance you won't be leaving with me.' It was hopelessly out of tune of course.

'And afterwards we drop into a quiet little place and have a drink or two.' But it didn't seem to matter... I sounded happy enough.

'And then you go and spoil it all by doing something stupid like...'

Killing somebody, I thought, and I think it was the first time that I really fully considered what I'd done.

'Oh pull yourself together for goodness sake... wimp!' My reflection said from the salon window. 'So you made some mistakes... so what. I've told you before, if you had just taken the time to get a grip on yourself and planned, you'd have been quids-in from helping these people by now.'

When Colin interrupted my daydream, I blinked to find myself staring at the slice of sharp lemon cake. I'd been thinking about Dr Carmen's mother and how only a few weeks before the old boot had deprived me of a whole cake. It might seem a mean thought, but I'd also been wondering if Karma and her son were in cahoots to ensure her comeuppance. I guess I still hadn't forgiven her.

'You met my brother.' Colin said, shattering my train of thought entirely.

'What?' I scowled, all I could manage in reply. Colin flinched at the unintentional, but unfortunately obvious irritation in my voice.

'At the farm.' he said, now sounding far less cheerful and confident than he had earlier.

'I'm sorry?' I asked.

'My brother, Connor.' He said. 'You met him near my parents' farm on Cattle Ford Lane.'

From within a distant fog that events and probably my recent double dosing on Prozac seemed to be erasing way too quickly from my memory, I recalled the country bumpkin that I'd asked directions from after the run in with my friend at Broughton Castle.

'Oh... yes... of course.' I said, rubbing my forehead. 'I'm sorry; I was away with the fairies for a moment just then.'

'It's not important.' Colin said, shaking his head. 'He just mentioned that you'd come out to the farm and lost your way.'

'Yes, that's right. I'd been out walking that morning. I wasn't exactly lost, but your brother showed me the quickest way back to town.'

'Oh, so you hadn't come up to find the farm then?'

'No.' I said, suddenly wondering if the question that I was really being asked was, had I gone there to visit him. Alas, before I could think of anything to soften my reply, I found myself adding, 'Not really. I'd been unwell and I needed some fresh air so I took a bus to Cattle Ford and walked home along the lanes.'

'I see.' Colin said, and I thought for a moment that he looked deflated. I could see disappointment lining his eyes. I remember at the time picturing Marcus and his mother and young Sammie from the restaurant and thinking 'Bloody hell... not another one.'

Not wanting to upset him any further, not only my favourite grinder but from what I knew of him a thoroughly nice chap, I turned in the settee to face him.

'Actually, your brother didn't seem to think that a sick bed visit from me would be a good idea. He told me I could wave to you through the window if I liked, but that you looked like a hamster. I'd have hated it if anybody saw me like that, so I didn't like to disturb you. It's good to have you back here though.'

'Thanks.' He said again, nodding wistfully.

'Another coffee?' He asked before turning away.

A second latté and, I'm afraid, a second slice of cake later, still comfy on the settee, I was once again lost in what was probably another paranoid daydream when a squeal of brakes and a screech of tyres on the road outside shattered my train of thought for a second time. Everybody in Starbucks except me dashed to the window. The car that had made the dreadful commotion, a small powder blue Mercedes that I could see easily from my seat, had mounted the pavement on the opposite side of the High Street. Although apparently undamaged, the car had obviously spun and was facing in the wrong direction. The driver, a woman who I instantly recognised, was frantically fiddling with something on the inside of the door. I reckoned that she was trying to get out.

I breathed a long sigh before I stood up from the settee.

'She's drunk.' The darker haired of two female servers who'd glued themselves to the window to my left, tut-tutted, the other, a yellow blonde with appalling ginger roots and a tidemark under her chin shook her head.

'Maybe the poor thing's had a stroke.' She said. 'You never know, the woman might be ill.'

'No, she's pissed alright.' An older regular customer at the coffee shop who was wearing a grubby and tired looking David Beckham baseball cap chimed in from his stool close to the front door. 'Look at her; she's all over the place.'

…And he was right; Marie Clarke was all over the place.

I made it across the road quickly, although I have to confess, begrudgingly. It was plain for everyone to see that Marie was in a terrible state. The pleasanter of the Clarke twins was hanging through the car window as I approached. I think, having failed to find the door handle, she was trying to climb through. Her breaths coming short and fast through a slack mouth, and her face wet, I guessed from a mix of cold boozy sweat and tears, it took a while for her to recognise me. When, eventually, she did, she slumped back into the car and started sobbing… loud wails that hurt my ears.

'I want to go home… take me home.' She pleaded.

I pulled the door open and helped her out of the car. For a brief moment, her eyes focused on my face and she seemed to recover herself, but then I eased my grip on her arms, and before I realised what was happening, she toppled backwards and landed with a hard bump on the pavement. As it happened, the fall seemed to sober him up. More shaken than hurt, I think, I helped her back on to her feet.

'What's going on Marie?' I said. It was not one of the most well thought out questions that I'd ever asked.

'My sister,' she wailed back at me in reply. 'Poor Jayney, I can't believe that she's dead… whatever am I going to do? I'm all alone now, just me… oh no, no, no.'

As you might imagine, while the distraught woman was clutching at my arm with tears filling her eyes and sobs welling in her chest, I felt rather a heel. Although I'd never set out to bash her dragon twin sister, Jayne the pain, round the ear with my straighteners, I couldn't deny, not even to myself, not even then, that however much she deserved it, I was ultimately responsible for causing her death. Believe it or not, I think, feeling an instant of overwhelming guilt I was about to apologise to Marie Clarke when thankfully she beat me to the mark.

'I'm so terribly sorry, causing such a fuss.' She said. 'I think I'd better get home now.' Then she tried to climb back into the car.

I shook my head and came to my senses.

'I don't really think that's a good idea.' I said, leaning between her and her Mercedes. 'Why don't we go for a coffee?' I suggested, taking her arm. 'I'll turn your car around and park it for you. You pop into Starbucks and find us a seat. We'll soon have everything straightened out.'

Well, I might as well have slapped her across the face.

'What the hell do you think you're doing?' She began. 'Get your filthy hands off me.' She shouted, sounding just like her horrible sister. 'Let me go… I just want to get home.' …and then she started flailing her arms and wailing again.

'I'll tell you what.' I said, wishing only that she'd stop making such an appalling noise. 'You're obviously upset, why don't you let me drive you home.'

Why I offered to drive I do not know, perhaps it had something to do with the fact that I'd recently dumped her sister into the local canal, perhaps I felt guilty for causing her grief, perhaps I just wanted to help her out. Whatever my reasons were, it was a silly idea, I hadn't driven a car in over fifteen years and back then, within seconds of starting the engine, I'd managed to smash the damned vehicle into a prison wall. The poor car went to scrap and I promised myself that I'd never drive again.

Actually, it was all Tristan's fault. Following the brutal events that led to him getting God, my lovely second cousin had been helping to make up the numbers at the particular correctional institution that fate had chosen for my run-in, and somehow – after another plea from his mother no doubt – having recently passed my driving test, I'd landed the job of collecting him upon his release.

I remember that I was tired and stressed after working a hot sticky day in the salon, which on its own, might explain my extreme reaction to what happened. I'd spoken to Tristan the evening before and although a nasal summer cold muffled his voice, I understood from his mutterings that I was to pick him up no earlier than six o'clock. It was all going swimmingly to plan. I finished work at about four thirty, grabbed myself a treat and a coffee from you know where, and was on the road to north-west London well before five. Fortunately, a pleasantly cooling evening and travelling against the flow of rush hour traffic, once inside the bounds of the M25, my route was easy and my little car and I made jolly good time. Having enjoyed my first proper outing in my nearly new vehicle, I arrived at Wormwood Scrubs cheerful and at only a few minutes after six parked my new fuchsia Suzuki Jimny on a gravelled square immediately adjacent to the main prison gate. I felt like an extra from Bad Girls.

I'd barely climbed out of my lovely little car when the clanking of locks and squealing of hinges began. I reckon that Her Majesty's Ministry for Prisons must employ someone to make sure that all the heavy doors and gates to such establishments are appropriately noisy… just as they should be of course. Alas, although the main gate was suitably huge and forbidding and the clanking of the locks made it sound as if the deepest dungeon in Christendom was being unbarred, the opening through which my second cousin appeared was disappointingly small.

Tristan looked dreadful. He was obviously poorly. Stooping to get through the narrow door within the gate, his posture barely changed as he stepped into the low evening sunlight. I waved and called to him from over the bonnet of my little car. He looked up and shielded his eyes against the sun but he didn't straighten up. When he saw me, or rather, when he saw my pinkish car, he made an exaggerated double take and despite his wan expression, I'm sure he raised his eyebrows. Then, still without straightening up, and through watery blood shot eyes, at last he raised a smile.

'Hello Tris.' I said, as he neared.

'Watcha Matey.' He replied, slowly and nasally, and then he added in a slightly more studied and drawn tone than his usual bluff. 'Bless you for coming.'

That was the first time Tristan ever blessed me and I can tell you that it came as quite a surprise. I'm sure that I must have nodded or smiled, or made some similar, and probably cynical affirmation of support, but I would never have believed then, that having found God in prison, my second cousin's faith would prove so strong (nor at times, those three little words 'God bless you' so bloody annoying).

Disaster struck almost with the turn of the ignition key. After pushing the passenger seat back as far as it would go, Tristan eased himself into my little car.

'Snug.' He said as I fired up the engine.

'Seventy to the gallon.' I tried in reply. He didn't look impressed. I put the car into gear and released the handbrake.

'It's pink Cuz'.' He said. ...And then, as if to punctuate the word, pink, Tristan sneezed.

I swear that the air pressure in my car increased two fold with the power of blast from my enormous second cousin's nose, my ears crackled and popped to testify. I felt physically shaken.

'Bless you.' I said, turning away and suddenly realising what a dreadful cold the poor chap actually had.

'Bless you to.' He said back spontaneously, as he would, it seems now, at every conceivable opportunity forever more ...and then we looked at each other.

I think that if Tristan hadn't sneezed again, we might have smiled and crooked little fingers and said 'Shakespeare' and 'Longfellow' to each other and maybe we'd have even chuckled. I think that maybe I'd have gone on to drive home in my little car and lived happily ever after as a motorist.

However, Tristan did sneeze.

The impact caught me full in the face.

A spray, a stream, an explosion of wet sticky snot splattered into my eyes and hair. Temporarily blinded and well and truly glue-gunned back into my seat I shuddered with horror. My first, and I have to say without the need of any further explanation, ill-timed prostate examination aside, it was the most disgusting experience of my life.

Bad enough you might think.

Unfortunately, preparing to drive away, with the hand brake off and the car in first gear and only a twenty-five yard straight run to the prison wall, thanks to an involuntary convulsion of... well... revulsion, my foot slipped off the clutch.

I'm quite sure that the prison guards were marvellous when they snipped away the canvas roof and prised us out of the wreckage, but when I saw what was left of my lovely little car the next morning I wasn't feeling kindly towards anybody.

Although I don't remember exactly what happened I do know that after the collision with the wall both Tristan and I were taken to the prison infirmary. When I woke sometime later that evening, my head had been bandaged, and my chest felt like an elephant had sat on it and wriggled. I do remember calling out. A very nice round woman with grey curls and a large red face that brought to mind scrubbing-soap, boiled water, and cold winter mornings, came and spoke to me. She explained where I was, told me that I would be fine and reassured me that she'd be close by if I needed her. I didn't... need her that is. For some reason that I still don't understand, I felt quite comfortable where I was, happy to sleep for those few hours in the homely prison hospital bed. Tristan, on the other hand, spending his first night of freedom in a temporary holding cell back inside Wormwood Scrubs, was not so thrilled.

I spent four nights in hospital in all and had to close the salon for two weeks after the accident. My injuries were mainly bumps and bruises. Nothing too serious, although one particularly nasty bash to my left temple had the doctor's worried for a few days. I think the most unpleasant part of the whole misadventure was that while I was recovering I went down with Tristan's cold. While the germ was a shocker, it wasn't so much the illness that bothered me, but more the vivid and everlasting memory of the way I'd caught it.

Marie Clarke stopped crying abruptly. 'Oh would you, how marvellous.' She said, jumping at my offer to drive her home. '...and then perhaps you'd like to come in for a little drinkies. I've just picked a nice Scotch up from the Co-op. It's so awful without dear Jayne. I don't know how I'll ever deal with the funeral. I'm not used to doing things on my own.'

...And that's how my unfortunate wrong got a whole lot wronger.

CHAPTER TWENTY-SIX

The first thing I noticed when I took the wheel of the neat Mercedes 'A' Class was not the polished walnut interior trimmings or the cream leather upholstery but the almost overwhelming smell of booze.

After making certain that Marie Clarke was securely belted in, I settled into the driver's seat, dropped the two empty Gin bottles that I found in the foot well over my shoulder, opened some windows and took stock of what I'd let myself in for. Just a glance beyond the steering wheel and I quickly realised that in the fifteen years since I'd driven, dashboard goodies and in-car gadgets had changed quite a bit. Faced with the unfamiliar array of knobs, dials and switches, I must have taken a pause too long.

'You need to use the key.' Marie Clarke said, swaying in her seat and looking at me as if I were stupid. They were her first and would be her only helpful words of the day.

'I know.' I snapped back at her.

'Well... stick it in the hole and get on with it man.' She said, slapping the top of the steering column with the back of her hand, and then she started to roar with laughter. 'I've said that a few times before, I can tell you.' She wheezed. 'Never in a car though, but there's always a first time, hey?'

A sharp elbow jabbed into my ribs. I didn't dare answer her. Instead, I pushed the arm away gently but firmly and found the ignition switch as fast as I could.

Thankfully, the car fired into life the second I even hinted at turning the key.

'Jubilee Grove.' I said. I hoped forestalling any further cringe-worthy suggestions.

'Jubilee Grove.' She replied, and then she started crying again.

In the event, I didn't even try to turn the car round as I'd suggested I would earlier on. I should have. I should have turned and steered south along the High Street, crossed the bottom of the one-way system and then taken Marlborough Avenue out of town and if I had, things might have turned out a whole lot simpler. However, for some stupid reason, anxiety I guess, I pulled away heading north.

By the time it dawned on me that I was driving in the wrong direction, we'd met the tail of a line of traffic that appeared to be diverting off the High Street into the lanes behind the bus station. It wasn't until my turn came to pull into the narrow road that I realised why, the wretched Easter egg hunt. On both sides of the High Street, beyond the bus station to my left and the entrance to the Brewery and Brewery Lane on my right, the narrow strip of the Borough Park straddled the town centre. Directly ahead of me, completely blocking the High Street, tidily herded into a day-glo orange and white plastic mesh pen were dozens of children baying presumably for chocolate eggs.

'Where the hell are we?' Marie Clarke said, suddenly coming to and realising, despite the effects of the booze, that something wasn't quite right.

'We're just stuck in traffic.' I bluffed.

'You're going the wrong way, you stupid man.' She said.

'I know... I know... but it really doesn't matter. We have to follow this lot now.' I said, waving at the cars in front and a policewoman who was directing the traffic. 'I'll pick the road out of town up as soon as I can.'

Suddenly, before Marie had a chance to throw any further comments at me, as I was about to turn the corner, a lorry carrying scaffold poles and wooden planks burst from Brewery Lane cutting between us and the children's holding pen. I had to slam on the brakes. Marie and I both shot forward in our seats. Marie screamed, and I'm afraid I may have yelped a bit too. In defence of my own outburst, I'd been nervous enough before I even started the car and being cut-up like that was hardly a steadier. As it happened, despite our split second of terror, the lorry missed us by a good few inches. However, once it had passed, I noticed the policewoman who was standing in front of the Easter egg hunters, pull out a note pad and pen and take down its number. Relieved that sometime soon, and preferably before he killed somebody, the driver of the lorry would at least get his wrist slapped, I was

227

busy concentrating on pulling back into the traffic when after a second glance I realised that the policewoman on duty was my niece. Although I tried to wave and even called her name through the closed car window, I'm sure we'd passed before she recognised me. I made a mental note to write to her mother.

Annoyingly, no more than a few yards round the corner we met the scaffold lorry again. I sighed and Marie physically shrank back into her seat. The lorry itself was a tatty green Bedford flatbed. It looked like it belonged in the 1960s rather than in the present day. A long pole hung several feet over the tailgate, much too far to be safe. Around the pole, somebody had tied a wad of red cloth presumably to warn following drivers of the danger. It reminded me of a huge boxing glove. For a fleeting moment, looking at Marie still cringing and whimpering in her seat I imagined the pole shooting back and punching her on the chin, knocking her out... shutting her up. I pulled up several yards short.

'Where are we now?' She said, leaning forward and squinting through the windscreen.

'We're near the bus station.' I said.

'Fine... then I'll get a bus home.' She said, and then she started fiddling with the door handle.

'No... no, don't worry.' I said. 'I'll soon have you home. I promise. Please just sit still.'

Thankfully, as I was speaking and before Marie could fathom the door handle, the traffic ahead of us started to move. We followed the scaffold lorry' with its giant boxing glove, very slowly past the bus station and the library, and finally out onto the roundabout at the bottom of the town centre. There, I'd hoped the lorry would get out of our way and turn left and head for the town by-pass north, alas, it didn't. Instead, the miserable driver took the same exit that I needed and pulled onto Marlborough Avenue. Although disgruntled, I followed him again.

At well over a mile long and wide between broad pavements, leafy Marlborough Avenue at least allowed the traffic to flow more freely. Marie Clarke's Mercedes 'A' class turned out to be a lovely drive. Smooth but not wallowy or bouncy, it purred along the road, quiet, easy, and comfortable. My confidence growing even after the near miss, I began to question if perhaps I'd been wrong to give up on driving after all. That maybe, when the money came through from Enid Fulton's bequest, I might take a peep around the showrooms and consider treating myself to another car. I remember, as I was driving along the road, I began to smile at the idea and I even dared look at a few of the cars parked on the kerbside and wonder which colour I might prefer. 'Not pink this time.' I thought.

Then… BOOM!

When the impact came, 'Boom' was the noise it made, not crash, or crunch, or smash. I didn't see anything, just a flash of red that whistled past my left shoulder so suddenly that I didn't even properly feel its force. Then, a nanosecond later, the front of the Mercedes hit the back of the lorry.

It is not true, as moviemakers would have us believe, that in moments of extreme drama the world slows down. In fact, it was all over in a trice and to tell you the truth, forget the benefit of slow motion details, wedged between the steering wheel and the seatback in a quiet cocoon of billowing white fabric, I hadn't a clue what had happened.

When the air bags deflated, although dazed, I glanced around to check where I was. While my head throbbed and my chest was stuck fast, I knew that I wasn't seriously hurt. However, I also realised quickly that I was suddenly quite alone, that Marie Clarke was no longer sitting next to me. For a moment I was puzzled, the passenger door appeared shut, her seat belt was still in its clasp, I could still smell her boozy breath… and then, when I turned, even just a little, I saw that the back of her seat was missing. Unable to move easily, I glanced into the rear view mirror. The horror that met my eyes, reflected in that small piece of silvered glass will stay with me forever. Put simply, the back of the car, the rear seats, and the hatchback door had gone and in the space where they had been, punched by the giant boxing glove and then skewered by the scaffold pole, swinging from side to side limp like a battered rag doll hung Marie Clarke.

I think it was then that I started screaming and to this day I'm not entirely sure when I actually stopped. It may have been when my niece, coincidently and fortunately one of the first police officers to reach the scene, came and spoke to me. It may have been when the firemen arrived to cut the front off the car. It may have been when they prised my fingers from the mangled steering wheel. It may have been when my reflection congratulated me on the 'Jolly good shot'. It doesn't matter. What I do remember is that my vocal chords gave out well before the thought.

It was Tristan who actually lifted me out of the car. My second cousin told me sometime afterwards that he'd had to push several uniformed people out of the way to get to me first, but that after my niece had called him he was so desperate to make sure I was okay he didn't think twice, he just came running. I think it was then that I first understood what a disappointment I'd likely be to him one day.

I suppose what surprised me most about the whole shocking incident, was that once the main furore was over, the blues and twos gone, the wreckage swept up and the road reopened, what a matter-of-fact procedure dealing with a motor accident actually is… even when that accident involves a fatality.

After the doctors had scratched their heads and pronounced me fit, and healthy, and very, very, lucky (they didn't mention my good looks), my niece and Tristan took me from the hospital to the Police Station.

The statement I gave was truthful and with my best recollection, but it was not very long. I wasn't charged with anything, but there was no promise that I wouldn't be either. When I'd done, the desk sergeant, a handsome blue-eyed chap, who I'd say to be in his mid 30s, but with the unfortunate name John Wanklin (probably of German descent but god I'd have raced for deed-pole), offered me a cup of tea.

'Thanks' I said. 'That would be lovely.'

'It must have been a terrible shock.' He said. 'Quite traumatic, a stiff Brandy would probably do you better.'

'Don't tell me,' I said. 'I don't suppose you serve anything stiff in here.'

'Afraid not.' He said, with a shrug, missing my attempted joke entirely.

Sergeant Wanklin then disappeared into what looked like a cupboard behind the desk. A moment later, I heard the sound of running water and the dull clunk of cheap china mugs.

'Milk? Sugar?' He called out.

'Both please John.' A voice called from behind me before I had the chance to reply.

I looked round to see Detective Sergeant Dennis Sapsead, the chap who'd interviewed me when Marjorie Warton disappeared and then again after Cecile Ablitt fell down the stairs. The swarthy policeman, who I thought, since I'd seen him last, was looking older and a tad more pudgy, was standing in the open doorway to the interview room where I'd just given my statement. As I hadn't seen any other doors in the room, my first thought was, 'how did he get there?'

I never found out.

'Hello.' He said. 'Well…' He chuckled sarcastically. 'Fancy seeing you here.'

From the tone of his voice and something in his body language, I could tell that Detective Sapsead would have liked any excuse to have sat down with me right then and had a bit of a chat. I guess I'd lost two more punters since I'd seen him last. I'm sure he knew that very well. To be honest, seeing him was all I needed. I didn't like the chap, I never had, and each time we'd met, he'd seemed to grow more and more antagonistic. Thankfully, before he had the opportunity to bushwhack me and start with any of the dozen awkward questions that no doubt he had, my niece and Tristan came back to the waiting area.

'I've just been given a tour around.' Tristan said to me, grinning from ear to ear. 'It's bigger here that you'd think Matey. They've got all sorts of stuff… a radio centre, a jail and even a room with a two way mirror.'

'We certainly have.' Detective Sapsead said. 'People often make the mistake of thinking that just because we are a small station in a small town, we can't deal with serious crime. Well they'd be wrong. We catch our fair share of villains. There's not many who get away with much around here.'

The detective said the last few words while looking only at me. I don't think that anybody else in the room took the thinly veiled threat to be more than a general comment, but the disquieting gleam in DC Sapsead's eye warned me at least to take him very seriously.

'...and I'm sure you're right too.' Tristan said, nodding enthusiastically, and then with perfect timing my lovely second cousin turned to me and added. 'How are you feeling now, Matey?'

Internally my whole being breathed a sigh of relief. The accident, Dr Carmen's blackmailing demands and Marcus's accusations were quite enough to deal with for one day, I couldn't face a suspicious local Dick who reckoned he was Sherlock Holmes.

'Not so great.' I said, fibbing just a tad. 'A bit sick actually... probably the shock. The doctors warned me that I might have a reaction. I think I'd like to get home.'

CHAPTER TWENTY-SEVEN

It is strange how sometimes anxiety and trauma completely befuddle the brain while at other times such stresses can allow one to think particularly clearly.

I told Tristan that I would be going to bed straight away, but I didn't. Instead, from a chink between the curtains in my bedroom window I watched my niece and my second cousin walk away down my garden path. Actually, they looked quite sweet together, him so big and her so small, an ironic antithesis of each other. Once on the road, they headed for Tristan's pick-up truck. My niece should probably have booked her sixth-cousin-in-law-twice-removed (or whatever they were to each other) on the spot. The thing was a wreck. Watching them pull away, from the black exhaust smoke alone, I couldn't believe that such a rusty old heap could possibly be legal.

When I was certain that they were gone, I sat down at my dressing table and stared into the mirror. My face looked pale and drawn and my eyes seemed to have dulled and shrunk back into their sockets.

'So here's the thing.' I said to my reflection before it had a chance to speak to me (a first actually, not that I realised it at the time). 'As I see it we don't have too many choices. Either we bow to demands or we take control.'

I didn't answer me at first. I just sat there staring back at myself, looking dazed, apparently thinking. After a moment or two, still keeping my eyes fixed on the mirror, I reached for the drawer on my right. Sliding the drawer open, I took out a blister pack of my favourite pills, popped four in quick succession, and then put the pack back.

'Do they help?' My reflection asked, breaking its silence at last.

I just shrugged and swallowed hard.

'Better than all that vodka I'm sure.' It said scornfully, and then added in an equal tone. 'What are you going to do now?'

Under the circumstances, perhaps the most remarkable thing about my reflections simple question was that for once in my life (or perhaps ours), without thinking too much, I knew the answer.

Looking back, I wonder now if it was missing the brake pedal so calamitously in Marie Clarkes dinky Mercedes that led me to the crazy idea for dealing with Dr Carmen. Although I have to say that, crazy or not, as it happened, nothing about that particular evening turned out quite as I planned.

Buoyed by my previous successful nocturnal adventures when I'd snuck back into town to sort out my troubles with Jayne Clarke at the canal, full of confidence and resolve, a stiff shot of gin (still no vodka) and possibly a few too many happy pills, I left my house an hour or so later, well after dark, probably sometime soon after nine. I was wearing the same old charcoal grey jogging suit that I'd worn those few days before, and just like then I set off across my back garden, through the hedge, and into the scrubby lane behind. However, instead of turning left and following the rough path west behind Gillycote Road, this time I turned right and climbed a fence into a neighbour's garden.

A soft glow from the waxing moon transformed neatly manicured lawns and borders in to a patchwork of sapphire and navy blue. Above my head, a million eyes watched my every step. Breathing slowly and steadily, from the fence, I crossed the cottage garden in five quick strides, tucking deep into the shadows beneath a laurel hedge on the far side. Although easy to traverse, much as my own, the small garden wrapped around one side of my neighbour's semi-detached house potentially leaving me exposed to view from the street. However, fortunately, close to the house, between my position and the pavement on Gillycote Road, my neighbour – a health worker of some kind - and his neighbour beyond had built themselves and now shared the use of what appeared to be, to the casual observer at least, a summerhouse. The wooden building straddled the boundary between their two plots in place of a fence panel. In fact, despite its ornate appearance and perfectly painted cladding, the structure was no more than a glorified tool shed, an unusual idea perhaps, but the arrangement seemed to work well. Never having been one for DIY or practical matters myself, on the rare occasion that I ever needed to use a tool, it was to one or other of these kind neighbours that I usually ran. They were both jolly clever chaps and usually very helpful. Between them they had a marvellous collection of tools and conveniently were often only to keen to demonstrate, not only the hardware required, but also their prowess in using it.

Crawling on my hands and knees careful to keep to the shadows, I made the shed's fancy veranda quickly and, I'm certain, without anybody seeing me at all. Not practised in the art of burglary I was nervous when it came to breaking in. From low on the short wooden walkway, I held my breath and reached up to try the most obvious approach first. To my pleasant surprise and relief the simple tack worked. The shed was unlocked. When I pulled at the latch the door inched open without any trouble at all.

Inside smelled like a mix of the first kick from Marcus's scooter and something nasty from the garden compost bin and was, alas, much darker than I'd hoped. Although I had a vague idea on which shelf I should be nosing, I didn't know precisely where the specific tool that I'd borrowed before and now needed actually was. Fortunately, although I'd been tempted to start rummaging in blind hope, I held my impatience in check and waited a moment or two for my eyes to adjust to the dimmer light. It was during the wait that I had a stroke of good luck when one or other of my neighbours arrived home. Initially, far from lucky, I feared the noisy arrival to be a disaster. When I heard heavy footsteps approaching and keys jangling, my pulse raced and my heart sank... but then, after brushing along the side of the shed, whichever timely neighbour had come home, opened their front door, promptly slammed it shut, and the lights came on.

From then on, my burgling became a whole lot easier.

Once I found the tool I needed, I tucked it into the waistband of my jogging bottoms, quickly and very quietly put anything I'd moved back more-or-less where I'd found it, and then peered through the shed window to look for my best way out. Unfortunately, my neighbour's good timing in coming home just when I needed them most was not now so helpful. Rather than being gently lit by a soft moonlight glow, outside, the neatly ordered garden that I could now see all to clearly, had been dotted with an array of miniature neon lights and was fairly bathed in a rainbow of pulsating colours. Just one glance at the home-grown aurora borealis and I quickly realised that getting from the wretched shed back to the hedge unnoticed would be virtually impossible. My shoulders sagged and my heart sank for a second time in as many minutes. Then, just when I was praying for a power failure or an inky black locust cloud to arrive with a charge from heaven above, as if my thoughts were being read, the lights in both the house and garden blinked out. My neighbour had always been a helpful chap, but an early sleeper and a psychic too? I didn't need Tristan that evening, I felt truly blessed.

I hedge hopped my way along the rest of the road. In spite of my bumps and bruises and the unbelievable traumas of the day so far, scrambling from garden to garden hidden behind my various neighbour's marvellously tall and jolly handy shrubs actually turned out to be quite easy. At the end of Gillycote, when eventually I ran out of suitably concealing foliage and the top end of the road into town met with the bottom of the road out, after almost bursting through a bush of forsythia into the path of an oncoming van, I crossed away from the main roads into Carpenters lane.

My plan was simple and in that I felt, perhaps smugly, rather clever. Using the steep banks and relative darkness of the unlit narrow lane as cover, I would follow the meandering single-track east and then south around the outskirts of town until it met with the Brewery canal. At the top of the canal – regrettably, closer to Enid Fulton's former home than I might otherwise have preferred, but diddly-doo – I would cut inconspicuously between the back of a terrace of houses that lined the one-way system and a strip of woodland that flanked the by-pass. There my brief nocturnal sneaking would all but end. Ahead of me, beyond a tidy swath of neatly trimmed green, would be the smart Queen's Park Estate. The sprawling jumble of comfortably large detached homes built sometime during the 1930s where Dr Carmen lived.

The point here was that not only did the roundabout route offer me good cover, but also I would be approaching the good doctor's house from a direction that no one would expect.

Unfortunately, most of my smug plan flew out of the window even before I reached the canal. Walking the route in almost total darkness, I kept a steady pace for about a mile and a half without needing to dodge anything or anyone at all. I was about to negotiate the final bend in the lane, peering into the darkness, maybe less than a hundred yards from the canal towpath, when a set of headlamps flashed in the road ahead of me. I ducked to my left immediately, into a cut in the bank where a pair of wooden gates cast the weakest of shadows onto an already gloomy gravel driveway. Working my way behind the gates, I took a long draw of breath and dropped to my haunches waiting for the car to pass. However, while the lights stayed bright in the road and I could still hear the rumble of an engine some way off, nothing and no one came past my hiding place.

I crouched quietly for several minutes before the usual mix of impatience and nosiness got the better of me.

Should I stay or should I go?

'You need to be careful.' A small voice inside my head said... and perhaps not so oddly, the voice sounded just like me. 'There's nothing to be gained by rushing. Take your time. Just sit here and wait. Don't get yourself caught now.' It added.

'Don't be stupid.' I replied moving my lips but speaking silently. However, peculiarly, although now I knew it was me speaking, the voice I heard when I mouthed the words didn't sound quite like my own. 'We need to get on.' I said. 'We need to get this thing done.' ...and this time within the unspoken words, I recognised a harsher tone and a clipped inflection. Close though it was to my own, I suddenly realised that the voice I was using, albeit silently, sounded dreadfully like my reflections.

'Please don't.' My own voice said in reply from somewhere deep inside my head. 'Please stay still.'

Alas, lost in the confusion, before the internal squabble - if that's what it was - had really begun let alone properly settled, I stood up and stepped from my hiding place into Carpenters Lane.

The car with the dazzling headlights was large and white and had now pulled into a driveway on the side of the lane maybe thirty yards around the corner. Although the lights were bright and still pointing roughly in my direction, the position of the car was such that the main strength of the beam hit the ground well before it reached me. Thankfully, even in my stupefied state as I inched along the road towards it I had the sense to keep to the shadows.

I'm not sure anymore, what it was about the car that particularly intrigued me. It might have been that subconsciously I recognised a familiar rattle or buzz in the engine noise. It might have been simply that at the time, I felt like James Bond, and it was there waiting to be spied on. Whatever it was, once I got closer and took a glimpse inside, I quickly wished that I'd resisted the urge.

Above the sound of the engine, as I moved in, I could hear raised voices and then a woman started shouting.

'Let me out.' She said. 'I want to get out.'

'Oh do shut up for goodness sake.' A deeper and vaguely familiar male voice, snapped back.

Keeping close to the bank, probably just nosey to hear more of what sounded like a juicy argument, I'd moved to within perhaps ten yards of the car, when suddenly the passenger door flew open. An instant later, a young woman with short fair hair came dashing out and a courtesy light inside the car flashed on.

'That's it run off... you silly cow.' The man called after her, and then, moving into the light, he leaned across and made a grab for the door.

When I saw his face, my whole body froze. However, rather than sensibly ducking into the hedge behind me, as the door slammed shut and the car's engine roared, I turned to run, slipped, and found myself falling backwards. Thinking back, I can't believe that above the tension of his own moment Detective Sergeant Dennis Sapsead would have noticed me sprawled on the ground as his car hurtled past, but at the time, in my state of panic, and I'm sure because the wretched man

238

seemed to have developed a spooky habit of turning up precisely when I least wanted to see him, I was convinced that he must have. Before the taillights of his rattling car were even out of sight, I leapt to me feet and made a bolt for the gateway where I'd hidden earlier.

Adrenaline surging through my system, after six strides, my breathing rasped heavy in my chest. Seven strides and my pulse beat like a drum. Eight and nine, although almost exhausted from the sudden explosive effort, I was nearly there, and then when my legs stretched for the tenth time, with my heart pounding and my head spinning, I heard a screech of brakes and a mechanical clunk. I froze again. A second later, although out of sight, I knew still not so far away, I heard an engine roar and the sound of tyres spinning on loose stones. Then I saw the taillights of Sapsead's car coming back towards me.

'Run Daniel Lyon run.' One of the voices in my head squealed at me, and boy oh boy, I never did as I was told so fast.

Beyond the wooden gates, out of view from the lane, and in complete darkness, a driveway curved in a shallow arc towards a thatched stone cottage. This time, convinced that I was about to be chased, and presumably, being possessed by some weird spirit of scared-to-death*ness*, I vaulted the gates rather than cower behind them, and then raced for the shadowy building as fast as I could. In the few seconds that it took the car to reverse back down the lane and slide to another teeth-rattling screeching halt, in my desperation, I'd managed to run the length of the drive, cross a broad lawn, and follow a path around to the back of the cottage.

…but phew! I was puffed.

Alone in the gloom, my pulse thumping at my eardrums, having scared myself half-silly, at the end of the path, I was relieved to find the shelter of an open porch. Carefully I peered inside. Two steps led up to a pair of glazed doors. Beyond the doors was dark, perhaps a sitting room, perhaps a study, I couldn't see. Crouching down on the top step, in a corner close in to the wall, suddenly all was silent. No scrabbling tyres, no following footsteps. I took a series of long slow breaths and tried to take stock of my position.

The gardens behind the chocolate box cottage were large and even in the darkness I could see that they were old and overgrown. The moon shone from behind me towards the east. Less than twenty feet to my right, a line of ten, perhaps a dozen, tall Poplars rippled gently in a breeze that until that moment I hadn't noticed. Spreading before me, terraced lawns fell away like a giant flared staircase towards a swath of huge shadowy shrubs. Beneath the veil of deep blue grey, the immense bushes knitted together with the rolling rise and fall of a heraldic serpent writhing on an enormous sail. Suddenly, in spite of my predicament, I found myself grinning. Blinking into the dense silhouetted horizon the image of my serpent began to change. Against the starry night sky, the wonderfully weird creature squiggled and squirmed against the back of my vision, and then at last turned to face me.

I think I may have yelped when I saw that my Prozac and adrenaline fuelled imagination had given my scary monster Marjorie Warton's ugly head. Instantly I forgot about Detective Dennis Sapsead. The wretched woman grinned back at me madly, reminding me of the disgusting dream I'd had shortly after Enid Fulton died. I shook my head and closed my eyes. For a long moment, as the burn of a filament lamp etched on a staring eyeball, the face hung on, gnashing its oversized teeth and slathering its overly long tongue. Then, as a candle snuffed out in the night, it was gone. I opened my eyes and realised that I'd been holding my breath.

Gulping at air, my heart still racing, and my body now dripping in a cold sweat, I crouched on the step hugging myself rocking backwards and forwards.

'This is no use.' I said aloud between breaths.

'I agree.' I answered, equally loudly.

'I told you... you should've stayed where you were.'

'Don't bloody start.'

'You have to get to the doctor.'

'I know, but I'm knackered... just give me a minute.'

It was probably while I was busy quarrelling with myself that what little sensible grey matter I had left was sorting out what I needed to do next. I remember a moment, after a couple of particularly cheap shots from either side of me, when thankfully I abruptly shut up and looked towards the bottom of the expansive cottage gardens. That moment felt like dawn rising. Suddenly I recognised where I was, that facing due east, the terraced cottage garden ran down towards the western edge of the Queen's Park Estate.

Realising that inadvertently I'd stumbled upon a shortcut, I didn't waste any more time dallying with dragons.

Following the pathway back around the cottage, I peered into the shadows back towards the drive. Beyond the gates everything seemed quiet and nicely dark, no more cars, no headlights, no more Sherlock Holmes. I breathed a low sigh and ran my hands through my hair. I remember it feeling damp and clammy, and probably a shade too long, not that that mattered, I was hardly on show. Once certain that nobody was coming for me after all, that Sapsead had more likely reversed back to continue his row with the girl than to chase me, I turned back into the garden and followed the path past the porch where I'd rested, to the far side of the lawns. There, a tall fence fronted by a low hedge - lavender I think – seemed to form a boundary line that from what I could make out in the gloom, ran a hundred yards or more, roughly in the right direction.

Using the fence as a guide, I followed the hedging and the edge of the lawns across and down four shallow terraces. Towards the bottom of the slope, the grass thickened beneath my feet and the moon disappeared behind the first of the large shrubs that had so teased my imagination. Ducking hurriedly between the shrub and its nearest neighbour, I pushed my way through a cluster of giant bushes to find myself standing at the top of a much steeper slope facing more-or-less where I'd hoped. Below me, its windows and streetlamps twinkling in the night like an organised reflection of the starry sky above, the Queen's Park Estate sprawled gently and grandly into the distance.

Negotiating the steeper slope didn't prove quite so easy. Although the first few steps were straightforward enough, when my feet caught in a longer tuft of grass, instead of sensibly dropping onto my bottom and sliding, rather stupidly I tried to jump it. While the tumble I took wasn't hard and I can't say that I hurt myself as I fell, the water I splashed into at the bottom of the slope was cold and slimy and smelled something like my grandmother used towards the end of winter.

Shuddering in disgust, I didn't so much climb out of the foul stinking pit as erupt. Holding my nose, cursing and spitting, and squinting to keep any more filth from my eyes, I couldn't see a thing. Stumbling wildly in the dark, I tripped and fell over again almost straightaway. While this time my landing was softer (more tufts of grass I guessed), something spiky prickled into my ankles. I reached out reflexively and immediately I wished hadn't. A thousand sharp barbs stabbed into my fingertips. I'm quite sure I swore dreadfully. Flopping onto my back and whimpering under my breath, I rolled away from the water's edge towards a bank of scrubby hedgerow and then I did the most stupid thing of all, without even thinking, I shoved my stinging fingers into my mouth.

Even now, I can barely think about that evening without feeling the need to vomit. The taste of the rotting whatever-it-was I'd put my hand in will stay in my mouth forever.

'You fool, you fool. Now look what you've done. You've probably poisoned yourself.' I said.

'It hurts.' I squealed.

'On just get up and shut up... making all this fuss... can't you do anything right? You're supposed to be keeping quiet... stealth remember? Now get up and get on.'

Shrugging crossly at the way I'd just spoken to myself, instead of following the snappy instruction, still nursing my sore fingers, I rolled sulkily onto my side and then pushed myself in towards the bottom of the hedgerow. The ground here was dry at least and less prickly thank goodness. Freezing cold and by now feeling pretty miserable, I looked back to where I'd fallen. Above me, the bank that I'd tumbled down loomed dark and steep, but much lower than it had from the top looking down. Silhouetted against the night sky, the large shrubs and bushes that only a few moments before had seemed so menacing, now looked like… well… smaller shrubs and bushes. Low down, a glint of moonlight, flickering across the rippling surface of the water I'd just clambered from, caught my eye. As the million tiny silver wavelets wriggled away from me, I quickly realised that rather than having splattered into a pool of stagnant sludge, as I'd feared, I had in fact fallen into a small stream. Indeed, running in a narrow culvert between the steep slope from the cottage garden and the scrubby hedgerow, under the moonlight, despite the foul taste on my tongue, and the revolting stench in my nostrils, the gently trickling brook actually looked rather nice.

Then I heard my voice again.

'Get up, I told you. Get up and get on.' I said, and even though I was whispering, now I sounded much angrier than before.

Turning towards the hedgerow, I wiped my face on my sleeve. A glob of something disgustingly slimy and yet with a nasty crust that popped when I pushed it smeared across my cheek. I shuddered, then wiped it off and hunkered down and tried to focus my thoughts. Through a small gap in the hedge, across a narrow yet broad garden yard, under the dim glow of a streetlamp someway off to my left, I could see the back of a house. Five windows, two doors, a small sunroom, three of the windows showed a light, two up, one down. Looking back across the garden, following the line of the plot, I reckoned that the stream or the hedge that I was lying under likely formed the garden boundary. Not having a clue which of the Queen's Park leafy roads the house actually fronted, rather than risk being caught crossing the garden, I guessed that if I followed either I'd soon find out.

As luck would have it, my guess was proved right within a very few minutes.

After stumbling fifty yards or so along the narrow bank between the hedge and the stream without any further misfortune, I came to a wall and to the entrance to a shallow drainage tunnel. Running along the top of the wall, at roughly my head height, a post and rail fence bounded a road. Using the keystone at the top of the tunnels brick arch as a foothold, I pulled myself up and peered through the fence. Immediately ahead of me, across a wide pavement and the narrow road, a white sign with black capital letters read, 'DUKES GROVE.' Perfect. Only one street over and a few of hundred yards from my target, I couldn't believe my good fortune. My nocturnal tumblings could hardly have dumped me in a better spot. Suddenly suffering the cold and the bruises and the soggy discomfort seemed almost worthwhile.

Finding my way to Dr Carmen's home on Princess Grove from the bottom corner of the cottage garden could hardly have been any simpler. Still playing at James bond, with oodles of adrenaline coursing my veins raising my flagging resolve, I fairly bounced over the post and rail fence and crossed the road in a flash. Beyond the road sign, I followed a footpath, between a line of parked cars and a high close-boarded fence, to the end of the road. There I turned right and then shortly after, right again. Jolly handily, wherever I turned my eyes, the posh estate seemed to be deserted. Everybody glued to their PCs or their TVs or even their Wiis, I thought likely.

When I reached Dr Carmen's house, I tucked myself behind a pillar in a driveway on the opposite side of the road. I checked my watch and then for the tool that I'd stolen from my neighbours shed. The time was nine forty two and I found the tool still tucked securely into the waistband of my mud sodden jogging bottoms.

Across the road, the doctor's house was still. The only light visible coming through a small diamond shaped pane of bull's-eye glass in the front door. To the left of the house, parked tail-in to the adjoining garage, almost blocking a wrought iron gate that I guessed led to the back garden, and mottled blue-grey and greyer under the moonlit shadows from a nearby Oak tree, Dr Carmen's shiny five series BMW glowered at me from across the road. I felt a chill run up my spine. My nerves fizzed an edgy rhythm under my skin.

'Get a grip.' I said to myself.

'Don't worry.' I replied.

But I did worry. In fact, perhaps unsurprisingly, as it was the first time in my life that I'd knowingly set out intent on bumping someone off, I worried a great deal.

I crossed Princess Grove a few yards on from Dr Carmen's house and then cut back towards the red tarmac driveway where the car was parked by ducking along the inside of the doctor's garden hedge. A yard or two before I reached the driveway, when I was directly in front of the house, an old-fashioned telephone bell started ringing inside. I stopped in my tracks and dropped smartly to my hands and knees. Between the first and second ring a light popped on in an upstairs window. Then I heard a series of muffled footsteps from inside. The telephone rang five more times before at last the call was answered and I reckon it was picked up from somewhere close to the front door. Lying prone, trembling, only a few feet away, although muted through the heavy wood, I recognised the voice immediately as Dr Carmen.

'Hello.' He said… then a pause. 'No, not yet.' I think he added. 'I leave early tomorrow morning.'

A moment later, after a curt 'Very well' and 'Goodbye', the call was over. I heard the telephone handset clunk back into its cradle and Dr Carmen's muffled footsteps stomping back up the stairs. It seemed to me that in that instant my pulse beat with the rhythm of his steps. Holding my breath, above the throb in my head, I listened hard. Somewhere close by, inside the house I reckoned, a door closed. Then the light in the upstairs window blinked out.

For some strange reason, I was suddenly freezing cold. Not chilled by the damp or the cool night air, but more I think from something dark and fearful in the pit of my stomach. Kneeling close in to the Juniper hedge, I rubbed at my arms and shoulders. My clothes were still wet and mucky and I was shaking.

'Come one, come on.' I said to myself. 'You've come this far, you can't give up now.'

Keeping my head low and my mind suitably blank, I shifted from my knees, and I crawled the remaining few yards along the line of the hedge, to the driveway and Dr Carmen's gleaming BMW.

A vague hotchpotch aroma of fresh polish, warm engine oil and tyre rubber clung to the air immediately surrounding the underside of the doctor's car. The smell reminded me of my father. His tinkering in the garage at home when I was child, my mother's grumblings when he came in late for lunch or dinner still reeking of petrol or grease. I remembered liking the smell... my father's smell... I breathed in an oddly calming breath. Lying flat on my back close to the Large BMW's offside rear wheel, I recalled my father's voice and the wacky motor maintenance lessons that he'd insisted on giving me as soon as I told him that I wanted to buy a car.

'What's that?' I might have asked him while pointing to some strange and previously unexplored part of the engine.

'That, Sonny-Jim ...' He might have replied, with a typically all-knowing look in his eye. '...is the whatsname doobreedangler, it connects to the left-handed flibbertygrubscrew on the gearbox when you need to fly... but you don't need to worry your head about that right now. Today we're going to change the rudder.'

I'm not sure if my father was a good teacher or a good mechanic, but my memories of the time we spent together in his garage are among the fondest of my youth. ...And even though I chose not to be a driver after all, even now if I needed to, if Mr Push needed a shove, I could still grind a valve, bleed a brake or adjust a tappet.

Sighing silently into the night air, I reached for the stolen tool from the waistband of my trousers. As I drew the icy metal from under my clothes, a stray glint of light from a streetlamp across the road caught on the shiny surface of the sharp steel jaws. Like the yawning maw of some weird jagged-toothed fish, the cutting edges snarled viciously in readiness. Careful not to drop the tool or to make any noise, while inching closer, thinking to ease myself under the car, I wedged the jaws tight into the gap between the rear tyre and the tar-Macadam driveway.

I think that it was sometime around then that I began to get an inkling that as Dr Carmen's flashy BMW actually sat closer to the ground than I had hoped it might, the chances of successfully tampering with anything underneath it would be slim.

As things turned out, the fact that my cunning plan to reach under the car and cut through a brake line failed so miserably and so quickly, and at such a basic level, didn't really matter.

Before I even had the chance to open wretched bolt cutters, a sudden series of metallic clunks and whirrs sounded immediately above my head. Then, an instant later, it seemed to me at the time at least, every single light bulb either in or on the wretched German car burst into life.

Reflexively twisting sideways in shock and surprise, I caught my foot under a sill and smacked my head straight into the car door.

'Bugger.' I'd said aloud, before I could stop myself.

A split second on, I heard the rattle of keys and a door slam.

'Who's there?' Dr Carmen called out, I reckoned from somewhere close to his front door.

Instantly, my heart jolted to a new beat, I think even faster and harder than ever before.

Sliding along the tarmac, desperate to get away unseen, I pushed myself along the ground towards the back of the car.

'Who's there?' Dr Carmen called again and this time I could tell he was much closer.

Scrabbling to my feet, I peered over the boot lid. The doctor, fully dressed wearing a lounge suit and tie and carrying a medical bag in front of him, was standing immediately opposite me, leaning against the bonnet of his dark BMW squinting into the shadows.

'I see you.' He snarled. 'Who are you? What do you think you are doing?'

I stepped away from the car and keeping out the light moved slowly toward the garage door. I guess, anticipating a possible dash to get away, Dr Carmen shifted his weight left and took a step around the front of the car, followed swiftly by another and then another. Suddenly I realised that somehow, stupidly, I'd manoeuvred myself into a corner. I looked up in panic.

'You...?' He said, seeing my face and recognising me at last. 'What the hell are you doing here?'

Then, as he took yet another menacing step towards me, his foot caught something on the ground close to the rear wheel where I'd been crouched. I knew what it was immediately. The heavy stolen bolt cutters that I'd wedged under the tyre. The tool spun from the doctor's foot, skittered ten feet across the driveway towards me, and then clattered into the garage door. The noise it made, I swear that if my skin hadn't fitted so well I'd have jumped clean out of it.

Dr Carmen stopped dead still. I started shaking again.

'Ahh...' He said, looking down at the incriminating snippers and then slowly back to his BMW, and then at me. 'I see. So you thought you'd play a little prank did you? Ignore my warning. Sort me out perhaps.' Then he looked at his car again.

'The Brakes...?' He asked, and his eyes told me that in just those few seconds he'd sussed my entire plan. 'I do so hope you haven't damaged anything. Repairs to this beastie cost a fortune and it would make me so terribly cross.'

I didn't answer him or give him a chance to say anything else. Having quickly realised, that without physically confronting the much larger man, my only hope of escape was over his shiny BMW, through the arched gate, and into the back garden... I did just that. He followed me of course, but I have to say that despite all I'd been through I was much quicker. In fact, by the time the doctor came after me huffing and puffing, around his car and into the garden, I'd already reached the far end of his swimming pool and was contemplating climbing the garden wall.

'Run if you like.' He said through heavy breaths. 'But you'll be running for a long time. Be quite certain that as soon as you're gone I shall call the authorities and tell them everything I know about you.'

The doctor's words must have rung an angry bell somewhere inside my head, because rather than shrinking back, suddenly I felt stronger and the notion of escaping the garden was the farthest thing from my mind.

So there we were, two grown men with nasty thoughts and I'm pretty certain, with even nastier intentions, facing each other from either end of a murky, not yet ready for the season, swimming pool.

'I'm not going to kill your mother for you.' I said, and, regardless of the fact that the selfish woman had stolen my favourite cake, I meant it. 'No matter what you do or say.' I added.

'You were prepared to kill me.' He said, and then he started walking around the side of the swimming pool. I copied his movement step for step along the opposite edge.

'I still am.' I replied.

Dr Carmen started laughing.

'You weedy runt… you don't seriously think that I'm frightened of someone like you, do you?' He said with a sneer.

'I'm not trying to frighten you,' I said. 'I simply mean that if it's a straight choice between you or your mother, then logically I choose you'

'Logically indeed…' The doctor laughed again. '…and precisely how do you intend to do it? Cut through my shoe laces with these?' He said. 'Snip snip.' …and then with a dramatic flourish, from behind his back, he pulled out the vicious looking bolt cutters that I'd stolen from my neighbours shed.

'I'd cut your fingers off first you little shit.' He scowled.

Although the thought made me wince, all the crunching bones and blood, for some reason Dr Carmen's threat didn't scare me at all. Still mirroring his steps around the pool, with my back to the conservatory where I'd eaten lunch only a few hours before, I had to step over the cable to an electric lawn mower. Although left in a loose coil on a paving slab close to the pool, the orange cable still connected the grass-cutting machine to a socket fixed on the conservatory wall. I guessed that mowing the lawn was one of the vitally important things that the doctor had to do after he'd dismissed me so curtly that afternoon.

Staring across the pool, I raised my arms towards him.

'Look, surely we can sort this out in an amicable way.' I said, using what I hoped was my most appeasing tone, although, I have to say that if I'm honest, I don't think I really believed that we could.

Dr Carmen seemed to agree.

'My dear chap... Don't you understand?' he said. 'You have killed people. At least two women that I know of and I'll wager there have been more. Why, you've even had a bash at sabotaging my car and killing me. Surely, you must realise that this knowledge alone puts me in quite a strong position. Now see, I've offered you a choice. Either our agreement stands as it is or I shall call the police. It's a simple as that. I'm not in the habit of negotiating with murderers.'

While the doctor's nonchalant use of the 'M' word came as quite a shock and it was certainly not a term I liked to hear, especially when used to describe me, really, I could only agree with him. His assessment was perfectly correct. As things stood, I was in serious trouble. I think, sensing my dilemma he stopped his pacing for a moment.

'I'll tell you what.' Dr Carmen said, now standing directly across from the conservatory window with one hand in the pocket of his suit trousers while the other swung the bolt cutters back and forth. 'Why don't we stop all this silly malarkey? You take a moment to consider your options, and maybe I'll fix us both a drink.'

Can you believe that for a moment I actually listened to the man?

Like a fool, while I was thinking about what Dr Carmen had said and whether I had any choices, I didn't seem notice him casually turn and slowly saunter back towards me from the far side of the pool. Instead of moving away promptly as I should have, gazing into the space between us like a hapless moron, I stood stock-still. In a matter of seconds, he was only a few feet away. Thankfully, as he drew nearer, something of the calm in the night-air shifted and I guess I came to my senses. My eyes blinked, my head turned, and suddenly Dr Carmen was lunging for me.

I literally frog-jumped sideways.

Landing with both feet grounded but with one foot on either side of a corner, teetering on the edge of the swimming pool, I almost toppled in. Crouching down quickly, I grabbed at whatever I could to keep my balance. Fumbling in the darkness behind me, my desperate fingers found the coiled cable to the electric mower. As Dr Carmen lunged again, I pulled on the cable. The orange snake, suddenly taut, struck perfectly. Dr Carmen tripped over it and I toppled backwards onto the grass.

Whether it was the shock of landing fully dressed in icy cold water or just sheer rage, I don't know, but the roar that came from Dr Carmen as he cart wheeled into the swimming pool was enormous. I'm afraid I scrabbled away and cowered behind the lawnmower. The doctor thrashed and spat in the pool making a terrible fuss. I watched him for a moment. His wild eyes and flailing limbs brought to mind the image of an ailing Wildebeest. I remembered watching a TV documentary on the BBC when I was a teenager in which a poor animal was filmed being caught crossing a Serengeti river by a hungry Croc. The beast's final demise was an awful sight.

I suppose it was then that the demon inside me realised what I was crouched behind, my own personal electric crocodile. It should have been a brilliant idea. Just another splash and maybe a fizz or two, that's all. While the doctor was thrashing and splashing in the murky pool, I stared at the lawn mower, the orange plastic cover, the sharp rotary blade, the electric cable still connected to the mains socket on the conservatory wall. Then, without a second thought, I jumped up, grabbed the whole kit and caboodle and hurled it into the swimming pool.

My throw was good. Even before Dr Carmen had reached the edge of the pool, the mower sailed over his head narrowly missing his ear and splashing into the water only inches beyond him. The doctor swung round, I saw his eyes widen and his mouth open as almost instantly he realised what I had done. As if pole-axed, the tall man, still wearing the lounge suit and collar and tie, suddenly stopped splashing. I thought he was about to fry, and so did he.

Alas, somewhere along the line, sometime between me hurling the mower into the air and it landing in the swimming pool, something hard thumped into the small of my back. I don't think I noticed it happen, but more that I felt the first sting of the bruise it left a moment or so afterwards. Suddenly distracted, I turned round to see what had hit me and found an orange electric plug attached to the end of an orange electric cable lying on the grass immediately behind me. Turning back to the pool, swiftly realising that my brilliantly improvised plan had failed completely, now my eyes widened and my mouth dropped open.

There was a moment, possibly two or three seconds, maybe more or maybe less, I don't know now and I don't think I knew then, when the water in the pool settled and as two desperate men our eyes met again and we mirrored each other's expressions, first fear, then confusion, then understanding. Then the fireworks began.

'You will regret that.' Dr Carmen growled through gasping breaths. 'Twice you bastard, twice you've tried to kill me and twice you've failed.' ...and with the words spat, with renewed vigour, he began a charge towards me from the centre of the swimming pool. Unfortunately, if perhaps at that point in my life, predictably, fear chose that most inopportune moment to treat the muscles in my legs to a critical dose of neurotic paralysis. Instead of carrying me away at a reasonable run, as wisely they should have, they left me frozen on the edge of the pool, waiting for the doctor to come and get me.

Although hampered by sodden clothes and heavy shoes, re-fuelled by a vengeful rage, Dr Carmen's ragged crawling stroke powered him swiftly through the water. In less time than it took me to breathe in and out twice, he'd crossed the pool and his head was bobbing up immediately below my feet. A long snaking arm slithered from the surface. A spray of cold droplets hit my face. Fighting against the ridiculous paralysing numbness, I reached for my knees, pulling and slapping and punching them, frantically trying to get them to work. It made no difference. My efforts were in vain. Like two useless stone posts, my legs were stuck fast on the edge of the pool. As an angry bumble bee caught in a jam-jar, a ball of panic buzzed furiously in my ears. My face glowed hot. Pins and needles scoured my skin. For a moment, I thought I might pass out, but then, suddenly, I felt a hand claw at my ankle and then an instant later, strong fingers take a grip around my leg.

I tried to pull back, to kick out, to fall over, to do anything to save myself, but now, seriously scared, my whole body simply refused to move. I glanced down. Dr Carmen was looking up from the water. His eyes wilder than ever and his lips curled into a maniacal grin. He mouthed something to me. Just one word I think... that word... the word of the moment, beginning with 'M' and ending in 'R'. I baulked of course. I may even have moved. I certainly felt something twitch. I glanced down again. Dr Carmen started to climb from the pool. His right arm pulled at my ankle. His left arm straightened against the tiled edge. Then, like a glistening sea-beast, hauling himself from the deep, his head dipped and his grey back curved upwards ready to attack. Wrenching my voice from its hideaway somewhere deep in the bowels of my soul, I screamed in terror... and then at last, when I feared all was lost and the dreadful man had me, I felt power surge back into my legs.

From here on in, I could tell you frame-by-frame, millisecond-by-millisecond precisely what happened, no equivocation, every detail, no ifs or maybes, no faffing around. I shan't of course; I'll just give you the bare bones.

I kicked out with my left leg, not forwards at Dr Carmen, but sideways away from the house. The fingers of Dr Carmen's left hand kept their grip on my ankle just as I knew they would, but his right arm shot wide, he looked up at me, suddenly realising what was about to happen to him, his face seemed to crumple, and then he went down... his chin smacking into the hard tiled edge of the swimming pool... kersplatt.

I stepped back and watched the doctor float unconscious and slowly drowning in a loose spiral back to the centre of the pool, a wisp of pink swirled in the water behind his head, tracing the arc of his drift. Slowly, like a sad windmill grinding to a weary halt on a dying breeze, everything in the neat garden on Princess Grove took a pause.

'Whoops.' I said quietly to myself.
'Yes indeed.' I replied.

CHAPTER TWENTY-EIGHT

Heaving Dr Carmen's medical bag through the gap in the hedge, I clambered up the bank into my back garden. I was cold and clammy, yet hot and exhausted. I hadn't intended to bring the bag with me. Annoyingly, Dr Carmen had left it on the bonnet of his BMW. I grabbed it as an afterthought as I sneaked past the car when I left. I felt I had too. I could hardly leave such an obvious sign of wrongness in plain view. Unfortunately, the bag was heavier than I'd expected and to be frank lugging it all the way home was a bit of a nuisance, it kept catching on twigs and bushes as I retraced my steps. I was tempted to dump the thing, maybe leave it in a thicket at the bottom of the cottage garden, but then my nosey bone engaged and I began to wonder – just out of curiosity you'll understand – what goodies might be lurking inside, so I carried it home.

Once safely in my garden, I opened the door to my garden shed. Crouching on the floor in the doorway, I scrabbled in the dark and quickly found the loose board, the second one in, immediately behind the door, and under which I'd hidden Marjorie Warton's small silver gun. The soft velvet pouch that I'd found in the miserable old woman's Birkin handbag was exactly where I left it. Picking the pouch up, I rested it in my hand. Inside I could feel the hard contours of the nasty little weapon and its five tiny bullets. To this day, I don't know what possessed me to steal it.

After putting the pouch back under the floor, I pushed it forward, closer to the front of the shed, to make room for Dr Carmen's medical bag. Although the heavy bag needed a good shove to squeeze it through the floors supporting timbers, a moment later I was replacing the floorboard and locking the shed. My curiosity for the contents of the doctor's bag would have to wait its turn.

Sitting on the cinder block steps leading to my shed, relieved to be home, I put my head in my hands and breathed a long heavy sigh. Forget the bumps and bruises that I'd picked up in the car accident that afternoon, hunched in the dark at the end of what must surely have been then the longest and most trying day of my life, my whole body ached. I stood up and stretched, scratched my fingers through my hair, and then bent down and returned the key to my shed's padlock to its hidey-hole crack beneath the cinderblock steps.

The cool evening air in my garden hung still and quiet with the hopeful scent of impending spring. Coming slowly and steady, my breath puffed ephemeral miniature clouds into the night. The swish of rubber on tacky tarmac and the low purr of an engine caught my ear. I looked up to the sky. Orion wasn't home yet. I liked Orion. I like stars. I turned towards my back door. I'd left a light burning in the hallway. A narrow beam leaked through a gap in the hallway door, crossed my kitchen, and then spilled its yellow tints through the kitchen window and onto the path immediately outside. Three short strides and I stepped into the pale glow. Somehow, just the closeness of the warmth of my home buoyed me. I think, despite the way I was actually feeling, through the tension and the fear, I smiled. My shoulders dropped. My limbs loosened. I inhaled deeply. Then a shadow from inside my house crossed the yellow shard of light.

Thankfully, I saw Marcus a moment before he saw me. My first instinct was to duck down and hide, perhaps to run away, but then the fat-brat looked up. Obviously, if I hadn't moved into the light, he'd never have seen me, but as I did and he did, there we were. I'm not sure which of us was the more surprised. I certainly hadn't expected to find Marcus in my kitchen when I got home, but I guess after my evening's antics, to his eyes I must have looked quite a sight. On another day, in other circumstances, Marcus's expression might have been comical. It might even have made me laugh. I'm not actually sure if he recognised me at first. His neck straightened, his eyebrows bunched. Then, I guess when he was certain that I was indeed me, his nose crinkled as if he'd smelled a nasty smell and his mouth turned down at the corners.

'What the hell have you been up to?' He said, staring at me in horror as I pushed the back door to my kitchen open.

'What are you doing in my house, is more to the point.' I said curtly in reply. His eyes dropped and for the first time since I known him, I think, for the briefest moment Marcus looked truly embarrassed.

'Ahh.' He said, somewhat sheepishly. 'Tristan called me. He told me about your accident. It sounded terrible. I came round to see if you were okay. When you didn't come to the door or answer your phone, well… I worried. The door was unlocked so I let myself in. I've only been here a few minutes. I haven't touched anything honestly. I was afraid you might be concussed or something.'

'Oh… I see.' I said, and although what he told me left me feeling a tad ungrateful, try as I might I couldn't disguise the surprise in my voice. '…and you only just got here?' I asked.

'Well, five minutes ago… I do care you know… I've been worried… and now, well… look at you. Wet and all covered in muck. What on earth have you been doing?'

Although Marcus did look concerned and I'm sure that in some strange *Marcusy* way, he probably genuinely cared about me, I couldn't help feeling that the motives behind his visit might not be entirely altruistic. Despite my misgivings, trying not to appear too ungrateful, I squeezed him a half smile.

'Just taking the air, then I had something to do in the garden.' I said, choosing to answer the question rather than to raise a new doubt. 'I just slipped down the bank that's all.'

'But you're soaking wet, and what in God's name are you wearing? Surely you…' Suddenly Marcus swallowed his words and stopped talking, and just stared at my dark charcoal grey jogging suit.

I looked down at myself, at my wet mud stained clothes, the filthy training shoes, the grime on my hands, then I looked back up at Marcus. I could see in his eyes and tell by his sudden tongue-tied pause that before he even finished speaking he'd recognised that I was wearing the same kit that I'd changed into the night he met me after I'd helped Jayne Clarke into the canal.

'What have you really been up to?' He said, slowly repeating the question but this time with a positively accusatorial tone. 'You haven't been raiding the dressing up box again have you?'

I held his eye for a long moment. I'm sure neither of us looked happy. His chubby face seemed somehow even chubbier, his eyes more weaselling. He had a spot on his chin and another on the side of his nose. The boy looked greasy. None of it was good. I was tempted to tell him that yes, I had, and that I'd been out murdering again, but then, that would have been a lie. Instead, still feeling fragile and dreadfully on edge, I turned away and slowly shook my head.

'I need to take a bath now Marcus, and then get some rest, it's been a long and very hard day.' I said.

'But we need to talk.' Marcus replied.

'I know... tomorrow... I promise... call me at the salon, maybe we can have lunch.'

Marcus shrugged, then nodded, then raised a finger as if he were about to say something else. I frowned. Understanding quickly that he'd best shut up, Marcus nodded again, this time more resignedly.

As I led the way to the front door, I glanced across the hallway into my living room. The light inside was jagged with shadows and bluish and came mainly from the street lamp across the road. I paused for a second by the door. On the telephone stand in the corner, next to my favourite chair, a small green neon light flashed an SOS sequence. I think held by the hypnotic rhythm for a moment too long, I probably seemed more interested in it than at the time I actually was.

'What's the matter?' Marcus asked. Having followed me along the hall he was standing directly behind me, too close for my liking, I could feel his breath on my skin. I could smell him, and that evening just his presence made me shudder.

'Oh, nothing.' I said, forcing myself to stay calm and composed 'Just the answering machine, I have a new message that's all.'

'Ahh,' said Marcus, 'I meant to tell you... The telephone was ringing when I got here, I picked it up but whoever was calling you hung up when they heard my voice. There's nothing recorded on the answer phone either. I checked the caller ID too, but the number was withheld.'

I looked the fat-brat hard in the eye. Understanding instantly that now he'd thoroughly cheesed me off, he squinted back at me and then he looked down at his feet. I knew that he'd been snooping. I hate nosiness. I wanted to punch him. More than that, I wanted to break something seriously heavy over his head. I think reading my thoughts or at least spotting the anger in my expression, Marcus flinched and turned away.

I pushed past him, straight to the front door, flipped the latch, and yanked it open.

'I'll see you tomorrow Marcus.' I said.

I dreamed that night.

Although I remember the dream vividly, it was nothing particularly special, just a short set of jerky images. I was taking a shower, or rather, I was trying too, in a bright white cubicle, but the shower wouldn't work. Looking from above, I watched me fiddling with the taps, then with the hose, then the showerhead, but nothing I did helped. After a while, a second showerhead appeared fixed high on the white tiled walls. Much bigger than the first, as soon as I reached out to touch the rose a powerful jet of water sprayed out and drenched me. Suddenly, instead of watching myself from above, I was standing in the shower, fully dressed in a woolly jumper, a shirt, and denim jeans, looking through a deluging curtain of steamy rain. Needless to say, that even in my dream state I understood that showering fully clothed was not such a great idea and so I started to undress. Pulling the jumper over my head, I unbuttoned the shirt, and I was about to undo the fly on the jeans when I noticed that under the shirt I was wearing another jumper. Dragging the wet fabric off my shoulders, I threw the shirt into the water pooling at my feet. The second jumper was a thicker knit than the first and not a pattern that I recognised from my own wardrobe. I took it off. Under the jumper, another shirt... and so it went on, a dozen times perhaps, maybe more, jumper, shirt, jumper, shirt, each one different, each one thicker, and each one heavier. Eventually the jumper became so thick and the shirt so heavy that no matter how hard I tried, under the force and weight of the torrential water, I couldn't move my arms, and neither the jumper nor the shirt would come off. Just as panic and claustrophobia were about take over, when I was beginning to think that I might be stuck in my sodden prison forever, I saw myself standing naked outside the shower cubicle. I didn't say anything, and neither did I. Yet, I think, somehow we both knew that if we could only get together we'd be able to break free.

Irritatingly, I woke with the lark on that Tuesday morning and so my dream never actually reached a satisfactory conclusion.

I think I felt okay. In fact, all-things considered, the bumps and bruises from the car crash, the frustrations and irritations of the bank holiday weekend, regardless of spending the night stuck in a shower wearing somebody else's jumpers, I felt surprisingly well. I got up and dressed quickly, popped a handful of Prozac, ate a breakfast of my usual favourites, and walked into town through St Michael's Churchyard and along the millstream path. It was a super morning, warmer that it had been recently and bright, spring had certainly fully sprung. By the time I reached town and Starbucks, far from feeling all doomy and gloomy at the prospect of a day at work, my close little world seemed a perfectly okay place to be.

'Morning all.' I chirped, as I pushed my way through the coffee-shop door.

Alas, instead of my cheery greeting receiving a similarly jolly reply, it was met by a wall of stony silence. Colin, Julie and another barista and two of Starbucks morning regulars stood in a line in front of the counter looking at me, all with soppy expressions on their faces.

'What is the matter?' I asked, suddenly worried that I might have missed something interesting and important.

Colin stepped forward.

'Are you okay?' He said. 'We didn't expect to see you this morning. Everyone's talking about the accident... that poor woman... the scaffolding pole... it must have been awful for you. Come in and sit down, I'll bring your Latté over to you.'

I know it sounds ridiculous, and I can hardly believe it myself looking back from now, but until that moment, I'd barely given poor Marie Clarke or the accident a second thought. Naturally, Colin and Julie were surprised to see me. Naturally, the others looked shocked. Covering my eyes with both hands, I pulled the smile from my face.

'I'm sorry.' I said. 'I'm just trying to feel normal.'

It was a lie… I did feel normal… I felt completely normal. I'm sure I shouldn't have.

I didn't stay long, just long enough to drink my coffee and nibble at a slice of sharp lemon cake. Colin was lovely, supportive words and warm smiles, Julie was sweet, and even the old guy with the David Beckham hat was kind. One of the two morning regulars, back on his stool in the window by the door, he asked me if I'd like to join him outside for a cigarette. I said 'no' of course, although the idea of a quick puff sounded wonderful, I hadn't smoked in dot-dot-dot years. I passed him on the street a few minutes after I finished my coffee as I walked to my salon. Sheltering under a porch with the woman wearing Marks and Sparks overall; they were both dragging on their fags as if their lives depended on the nicotine.

'Chin up, son.' He said, as I went by.

I nodded to him and faked a wan smile. Before I turned away, the wrinkly chap leaned in to the woman from Marks and Sparks and whispered something into her ear. After he'd said whatever he said, she looked at me sympathetically and then mouthed, 'Ooh… nasty', through her screwed up face. I pursed my lips and raised my eyebrows in a miniature shrug back, and then I walked on wondering if really she'd meant me. If that was it, then perhaps she was right, maybe I was nasty.

I unlocked my salon door sometime around nine, although to be honest I don't think right then I had a clue what time it actually was. The morning didn't feel so good anymore. My salon felt cold and lifeless. My feet seemed to sink into the floor. I picked up the mail from the doormat. Some of it was damp from the rain over the weekend. I'm sure it would have been the usual stuff, bills that my failing business couldn't pay, news that I didn't want to hear, and a heap of junk mail most likely from insurance companies and cut price supermarkets. However, somewhere in the pile - I remember the simple buff envelope and the scrawled italic handwriting catching my eye - was a letter from Elaine Hennessey my solicitor. I peeled the envelope open in the staffroom over another cup of coffee and a gingernut biscuit. Inside were several sheets of A4 paper and a smaller compliments slip. While the larger sheets were type written and formal, when I unfolded the compliment slip I found it smothered in the same flamboyant scrawl used to address the envelope.

Read and Enjoy. The heading told me; I did as instructed.

Hi Sweety. Elaine's note began.

Please find enclosed a full statement of Enid Fulton's estate, a short transcript of her bequest to you, and a printout of the final settlement referring to the bonds in question.

As I suspect the figure in the very last column on the very last page will come as quite a surprise (it certainly did to me) you may want to contact a personal finance advisor ASAP.

I know a few good names.

Call me soon you lucky chap.

Fondest regards.

Elaine.

She signed off with two kisses.

I put the note down, took a long slurp from my coffee cup, and as I'm certain anyone would, I turned to the last page of the A4 sheets straight away. Fifty thousand, had been suggested, twenty would've have been great, ten would have bailed me out of trouble with the bank. Using my finger to trace down the column of figures, when I reached the bottom and stopped and then read the numbers aloud my knees nearly gave way. I could hardly believe my eyes. I blinked hard, and then folded the pages shut, put them back in the envelope, took a breath, and then opened them all over again... slowly. When I got to the last page, thank goodness, the figures read the same. Not twenty thousand pounds as I'd allowed myself to hope. Not fifty thousand as Elaine had estimated when she'd first spoken to me several weeks earlier. No. The figures printed in the boldest black ink and double underlined in the bottom right hand corner of the very last page read, one hundred and forty four thousand, five hundred and eleven pounds and sixteen pence... my gob had never, ever, been so thoroughly smacked. To say that my spirits and emotions, indeed my life, were suffering a big dipper ride of insane and outlandish proportions would have been... well actually... it would have been about right. I sat down where I was, on the floor, in the staffroom, and as I remember, once again I think I began to cry.

Sometime later, maybe twenty minutes, maybe half an hour, the telephone in the salon started ringing. Realising that I needed to pull myself together sometime soon anyway, I stood up, dusted myself down, wiped my eyes and pushed my hair into place, and then tucked those most wonderful pieces of paper into my trouser pocket. I picked the telephone up between the sixth and seventh rings.

'Good morning.' I said. 'How may I help you?'

'At last.' The familiar voice came back in my ear. 'I was beginning to wonder if we'd ever get to speak.' It was my friend.

Although it felt as if I'd been waiting for the call for half a lifetime, as it happened, neither of us said very much. It wasn't that chatting felt particularly awkward or uncomfortable, but more, I think, that neither of us knew quite where to begin. In the end, we gave up our stuttering attempts and agreed to meet for lunch at one o'clock at Le Petit Paris on the High Street. I was so happy I would have cancelled anything. After we hung up, I dashed to my appointment book. The day ahead panned out easily enough. Three clients in the morning, but only two later in the afternoon, a gap of two and a half hours spread right across lunchtime, perfect, nothing needed changing at all. In my excitement, I'm afraid that my promise to meet Marcus didn't even cross my mind.

It was almost ten o'clock before I properly opened the salon. My first client of the morning was new to me, Prudence

Percival, a recommendation from Sylvia Cokeley, the vicar's wife. When I checked the book, I remembered that although as far as I could recall we'd never met, somehow I recognised the almost comical name. The image of an outrageous sitcom character had sprung to mind when I wrote it down, a Mrs Slocombe, a Sybil Fawlty, or a Hyacinth Buckett, sometimes I feel all of them could be customers of mine. Whatever I was thinking then, my jovial thoughts were quickly shattered a moment after the woman in question actually stepped through the salon door.

'Cooee! Good morning.' She called from the reception desk.

Completely preoccupied with the prospect of my lunchtime assignation, I was trimming my hair when she arrived.

'Hold on.' I called back. 'I shan't be a moment.'

'It's only me… Pru, Prudence Percival… Mrs.' she called again. 'I have an appointment at ten o'clock.'

Hearing the woman's clipped nasal voice announce her own name so precisely, suddenly a huge gonging ringing sound exploded between my ears. 'Pru, Prudence Percival', the words, the name, jolted in my memory like an electric shock flashing the picture of a small dumpy woman dressed in beige with a white scarf and bottle dyed flaming red hair across the back of my eyes. Still holding my scissors, I moved to my left across the salon and peeped through the tall floor to ceiling mirror to the reception area. I could see her standing between the reception desk and the door, and she could see me. Of course, I recognised her name. Of course, we had met before. Prudence Percival was the flower woman, the iced bun with the cherry topknot on Cecile Ablitt's front doorstep. I met her on that drizzly Sunday morning when Cecile fell down the stairs while I was wearing her Chanel suit and Prada heels.

'Marvellous,' I said, swallowing hard, 'take a seat; I'll be with you right away.'

I've often thought that one's greatest protection in a hairdressing salon, along with a good stern receptionist, is the mirror. Standing, effectively, between the hairdresser and the client, the mirror raises a subtle barrier, gives distance, and a certain degree of anonymity by turning everything, including faces, round the wrong way. A mirror provides context, a frame if you like, in which the client and stylist know their relative place. Recognition beyond that place is often not an issue, pass in the street and often neither client nor stylist would recognise each other. It is all terribly important. Ask any long serving coiffeur or coiffeuse and they'll tell you, that while they may love a cosy chat, maintaining personal space is essential, room to breathe, room to perform, room to hide a sneaky smirk or a craftily raised eyebrow. Angles of reflection and the distorted optical distance between people looking at one another through a mirror allow this. My personal preference was always to work with small mirrors, through smaller mirrors I could move in and out of view at will without a client ever noticing what I was doing. I'm sure other stylists and salon owners have their view.

However, at that particular moment, when my eyes met with Prudence Percival's through my large floor to ceiling mirror I felt completely exposed and cursed the day that I ever invested in trendy shop fittings and installed the huge thing. Desperate to remain unrecognised, I turned away quickly.

I suppose I used the extra time that I took fiddling with my hair as much to work out how best to deal with Prudence Percival incognito as I did to tidy my appearance. Regardless of my dilemma, somehow I managed to stay calm. After four or five minutes, when I finished trimming and fluffing around, while standing half hidden behind my favourite dressing table, I called her into the salon. I asked her, a tad more firmly than I'd intended to, to take a seat in a chair by the basins. Thankfully, probably concerned for the safety of her own hair and therefore keen to keep me onside, she behaved very well. Like an eager puppy in training, she followed my slightly barked command to the letter. Once safely at the basin, I moved in behind her and that was where I stayed throughout her appointment. Using every ounce of guile that I possessed, once I'd shampooed her hair, I led her across my salon backwards, dodging carefully between only the smallest mirrors. Indeed, quite remarkably, I can tell you, that for the entirety of the lovely Mrs Percival's wonderfully timed

− NOT - forty-five minute visit, I successfully steered her around my salon, washed, cut, and even dried her hair without facing her directly at all.

Despite my initial apprehension, happily, while we chatted she seemed oblivious to who I was, despite the fact that we had faced each other so closely on Cecile's doorstep there seemed to be no recognition at all. I felt my subterfuge was going extremely well. As it turned out, although her hair colour was disgusting and her style vile − don't worry, I told her that things would have to change - the odd dumpy woman wasn't such a bad sort. I remained quietly confident. That was, alas, until the very last minute. After she'd paid her bill - thirty or forty quid I think, I can't remember exactly how much I charged her although I'm sure I was worth every penny - I thought I'd heard the door close. I thought the blessed woman had gone. When abruptly, while I was lost in a silly moment of smug self-congratulation, she came back into the salon to hand me a tip and caught me completely unawares.

In fact, she caught me face to face mid yawn. Unexpectedly less than a foot apart, we stared at each other very closely indeed. I shut my mouth and swallowed hard. I may have smiled. I may have grimaced. Whatever I did, almost instantly, Pru Percival's expression changed, her eyebrows arched, her forehead furrowed, her mouth dropped open. Suddenly seeing something in my face that she hadn't seen before and that she most definitely did not like, Prudence Percival stepped back.

'I just wanted to say thank you and to give you this.' She said holding a few coins out towards me, and while her eyes held mine, all of a sudden, she sounded terribly flustered and looked frightened. 'M…my hair, I just wanted to say that it looks l…lovely, thank you, v…very much.' She stammered. Then she turned quickly away and scuttled from the salon without even saying goodbye.

I did nothing.

Perhaps, in hindsight, I should have, perhaps I should have followed her. Perhaps I should have helped her with the fear, but I didn't, I simply let her go. In fact, I let her go and then did my best to forget everything about the woman, and that we'd ever even met.

———————————————

Lunch was delicious… I think.

Sammie served us. She smiled a lot while she did it and even winked at me a couple of times through dessert. I think she knew something important was up. My friend thought she was lovely. After we'd finished eating, she cleared the table and then brought us both coffee and a couple of caramelised biscuits… my favourites.

'You can stay here as long as you like.' she said. 'We don't need the table until this evening.' Then she did a girlie little curtsy and floated away, back through her brother's restaurant.

My friend smiled.

'She's Charming, how do you know her? …Do you come here often?'

'No.' I said, chuckling lightly at the jokey cliché. 'This is only the second time I've eaten here actually. Meeting Sammie was a coincidence really. I cut her hair one afternoon, and then when I came here for dinner, as a treat after a hard day in the salon, we got chatting. She's a sweetie; she lives near me with her parents on Gillycote Road.' Then I dropped my voice to a confessional whisper and added. 'To tell you the truth, when I'd eaten my dinner that evening, Sammie finished work and we walked each other home. I know this will sound daft now, but somewhere along the line I grabbed the wrong end of an awkward stick, and I thought she fancied me… silly… but now, would you believe it, she's dating Tristan.'

'Tristan, good lord, I'd almost forgotten about Tris. How is the big fellow? All grown up now I suppose. Not still causing everyone trouble I hope.'

'No no… Tris is mostly fine these days, still a bull in a china shop at times, but Jesus saved him a few years back and now he's quite the pillar of his local church. Thank god for God, that's all I can say.'

My friend smiled again.

...and so our conversation went on, a light and gentle catching up, much as it had throughout our 'probably' delicious lunch, no recrimination, no embarrassed pauses, only happy tears. It was lovely... It was just as I'd dreamed it would be. It was all I'd ever wanted.

Then Marcus started hammering on the restaurant window.

CHAPTER TWENTY-NINE

The police arrived at my little house on Gillycote Road at five o'clock in the morning. Fortunately, my very good friend had already left. I was wide awake and chatting to myself in the mirror, something about Marcus's jealousy I think. I wasn't angry, but more frustrated. I had a large glass of vodka with sugar and three or four Prozac capsules in my hand. I downed the lot in one swig when I saw the police cars pull up outside.

I knew.

The burley Bobbies didn't so much knock on my front door as smash it into little pieces. A moment later and it sounded as if a herd of Rhinoceros were charging into my house. I don't know why they had to be so aggressive. Surely, they must have known that I wouldn't run away. I tried to get dressed while they were coming up the stairs, just jeans and a white tee shirt, nothing special. As I pulled the tee shirt over my head, I noticed a mark on the sleeve, a dark brown smear. I cursed it and I'm sure it cursed back. I guessed it came from a chocolate cookie that I'd been munching while I was ironing. I remember wishing that I had the time to choose another tee shirt from my wardrobe. I like to be clean. Alas, time was a commodity suddenly in short supply.

Detective Dennis Sapsead was the first in to my bedroom. Fair enough, I suppose. Although I don't know how he'd managed to work it out, I reckoned he deserved me. His eyes were cold and expressionless when he came in. His hair looked a mess, his skin looked waxy, and he needed a shave. Already resigned to my fate, I held my arms out ready for the handcuffs. He didn't disappoint, he didn't say a word; he just reached behind his back, pulled a pair of the grim manacles from his belt, and then snapped the cold metal in place around my wrists.

The detective led me down stairs quite gently. At the bottom, in my hall, another and younger plain clothed policeman who I didn't recognise, but who reminded me of a thin Boris Becker, read me my rights. When he asked me if I understood that they had come to arrest me on suspicion of murder, I nodded and then smiled at him. I hadn't meant to smile. I can't say that I felt particularly happy about anything. Unfortunately, the accidental grin seemed to bother the chap. He turned away apparently angry and then muttered something under his breath. I looked to Dennis Sapsead, not so much for reassurance or comfort, but more for some kind of explanation. The senior officer held my eye for a moment but gave no hint, and then he also shook his head and turned away from me. It was only later, much later, in a different existence, when I discovered that the younger detective was engaged to marry my niece that I understood. Not so much shocked at my crimes as I'd thought likely, but disappointment and embarrassment all round.

They wouldn't let me put my shoes on. I'd watched lots of high-octane American cop movies over the years, so I knew full well why. They needn't have bothered, as I told you before, I wasn't about to run away. I didn't mind though. At least I didn't mind bare tootsies until it came to walking down my garden path. Spring that year on Gillycote Road it seemed had sprung a whole crop of early baby thistles and other prickly weeds and had planted them in every crack and crevice. In just those few short strides to the waiting police car, my poor toes found most of them out I'm sure… and, of course, my stone pathway was also jolly cold.

When I ducked into the police car and a uniformed chappie slammed the door shut, I looked back at my house through a smeared window. In the grey-light between night and dawn my small semidetached home looked sad, somehow… let down. I wondered when I'd see it again, when I'd sleep in my own bed, when I'd eat at my own table. In fact, as things turned out it wouldn't be so long as I then feared. However, as I didn't know that at the time, despite making a solemn promise to myself in the mirror not to cry, a hard lump grew in my throat. I didn't actually shed tears. I think perhaps, that the quantity of Prozac that I'd recently been consuming helped carry me past properly crying. Indeed, as the car pulled away, I remember feeling oddly calm. The only real worry I remember having, was that after all the bashing and crashing, my front door might be left open to burglars. I think even then, even at that most crucial point of extreme crisis, when I should have been frightened I still didn't really believe that I'd done anything so terribly wrong.

I no longer remember the more unsavoury details of the period between my arrest and my ultimate incarceration. I know that in general with only one or two minor exceptions – most notably the press - people were surprisingly kind and understanding. I saw numerous doctors and lawyers of course. Elaine Hennessey my own solicitor and, I liked to think, a personal friend, was marvellous. Albeit for a fee – which thanks to Enid Fulton's wonderful bequest at least I could afford - she oversaw the wrapping up of my business, the eventual sale of my mother's home, the management of my assets and the letting of my little house on Gillycote Road. Quite remarkably, and rather nicely I thought, purely as friends I was sure, Colin and Julie, my favourite baristas from Starbucks eventually took the tenancy of my house. While I was still on remand, maybe a month before my trial, I received a lovely letter from Colin. While I can't pretend that he was supportive of my unfortunate criminal position, he did at least promise to look after the place until I came home. I do so miss the optimism of youth.

As for the other lawyers, they were a dead loss. Some, it seemed, saw my high profile case as a chance to further their career. Some came because of the media interest, others because it was their duty. Some were assholes and some, I am sure, were genuine. However, not one of them had good hair and none of them presented well, and in the end, I declined them all. It didn't matter; I knew what I wanted to say anyway.

The doctors weren't much better. A steady stream of them started visiting my various prison cells within a few days of my arrest. On reflection, I think the first old chap that came to see me was the best. Highly qualified I'm certain, and looking like a bespectacled garden Gnome, he didn't say a great deal. He just took me to a consulting room in one of the prisons - I forget which one - sat me in a plump and comfortable chair opposite his own plump and comfortable chair and asked me simply 'why?'

'Why what?' I said.

271

Instead of answering me, the old fellow steepled his wrinkly fingers against his equally wrinkly chin and promptly fell to sleep. 'What the heck', I thought, I was tired and my prison cell bed wasn't the most restful, so I snuggled down and did the same. An hour or so later, after several heavy knocks on the door went unanswered, my personal jailer and another prison guard burst in. Bleary eyed and yawning, I jumped out of my chair and stood to attention as quickly I'd learned they expected me to, but the old grey wrinkly doctor stayed exactly where he was, apparently fast asleep. I was hurriedly bundled back to my cell. Later that evening I heard that the poor old fellow was dead. A stroke or his heart probably, I never found out which, but I couldn't help wondering if they'd try to pin him on me too. After that, I think I lost interest in doctors, although after my conviction, when the judge had studied the medical reports that she'd requested, and it seemed that my new life of confinement might need some interest, to appease the old dear I did agree to continue seeing the prison psychiatrist once a week.

Tristan was great naturally... and his mother.

They both visited me fairly regularly while I was on remand and my cousin wrote to me almost every day. They were lovely letters too. I've kept some of them. In fact, I was reading one, on my balcony, only the other day.

My dearest cousin.

It started, as they all did, with possibly the most coherent line of the whole letter.

Today I have been dealing with varmint caterpillars. While I like to see the butterflies around my buddleia - they are pretty in the sunshine - I do so hate the crawling little blighters that they deposit under the leaves of my broccoli and sprouts. I hope that you are well and the food is better than it was when Tristan was a guest of Her Majesty. Also, the cauliflower is being eaten alive. Indeed, their leaves are starting to look like green lacework. I do miss having a regular man about the house, a strong arm does come in handy.

I can't believe that all this has happened. I know you're not a bad man. You had such a lovely smile when you were a boy and perfect teeth. Can it be true? Whatever were you thinking? I worry for your Mother. Maybe it is fortunate that she is dead.

I shall try to use the powders I got from Mr McKluckie at the nursery. You probably don't remember him, but he has a scar from the Falklands and he is a wonder with Brasica. If that doesn't work I'll try smoking them out, but I think the damage is done now.

You might like to know that I will be preparing one of your very favourite roast lunches this Sunday - leg of lamb most likely, unless the meat-man at Sainsbury's has on offer on beef, with crispy King Edwards - for Tristan and his young lady, Samantha, and we shall be thinking of you.

Until our visit.
As always, my very fond regards.
Your ever loving Cousin.
xxx

Kisses too, she'd always been a good egg my cousin.

I suppose the biggest sadness for me during the whole sorry affair, was that just when I was rekindling my relationship with my very special friend, a few overly zealous vindictive and nosey policemen helped either by a mealy-mouthed telltale ginger minger, or a green-eyed fat-brat bastard – at the time I wasn't sure who - had to go and spoil it all.

When it came to my trial, apart from dear old Enid Fulton, who, thanks to a brilliant diagnosis by the late Dr Carmen, was happily, certified dead from natural causes, and the responsibility for the disappearance of nasty Marjorie Warton, I was convicted of everything that they threw at me. Very much against the advice of, but with guidance from Elaine Hennessey, pigheadedly - I realise now - I handled my own defence. Alas, although I thought I made a reasonable crack at it, my denials and arguments didn't prove to be terribly effective. Hindsight can leave one feeling so silly. In fairness to me, the police were damned lucky. From inadvertently tracing a half-literate report on my broken shop window from November of the previous year, that briefly mentioned Marjorie Warton's disgustingly expensive and unfortunately distinctive Birkin Handbag and opened a right old can of worms. To somehow discovering microscopic deposits of Jayne Clarke's blood, in the cracks on my salon floor some fifteen feet from the place where the accident actually happened. An area, incidentally, that I'd thoroughly steamed, scrubbed, and bleached three times over. Detective Dennis Sapsead was either a genius or just downright jammy. Bah! Two plus two equals guilty I guess.

'It was the blood what swung it guv'nor.' The odd-looking court Jailer told me cheerfully as he led me from the dock.

I made no confessions I promise, not then, not since then, not ever. Thin, though his case was, my favourite Detective Sergeant had somehow magically turned up too much evidence and produced too many - in my opinion, spurious – witnesses for the predominantly female, middle-aged, middle-class, jury to ignore.

Ultimately, psychiatric reports pending, despite my continued protestations of blamelessness, the court sentenced me to an indeterminate term of imprisonment with a denial of my right to appeal and a recommendation from the judge – the old sweetheart - that I serve no less than twenty-five years. Although probably not for the most obvious reasons, I have to say that her almost casual afterthought suggestion of a minimum sentence quite cheesed me off. I'm sure that she was a very nice woman and I'm sure that usually she was consistent in her work. However, although twice during her summing up the slightly blue-rinsed but otherwise good for her years judge mentioned the 'serial' nature of my crimes - which is usually serious stuff - she failed to act upon the remarks properly. Ordinarily, when handed a life sentence, serial murderers serve just that, jail for the remainder of their natural span. I know it sounds silly, and perversely, wildly against my best interests, but regardless of the circumstances, guilty or simply misguided, a chap doesn't like to feel undervalued.

PART TWO.

CHAPTER THIRTY

I have to say that I never liked prison. I knew it wasn't my kind of place as soon as I arrived there all those weeks and months ago, and apart from the few friends that I made, and the first visit from my 'perfect' appeal lawyer, nothing much happened during my stay to improve my opinion.

They delivered me on a Thursday, on a wet Thursday afternoon, on a wet Thursday afternoon late in November. The place was a mess I remember. Thanks to some government refurbishment programme to combat prison overcrowding, the grey 1960's cast-concrete edifice looked more like a construction site than a jail. I only mention the muddle, and the rain, and the time of the year, because the combination of the three sort of matched my mood at the time… soggy and sad and in need of repair.

I don't know what I'd naively expected… Summer camp I think. Butlins meets Kellermans perhaps, just with padlocks on the doors, communal showers and not so much dancing. It certainly wasn't that. The first face to greet me properly was no Patrick Swayze. The small pinched features wore a scowl only marginally less welcoming than a Thames sewerage outfall at closing time on a Saturday night, and had more pockmarks than the new moon has craters at that most special time of its cycle. Deakin was the name behind the snarl… Mister Deakin with a capital B, Lance to his friends – although there couldn't have been many - and the senior sourpuss prison officer of the landing I was headed for, and who looked to me like the archetypal screw. The wiry brute didn't so much show me to my cell as drag me to my new home from home by my earlobe. I guess it was my own fault. I made the mistake of trying to cover my innate awkwardness in new situations by cracking a little funny. I should have known better. After all the time I'd spent on remand, I should have learned by then that having a sense of humour is not high on the attribute list among prison officers.

'Oh for god sake… just what I needed, another bloody comedian.' Deakin sighed irritably instead of laughing.

All I did was ask for the key to the bridal suite and copy of the Times with my breakfast tea. Actually, although the Times and the tea weren't such a bad idea, I found out jolly quickly – although not through personal experience thank goodness - that the Bridal suite was the last place in my particular prison any nice person would want to visit.

Although Deakin's assault on my earlobe was not especially uncomfortable – I have a reasonable pain threshold when anxiety takes hold - being marched from the stairwell, across landing No.2 and into 'B' corridor and to my new home from home, like a naughty schoolboy, certainly drew more attention to my arrival than was probably ideal, and I don't suppose it did my 'nick' credibility any favours either.

'The wimp has arrived.' I might as well have been shouting as I hopped and skipped to keep pace. By the time we reached the tiny cell at the end of the long corridor, we'd passed twenty-three others; I reckoned half with an ugly mug peeping out through the spy-hole in its door, and all jeering me on.

It could have been worse. I quickly learned that on any other day of the week my abject humiliation might have drawn double the audience. As it was, Thursday on my particular wing turned out to be visiting day and after lunch, rather than returning to their cells as they usually would have, a number of 'B' corridor's otherwise unemployed special guests had been herded into calming green ready-rooms somewhere down below to wait a brief turn with their loved ones. I suppose I should've been thankful for the minor mercy. In reality, however, I knew that in all likelihood the damage had already been done, that word would soon spread, and for the time being at least, Deakin's peevish display of rotten authority, would quickly tag me as a potential victim. I cursed him then as I curse him now.

'In you go.' He said, releasing my earlobe only after an extra twist, and then giving my behind a shove with the side of his boot.

My ears crackled as a further rumble of jeers and catcalls echoed towards me along the corridor. Deakin ignored the din and grabbed the long shiny steel handle on the door.

'You're a lucky girl tonight… You've got this cage to yourself.' He grinned. 'Don't worry though, we'll move you soon enough, maybe tomorrow, to somewhere more interesting, I'll find you a double and a nice roomy… maybe two. We wouldn't want you to feel lonely now would we?'

Then, without slamming it, the Senior Officer pulled the door to my cell firmly shut. For a moment or two, he stood immediately outside the door looking up the corridor with the back of his head blocking most of my view out through the spy-hole. From my place, standing alone in the very centre of the small stark room, I closed my eyes. Although I couldn't see Deakin, I imagined the scene as he saw it. The smug expression on the officer's pockmarked face as he listened to the last, of what I'm sure he considered to be, cheers of approval for his wonderful jape die away. In my mind's eye, his jaw shrugged up and to the left, he pulled the peak on his cap low over his eyes. I imagined his head nodding slowly and deliberately as he took a breath of callous self-satisfaction. A part of me vowed revenge at that point. A minute later, when at last the catcalls and jeers had faded completely, I heard a key turn in the lock and then, when I opened my eyes, the wretched man was gone.

I think it was probably only then that I first understood that I wouldn't be able to cope with being locked up for very long, that the idea of serving a full life sentence didn't really appeal. I shrugged my shoulders to myself and let out a long slow sigh, and then, shoving my hands deep into my trouser pockets, I turned away from the door and looked around my new little room. There wasn't much to see really and certainly nothing to enthuse about. Four almost square white painted walls, a bed that seemed to me to be lashed together using bent scaffolding poles and sackcloth, one small metal chest of drawers, a tall narrow cupboard, and a weird looking plastic and stainless steel toilet which had a hand basin arrangement moulded into the top of its cistern. With everything other than the walls, toilet bowl, and sackcloth bedding, painted in an insipid brownish-grey, the style genre that my particular prison seemed to favour most could well have worn the label 'indestructible utilitarian chic', only without too much 'chic'. Under other circumstances the decor would probably have been considered trendy… Alas, somehow, it didn't work for me.

With nothing much to do and nowhere to go, no company or offers for lunch, bored, fed-up and fidgety, I did what I suppose most people finding themselves in such situations might do, I lay on the bed – which happily turned out to be more comfortable than I'd expected – and I took a nap. Despite the unfamiliarity of my surroundings, exhausted from the upheaval of moving home I suppose, I fell asleep easily enough, and I as I recall, I think I slept for a couple of hours or maybe even more. While I don't remember dreaming – another of life's little luxuries that holidaying at Her Majesty's pleasure seemed to steal from a chap – I do remember waking up with quite a start when I heard a familiar voice close by, seemingly whispering in my ear.

'I can't share a cell with anyone else.' It said. I heard it very clearly. My eyes blinked open, I remember sitting up on the bed and looking around the room with my heart thumping in my chest.

'I really can't… and neither can you.' The voice continued.

Of course, when I looked around through bleary eyes there was no one there. I was completely alone, my little room was entirely empty… just me, and my new bed, and my weird toilet, and… well… me.

Now here's the thing… Since the moment of my arrest, when nasty Dennis Sapsead burst into my house so early on what I am quite sure would have been a lovely spring morning, during all the lonely trials and tribulations, and the long time I spent all on my own on remand, I never spoke to myself once… not once.

'We'll have to think of something… YOU will have to think of something. I mean to say, we're hardly the sharing type now are we? Surely you understand that.'

Just like that. After months and months of apparent abandonment, without so much as a 'Good afternoon.' or 'How are you today?' there I was, popping up, out of the blue, just when it suited me, making unreasonable demands. It was oh so typical. The snag was that while I would have liked nothing more than to ignore me and go back to sleep, irritatingly, with less than a moment's thought I knew that I agreed with myself completely. I knew that I was quite right. I couldn't possibly share such a small space with another human being, and certainly not two. Yuck, the very thought, something would indeed have to be done, and considering the restrictions of our tricky situation, I reckoned it would be me that would have to do it.

'But what?' I wondered aloud, more to myself than to me. Needless to say, cussed as ever, my reflection didn't come up with any helpful ideas.

As it happened, a possible solution to the dilemma that Mr Deakin had so mischievously posed came more quickly than I might have expected, and not from the lengthy tortured discussions with myself that I'd feared, and self indulgently, I confess now, had even hoped it might, but from a chance and, at the time, rather frightening encounter in the dining room only a little while later that very evening.

Before I was fully awake or had even been able to properly chastise myself for letting me down so badly let alone come up with any clever idea of my own, something heavy thumped against the door to my cell, and a moment later, I heard the sound of an electric buzzer and a key rattling in the lock.

'Up you get Princess.' A prison officer, who I hadn't seen before, called to me as the door swung open. 'Supper time comes but once a day, and you, you lucky thing you, will be dining with the rest of the brethren this evening and not on your tod as you might have been told.'

In fact, I couldn't remember anybody mentioning supper at all. I stood up quickly, rubbed my hands together eagerly, and probably smiled at the chap. To tell you the truth I was starving hungry by then and the prospect of getting something to eat seemed pretty darned good to me.

'I'm glad you're so happy to see me,' the officer chuckled, 'but I wouldn't be too cheerful if I were you. Least ways, I wouldn't go grinning my way into the dining room, like it was some kind of ladies meet-n-greet, if I were you. Do you know what I mean?'

Although, largely thanks to my various Psychiatric Doctors various analyses and subsequent recommendations, I'd spent most of my incarceration, so far, away from fellow prisoners and thus prison politics, I understood exactly what he meant. Prison is a fairly… or maybe I should say… an unfairly feudal place, easy enough to understand from the outside looking in, but get the slightest thing wrong inside at your peril. I was the new kid on the block, fresh meat, and thanks in part at least, to the lovely Mr Deakin and his kind ear-tweaking help in introducing me to my fellow inmates I had a few things to try to put right already.

I nodded and dropped my smile to the floor.

The prison officer nodded back. 'Follow me.' He said.

Of all the things that a fellow has to learn to get used to in prison - in my experience and so far as my delicate sensitivities are concerned anyway - probably the worst is the constant noise. I can't say that it was something that I'd ever considered before my incarceration. However, while in the outside world, noise is something that, to a greater or lesser extent a least, one has some control over – I mean to say, you don't have to be wherever you are do you? In prison, you are stuck with it, noise is everywhere and everywhere is noisy. Forget the dreadful din from the construction workers in my particular prison, the banging and hammerings of the government's wonderful refurbishment programme. I'm sure it applies to prisons in general. The very fabric of the buildings is noisy, the way they are constructed, the fixtures and fittings are noisy, even the type of person that the institutions themselves tend to attract is noisy.

Stepping from my small room and turning right onto 'B' corridor a sudden high-pitched scream echoed from somewhere distant ahead of me and made me jump. I stopped and glanced towards the sound. Beyond the end of 'B' corridor, directly across the more brightly lit landing where I reckoned my escort and I were heading, perhaps ten yards or so into another long line of cells, a door swung open. A sign fixed to the ceiling above the open door read 'A'. Suddenly, like a miniature rugby scrum, a huddle of navy blue uniforms burst from the open doorway. Peering ahead, between the uniforms a leg appeared and then two arms, and then I heard more screaming. A moment later, en masse, the prison officers lurched forward, and then swayed, and then as a group, they fell to the ground. I worried for the poor soul underneath. I turned back to my own prison officer who raised a shrugging eyebrow. He wasn't interested. Staring back at me from a few yards on with his hands on his hips and with the body language of someone who'd been waiting at a bus stop for far too long, 'Come on…' he said impatiently. Then as he turned away from me and headed along the corridor, he added, and I think speaking more to himself than to me. '…probably just one of the girlies who didn't want to come home after visiting, they all squeal, he'll be off to the block soon enough, you'll get used to it.'

Resigned to do as I'd been told quickly and not to make unnecessary ripples, I tucked my chin into my collar and followed the officer along 'B' corridor onto landing No.2, at the top of which a barred door swung open as we approached. Although I'd walked the route in the opposite direction with the dastardly Deakin only a few hours earlier, somehow now nothing seemed familiar. Perhaps it was dimmer evening light. Perhaps it was a smell. Perhaps it was just something unspoken left hanging in the air. Whatever it was, for no obvious reason, suddenly, I felt completely lost. Anxiety welled up at me from the soles of my prison boots. A tremble ran through me. Less than a second later, my officer coughed and then beckoned me through the door. I bit my lip and cautiously crossed the threshold. Beyond the door, the landing narrowed into an open stairway, Stairwell No.2, the sign on the wall read. Metal gratings clanked and echoed beneath my feet. The door slammed shut behind us and as it did, over the noise from the builders at work on the ground floor, a rat-a-tat-tat of shouts came from above. Moving towards the downward stair, my prison officer turned and roughly grabbed my elbow, I looked at him in alarm, afraid that I'd done something wrong.

'Don't worry.' He said, at last a glimmer of amusement in his eyes. 'Health and safety that's all. You can kill yourself by falling from the very top to the very bottom of this whole bloody staircase, any time you like, just so long as you are on your own, but if I'm escorting you anywhere in this prison, we go by the book, and you stay healthy and safe… do we understand?'

I nodded and smiled, I relaxed my arm, and I think that maybe, for some silly reason, I may even have giggled.

The prison officer stopped in his tracks immediately, then turned back to me again and glowered. 'I thought I warned you about all that cheerful stuff before.' He said sharply. 'I thought I warned you that this is not supposed to be a fun place.' Once again, like before, after swallowing hard and blinking a silent apology, as a child might when scolded by an angry parent, I dropped my eyes to the floor, and hoped that my smile would quickly die and slither away.

The dining room was far bigger that I'd imagined it would be - eight tables long by four wide - easily seating a hundred and fifty men. As with my little room, it was painted in a stark glossy yellowing white with attractive matching brownish/grey trimmings (no signs of refurbishment here). The tables and chairs, as an extension of the prison's 'indestructible utilitarian chicless-chic' theme, looked as if they'd been remodelled from some kind of cast iron that in a previous existence might well have been used to pen condemned swine in a slaughter house… smashing. Beyond the interesting tables and chairs, set into the wall opposite the main entrance, and manned by several interesting looking chaps, all of whom I reckoned were my fellow inmates, three wide serving hatches held the primary gaze of most of the evening's diners. Each of the culinary glory holes sported its own eager queue, as I'm sure that it disgorged a plethora of fine local fare. I suppose, that in a sort of 'IKEA' meets 'Colditz' way, it was all jolly well thought out. Neat, tidy, and to the point, all we needed was a pot of Swedish meatballs and maybe in some people's eyes – trendy do-gooders from small towns like my own probably – it might have been the perfect calming environment for poor criminal types to dine.

'Get food... find seat... eat.' was all that my prison officer said to me once we were inside. Then, with the instruction given, he took a sideways step to position himself next to a similarly proportioned and equally stern looking colleague who'd struck a tough-guy pose close to the entrance to the dining room. As ever, when finding myself thrown into new and challenging circumstances, affable acquiescence being my middle name, I followed the instructions quickly, braved my way further inside, and again did my best to do exactly as I'd been told.

Closer to the serving hatches - perhaps halfway through the sea of tables and chairs but still a good few yards from the tail of either of the queues that I was hoping to join – I found my way forward blocked. A group of rough looking men, who, although no longer eating, were huddled around a table between the serving hatches and me, had pushed their chairs into the aisles between the tables. Thinking about it now of course, having spotted a fresh face heading their way, I'm sure that the Oiks had blocked my path deliberately to stop me getting to my dinner. However, at the time, choosing to avoid any hint of cowardice, instead of sensibly turning away, when I reached their table I spun a nifty sharp right, with the simple and obvious intention of making my way around them and then past the next table over.

Although I doubted that any of the uncouth thugs appreciated the deftness of my neat heel-turn, following my sappy introduction to my fellow inmates perhaps I shouldn't have been surprised when as I whisked my way sideways with a tidy Chassé back to my original path, once past the next table along, the whole misshapen cast iron kit and caboodle came hurtling towards me. I dodged it of course. A quick nip to my left and then a neat body swerve back to my right. The table barely brushed my hip before it crashed into another where a big chap with long greasy hair sat alone eating his dinner. His plate - piled high with food - spun away from his lunging knife and fork and clattered onto the floor beyond. I glanced back to the tables of oiks and then to the big chap, he looked suddenly mortified. Actually 'big' doesn't quite do the chap in question justice, 'big' rather implies that he was simply larger than average. In fact, although not blessed with the tall muscular hugeness of my second cousin Tristan or the taller and even more muscular hugeness of his friend Mr Ripper, Edward Ewan Edwards, as later he introduced himself (probably only a guest of Her Majesty because of an inability to runaway at any sensible speed), was positively enormous. Thirty-five stone at least, a great dollop of a man, rounded and bloated, like a six foot five inch Ostrich egg, in truth, Edward Ewan Edwards was not just large, but actually quite obscenely obese.

It was about then, while I was keen to get away but also while desperately trying not to further antagonise either Edward Ewan Edwards or any of the men who had shoved the table and were still glaring at me hard, that I noticed the first wafts of an unpleasant smell. Initially, my nostrils found it difficult to distinguish precisely what the nasty whiff was. A mix of boiled greens, stale underpants, and rotten potatoes, I wondered, or of old egg and ripe French cheese. However, as I hurriedly tried to cut behind Big Mr 'E' and away from the rough chaps, towards the serving hatch queues, the stronger and more disgustingly familiar the smell became.

'Why did you do that?' Big Mr 'E' asked, pointing with one large chubby finger to his ruined dinner on the floor while shooting the other out to stop me before I could entirely circumnavigate his vast girth.

'What?' I said. My good old single syllable stump the only coherent reply I could manage.

I looked into his great blotchy face and winced. Suddenly I knew precisely where the awful stench - a revolting mix of rank body odour, appalling bad breath, and I reckoned probably much worse besides - was coming from. Although our exchange so far had taken only a split second, my annoying inner eye and the silliness of my imagination instantly colluded to concoct a vision of the huge man being inflated further, up to and beyond bursting point, by a giant candy striped bicycle pump. Fearing an explosive splattering of the grossest proportion, I shook my head to clear the thought as fast as I could. My nostrils shrank. My stomach lurched. Edwards' grip on my arm tightened.

'Why did you do that?' he asked again, and this time with more menace in his voice. Then heaving himself up from his poor straining chair, he punctuated his question by rocking towards me like a wobbling Weeble and shoving his face far too close to mine. Hot foul breath engulfed my face and head in a thick pungent fug; a spray of noxious sticky spittle blurred my eyes, and for a fleeting moment, my eyelids seemed glued together.

If my stomach hadn't reacted to the assault on my senses so violently and in such a frightening hurry, I might have told the smelly round giant, that it wasn't actually ME who'd spoiled his quiet dinner. I might have told him to ask himself where he thought someone of my slight stature might have found the strength to shove such a heavy iron table with such enormous force. I might have pointed a finger towards him and poked him in the eye. I might have been quite cross. I might have... but...

Whoosh.

For a moment the world stopped. The dining room fell silent. Eyes turned in my direction. Knives and forks froze mid-motion.

My feet went cold. My eyes watered. Reflexively, I wiped my chin with the back of my hand. When my vision cleared, Edward Ewan Edwards was staring at me with a look of disbelief fixed in his beady eyes, and a splatter of something unpleasantly sticky and worryingly greenish on the side of his face. It was dreadful. I was certain that at any moment the big man would hit me or at the very least drop me to the floor, and then sit on me and squish me into the ground. As if sensing my terror, Edwards' eyes narrowed, almost disappearing into his puffy cheeks. If I could have seen his mouth, I'm sure it would have been snarling at me. I started to turn away, a sort of slow-motion flinch, but then for some strange unknown reason, a flash of insanity perhaps, or a sudden attack of masochism, goodness knows, I stopped myself, and something or perhaps someone – you know who maybe - seemed to take over inside my head. When my eyes met Edward's, I felt my top lip crease into a smile, not a weak smile either but a whopping great cheesy grin, just the sort of whopping great giggly grin that at around that time seemed to be getting me into trouble generally.

'Oh deary me… whoops! I am so sorry. Shit happens I guess.' I found myself saying surprisingly calmly, and I think I said it with a smirk as well, with no hint of apology or fear in my voice.

Edward Ewan Edwards just held onto my arm and although his eyes seemed to be vanishing further into the folds of skin on his face, I'm sure he continued his stare.

'Can't help myself I'm afraid, whenever I'm scared I either seem to puke or poo myself.' I said. 'It's jolly embarrassing. I reckon you got the better alternative actually.'

It wasn't entirely true. In fact, throwing-up as I did so suddenly shocked me as much as it must have horrified him. Usually, when I'm frightened I just collapse into a useless crumpled heap on the floor, the proverbial 'quivering wreck'. I don't remember ever puking or pooing myself before. However, at the time and under the circumstances the lie itself didn't seem to matter. I reckon, in my panic, I was thinking that if he was considering smashing me to smithereens, the prospect of further, and possibly even more unpleasant, repercussions might just give him cause to think again.

With Big 'E' still looming over me, I took a huge breath in and sort of scrunched my lips together in what I think was supposed to be some kind of oral shrug. The air between us fizzed for a second or two. I could sense the eyes of the group of rough chaps on the next table down burning into the back of my head. Then big greasy Edward Ewan Edwards did something that quite took me aback. Instead of leaning over me so threateningly, he straightened a bit, and then bent carefully to one side, and this time so that his mouth was close to my left ear, then he cupped his hand hiding whatever he was about to do. I think I half expected him to spit some foul threat into my ear, or worse, to bite my shell-like clean off, but he didn't.

'I'm very sorry…' He whispered softly instead. 'Don't worry; I won't let it happen again. I know what it's like to be frightened, it's a horrible thing, fear, I won't scare you anymore, I promise'

I couldn't believe my ears. For a while afterwards, I wondered if perhaps somewhere along the line, some small thing that I'd done or said had struck a chord with the fat chap. Although his choice of words seemed odd, I wondered if somehow, by standing up for myself, I'd gained the brutes respect. Actually, I later learned that it wasn't quite that. However, when he let go of my arm, and turned around and simply walked away from his table, wiping his face with a napkin and leaving his food on the floor and me alive and in one piece, I felt confident that as far as the thugs who had shoved the table at me were concerned, indeed as far as most of Her Majesty's on-looking dinner-guests were concerned, it might as well have been.

When at last I made it to the serving hatch, I chose a meat curry – it could have been Lamb or it could have been a road-kill hedgehog - with plain boiled rice for supper. Aware that the eyes of my fellow diners were on me, I sat as far away from anybody else as I could. The officer, my officer, who'd kindly escorted me to the dining room earlier, came over and spoke to me as soon as I sat down.

'Not many people do that.' He said.

I looked at the food on my plate, then at the ceiling, then at the prison officer. I felt the warm swell of self-satisfaction rise in my chest. I tried to act cool.

'I guess he just didn't want to take me on.' I said, blagging it ludicrously, but nevertheless doing my best to look both tough and nonchalant at the same time... and then for the second time that evening, I made my mouth do a sort of oral shrug... I think Elvis Presley used a similar affectation in the film 'Jailhouse Rock'.

The prison officer looked at me curiously, and then he also did something for a second time that evening... he smiled.

'What?' I said.

'Well... It's just that I think you've got hold of the wrong end of the stick.' He said. 'I don't think Big Eddy would want to take you or anybody else on, especially not in here. He might pick your pockets if you're not too careful, but unless you're an old lady trying to keep hold of your pension book or handbag he's not the sort to start punching.'

'So what did you mean then?' I asked. 'Not many people do what?'

'Not many people like to get too near to Big Eddy.' He said. 'Couldn't you smell him? The man hasn't washed, or showered, or cleaned his teeth since the day he was banged up, he's disgusting, if I had my way even his clothes should be burned.'

'Well yes… Now that you mention it I did notice that he smelled a bit high.' I said. '…But surely, can't you just take him to the showers and make him wash?'

'Waterphobic.' He said.

'What?' I said.

'Well… the word is hydrophobic actually; apparently it's an acknowledged medical condition, like a disease. Big Eddy is hydrophobic. He suffers from hydrophobia, he is scared of water, now we can't just chuck the poor chap in a bath full of his worst fears can we… health and safety… I've told you about keeping safe and staying healthy already. So no… with Big Eddy, most people just keep their distance. We keep our distance. Even the Doc keeps his distance. No one has much to do with Eddy Edwards, not many even talk to him, and I can tell you now that even though he has one of the old double cells, there's not one person in this place would share with him.'

I know that it sounds absurd now, especially given my penchant for personal cleanliness, but at the time, the officer's last few words flashed at me like an electric light bulb blinking on with a full 240-volt charge inside my head… a wonderful moment of hope. With the chance of an answer to my 'sharing' dilemma stored safely if somewhat daftly in the back of my mind, suddenly, for the remainder of my first incarcerate day, my surly prison officer looked fresh faced and oddly attractive, the decor in the dining room more cheery, and even my hedgehog curry seemed to taste perfectly okay.

'…and I wouldn't blame them one bit.' I said. 'The very idea of being forced to occupy the same cell as anyone so utterly filthy would be wholly unacceptable.'

CHAPTER THIRTY-ONE

A juicy chunk of pineapple, topped with a scarlet cherry and neatly run through by a small pink plastic sword, nestles on the edge of my Pina-colada. Gripping the diminutive weapon between forefinger and thumb, I dunk the chunk once and then twice before biting into the succulent flesh. A trickle of sweet nectar escapes my lips and then runs down my chin dripping onto my bare chest. Somewhere behind me, a soft splash, and a musical liquid tinkle tells my ears that another beautiful sun bronzed body has slunk silkily into the glistening waters of the cool infinity pool. In the distance, an exotic bird calls for its mate, a child - playing in the warm sunshine - chuckles, a minaret bell rings, and then... something harsh and cruel shatters the wonderful moment.

'Up you get princess.' Deakin's trite words, punctuated by the already familiar sound of my cell door buzzing and clicking, and then banging open, drag my senses back to the sad truth. Instantly, disappointment and dread flood every molecule in my body. I roll over with sigh and a wrongly long trailing yawn as I wake feeling unbearably sick.

As I remember it, and regrettably I do remember it very well indeed, that first prison wake-up call heralded probably the worst few days of my life. In fact, I don't think that anything in particular actually happened on that specific day to make it any more appalling than any other, but more that on waking that morning, after months of denial and self-delusion, the grown-up reality of the terms and conditions of my ultimate incarceration had at last sunk in.

I'd never felt so awful, not when my father died, nor after my mother's funeral, not even when I was first arrested and realised that the indefatigable Detective Dennis Sapsead's irritating nosiness had blown any real chance of a reconciliation with my very good friend clean out of the water. Before I'd even opened my eyes, an overwhelming thick grey soup of hopeless pointlessness swirled up from the floor filling my ever pore and my every sense. To say that suddenly, and most naively, unexpectedly, the moment I woke I found myself drowning in an anxious depression of Churchill's legendary 'Black Dog' proportions might now seem an exaggeration, but I know, that then, that's exactly how it felt. Just raising my head from the skinny prison pillow took, it seemed, every ounce of my strength and every morsel of my energy. I slumped sideways and all but rolled onto the floor.

'Ah! Got a dose of Nick flu, hey?' Deakin's irritating, but, I realise now, undeniably accurate diagnosis, was made without a moment's hesitation. The accuracy and casualness of his assessment should have annoyed me. At almost any other time in my life, metaphorically at least, I might have spat at him. Instead, I peered up at him and blinked helplessly through myopic eyes. The wiry man was standing in the open doorway to my cell looking at me on my knees, one hand in his pocket while in the other he held and swung a magic silvery key. Of course, I didn't have a clue what he was talking about at the time.

'I can spot the symptoms a mile away.' He said. 'We'll put you on watch, you'll either get over it or you won't.' Then, straightening up and tucking the key to my cell, actually, the magic key to all the cells on 'B' corridor, back inside his jacket, he added. 'Your breakfast is at seven forty, the showers are at the end of the landing, it's ten past seven now, so you have fifty minutes to get up, get clean, get fed, take a stroll along the prom (the sarcastic sod), and then get back here. It's up to you whether you do or whether you don't… nobody will worry too much either way.' Then Deakin turned and pulled my door shut behind him.

I didn't do breakfast or lunch. I didn't shower or clean my teeth. I didn't even wee or poo. In fact, I hardly moved at all. I think I spent most of the day, and possibly most of the next day and even the day after, sitting, sometimes rocking on the floor in the narrow gap between my weird toilet and the metal chest of drawers.

When I think back to that time, and believe me I wish that my sorry mind would erase all the memories completely, I find tracking the passage of time, almost impossible. Forget the hours and minutes and the time of the day, after a while, none of us can remember precisely when or for how long we do anything in terms of real time. It's the sequence of the events that becomes important, and for me, those first few days in proper prison are now just a jumble of nasty random recollections.

At some time or other, the prison officer who'd escorted me to the dining room on my first evening in my particular prison, came in to my cell. The chap, who I now realise, bore more than a passing resemblance to a young Jimmy Stewart, but just with harder eyes and fairer hair, squatted down close beside me on the floor. Resting his elbows on his knees, he steepled his fingers together thoughtfully then touched his two index fingers against the tip of his chin. While I noticed then and I now remember everything he did in quite some detail, - including the fact that his nails were dreadfully badly bitten and especially those on his right hand - I don't think that while he was there in front of me I actually looked at him at all.

'It's no good you know?' He said – and I wasn't about to argue the point, with all the strength and enthusiasm for life of the average garden slug, I think I felt pretty crap at the time, and 'good' was hardly a word I'd have used to describe anything.

'We can't let you stay like this for much longer. Mr Deakin just won't put up with it.' He continued after a moment. 'He'll write a report, then the doctor will come, then they'll take you away… and that won't be good for anyone, now will it?'

Then, after saying, what I reckon he'd been sent along to say, prison officer Jimmy, his knees creaking as his long legs straightened, stood up directly over me. Momentarily his shadow, softening the harsh light in my cell quite nicely, seemed somehow comforting I remember. I think that maybe I moved a little. Maybe I breathed a slight sigh. I don't think I said anything, but suddenly, Officer Jimmy was back down on his haunches. The shadow was gone. He leaned towards me. I felt his hands grip my shoulders.

'For Christ's sake man… Deal with it…' He shook me once, then twice, and then he pulled away again, looking at his hands as if they were suddenly soiled, he sniffed the air around me. 'God...' He said. 'You're starting to smell like bloody Eddy Edwards already.' Then, before I realised it, he was gone.

Sometime, either before or after prison officer Jimmy's visit, I don't suppose it matters which, a man, who I later learned to like very much and even trust (a fellow happy camper on my corridor it turned out), brought me some food. It wasn't much, just an apple, a couple of rich tea biscuits (one of them was broken), and a half-eaten packet of Trebor extra strong mints. The man didn't say a word. He must have tiptoed into my cell unnoticed by the prison officers; put the apple on my bed, the biscuits on the edge of the metal chest of drawers, and the extra strong mints on the floor immediately in front of me. Never having even been introduced, in my experience of prison etiquette, it was a rare kind thought.

Of course, the thing that I remember most vividly of all from that time is what I think of now as 'the nothing'. I'd never experienced anything like it before and I hope that I never have to experience anything like it again. Thankfully, most people never have to experience it at all. It is quite simply, in my opinion at least, one of the most disgusting things for a human being to have to endure. 'The nothing' is not something that can be easily explained, it is, after all, sort of... nothingy... a waking emotionless sleep perhaps, a bland-middleness, a couldn't-carelessness, an emptiness, a 'Greydom'. When 'the nothing' first took me in, it consumed every part of my very being. While it is easy enough to understand the idea of misery or fear or even abject loneliness, all dreadful of course, with 'the nothing' well... there's nothing much to get a handle on. I couldn't tell you that I felt suicidal or even especially wretched, because really I didn't. Somehow, it was even worse than that. I just felt empty I guess... nothing.

Then, one morning, or maybe, one afternoon, or evening, honestly I've no idea which, I woke up with a start, no longer on the floor, but snugly tucked into my grey prison bed and choking on the remnants of a half-sucked extra strong mint. I've no idea how I got there, just as I don't remember ever popping the sweet into my mouth. Actually, it really pissed me off. Neither of us has ever been a fan of peppermint. However, on waking, coughing and spluttering as I mentioned, the anger we felt towards that tiny piece of minty confectionery was out of all proportion to the small crime the wretched thing had actually committed. Before I knew quite what I was doing, although only half conscious, I'd flung my blanket aside, spat the sugary sweet clear across my cell, then chased it to ground, stamping it to dust a dozen times over.

'What the hell is going on in there?'

The voice belonged to good ol' Senior Officer Lance Deakin, and surprisingly, he sounded more apprehensive than angry.

I didn't reply, instead, I gave the nasty sweet an extra strong kicking in the direction of the door. As a dozen or so tiny fragments of white mint chips disappeared under the threshold, Mr Deakin's distorted eyeball appeared in the small spy-hole in my door.

'What?' I said, glowering angrily.

'Nothing.' Deakin said, pushing the door open and shrugging his shoulders.

'I'm hungry.' I said.

'Well whose fault is that? You haven't eaten anything for ages. It serves you bloody right.' Deakin said.

I'm not going to pretend that from that point on it was all plain sailing, because it was not. In fact, it took me several weeks and many hours of help from the prison psychiatrist to shake off the spectre of Winston Churchill's depressive 'Black dog', and then several months more to fully straighten my head. If one good thing came out of my, thankfully 'mini', breakdown, then it was that somewhere along the line, some wonderful person, an officer perhaps but I think more likely my doctor, decided that until I'd sorted myself out and learned to become more accepting of my new lot, I would be allowed to remain in that first little cell all by myself. I can't begin to describe to you the relief I felt when they first told me. Not least because while I'd recognized that the Big Edward Ewan Edwards 'get down and dirty' approach to gaining the privacy that I so badly needed, might have been an effective option for him, the prospect quite revolted me.

Now, thank God, for the time being at least, I could sleep both undisturbed and wearing clean underpants.

Three days after hauling myself from the brink of my own personal pit of despair, on the last Thursday of that November, my cousin and her son, Tristan, came to visit.

I got the call in my cell at about one o'clock. Mr Deakin came to tell me personally. I'd just finished a bowl of vegetable soup - a clever recipe, probably nutritious enough, but one with the flavour somehow completely removed – and I was feeling reasonably relaxed, when the senior prison officer knocked on the door.

'Ahem.' Deakin coughed, rather than actually saying anything intelligible.

'Hello.' I called back.

The lock clicked, the door buzzed and then swung open slowly and Mr Deakin peered inside.

'Oh… I see you're alone,' He said. 'I wondered if the Doc was still with you.'

'No.' I said. 'I think he trusts me to eat on my own now. He told me that he'd look in again later.'

'A good man… Doc Metcalf.' Deakin said solemnly. 'A rare sort in here… you're a lucky chap.'

I nodded, then picked up my moulded plastic tray, my moulded plastic bowl, and my moulded plastic spoon, and placed them on the top of my weird moulded plastic toilet. Since my ignominious self-crumpling, followed, I reckoned, by a word or two about the negative impact that incarcerate suicides have on the public's perception of the prison service from my particular prison's psychiatrist the handsome Dr Martin Metcalf, Deakin's attitude towards me seemed to have softened some. He leaned forward as if asking for permission to come into my room. I nodded again. He stepped inside and then removed his cap.

'Well, I have good news… you have visitors.' He said. 'Relatives I believe. A Mr Tristan Blandy and his mother, I don't have her name, but… well… a rather attractive woman, Mrs Blandy I suppose. They're waiting for you now in the visitors' ready rooms. I'll take you down whenever you're ready.'

The walk to the bottom of my prison through the various security gates took almost fifteen minutes. When I arrived at the door to the visitors' rooms, the clock on the wall outside showed, one, twenty-three and ten seconds... tic tic. Standing, waiting for the door to be opened, I glanced down at my feet and then at my clothes, at the soft plain round toed leather shoes, at the 'previously enjoyed' navy cotton trousers, at the almost worn-out blue sweatshirt. At that moment I'd never felt more like a prisoner. I nearly turned around. I very nearly asked to go back to my cell. Thankfully, before I could think myself any further downhill, Deakin opened the door.

'Oh my, my, my, look at you.' My cousin shrieked as soon as she saw me from the farthest side of the room. She covered her mouth with her hands in horror. Suddenly, the visiting room fell silent. All eyes were on my cousin... and then on me. An instant later, my cousin was up from her seat and rushing towards me. 'So pale and so thin, and those dark circles around your eyes, and your hair it's so long and... oh. 'She stopped and shook her head. 'Just look at you, just look at you.' She repeated again, and then again, as she bustled her way between the tables and chairs, knocking one poor visitor this way and another that.

A moment on and I was got. Two plump arms engulfed me. My cousin's warm rosy cheeks pushed hard against mine.

'You need a shave...' she said, squeezing me harder then finally pulling away, '...or at least, the use of a decent razor.' Then she stepped back and took my face in her hands.

'It's so good to see you. They told me you've not been so well... and now I can see. Me and Tris... well... we've been so worried.' Then she looked over to her son. I'd noticed several inmates warily eyeing his hulking physique when I came into the room. Tristan was sitting patiently if not inconspicuously on a small settee in the far corner of the visitors' room, grinning at me. My cousin shook her head and then narrowed her eyes and scrunched her lips together. 'Well at least, I have been worried. Now come on over here. Let's sit down. Let's talk. I brought you cake, your favourite Lemon Drizzle. Will they let you eat it? Tristan says probably not. They made me put it into a locker with my handbag and Tristan's penknife. Maybe, if I asked the nice man in the hat?' My cousin pointed and then smiled at Mr Deakin, who promptly flushed and looked away, and then quickly scuttled out through the way we'd just come in.

Eventually, after several minutes more of nonstop chatter and hair ruffling and cheek tweaking, my cousin and I made it back across the visitors' room to where Tristan, having moved to a table and chairs, was waiting for us.

'Hullo matey.' My cousin's son, my second cousin said when finally we sat down. He stood up, then reached his great hand across the table and grasped mine. 'You look crap.' He said. We shook hands firmly and then embraced in a very manly and awkward fashion.

'Thanks Tris.' I said. Then he put me down.

As it turned out, Tristan's and his mother's surprise visit on that particular Thursday afternoon helped me out in more ways than at the time I could ever have dreamed it might. As I'm sure, you can imagine, after my unfortunate introduction to the prison, just seeing a familiar and friendly face gave me quite a boost, and despite a lull in my feelings when my diminutive family made ready to leave, ordinarily, one might have thought, that would have been good enough. However, just as my cousin stood up to say good bye and was brushing at the very ample front of what I must say was her snugly fitting woollen dress – she'd scrubbed up pretty well that day I seem to remember - Mr Deakin came back into the room. Their eyes met straight away. My cousin didn't waste a beat. Quick as a flash, she was moving across the floor, her hips swaying from side to side as she sashayed between the tables. With bosoms to the fore, she fairly charged at poor Mr Deakin. Despite her years, when my cousin turned it on, as she was without doubt now doing, the power of her sex was a revelation to me. The eyes of the room were suddenly all on her. My senior prison officer didn't stand a chance.

'Now you look like the kind of man who simply *must* be in charge.' She said, her eyes flirting outrageously, she stopped immediately in front of him and provocatively straightened herself up. For an instant I was afraid that my cousin was about to grab the wiry senior prison officer and plant her lips firmly on his chops. Thankfully, the moment passed with no more than a heaving breath and a long look passing between them.

'I wonder…' I heard her say in a lowered sultry voice, '…if you have the authority to allow me to give my young cousin over there,' she pointed at me but kept her eyes firmly on Mr Deakin, 'a slice of his very most favourite cake.'

Quite unbelievably, perhaps even pathetically, Mr Deakin fell under her spell headfirst, hook, line, and sinker, straight to the bottom… well I reckon the thought of it at least… that is… the thought of my cousins, pleasantly large, well formed, curvaceous and I'm sure, wonderfully womanly, bottom.

Ten minutes later, a mesmerised, dare I say it, a giggly Mr Deakin, my cousin, Tristan, and I were sitting cosily, drinking tea and eating large slices of deliciously moist Lemon Drizzle cake in a small, and although obviously undergoing redecoration, reasonably comfortable ante-room only a short way along the corridor from the visitors' room.

Good enough yet?

Well not quite.

When we had finished our tea and chats, and at last my visitors were required by regulations to leave, as Tristan and I followed my cousin and my senior prison officer the short distance to the security gate, we passed two other officers who were escorting a brute of a man back in the direction we'd just come. His head bowed and eyes glowering, the chap reminded me of Cindy Dobson's husband and Tristan's friend, Mr Ripper, only he was even uglier, and with longer matted hair and nastier scars. Caught in a narrow passage between a wire mesh barrier and a line of scaffold poles, as we were ushered to one side to let the men past, Tristan reached a hand out and grabbed hold of the ugly chaps arm. I thought he'd gone mad, but then as cool as you like, my cousin's son leaned forward and said:

'How's it hanging John?'

Obviously surprised, ugly John turned quickly and shot Tristan an angry glance. Then, an instant later, a flash of recognition crossed his face and the brute stopped in his tracks jolting his two guards to a sudden halt. Both officers harrumphed but neither of them seemed keen to make a fuss. Ignoring them completely, John didn't so much speak his reply as growl it.

'Good thanks Tris.' He nodded easily, any trace of anger falling away. 'I didn't know you were in here lad?'

'Just visiting today John, family… my cousin here actually.' Tristan said, and then he rested a hand on my shoulder, looked ugly John squarely in the eye, and added. 'Keep a watch mate.'

John looked down at me, pursed his lips, scratched his chin, and then nodded slowly.

'Family Tris…? Take it as read son; I'll put the word out.' He said.

A moment later, the brute and the two officers moved on. Strangely, although I never saw him again, not once during my entire stay with Her Majesty, I have to say, that after his promise to Tristan, neither did I see any more dining tables hurtling in my direction.

Tristan, his mother and I were standing by the visitors' security gate with Mr Deakin. My cousin was hugging me, Tristan was whispering over her shoulder in my ear, telling me, that from now on, everything would be okay, and Mr Deakin was watching the three of us. Something in the bemused expression on my senior prison officer's face, and from the cake crumbs on his chin, made me wonder if he knew what the heck had just happened. Tea and chats one minute, heavy inmate politics the next, right or wrong, or just plain odd, I don't think he had a clue, I certainly didn't.

'I'll be back soon… you start eating properly now… do you hear me?' My cousin called as she disappeared through the security gate. Turning at the last minute, she smiled at me, and then she winked at Mr Deakin. Neither of us responded, although I did give her a final wave. I remember feeling quite dazed. I think that in a strange way after all the excitement I needed to get back to the safe four walls of my own little room.

CHAPTER THIRTY-TWO

I ate my first proper meal, after my inadvertent fast, sometime later that evening with my cousins reprimanding words still ringing in my ears. As it happened, despite my preference for privacy, I ate it in the dining room with a hundred or so other inmates, and more specifically, in the immediate company of Edward Ewan Edwards. None of it was intentional.

When I got back to my room after visiting, I found Dr Metcalf waiting for me. He was sitting on my bed leafing through some papers that he must have brought with him. Keen to reach my home from home, I shoved the door open a touch too hard and rather barged in. I made him jump, as if I'd caught him doing something he shouldn't have been. Dr Metcalf, or Martin, as he always asked me to call him, stood up quickly and dropped a few of the papers that he'd been reading on to the floor. Just two or three sheets, all face up. When I crouched down to help pick them up, he tried to shoo me away as if he was chastening a naughty dog. It was the first time since our thrice-daily chats began that he'd spoken to me other than gently or kindly.

'Don't touch, leave them alone. Let me deal with it.' He snapped authoritatively. 'I can manage, leave them be, okay!' However, I could tell instantly that it wasn't okay. By the tone of his voice, I could tell that all of a sudden, my usually *ever so patient* doctor, was now very agitated indeed. I gulped hard, and still wobbly after all, I actually found myself fighting against tears. Despite his curtness and his obvious wish for me to do otherwise, somehow through the upset, I couldn't help but stare at the scattered paper on the floor. Now it's an odd thing, but I remember that when I was young and at school, sometimes I could spend an hour reading one sentence on a blackboard and still never get the gist. The white chalk marks might as well have been Egyptian hieroglyphics. Yet right then, with Dr Metcalf flapping around my cell like a pigeon that had dropped the juiciest worm into a pile of cat poo, just from the briefest glimpse of those few apparently insignificant sheets of paper, I twigged the fullest nuance of every scribbled word.

A name... my name, phrases like 'Self absorbed', and 'Self obsessed', words like 'irrational', and 'delusional', and 'suspicious' and 'psychosis', all glowed far too brightly. All there, all jumbled in blue Biro, and yet somehow, at that moment at least, all perfectly clear.

I told Dr Metcalf that I wanted to rest, that I'd had a busy afternoon with my family, and a nap would be grand. Either he believed me, or he didn't, I can't say that I cared very much. After he'd gathered his papers, and I think had convinced himself that I hadn't seen anything of any particular significance, he left me alone... and I was just fine.

At six thirty two, having slept for a couple of hours, exercised my bowels, washed my hands and face, and cleaned and flossed my teeth, I left my room for the dining room.

I spotted Edward Ewan Edwards sitting alone at a table one row in and two across from the entrance to the hall. The bulk of his enormous rolling back was towards me and shielded my view of the table. I carried my tray from the serving hatch straight to his table and not to any other, not through any need to dine with him in particular, but more because of the guaranteed spare seat, and at the time - although I couldn't have explained why - it looked to be the most comfortable place in the room. Naturally, I sat a good distance from him. Actually, for obvious reasons - nasal safety primarily – I sat as far away from him as possible, at the very end of the table. When I first took my seat, big bad Edward ignored me. I said 'Hullo', politely of course, and I probably smiled, but I remember he didn't reply. When I looked at his plate, although his serving was far larger than my own, I saw that coincidently, we'd chosen the same spaghetti option from the menu. The alternative, which I guess we'd both sensibly avoided, being a scoop of disgusting brown gloop pie with a detachable cardboard puff pastry lid.

Edward wasn't a twirler like me. Instead, he chopped his spaghetti into short sticky maggot sized pieces with the side of his fork, and then shovelled large disembodied chunks of the resultant mess greedily into his mouth. Edward Ewan Edwards' mouth was big, his plate was big, and indeed,

Edward's plateful of spaghetti was at least three times the size of any other that I'd seen. When I first sat down, I wondered how he'd managed to get such a large portion. Waiting in line at the serving hatch it had soon become obvious to me that neither hierarchy, nor fear, nor favour, determined the size of anyone's meal, the portions were dished out so haphazardly, and by such apathetic trustee servers, that I'd felt lucky just to get what I'd asked for. As it happened, the answer to the riddle arrived only shortly after I took my seat when, rather than crossing the hall to the waste-bins, the first of a regular trickle of lazy fellow diners mooched up to Big Ed's table, conveniently close to the exit, and promptly dumped his leftovers onto Edward's plate. I couldn't believe my eyes, it was disgusting, and neither could I believe it when, rather than baulk at the affront, my tablemate actually nodded his thanks and continued tucking hungrily in to his freshly (or perhaps not) enhanced meal. Quite incredibly, during the half hour or so that I spent in the dining room that evening, the stack of plates at the end of our table rose to fifteen and I'm sure I left before the last arrived.

Sometime during our meal, maybe when the plate stack was only seven or eight high (I wasn't counting closely and the supply of leftovers was steady), I thought I'd take another bash at communicating with the big chap. As the spaghetti was actually unexpectedly good, I plumped for the quality of the cuisine as a positive starting point.

'I've always loved the Bologna region.' I began with a cheery tone. 'I once stayed with a friend who had a holiday home there. I remember eating Spaghetti Bolognaise in a small Ristorante on the Piazza Maggiore. Do you know? I think this may almost be as good. I wonder if the chef here is Italian?'

Okay, so it was probably a silly suggestion, but I had to try something. I'm sure that if the conversation had progressed, as it should have, I might have mentioned the odd negative. The lack of ambience or a decent wine for example, but as Edward Ewan Edwards remained entirely unmoved by my attempt at polite chat - he didn't even look up from his food - I gave up on the Italian job and thought I'd try another tack. Perhaps keep it simpler, with a straightforward question.

'Did you have any visitors today?' I tried. I knew as soon as I opened my mouth that I'd picked another duff one. I knew already that apart from when it came to eating, Big Ed was virtually a recluse, and then one had to ask oneself, why on earth would anybody in their right mind want to visit such a greedy smelly blob. From Edward's reaction, it seemed that my estimation was about right; he ignored me completely, keeping his face firmly buried in his plate of spaghetti.

Stubborn to the last, rather than admit defeat and simply eat the remainder of my meal in silence, I decided that I'd give big Edward Ewan Edwards one final chance, and this time, although surprisingly I was enjoying the food, I had the daft notion to use my dinner as a tempter.

'Gosh, this is filling. I don't think I can manage another mouthful.' I sighed, rubbing my tummy more theatrically than was absolutely necessary I'm sure. 'I don't suppose you could help me out could you?'

Well, I might as well have waved the entire culinary contents of a naughty Nigella cookbook under the big fellow's nose. What I'd thought Big Ed would see through as an obvious ploy worked like a magic charm. Immediately, Edward Ewan Edwards' head was up from his plate, his eyes were alert, and although he didn't actually stop munching, I reckoned that I had least 50% of his attention.

'Ahh, it's you.' He said between chomps, suddenly taking notice of me as if I'd only just sat down. 'I haven't seen you for a while. I hope you're feeling better than last time.'

'Well yes I am much better, thank you very much.' I said.

I suppose that having vomited over the poor chap within only a few seconds of our first encounter, I shouldn't have been surprised that he asked how I was feeling, he was probably concerned that I might do it again. Absently, I took my fork and twirled a mouthful of spaghetti into a neat coil and I was about to pop it into my mouth, when quick as a flash, Edward grabbed my wrist. The instant he moved closer a nasty waft of stagnant air filled my nostrils. I recoiled automatically. He didn't seem to notice.

'I thought you were giving that to me.' He said.

'Oh… yes of course.' I said, dropping my fork as if suddenly it carried an electric charge. 'Of course you can have it. I really am most dreadfully full.' I lied, while trying not to inhale. I pushed my plate towards him and only then realised how little I'd actually eaten.

'You'll never grow to be big and strong, will you?' Edward said. 'Not like me.' Then he looked down at himself and somehow managed to puff himself up even bigger.

'No.' I said, and I wanted to add, 'Thank god.' but fortunately good sense squished the temptation and instead I leaned back in my chair and for some insane reason I asked him if he'd mind very much if I joined him for dinner again tomorrow.

This time my question made the round man pause, he thought for a moment, tapped his chin with his fork, and then he cocked his head to one side and said. 'I'm not usually much of a one for other people's company, but you don't seem a bad sort, so you may do as you like.' As he was speaking, Edward was slopping the remainder of my spaghetti on top of his. Then, as soon as he'd finished, his head went down again. I took what he'd said as a vague affirmative and his getting back to the more serious business as my cue to leave.

Sometime later, when I was back in my room, while waiting for the locks to clunk shut for the night, I stood in front of my small shaving mirror - somewhere away with my own particular fairies - looking at my reflection. Although I wasn't smiling, and despite the various ups and downs of the day, and my dreadfully outgrown hair, I felt better that evening than I had since the day I'd arrived at my particular prison, almost exactly a week before.

'On balance…' I said to myself aloud, naively I suppose now. '…I think that today has probably been a good day.'

I wish I hadn't said it now obviously. I wish I'd kept my big mouth shut.

'Are we barking bloody mad?' My reflection snapped back instantly, and with a snarl and with a venom in my voice that quite shook me.

I stepped back.

I blinked my eyes wide open.

I forgot the dreadful state of my hair.

'No…' I said, gathering myself defiantly although speaking quite calmly. 'No! Actually I don't think so, in fact, today I don't feel mad at all.'

'On balance a good day? Are you quite serious? We're in bloody jail you fool. You got us caught remember… banged up… nicked. A good day indeed, pah! The only good day that either of us is likely to have anytime soon will be the day that YOU get us out of here.'

'I didn't get us caught… that was you. That was your fault.' I said, and I wagged my finger into the mirror to show myself just how angry I'd made me.

'My fault… My fault?' My reflection screeched back at me, waving my arms in the air. 'How bloody dare you? After everything I've done for you, after putting up with your soppy moods and that pathetic episode last week, you try to throw the blame at me. You must be mad! Look at you. you must be barking mad. If you ask me we were better off when you were dosed up on medication.'

Now that really pissed me off.

'How dare you.' I said, speaking slowly and deliberately through tightly clenched teeth. 'I've a good mind to shut you up forever.' I waved my fist into the mirror.

Just then, in the midst of the row, possibly, when I was considering smashing the wretched glass and finishing my reflection off once and for all, I felt a prickle run up my spine and had the feeling that I was being watched. I spun from the mirror to see Dr Martin Metcalf looking at me through a crack in my cell door. Our eyes met. A moment later, whether cued by him or just through an electronic coincidence, my door closed, the locks clunked shut and lights in my room blinked out. I ran to the spy-hole in time to see my sorry mind-shrinker's dishevelled head silhouetted against the bright corridor lights behind him. Too late, he ducked away, embarrassed by his snivelling prying nose, I hoped. Kicking the door, I screamed something bad.

I went to bed straight away. The lights in the corridor faded until the glow from my spy-hole eventually blinked out. Having lulled myself into a false sense of hope, I let the darkness and I think, more tears, overwhelm me. I wrapped myself in my blanket like a Swiss roll, so tightly that I could barely breathe. When sleep took me in it was both hot, and sticky, and fidgety and cold.

The night was again dreamless.

Early in the morning, when I decided to wake up, I had black circles under my eyes, my face was puffy, and both my hair and my blanket were wet.

'Soppy moods... indeed.' I thought aloud and winced. The words my reflection had used the evening before, and the way I'd spat them, stung me. Rattling and clattering against the inside of my head, each syllable like a shiny ball bearing and my skull an arcade pinball machine.

...and the worst thing about it? You might ask... was that once again I knew that I was right.

'On balance... a good day...' indeed... Pah! What a fool I was.

If I'd learned nothing else, dammit... surely, when it comes to me, I should have known by then that I was usually right.

Although my second week in prison was a marginal improvement on the first, on the first three mornings following my dreadful falling out with myself, I woke with a heavy heart knowing that the day ahead would likely be a struggle, and broadly speaking as each day progressed I didn't disappoint me. However, almost immediately after my cell door clicked unlocked on the fourth morning - the morning of the first Monday in December - I was surprised, when, instead of hearing Mr Deakin's cheery tones (I jest), a deeper, more resonant baritone voice bade me 'Good morning' and asked 'May I come in?'.

Unfortunately, I was sitting on my weird plastic toilet at the time, waiting for my bowels to engage the AM movement, while I absently wondered if I could brighten the lavatorial contraption by drawing patterns on the cistern with different coloured marker pens. It probably wouldn't have worked. Anyway… caught unprepared and although eager to meet the person behind the creamy baritone voice, preferring to do so with my trousers around my waist rather than around my ankles, I shouted 'Hold on'. Then, immediately afterwards, remembering the polite prison codeword for such tricky situations, I added 'Business!'

Immediately I used the 'B' word, the door to my room stopped moving and tentative fingers reached in and swiftly pulled it to.

'No problem.' Came a muffled reply from behind the door. 'I'll just wait for you out here.'

'I'll be with you in just a moment.' I called again.

Of course, the distraction entirely ruined the scope of my ablutions. I gave up trying almost immediately. …And so, only a minute or two later, having quickly washed, found myself a nice pair of French navy trousers, a freshly laundered pastel aqua sweatshirt, and donned a pair of rugged sensible black leather shoes (it was winter after all), feeling brave and reasonably ready to face the day, I stepped outside my cell to meet my gentleman caller.

'Good morning and I'm sorry to have kept you.' I said, before I'd even looked at my visitor. My initial surprise at hearing the unfamiliar voice was immediately compounded, when I found a fellow inmate standing outside my door and not the prison official that I'd expected.

'Hullo.' He said, turning towards me. The man was about my height and build, with a mop of black curly hair and he wore a gold ring in each ear. I saw straight away that he had a kind face, a sort of lived-in Will Smith just with normal human sized ears. 'I'm really sorry I bothered you so early.' He continued. 'I just wondered how you were doing, that's all.'

'Oh!' I said, taken aback. Although my experience was limited, so far I hadn't found prisons to be the most caring of places. 'Well, thank you very much… I'm getting there I guess.' I looked at him and smiled. He smiled back.

'I had my share of troubles when I first got here too…' He said. 'You know… depression, bad thoughts, that kind of stuff. That's why I came to see you the other day. When I heard you were in trouble,' He tapped his temple with his forefinger. 'I thought I might be able to help… but boy-oh-boy, you were down low, too deep for me. Deakin and the others said that I was wasting my time. But I just wanted you to know that at least someone in this place gives a damn, that's why I left you the apple and the biscuits, it was all I had but…'

'…and the extra strong mints.' I said, suddenly realising that here was the fellow happy-camper who'd tiptoed so kindly into my cell when I'd been poorly. 'That was you? That was so kind. Thank you so much. I think it really helped.'

The man smiled and held out his hand.

'Phillip Johnston.' He introduced himself. I shook his hand firmly and then looked at him. The name seemed oddly familiar and for a moment, I thought his smile did too. However, although a jolt of déjà vu flicked me full on the nose, no solid memory came to mind.

'I'm at the other end of 'B', apart from the fat guy and you, until they finish the refurb' the only other single occupancy cell on the landing.' Phillip said, and then with a half shrug and a look that I reckoned was tinged with embarrassment and regret, he added; 'I get angry sometimes if I don't get my own way, so mostly I'm best left on my own.'

'Well Phillip.' I said. 'Unless you'd prefer to be left alone now, do you fancy some breakfast? By the clock, we have less than twenty minutes.'

'I was heading down that way.' He said. 'But the thing is… I've seen you eating with the fat guy these last few days. Don't get me wrong, I've nothing against big people and I do have a strong stomach, it's just that I don't think my nose is up to him this morning.'

I laughed out loud at that… and I think it may have been the first genuine laugh that I'd squeezed out since lunchtime on the day before my arrest. It felt surprisingly good.

Over the next couple of weeks, for me at least, the incarcerate life in my particular prison improved quite a bit. With thanks, albeit begrudgingly, to Dr Metcalf and I think to

HMP's ongoing refurbishment work at my prison, I still had a room of my own. Thanks to Tristan, I enjoyed relative safety among the livelier residents. And rather untypically, thanks to me, I seemed to have made a couple of new friends.

While Phillip Johnston and big Ed E Edwards never got on with each other very well, I found the distraction of either of their company very helpful. I might eat breakfast with one, dinner with the other, and depending on the sensitivity of Phillip's nostrils and Big Ed's sociability, if I could manoeuvre them to opposite ends of a table, just occasionally, as a motley trio, we might eat lunch together.

Phillip turned out to be an exceptional chess player, a surprise thinker in fact. During one recreation hour in the games room, a daily treat that followed lunch on Tuesdays and Fridays, and dinner on every other day of the week, while trying to convince me that I should read more broadly and substantially, he checkmated me three times in three short successive games. While I'd never been especially good on the chequered board, I'd never been a good loser either. It shouldn't have bothered me, but alas, although I didn't let it spoil our burgeoning friendship, I'm afraid it did. In fact, I'm afraid that I found losing so badly, dreadfully irritating. I left the chessboard with my face long and my shoulders slouched.

Providentially (as it turned out) on that particular day Big Ed had been watching us play, and I think, secretly jealous of the attention that I'd been giving Phillip, he was quietly pleased with the sorry outcome. Without saying a word, as I slunk deflated from the table Edward patted my arm and then, in what I took as a gesture of consolation, he handed me his most prized possession, his iPod. I knew what it was of course, I'd seen clients using them in my salon and apart from when he was eating Ed's ears were rarely empty, but I'd not actually played with one before. I looked at the odd little silver/grey box quizzically. Never having been a gadget man it didn't look much to me. I shrugged my shoulders. Edward raised a large chubby finger and gestured for me to be patient, and then he reached for his toy. After a moment's fiddling with the button wheel mechanism, Ed shoved the tiny ear-thingies unceremoniously into my ears, and then he squeezed the front of the iPod and smiled. Almost instantly, the rich thundering opening bars of Rimsky Korsakov's Scheherazade filled my head.

The miniature – and suddenly wonderful - gizmo was a revelation, quite fantastic. A while later, when my mood had mellowed, and our hour of social recreation was up, when Edward managed to prise the thing from my grip, he explained that somehow beneath the marvellous machines diminutive veneers, he had managed to cram an amazing two hundred hours of music. From Opera to jazz, from Classical to rock, pop and reggae, when Phillip finally gave up on the chessboard and in my delight I told him, I think even he was impressed. I decided right there and then to add the natty gadget to the very top of my Father Christmas's good boy list for that year, even above the shampoo and conditioner that I'd begged my cousin to send.

My cousin and Tristan came to visit me again, twice in fact, one scheduled and one a surprise. On the first visit, on the HMP scheduled second Thursday of the month, although my cousin may have been sitting at our table, I'm not entirely convinced that she had come to see me at all. It seemed that for most of the visit her attention was taken up, not with reassuring family chatter with her poor inmate cousin as one might reasonably have expected of a prison visitor, but almost entirely with nodding, and winking, and flirting with Mr Deakin, who very conveniently remained posted on duty close by. It was all dreadfully cringey. Believe it or not, when it came time for Tristan to take his mother home (which wasn't soon enough in my opinion), I'm sure that she and Mr Deakin blew each other a kiss. Right there in the visiting room, in front of everyone, and all after just one previous meeting. She told me that it was my senior officer's bashful grin that did it for her. Bashful grin indeed, if I'd had any 'Nick-Cred', it would have fallen through the floor.

In some ways, the third visit was even worse. Less than a week later, although I had no idea that they were coming to see me, it was quickly obvious that Mr Deakin certainly had. I reckon he'd spruced himself up for the occasion, polished his buttons and boots, and even combed his hair. When my senior officer escorted me downstairs, a courtesy that was unusual in itself, we left a wafting trail of cheap aftershave in the air behind us. It caused quite a stir on the landing, heads turned as we passed by, catcalls and odd looks; I'd never been wolf whistled so much in my life. It didn't seem to faze my escort, but then, I reckoned that his mind was elsewhere.

When I saw Tristan leading my cousin into the empty visiting room, I guessed straight away that she had done much the same as Mr Deakin. Rather than scruffed up into a shabby old scrunchy band as it most often was, that afternoon my cousin had washed and curled her flaxen hair and had left it falling loosely around her shoulders. She was wearing a snugly fitting scarlet dress. She wore make-up on her face, and looking back now, I think that in the few days since I'd seen her, somehow, she might even have lost a few pounds… And perhaps most importantly of all, my cousin's eyes sparkled. Tristan and I exchanged a glance that turned into a smirk. He and I sat down at a table towards the back of the otherwise empty room. My cousin did not. Instead, she walked straight past us, straight to Mr Deakin, and then planted a kiss, smack on the senior prison officer's chops.

Well my goodness… my cousin the forward hussy, I reckon it's always the quiet ones, but who'd have thought it… what a girl.

Later that day, after dinner, when I was back in my room, but before lock-down, Mr Deakin came to see me. He was out of uniform and although he looked somehow pleasanter in his civvies, he also looked worried. Unusually, he closed my cell door behind him, and then he sat down on the end of my bed.

'Is this going to be awkward?' He said.

'What?' I said. …my God I can be dim sometimes.

'I could move to another wing… I'll probably have to move to another wing, maybe even to another prison.'

'Why?' I asked. …I told you that I could be dim.

'When people find out.'

'Oh… I see… about you and my cousin… Well you needn't worry about me, I'm not about to tell anyone.'

'What?' Deakin said. Now it was his turn to be dim.

'Think about it Mr Deakin.' I said. 'It's not rocket science. This place is tough enough for me on the best of days, the last thing I need is for everyone to know that my cousin is shagging their favourite screw.'

'Shush.' Deakin pushed his finger against his lips and looked over to the door. 'Not so loud.' He whispered.

'Whoops.' I said. 'I'm sorry.'

'That's alright, I'm just edgy I suppose.' He said. 'Look… let's just say that I owe you one… okay?'

After Deakin had gone, I made ready for bed. I had a wee, washed my hands and face, cleaned my teeth and squeezed a spot or two in the mirror. I thought I was safe enough. My reflection had been remarkably quiet since our row, so I wasn't expecting me to say anything. However, as I wiped a small gooey smear from the glass, I heard my voice all too clearly.

'Quite a result.' I said.

I looked deeper into the mirror, into my eyes. My reflection winked at me.

'Perhaps things are looking up.' It said.

Although I didn't say anything back, towards the end of that third week, I had to agree with myself.

CHAPTER THIRTY-THREE

Precisely one month after I arrived at my particular prison, on a chilly Christmas Eve afternoon actually, just over a week after my cousins surprise visit, Mr Deakin came to my room and told me that I had another surprise visitor, two of them in fact. I think I was quite excited; it was nearly Christmas after all. However rather than being gift bearing family or friends as I might have hoped, my new visitors turned out to be two policemen, who, because of the ongoing construction work downstairs, had arranged to see me, not in an interview room as would ordinarily have been the norm, but actually in my cell. Although I didn't know it at the time, my surprise visitors - a young sergeant with thick glasses and an annoying tic that contorted the whole right side of his face, and a silver-haired but otherwise not unattractive inspector – were not just any old police officers either, but two senior members of some sort of internal investigations department.

Too important to wait until after the holiday season, I don't know quite what I expected of my constabulary visitors when they appeared at my door, mulled wine and chats maybe, or some nice warm mince pies and a natter about baby Jesus and all things Christmassy. Silly, they were policemen after all, and thus, I should have guessed that all they'd really want to do was what policemen seem to love best… poke their noses into my business and ask questions… lots and lots of nasty niggling questions. If I'm honest, forget my earlier whimsies, I'm sure that baby Jesus wouldn't mind, when my two policemen first introduced themselves, I thought I knew exactly what they wanted. I'd thought it likely that they'd come to see me in the hope that now, having had some time to reflect, at last I'd come clean over the fateful and unfortunate incident with Marjorie Warton. What had really happened? Where had I hidden her body? I still find myself trembling anxiously at the memory of that battered red wheelie-bin spinning in the jaws of the snarling metal monster at Mr Ripper's dump. Facing the two men across my small grey bedroom, feeling small, and certainly alone, but with absolutely no intention of telling them anything new at all, I steeled myself.

As it happened, I needn't have worried. Although, after an initial pussyfooting, gentle probing, their questions gradually came thicker and faster than I found entirely comfortable, I have to say that throughout the entire interview both policemen were thoroughly charming and not at all typical of their sort. It turned out that my visitors weren't actually terribly interested in revisiting any of my little mistakes after all. It seemed that what they really wanted to discuss was my relationship with my favourite Mr Nosey, Detective Sergeant Dennis Sapsead. From what I could glean, reading between the lines of what were mostly not terribly subtle questions, I quickly realised that dear, diligent, but sadly overly meddlesome Dennis seemed to be in some kind of trouble. Of course, speaking only from my own point of view, I reckoned that the man was probably deserving of anything horrid that the world sought to throw away.

Nevertheless, you know me, always keen to help. What better way to assist the authorities in weeding out a wrong'un, than to speak up the moment one has an inkling that something or, more importantly, that someone, is not quite right.

'In a gay bar in Soho I think.'

I said flippantly, and in hindsight perhaps stupidly, in reply to the eventual question. 'Remind us… when and where did you first meet Detective Sapsead?'

In my defence, at that moment, I couldn't quickly recall where or when I had met the wretched chap. So, not yet realising the importance of whatever I might say, and not wanting to disappoint or let either of the policemen down, quick as a flash, I made up the daft answer thinking that it might add to the fun. I didn't expect them to take me seriously. In fact, I was certain that they knew the answer all along. While the younger policeman, the sergeant with the glasses, raised half a smile, and for a second or two at least stopped twitching, the older chap just looked at me sadly and then like a disappointed grandfather or aged uncle he slowly shook his head.

'No... I'm sorry.' I said, not only suddenly feeling foolish, but also at last remembering when I had first met the creep.

'He came to see me in the salon a few weeks after Christmas last year. He was enquiring about a client of mine who had gone missing.'

'Marjorie Warton?' The older policeman responded immediately.

'Yes,' I said. Alas, just hearing the Wart hog's name spoken aloud instantly made me feel uncomfortable. I squirmed in my seat. Crossed and then re-crossed my legs. Definitely dodgy body language, I knew, but I couldn't help myself.

'...and how would you say Detective Sapsead behaved towards you?' He asked.

'How did he behave?' I said.

'Yes, was Detective Sapsead polite and friendly, or was he rude and aggressive?'

'Well... he was okay... I suppose.' I said. 'I could tell he didn't like me though.'

'Now why do you say that?'

'I could tell... you know... I'm intuitive like that. I can always tell when people don't like me.'

'Yes, I understand, but did Detective Sapsead say anything, or do anything in particular that made you think that he had something against you personally?'

'Let me put it this way.' I said. 'Sometimes when you meet a person, they don't have to open their mouths, they can just look at you in a certain way and you know that, well... that you are just not their sort. If you put me on the spot, I'd say that the moment Dennis Sapsead clapped eyes on me in my salon, he knew that he didn't like anything about me. I'm not sure why, but as you're asking, I'd guess that dear Dennis made a snap judgement, maybe an incorrect judgement about who, or perhaps what, he thought I was, and who knows... maybe he just didn't like my sort.'

'I see.' The older cop said, and I think he was about to add something, but before he could phrase his question, the younger cop butted in.

'Would you say that Detective Sapsead was out to get you from the start?' he asked.

'*No faffing around with this one.*' I thought, straight to the point. Bang bang. I noticed the older cop frown.

'Mmmm.' I said, but before I could think about it further, or begin to answer the question properly, the older cop overrode the younger with another more carefully worded question of his own.

'When Detective Sapsead came to see you about Marjorie Warton on that day in January last year, did he give you any indication that he might have already decided that you'd done something wrong?'

I hesitated.

'No, I don't think so, why would he, of course not.' I said, and then I took a moment to think about what the policeman was actually asking me. Did I think Sapsead knew? Had he always known? Had he accused me right there and then, on the doorstep of my salon? *No, he hadn't, had he, surely not, not during any of our conversations, not in so many words anyway, not until the very end at least.* All of a sudden, that belief struck me as being odd. 'Denial or delusion?' I guess I should have asked myself. Sitting in my small room under the scrutiny of the two policemen, I closed my eyes and thought back. Although, during that first interview, my mind had been lurching through the early, elated, stages of an over confident 'what-the-hell' Prozac fog, now my memory of the event was suddenly crystal-clear. Detective Sapsead had never given me any indication that he thought I MIGHT have done something wrong. No, thinking back to the moment, I realised that the most powerful impression I had from that first conversation was that even so early in his investigations, somehow and for some reason the miserable detective had indeed already decided that I HAD done something wrong, and was out to find a way to prove it. I suddenly wondered if perhaps, so buoyed by the drugs and so keen to lie smugly and play clever games with the nosey man, I'd simply failed to see the danger.

I think all the blood drained from my face. I opened my eyes.

'Are you alright?' The Inspector asked.

318

I took a deep breath.

'Why wouldn't I be?' I said, although truthfully, I was feeling decidedly 'alwrong'. What else had I missed? What else had I avoided noticing?

We took a break for a few minutes, about then. They left me alone in my cell. I think I was in a bit of a daze. I think we all used the toilet. Despite quaking bowels, I didn't make any nasty smells in my room. Such a small space, it didn't seem fair somehow. When they came back, the Sergeant was carrying a tray with three glasses of water on it. I said thank you, but I'd wished he'd brought coffee. Oh how I yearned for my Starbucks, Colin, a tall skinny latté, and a huge slice of sharp lemon cake… or then again, a bottle of vodka might have gone down well.

We sat as we had before, with me on my weird plastic toilet – with the lid down naturally – and the two policemen sitting at either end of my bed, only now they were sitting the opposite way round, with the inspector at the head and the sergeant at the foot. Now, closer to me, the younger sergeant sat up straight and appeared to be taking the lead. He pulled an A4 ring binder from a briefcase that the inspector had been carrying with him when they arrived. He flipped through a few pages and then stopped at the second of two blue file-markers somewhere near the middle. I think that he wanted me to know that he was reading his questions from an already prepared list. I couldn't have cared less.

'Did you, at any time before your arrest, allow Detective Sapsead free and open access to your home or to your business premises?' He asked.

'What.' I said. 'Of course not. Why would I want to do that?'

The Sergeant twitched and ticked a box but he didn't reply.

'Did you ever provide Detective Sapsead with a key to either of the said premises?'

'Certainly not.' I said.

He ticked another box.

319

'Did you ever give Detective Sapsead permission to remove any property or item from either your home or your business?'

'No.'

'To the best of your knowledge, did Detective Sapsead ever bring anything, substance, material or otherwise, into or onto any property or premises previously or presently under your control or ownership?'

'What?' I said, not absolutely certain what Twitchy the Policeman had just asked me.

'Did he ever leave anything in your house or shop?' He said, simplifying the question.

'Oh... I don't know... I don't think so.'

'During your dealings with Detective Sapsead, did you ever have cause to consider that he might have been acting or behaving in any way inappropriately?'

As the sergeant looked at me and waited for my answer, suddenly I thought I knew where he was going. I suddenly realised that for some reason he and his colleague were investigating the possibility that Dennis Sapsead had set me up.

Now, here's the thing. I could have said no straight away. I could have tried to explain to the nice policemen how I was feeling when I first met Detective Sapsead. That I didn't think I understood what was going on. That my mother had lately died, that I'd recently, accidently, bumped off one of my best customers, that I'd been taking medicine and that I'd not been quite right. I could have behaved and acted entirely appropriately.

Instead, I looked around me, at my grey, claustrophobic, nasty little prison cell. The walls seemed to be pulsing in time with a rhythm inside my head. 'Let me out. Let me out. Let me out.' I cocked an ear to listen, to feel the beat, and then I stood up. I walked behind my weird plastic toilet, reached over the chipped basin, and then pulled my shaving mirror to face me.

'What?' I said to myself, although thankfully not audibly to either of the cops.

'I need help.' I said. 'I need help. I need help. I need help.'

When I turned from the mirror, both of the policemen were staring at me. Both policemen looked expectant, almost hopeful, so I gave them something, something that I thought they wanted, the same something that I'd given Dennis Sapsead... I gave them a pack of plausible lies.

I woke early on Christmas morning, not so much full of seasonal cheer, as with thoughts of revenge on my mind. It was the first time in my life that I'd felt the emotion so acutely, and surprisingly, I have to say that it felt good. While Marcus Hendy-Coombs still seemed to be the primary focus of my anger (although he'd never had the courage to point the finger in court I was still convinced that, in a fit of jealousy, it was he who had tittle-tattled), now, perching between my bunny boiling stalker and the snitching, bottle-dyed redhead, Prudence Percival, who'd recognised me at my salon after meeting her at Cecile Ablitt's house, suddenly Dennis Sapsead was running a very close second.

When Sergeant Twitcher and the older Inspector, left my cell, I wanted to shout after them. I was furious, frustrated that after spending less than an hour with them, having at last enjoyed a few calmer days, my head was once again spinning. The moment the door closed, I'd slumped down on my bed with my head in my hands and my hands in my pillow. I'd lain there for several minutes, perhaps hours, maybe all night. I didn't cry. Actually, I don't remember feeling even remotely like crying. When I stood up, I ran my hands through my long hair, twisted it into a loose ponytail, and then I stepped over to my shaving mirror. I glared at myself. I looked crap, my hair was appalling and badly needed cutting, and my skin was desperate for moisturiser.

'Go on then, tell me it's my own fault.' I said.

My reflection just stared back me like, well... like reflections are supposed to I guess.

'Go on; tell me that all they did was open my eyes to what I already knew.' I said.

Still my reflection did nothing.

'Tell me that I'm being ridiculous; tell me that they were just doing their job.'

I felt a flush of blood push against the inside of my face.

I drew back from the mirror, clenched my fist, and then swung it at the glass.

Nothing broke, disappointingly, neither my hand nor the silvered glass. Instead, as the mirror swung on its hinge and crashed against the wall, the face that it reflected - my face - contorted and then appeared to grow larger, larger actually than the frame holding the mirror itself.

I didn't hear my voice then, more, I felt it run through me like a deeper vibration, perhaps like a distant whale song through an oppressive lumpy sea. It was both scary and soothing at the same time.

'We need to be free.' Was all it said.

Phillip Johnston knocked on my door within a few seconds of the locks clicking open that morning.

'Merry Christmas.' He called. It was marvellous, truly perfect timing. Although my hand hurt like hell and I might have been shaking, I drew away from the mirror, grabbed a towel and made as if I'd been washing my face.

'Hi Phil, come in.' I called as calmly as I could.

The door inched open although Phillip stayed where he was in the doorway. He was carrying what looked like a roll of brightly coloured Christmas gift-wrap. When he saw me looking at the tubular package, he smiled, and then raised it to his shoulder as if he was presenting arms at a military parade. The image seemed suddenly familiar, and rattled at something distant but perhaps also unpleasant in my memory. However, before I could mull the thought further, as befit his pose, like a clockwork soldier, Phillip marched into my cell.

'I come bearing gifts.' He said in a clipped voice, and then he swung the roll of gift-wrap in a wide arc from right to left until in ended horizontally under my nose. Another jolt to my memory, although, I think rallying slowly from such a poor night's sleep, I still couldn't twig why.

'Wow!' I said. '…and what have we here.'

'Open it and see.' Phillip said, his smile widening as he lowered the tube into my hands.

'I will, and thank you, thank you very much Phil.' I said, our eyes met and held for a moment, and something simple but fundamentally okay passed between us.

Taking the gift from my new friend, I sat down at the end of my bed to open it. Looking more closely, I could see that the long tubular roll of gift-wrap was in fact a carefully wrapped parcel with a small hand-drawn Father Christmas label Sellotaped across its middle.

'*Thanks man and have a happy Christmas.*' The label read.

Peeling open one end of the outer wrapping, inside I found a roll of fabric, canvas I thought but more likely an old bedsheet. Pulling carefully, I unrolled it on to my bed. I started to laugh immediately. My Christmas present was wonderful. Phillip had painted me a picture, a bright and witty caricature of himself with Big Ed and me. Big Ed' was enormous, and filled the background like a giant bloated baby, he had one arm around Phillip and the other around me, as if we were a couple of Teddy Bears. Phillip looked disgusted, his nose tilted and his nostrils were flaring wildly, not so much Will Smith anymore as a black Kenneth Williams. I, on the other hand, was depicted as some kind of wan cherub, all drifty and drafty and balletic, just with a peg on my nose, curlers in my long hair and I was clutching a copy of Paradise Lost.

'Bloody cheek.' I laughed, feeling genuinely cheered. 'It's fantastic.' I said. 'Have you shown it to Ed yet?'

'No man. He was too smelly yesterday, and let's be honest, if you look at what I've done to him in the picture, it's probably best if he doesn't see it. I'm glad you like it, but keep it in here, where he doesn't even have to know about it.'

I peered at the sketch and laughed again. Phillip was a talented artist, it seemed a shame to hide his work away, but he was probably right. While the caricature of Edward Ewan Edwards was plainly acidly comical, in reality the big chap's sense of humour was limited. A loud belch and Ed might snigger, a fart and he'd chuckle, and should anybody dare to slip on a banana skin or anything similarly slithery then Ed would probably be rolling on the floor with them. Nevertheless, I had to agree with Phillip, I didn't think our friend would find the picture funny.

With one small exception, Christmas breakfast in my particular prison turned out to be much the same as any other breakfast that the institution had served up that year... dry yet somehow greasy, tasteless yet somehow salty or sweet, and entirely unappetizing yet somehow I always managed to eat it all up.

'The small exception?' you might ask... well two of them actually... boiled eggs - the Governor's idea apparently – a brace for each man; oh the excitement, oh the treat, oh the binding joy.

After waiting for Edward at the bottom of stairwell number two for a few moments (he was always a slowcoach on the stairs), the three of us eventually sat down for our sort of 'family' Christmas breakfast at about 7.45 am. I can't say that I remember actually noticing the time, just that our turn to eat usually came at around 7.30 and I'm sure that we were a few minutes late. Phillip took the seat at one end of the table, with Edward at the other, while I sat in between them facing the serving hatches with my back to the door from the wing into the dining room. As usual, the dining room was busy and noisy, very noisy indeed. While everyone seemed cheerful enough, even then, there seemed to me, to be a hint of impending mischief in the air.

At about eight o'clock, maybe ten minutes or so after we'd sat down, by which time, you might be interested to know, Big Ed's spare cereal bowl was already brimming over with boiled eggs, Mr Deakin and a group of prison officers, perhaps a dozen smart looking chaps, came into the dining room. The uniformed men took their place in the corner of the room where several tables had been moved aside, and a small dais raised. Quietly, but quickly, the men stepped onto the platform and formed two equal rows facing the increasingly curious breakfasters. A moment later, after no announcement and with no preparation at all, the group started singing a hearty and rousing, 'Good King Wenceslas Looked Out.' Impromptu or rehearsed, I don't know, but on that Christmas morning, the ensemble of carolling screws sounded fantastic. Wriggling goosebumps ran up my spine, a lump grew in my throat, and to use a favourite phrase of my mother's, 'I fair welled up'.

As I remember, the small band of Her Majesty's Prison Service Officers sang for about a quarter of an hour, before the first egg hit Mr Deakin. I don't think anybody realised what had happened at first. One moment my senior officer was leading his choir into the penultimate verse of 'Once in Royal David's City.'

> *'For He is our childhood's pattern;*
> *Day by day, like us, He grew;*
> *He was little, weak and helpless…'* He was singing. Then

the next moment… kersplatt, an egg knocked his hat off.

Of course, once it started, and the lid was off the boxed frogs, pandemonium quickly spread. Amid roars of laughter, one after another, from somewhere behind our table, a mortar bombardment of boiled eggs rained over our heads and then down upon the poor defenceless officers' choir. I don't think one of them escaped unsplattered. I saw Mr Deakin take several more hits. He looked furious. While Phillip ran towards the doors for cover, I hid under the table with Edward. My hasty dive for safety definitely proved the less sensible. Christmas or not, I quickly discovered that, on that particular morning, the larger of my two new friends smelled appalling. Peering out through watering eyes a while later, when the melee appeared to have died down, wishing that I'd followed Phillip, I had to wonder if I might have been better off sheltering with the egg-spattered choir.

The most remarkable thing about Christmas that year, was that even stuck in my particular 'indestructibly chic utilitarian prison', and despite the punitive mass lockdown following the morning's magnificent flying egg display, and worse, missing my cousin's Christmas lunch, somehow, the day actually still felt Christmassy. Forget the carols (yes, a peeved Mr Deakin piped more into our cells during the afternoon), forget the decorations (yes, we had a tree and tinsel too), rather cheesily, it was the smiles that did it. Honest guv', even banged up in the nick, for that one day, in spite of the absence of real Christmas comfort, and of families and friends, almost everyone found a reason to smile, even me.

Oh... and although Father Christmas failed to bring me an iPod as I'd requested, thanks to my cousin remembering the shampoo and hair conditioner on my Christmas list at least, for the first time since Dennis Sapsead gave me the lift to his police station all those months ago, my long hair was soft and glossy all day long.

CHAPTER THIRTY-FOUR

I find it hard to imagine a more incongruous sound than the crisp click-click-click of a properly worn stiletto heel echoing its way along the corridors of an all-male prison. I'd like to say that I recognised the sound instinctively, but I didn't. In fact, waking from my after-lunch nap in my room on that first Monday in February, I'm not entirely sure what I thought might be heading my way along 'B' corridor.

Knock-knock-knock.

I stood up from my bed slowly and stretched. Something in the air tickled my nose, something pretty, and something out of place, perfume perhaps, maybe Gaultier. Tucking my sweatshirt and smoothing my trousers, I stepped towards the door, bent slightly, and then peered through the spy hole. Immediately outside I saw a chest, a lumpy chest, a woman's chest I quickly decided, which pretty much filled my view.

I opened the door.

'Darling!' A voice that I recognised instantly greeted me at once.

I blinked my eyes wide. Elaine Hennessey – surprise surprise - my solicitor and, I hoped still my friend, was standing outside my cell between Mr Deakin and the officer who I'd not seen on the wing recently but who'd taken me to dinner on my first evening at my particular prison. While Elaine's escorts looked stern, and frankly, cheesed off, Elaine herself looked radiant. Dressed in a beautifully tailored charcoal pinstriped suit, her dark hair was immaculate, and her makeup and teeth perfect. Her head held high, the finest of woman. Although I smiled all round, not just at lovely Elaine but also at the prison officers, only Elaine smiled back.

'Good lord.' I said, straightening up, and then I opened my hands out in a sort 'what-the-heck...?' gesture.

'You might well ask.' Elaine said. 'Invite me in sweetie, and all shall be revealed.'

Still astonished to see her actually at the door to my room, moving to one side, while shaking my head in disbelief, I pulled the door further open and ushered her in. Elaine began to take a step forward but before she could cross the threshold my former dinner-date officer moved directly in front her, physically blocking her way.

'Just a second Miss, if you don't mind.' He said. 'If you'll allow me to go in first, I'll just secure the room.'

Obviously miffed, I think more at being called 'Miss' than being obstructed so clumsily, Elaine stepped back, she looked at me, then looked at the officer and then at Deakin, and then she smiled a chilly smile.

'You will do what?' She asked.

'We're just taking precautions Miss, this is an unusual situation.' Deakin said, as the younger officer stepped into my cell.

'Well if you are quite certain that it's absolutely necessary, hurry up and get on with it will you. I need to speak to my client and I haven't got all day.' Elaine said. She was wonderfully commanding. Deakin nodded courteously and then leaned past her into my cell and spoke to his colleague:

'I'll carry on here.' He said. 'You nip back to the landing office and find some chairs.'

'Oh please, don't worry about the chairs.' Elaine cut in and said to the younger officer before he had the chance to leave my cell. Then turning to Deakin she added. 'We'll be fine, I can perch on the end of the bed here if I need to sit down, so you two can just run along when you've finished your checks, I'll call you when I'm ready to leave.'

'Oh I'm Sorry Miss.' Deakin said, his expression changing to a frown. 'You misunderstand me; the chairs were for all of us. I'm afraid I can't allow you in a cell with our friend here unchaperoned.'

'Oh... Now why ever not?' Elaine said, and although she said it confidently and with a plausible degree of indignant surprise, I had the feeling that she might've been expecting to have to say it.

'Because... Miss.' Deakin began, then he looked at me, then at her, and then back at me again. 'Because...' Then he turned to Elaine so that his back was to me. 'Because... well... Prison regulations Miss.' Now Deakin moved closer to Elaine and lowered his voice so that it was only just above a whisper… I could still hear him though. 'Because your client is only here because he has a habit of doing away with nice ladies like you Miss.'

I think I breathed in and out and laughed and coughed all at the same time. Suddenly I couldn't do either. Horrified at what Deakin had just suggested, my face reddening rapidly, I sat down on my bed and caught my breath. Thankfully, before I had the chance to let myself down by shouting something *Tourettesishly* rude at the stupid man (my cousin would hear of his outrageous behaviour in the strongest terms), my knight in shining corsets, Elaine Hennessey, once more took control.

'Don't be so bloody ridiculous man.' She said. 'Look, I am his Lawyer; I am here quite legitimately to meet with my client. I don't care about your wretched refurbishment works. If, for whatever reasons, your establishment is unable to provide me with proper private conference facilities then that is your lookout. You may wait close-by outside the door if you wish, but I insist that my client and I will have privacy.

'Safety Miss, that's all that I'm worried about. It would be more than my job's worth… I mean… if anything happened to you Miss, Me and….' Deakin paused to look at his younger colleague who still hadn't made it out through the door, and was about to add to what he'd said, however, Elaine didn't miss a beat.

'I am quite confident that my physical well being is not under threat, thank you very much.' My sterling solicitor snapped. 'Now officers if you please…' She said, then she pointed to the door, and I think that all four of us understood that the conversation was over.

Deakin's face darkened. 'Miss.' He nodded grudgingly. Then he turned to the door to see that his younger colleague had at last escaped. 'We will be outside.' He said. 'But I will not be locking the door, call if you need assistance.'

Elaine's eyes flashed angrily for a brief moment, then from somewhere deep and obviously uncomfortable she squeezed out a smile and nodded. 'Of course.' She said. 'Thank you.'

We sat at either end of my bed, me at the head, Elaine at the foot. With my face cooling and my breathing returning to normal, I looked at her and I shrugged.

'Thanks.' I said.

'¿Por qué.' She replied absently, while she was looking for something in the small case that she had brought in with her.

'For… trusting me I guess.' I said. Elaine stopped fiddling in her case and looked up at me for a moment.

'Oh, darling, don't be silly. I'm a lawyer for goodness sake. Trust… I barely understand the word.' She said with a flippant smirk, and I suddenly felt deflated. I think, noticing my face drop, she leaned forward and patted me on my thigh. 'Oh, please don't be offended. It's not a matter of trust anyway. These days one doesn't know what to believe in. Now, let us get down to business. We have one or two financial matters to discuss and then there's the 'Biggy'.'

'The 'Biggy'?' I asked.

'Yes….' She replied. 'That's why I'm here of course. A whopper biggy actually, ooh I do so hope we are going to have fun with it.'

I smiled then, in fact, I grinned, not because suddenly I felt any happier, but I think simply because I found Elaine's mood and positivity somehow infectious.

As it happened, we spent only ten minutes or so dealing with my financial bits-and-bobs before we tackled Elaine's 'Biggy', so I didn't have to wait long to quell my excitement. The money stuff was mostly boring. Interest, or rather the lack of it, on the various failing investments that I'd made with the money that lovely Enid Fulton had left me. My salon had at last sold, Elaine told me. I say sold, that's a joke, after the police noseys had finished tearing everything to pieces I virtually had to give the place away. Seventy-nine years left on a ninety-nine year lease for under fifty grand… ludicrous. Finally, Elaine told me that the tenants in my house, my favourite coffee-shop barista Colin from Starbucks and young Patchouli oil Julie had been paying their rent regularly and were going to have a baby, did I mind having children in the house? I had no idea, I thought Colin was gay and Julie would've been too spotty for that sort of canoodling. Wow… of course I didn't mind, but it just goes to show, you daren't assume anything these days.

When, eventually, we got round to the 'Biggy', Elaine put the various bank statements and other financial papers that she'd been reading from, back into her small leather case. Then she took out a thick brown envelope that straight away I noticed had 'HMG Home Office' written in large black letters across the front. Reaching forward, Elaine dropped it on my lap with a flourish like it was a surprise birthday gift.

'What's this?' I asked.

'It's the 'Biggy'.' She replied, raising her eyebrows.

Now I'm not going to pretend that between the visit I'd had from the County Police Service's Internal Investigations unit before Christmas and Elaine Hennessey's visit then in early February, I wasn't well aware that some legal machinery had been set in motion. Of course, I was aware that something was going on, but what I didn't know was how or even if those whirring cogs might affect me. I had the feeling that I was about to find out, I had the feeling that it might be good news and that Elaine was about to tell me why. I looked at the thick brown envelope. My fingers twitched. I wanted to rip it open. Suddenly, an impatient zing ran through my waterworks and I felt that I needed to pee. I crossed my legs and did my best to sit still.

Closing her briefcase, Elaine looked at me quizzically for a brief moment, and then smiled to herself and shook her head.

My eyes widened. My feet fidgeted. I'm certain that I must have had to stifle a giggle.

'Now Darling, before you get too excited.' She said. I'm sure realising that she was already too late. 'I want you to put that envelope under your pillow. I don't want you to open it now. I want you to listen to me carefully and then when you've had a chance to think about and digest what you've heard, I want you to read the papers thoroughly, maybe later on, when you have plenty of time. What I'm about to tell you… the gist of what that envelope contains… with good fortune and a fair wind may just be a glint of light at the end of your proverbial tunnel.'

'A glint?' I thought, and once again, I felt a tad deflated. My proverbial tunnel seemed jolly long to me and after the 'Biggy' build up that Elaine had spun me, I think I was hoping for a laser-beam or a half-decent flash at least… somehow a 'glint' sounded so insignificant, so tenuous. Taking the envelope from my lap, I breathed a sigh to myself, and then held it in both hands for a second or two before doing as I'd been told and slipping it beneath the pillow at the top of my bed.

Nodding her approval, Elaine stood up and turned to face me from a place between the door and my weird plastic toilet. She interlaced her fingers and inverted her hands as if she were offering me something that wasn't there. Then, her eyes moving between my own and the ceiling as she spoke, my solicitor started to talk.

'This all stems back to your time on remand and your trial. You'll remember all the shenanigans we had soon after your arrest, the trouble with the search warrants, you refusing representation, our falling out. Well, I have to say, that in light of what I now know, in light of what I'm about to tell you, one has to wonder whether perhaps if you'd been more canny then, more helpful, a little more concerned for your own liberty and welfare, you might not be languishing in this luxurious establishment now.' Elaine pursed her lips, tipped her head to one side, and all but wagged her finger at me. I'm sure I felt suitably told off, but I'm equally certain that my patience was ebbing and my eyes would have been urging her to get on with it. I remember staring at her hard. Thankfully, she seemed to get my drift quickly enough, and leaving any further reprimands for another time, finally moved on to the meat of the matter.

'Okay.' She said, now holding her hands up defensively. 'Essentially, it would appear that at least some of the charges that were originally brought against you, and in particular those concerning Marjorie Warton and Jayne Clarke, were never as cut and dried as they had first appeared. Evidence that I think you had taken as being irrefutable, in some cases didn't actually exist. There were also chain-of-event inaccuracies, and it would seem that some of the prosecution witnesses might have been encouraged to agree and then sign statements that were either not their own or that they themselves knew were not strictly true. Then, we come to Detective Dennis Sapsead. I know that you met with the Internal Investigations chaps a while ago and from what I can see in their report, you did a good job in confirming their doubts. Sapsead is definitely in trouble. Tampering with, or falsifying evidence, interfering with the scene of a crime, altering witness statements, are just some of the accusations that are being levelled against him. Together with your input, the report is quite damning. You have a copy in the envelope, along with several other documents that in my opinion at least, all point to one simple conclusion… that if your trial wasn't unfair and your conviction unsafe, then at the very least the judge's position on the denial of your right to appeal is now entirely untenable. If I were you I would be instructing fresh counsel immediately.'

Having said what she had come to say, Elaine folded her arms across her chest and then grinned at me like the Cheshire cat. I reckoned that she was feeling pleased with herself.

'Wowee!' I said. 'Tell me, has anybody ever mentioned that you are truly spell-binding when you are in full flow?' I asked.

'Actually… yes.' Elaine replied, and then she sort of cocked an eyebrow, pursed her lips, and shook her head up and to the right.

'So, what does all that mean?' I asked… It was a genuine question. I had been listening. I just got muddled towards the end, that's all. Elaine shot me a withering glance that told me instantly that she thought I'd said something stupid.

'It means.' She said. 'It means, that, while I am not an expert in the process of criminal law, in my opinion, if everything turns against Detective Sapsead as I suspect it will, you could very well stand a fighting chance of getting out of this place sooner than you might've hoped. However… listen to me... you will need to act promptly and to employ the very best specialist lawyers. If you want my help and support, then under no circumstances must you even consider representing yourself.'

'Crikey!' I said, nodding earnestly. 'Crikey indeed.'

Elaine left my room at almost exactly four o'clock. I remember the time because as she was leaving with Mr Deakin, Phillip Johnston appeared at my door to suggest that during the recreation hour before dinner he and I should play chess. Before agreeing to the challenge, I checked my watch to see how long I had to prepare. With dinner at seven, only two hours, not long enough that day, so I declined the invitation, but while he was there I introduced Phillip to Elaine.

'This is my friend Phillip Johnston.' I said.

When Elaine looked at Phillip, I couldn't help noticing that a dark cloud slid across her face. Having obviously recognised him from somewhere, the newspapers or TV I guessed, she glanced at me, frowned, and then looked back at Phillip. Spotting the obvious glower, my friend turned his eyes to the floor. Suddenly I felt awkward.

'Friend?' Elaine said, and although it came out as a question, I had the feeling that my solicitor didn't really expect an answer.

'Yes, Phillip is my friend.' I said anyway.

Alas, my reply now earned me a full-blown grimace.

Elaine shook her head, then leaned in towards me and whispered quietly in my ear, although I'm afraid not quietly enough, 'Maybe as an innocent man you should choose your friends more carefully darling... or at least pay more attention to the front pages... your friend here is notorious dear, the man is a killer and a thief.' She said, and then she pecked me on the cheek, and added cheerily as she pulled away. 'I'll have my secretary send you the names of a few good criminal lawyers... if that's not a contradiction in terms.'

A moment later, after chuckling at her own joke, Elaine was off with Mr Deakin and my former dinner-date officer, click-click-clicking her heels along 'B' corridor.

'Who and what was that?' Phillip said contemptuously when they finally turned out of sight.

'My last shot at freedom, I think.' I replied.

CHAPTER THIRTY-FIVE

In all, it took me five and a half hours to read through the various papers that Elaine Hennessey left with me, and I have to say that, probably because of their pertinence to me, I found them all absolutely riveting. Once I'd started reading, I could barely put them down.

In some respects, when the lights went out in my room and the door locks clicked shut for the night, I felt a sense of relief. It had been long day. The print on the pages had started to jumble. I was exhausted and already in bed. Fumbling in the dark, I returned the pieces of paper to the envelope and then tucked the envelope under my pillow. Lying down, I rested my head back and let out a long slow breath. A low ringing started in my ears, then sank to a whine, then faded to a whistle, and was gone as quickly as it had started. I swallowed hard, something in my head popped and then buzzed and then... silence. Well. Prison silence anyway... the usual racket in the background... shouts and yelps and the banging of toilet seats.

I knew that I would chat to myself that night. I knew, because I needed to talk things over with somebody, and who else did I have? Dozing on my back, I stared up towards the ceiling, my thoughts swirled with the gloomy patterns behind my eyes, red to black, black to blue, and then to a roiling purple. Somehow, the intensity of the colours and the urgency with which they moved between my mind and my vision seemed significant... angry... vengeful.

'So he's a cheat as well as being too nosey for his own good.' I said aloud, but careful not to speak so loudly that anyone outside my cell might hear. 'It makes me sick to think that a policeman could be so dishonest... Breaking into my home and stealing my lovely Chanel suit. Taking some of poor Jayne Clarke's blood from the mortuary and then poking it into the cracks between the tiles on my salon floor indeed. I knew that I'd cleaned that floor properly... the devious bastard. I can't believe that he could have stooped so low. Whatever is one to think?'

I asked the question openly, it hung in the air for a long moment like a curl of acrid smoke, until from somewhere in my room, I don't remember it having anything to do with me, I heard a much calmer voice than my own reply.

'I think we shouldn't trust anybody. I think we should get out of here as soon as we can, and any way we can, and then we should get even.'

I can't say that the answer took me by surprise. I sat up in bed blinking into the darkness, then, going with my own flow, I said. 'That's very easy for you to say, but this is a prison you know, the doors are locked. What do you expect us to do? Just get up tomorrow morning and stroll out through the main gate.'

This time the reply came instantly. 'There will be opportunities, you mark my words.' It said. 'You will spot them, we will spot them, trust me, if we work together we will succeed just you wait and see.'

I didn't sleep terribly well that night. I was hot and then cold and I tossed and I turned while mulling things over. I didn't talk to myself anymore. There didn't seem to be any point. When I thought about it, we had nothing much to say. After my suggestion to escape, for the first time since I'd first winked at myself through the tall floor to ceiling mirror in my salon, I knew exactly what I was bound to say... and of course, now, I always agreed with me completely.

Breakfast was appalling. The eggs were like polystyrene, the bacon like leather, and the baked beans appeared to have been squished into an orangey mush soup. I sat at the table closest to the dining room doors opposite Big Edward, who, I remember, looked even more sweaty than usual that morning, and smelt particularly high. Unusually, Phillip Johnston had neither knocked the door on his way past my cell nor apparently yet come down.

'He was grumpy yesterday evening in the recreation room.' Big Ed said. 'I don't know why. When you didn't come out to play, I went back to my cell. I think he might have been sulking because you wouldn't play chess with him.' Big Ed suggested.

'He always beats me. It's no fun losing every time.' I said. '...and I was busy, I had stuff to think about.'

'Well it might have been that woman then.' Ed said.

'What woman?' I said.

'Your woman... the posh woman who came to see you, her with all the clothes and the lipstick and the scent... everybody's talking about her, apparently, she smelled very nice... good bosoms and shoulders.'

'Oh... Elaine. She's not a woman, she's my solicitor.'

'Yeh, well whatever... I reckon she pissed Phil off.'

'She's okay; I just don't think she took to Phil that's all.'

'He said she called him a tealeaf.'

'A what?'

'A thief.'

'Oh... is he?'

'Well... yeh, he is, but it's not for women like her to come in here all hoity-toity like and start telling us all about what each other has done is it.'

'Gosh... no.' I said. 'I suppose not.'

'I mean... I've never told you what I done, and you've never asked, have you? That's the way it is. I don't know you, and you don't know me, except for in here that is... and that's for the best. Most of us don't want to know. Now, your woman has gone and spoiled it, hasn't she? Your woman has gone and told you that Phillip was a tealeaf, and I expect she told you that he used to mug people with an iron bar too, and that some poor blighter died. Spoils it for everyone that kind of loose talk; during the war they used to shoot people for that kind of thing.'

I'd never heard Big Ed string so many words together before, not only had he stopped eating but he'd used multiple sentences too; it seemed to me that Elaine had upset both of my friends.

'I didn't pay much attention to her actually.' I said, trying to defuse the sudden awkwardness between us. 'I heard what she was saying, but... well... I guess I had other things on my mind.'

'Well... there you go... now you know, don't you? Our mate Phil was a bad lad outside.' Ed said angrily, and then he added with an air of finality in his voice. 'Just like most of us here I reckon.'

I pushed my bacon and the polystyrene egg on top of the orange bean mush, then leaned across the table and forked the whole sloppy mess on to Big Ed's plate. He didn't say thank you or even look up, he just dived in at it like a man who hadn't eaten for a week. After I told him that maybe I'd catch him later, I pushed my chair under the table and headed for the door. Mr Deakin was standing outside.

'Are you expecting any visitors this week?' He asked, his eyes looking hopeful.

I smiled to myself.

Although Tristan had been to see me a couple of times since Christmas, my cousin had been poorly with something that her son had called 'Piggy-flu' and she hadn't visited me for a while. Although she'd written me numerous letters and kept me up to date with family matters, I reckoned that my senior officer was missing her.

'Now that is a very good question, I wonder, who could you possibly mean?' I said, being a deliberate tease, and then I added; 'Yes, I am indeed expecting visitors this week, but who they might be and what they might want, well that would be for me to know and for you to discover.'

Mr Deakin nodded and shrugged, and then shot me a squinty sarcastic half-smile. My senior sourpuss prison officer didn't look happy.

Walking from Stairwell number two onto 'B' corridor, I asked at the landing office if I could call in on Phillip Johnston's cell on the way back to my own. The officer I spoke to looked up from the magazine that he was reading, then shrugged at me.

'You can if you like, but you won't find him there.' He said. 'Our Phil had a bit of a paddy in the rec room yesterday evening. So we sent him on holiday to the block.'

'Oh...' I said. 'When will he be back?'

'He won't be coming back.' He said. 'This is the cushy wing, for newbies and good boys. Everybody knows that, but like everything in here, it's three strikes and you're out. Your mate Johnston has struck out half a dozen times already. He's had too many second chances. He's always been a liability. He might've been better since you've been around, but take it from me, after last night's performance, he'll be off to a tougher wing, and he won't be coming back here.'

I walked back to my cell feeling seriously glum and disappointed. Yet another friendship had bitten the dust. I went to my shaving mirror straight away.

'You're right.' I said in a low voice to my reflection. 'Whatever it takes, we have to get out of here as quickly as we possibly can.'

CHAPTER THIRTY-SIX

The list of likely candidates for the salubrious position of my primary defence lawyer arrived from Elaine Hennessey's secretary shortly after breakfast on Wednesday morning. Less than forty-eight hours. Jolly efficient I thought. It was not a long list, five lawyers, four men and one woman, none of the names stood out. With nothing to go on other than Elaine's apparently universal recommendation and some interesting initials, rather than picking randomly, I decided that, to hell with protocol, if I could I'd interview all of them and would start as soon as possible. Therefore, after reading the accompanying letter, in which Elaine expressed only the mildest of preferences for lawyer number two on her list, a chap called John Banks, straight away I put a request in to the Wing Governor's office to use a telephone.

'Five calls.' The officer on duty at the time snapped at me. 'You've got to be joking, nobody gets five calls.' Then he paused for a moment and added as an afterthought. 'How much money have you got?'

'I've got money.' I said indignantly. 'But these are official calls; I need to speak to my lawyers.'

'You have five lawyers? Blimey mate… most people make do with one, and that's rough enough if you ask me, what the hell do you want five for?'

'You may well ask.' I said, and because I couldn't see any reason why not, and because he had asked so nicely, I told him what I was hoping to do and that I wanted to appoint legal representation to handle my appeal as soon as I possibly could. Alas, the moment I mentioned the word 'appeal' the officer in the Wing Governor's office started laughing.

'Now I know that you're taking the Micky mate.' He chuckled. 'You… an appeal… Look, you're a nice fella, you've been no trouble on the landings, and most of us think you're okay. I don't know who's been winding you up to this, I'm no expert, but I read the papers, I saw it all on the news, if anything looked like a slam dunk mate, your conviction was a hummdinger…' Then the officer started chuckling again. I stood there squirming. After a moment or two, he wiped his eyes with a tissue (rather unnecessary I felt), and then to my surprise, he reached to one side and pulled a telephone over towards me from an adjoining desk.

'Here.' He said. 'Try this; I could use a good laugh.'

Almost an hour later, after actually making six telephone calls, after I'd hung up the handset and returned the pen that I borrowed from the duty Wing Officer's desk-tidy, I stared at the sheets of paper that officer had given me and scanned through my scribbled notes. Out of the five lawyers on the original list, I managed to discuss my case briefly with four, all of whom remained firm possibilities. The one failure, my second call, ironically, to Elaine's apparent favourite, John Banks from Banks Banks and Windie in Surbiton Surrey, turned out to be an elderly gentleman with a wonderful timbre to his voice (very Richard Burton). The old lawyer's secretary told me that I was in luck as I'd caught him leaving his office on his way to attend his own retirement lunch party. After she reluctantly put me through, although the chap listened to me for a while, the instant I mentioned the words 'Habeas Corpus', 'Murder', and 'Appeal' and the possibility of a complex case, I could almost hear his old bones freeze. 'I'll have a colleague call you.' He promised. 'Chris Tensely-Evans... fine lawyer, fantastic brain. Give my secretary your number and give me a few days, and we'll be in touch.' He seemed a amiable enough fellow, and if what his secretary had told me about his imminent retirement was true, I could hardly blame him for passing on what might have been a hot potato, so I thanked him very much and told him that I'd look forward to hearing from his colleague soon.

Of the four other lawyers that I spoke to, all appeared to be interested in my case, three gave me good vibes and positive feedback, and quite amazingly two agreed to contact my Wing Governor straight away with a view to arranging a meeting before the end of the week. Overall, quite a result, I felt good.

My last phone call, the sixth and the call that once again confirmed my initial judgement that some prison officers aren't so terribly bright (the chap in the Wing Governor's office might have been eavesdropping but he obviously couldn't count), was to Elaine Hennessey. It was not an essential call, but as I had the chance, I thought that I might as well bring her up to date. I think, or maybe I hope, that she was eating her lunch at the time, a particularly delicious sandwich perhaps; either that or when I called she was up to something rascally and delightfully unladylike in her office. Although our conversation was brief, my ordinarily 'very in control' solicitor seemed keen to punctuate our conversation with quiet almost secretive asides that I couldn't quite make out, and odd squeaks of pleasure… intriguing. However, doing my best to ignore the 'Oohs' and 'Aahs' and even the occasional whispered 'Oh yes' (maybe somebody was giving her great mayonnaise), I gave Elaine the names of the two lawyers who'd promised to see me later that week, a *somebody-or-other* Giles and a woman with a foreign name that I can't now remember, and I asked her what she thought.

'Well they are all good darling.' She said. 'It's a shame about John Banks though, he might sound like a bit of a duffer, but the old fellow still thinks like a fox and with chambers in the Suburbs, Bank Banks and Windie might fit more comfortably into your budget. I'll tell you what, I'll call his office this afternoon and maybe send a few bits and pieces over, and if the others don't suit you, you never know, John's lackey might yet be the biscuit.'

I barely heard Elaine's last few words. 'Budget?' I thought. The nasty word hadn't even crossed my mind. I knew that I had money in the bank, quite a lot I reckoned, I'd hardly spent a penny on my first trial, not even of Her Majesty's cash, but I hadn't considered how much I might need to put up a fight in the appeal courts. Suddenly concerned, I smiled into the telephone at Elaine. People do hear smiles you know. Smiles sound happy and confident, just as frowns can sound stupid and pissed off.

'Let's hope so.' I said, then I gave chuckle, and then as casually as possible, I asked.

'Just what is the state of my finances right now, how much could I lay my hands on if I really needed to?'

'Darling… we went through all that only the day before yesterday, I knew you weren't paying attention.' She tutted at me through her teeth. '…But well… off the top of my head, if I remember correctly, I'd say that you should have access to something approaching a quarter of a mil', in fairly liquid funds that is. Of course, I could always arrange to mortgage your house if we need more.'

'MORE…?' I said, suddenly horrified. I felt the blood drain from my face and leaned on the wing office desk for support.

'More…?' I squealed. 'How could we possibly need more than a quarter of a million quid?'

'Darling…' Elaine's tones were instantly silky and smooth and her inflection oh so wonderfully reasonable, no 'Oohs' or 'Aahs' and no squeaks of pleasure either. 'I'm afraid that the finer pursuit of justice in the UK today can be terribly expensive, but then… the money's no use to you where you are is it? … and one has to consider the alternatives.'

'That is exactly what I am doing.' I said.

On my way back to my room, my escort started whistling. A tune from Phantom of the Opera, the song that Christine and the sneaking Phantom sang on the roof of the Opera House I think. The prison officer actually whistled it well I remember, perfectly in pitch. With the aid of the echo from the hard prison walls, the man's rendition of the simple melody was haunting. Following silently, bathing in the sweetness of the tune, I lost myself for several moments. The Phantom musical was my mother's favourite. She braved the West End to see it a half dozen times, both the first and the last time with me. The first was the best naturally, with Michael Crawford and Sarah Brightman back in the Eighties, I've always secretly been in love with them both, he so charismatic, and she so lovely.

Whilst I have to confess that when it comes to Lloyd-Webber, Joseph is more my cup of tea, I love the simple variety of the music, I treasure the memory of those trips to town with my Mum. Eyes wide with excitement like a child at Christmas; she'd clutch my arm with both hands as we strode eagerly from Piccadilly up along Shaftsbury Avenue. The lights and the bustle enthralled her. After the show, we'd eat. 'Oh anything exotic.' My Mum would say when I asked her what she fancied. For Mum that meant Chinese. She liked red and gold. She never ate much. More of a cottage pie than Cantonese Duck, my Mother. We had fun. I still can't believe that she's gone. If only I'd realised. If only I'd been there with Richard and Judy.

By the time my escorting officer left me in my cell, I had tears in my eyes, a mix of both happy and sad. I sat on my bed, wiped my face with the pillow, and tried to gather my thoughts. One moment up, the next down, a loop the loop of emotions, a switchback ride for the soul, even stuck in the predictability of my particular prison, that's how my life seemed right then. I can't say that I felt depressed or unhappy, because I don't think I did, I think I just felt confused at that moment and perhaps rather crossly frustrated.

Thankfully, before I could screw myself any further into a knot of 'if-onlys', shortly after lunch Dr Martin Metcalf knocked at my door.

'May I come in?' He asked through the crack (always polite even though he seemed nervous since our little spat).

I pulled the door open, and without saying anything, I ushered him in.

'How are you doing?' he asked.

'Very well thank you, marvellous actually.' I said overly enthusiastically and with a cheesy grin, although I'm sure that neither of us really believed me.

'I heard that you'd been asking about Phillip Johnston, and I thought that I'd come along and fill you in on what happened last evening in the recreation room.' Dr Metcalf said. 'May I sit down?' Then, oddly, the doctor pointed to my weird plastic toilet indicating that he wanted to use it as a chair. Whilst I am quite certain, that by then almost everyone in my particular prison, both inmates and officers alike, were well aware that I always kept my personal lavatory spotlessly clean, I have to say that I was quite surprised (such uncommon trust in such an unreliable place). I shrugged and then nodded. The doctor nodded back and then lowered himself down and perched on the edge of the rim like a woolly frog on a wobbly rock. He looked entirely uncomfortable.

'I gather Phillip has become friend of yours.' He said, now crossing his legs and balancing precariously on one buttock. The new position seemed insanely awkward.

'Yes.' I said.

'Friends are hard to come by in places like this.' He said.

'Yes.' I said.

'Phillip has issues.' Dr Metcalf said, and then he fidgeted sideways and uncrossed and re-crossed his legs. 'Phillip is an angry man. We have been working together for some time, but I'm afraid, that yesterday in the recreation room, Phillip's anger got the better of him.'

'Yes.' I said.

'You see, well, the thing is, I mean, well, Phillip, you know, and his issues, and his anger...' Now the doctor uncrossed his legs again and sat astride my toilet this time with a hand on either knee. '...well you mustn't blame yourself for the situation... your visitor, the woman who upset him. I mean now that he's gone... with his issues and his anger. You weren't to know that he might be sensitive. It wasn't your fault so you mustn't worry, that's all I'm saying. You were told that Phillip has gone, weren't you?'

'Yes.' I said.

'Good... Good... There, now that's much better. You'll make other friends. You see, it's good to talk. Now... do you need anything to help you sleep?' The doctor asked standing up from my toilet. 'How's that lovely cousin of yours, the poor lady with swine flu who Mr Deakin so admires? Family can be such a help at times like these when ones morale is at a low ebb.'

I looked down to the floor, trailed my fingers through my hair, and shook my head slowly in exasperation.

As it happened, I am sure greatly to my doctor's relief as well as to Mr Deakin's delight, the following day, on the Thursday, now fully recovered from her ailments, my cousin came to visit me.

I was in the dining room finishing my lunch with Edward when the visiting bell sounded, two rings and a half muffled announcement over the brand-new PA system (apart from at last having reliable hot water in the showers, as far as I could see, the only improvement that had actually been completed and put to use since the prison refurbishments began). It was great timing actually, Edward was being his usual non-communicative self and was having a bad time with his pungency again, and it seemed that I was especially nasally sensitive that day.

BING BONG... the new bell boinged.

'Odds on corridors B D and F, to the ready rooms at the visitor suite please.' A pleasant though solemn female voice announced over the Tannoy system.

You know, in my experience, new and efficient doesn't automatically equal better. Naturally, when the nice lady called, everyone and anyone from the odd numbered cells on B D and F corridors, who thought that they might have even a sniff of a visit, came running. I am sure the whole wing was instantly in furore. Only the day before and we'd have had a barked command from a hairy-necked prison officer and then a personal escort downstairs. ...And did she really say 'to the ready rooms in the visitors' *suite*'? Surely she did. Ridiculous - the visitors' room, in fact, most of the ground floor including all the main offices and the infirmary, even parts of the secure areas beneath the wings, was still a dusty construction site. I'm afraid that the slow progress of my particular prison's refurbishment programme had become something of a joke.

Following behind the crowd of rattling feet from the bottom of stairwell number two along a narrow passage between the reception area and a tall wire security barrier, I entered the visitors' room on the ground floor at about twenty past one. I saw my cousin straight away. She was sitting at the table furthest from the door, opposite Tristan and another person, who although she had her back to me I guessed from recent letters would likely be Sammie Gough, not only formerly my favourite teacher/waitress but as of New Years

Eve apparently now also my second cousin's fiancée. Unfortunately, standing close by, I also saw Mr Deakin.

Although I kept my head down while I pushed my way between the tables, my cousin spotted me before I was halfway across the room.

'Cooee!' She called at the top of her voice, and then she stood up and waved excitedly with both hands. I know that it was only my cousin being well... my cousin, she has always been an effervescent sort, but I was only a few feet away and everyone in the room stopped and looked at us. I'm afraid I cringed. She was obviously feeling very much better.

'Oh look at you.' She said at the top of her voice as I approached the table. 'Come here with you and give me a hug.'

Of course, I did as I was told happily, but as soon as I'd done my family duty and hugged the woman, half of the people in the visitors' room including Mr Deakin started to applaud. I was mortified.

'Okay, that'll do. Let's sit down.' I said, pulling at my cousin's sleeve. It was only then that I noticed what she was wearing. Dressed in a snug black and gold chiffon number from which her ample figure seemed keen to escape, my cousin looked more like she was off out on a night of razzle-dazzle rather than visiting one of Her Majesty's more serious Prisons. I tried not to stare like I suddenly realised everybody else was, but it was hard.

'How are you?' I said, more to distract myself than because at that moment I actually felt that I cared... I did care really of course, but sometimes people do push the boundaries.

'I am much better now, thank you indeed.' My cousin said. '...But look at you with all your long hair and your chubby cheeks. You're looking much better too, much healthier and certainly bonnier than the last time I saw you.'

Well... frankly I didn't know what to say, I knew my hair had grown (I should've trimmed it up, but somehow I liked the feel of it keeping my neck warm), but chubby... chubby cheeks... bonnier... bloody hell. I didn't even try to hide my pissed offness. I just feigned a snatched smile, snubbed my nose, and turned away from her to Tristan.

'Hello Tris.' I said with a tiny shrug of my chin. 'How are you and Samantha?' Then I looked at Sammie and grinned, and I think that I was about to tell them both just how excited I'd been when I'd heard about their engagement, when I spotted the look on the girl's face. Her jaw clenched tight, her eyes unable to hold mine or even to stay fixed on anything much else in the visitors' room for that matter, she looked dreadfully uncomfortable, embarrassed to be there, I thought likely. Perhaps I shouldn't have been surprised, after all, it's not every day you visit a real live murderer in nasty old prison is it? Suddenly I felt sorry for her.

'Thanks for coming.' I said quietly and trying to aim my words somewhere between the two of them. 'I'm happy for you both and it's nice that you've come to see me and I wish you all the luck in the world.'

Sammie nodded at least and even managed to squeeze the briefest of smiles from between her lips. Tristan smiled too.

'Thanks Cuz'.' He said. 'We can't stay too long today. Sammie has to work this evening, but we wanted to see you before we announced the wedding date. I wanted to ask you to be my best man. Obviously I know that you won't be able to do it, but I wanted to ask you anyway.'

'Thanks Tris… I would have loved to be your best man. When are you going to get married?' I asked.

'In the summer, early in June probably.'

'Aahh… blue June skies…' I breathed a sigh. 'My favourite month of the year, but you're right, I'll be away I think.'

We chatted on as we were for a while longer. My cousin and I made up thank goodness, although she barely sat down and actually spent most of her time in the '*Visitors' Suite*' nattering flirty asides with Mr Deakin. Sammie loosened up some… although I have to say not much, and even when she did, after ten minutes or so, she made her excuses and left the table for the bathroom. I didn't see her again that day. Tristan was a brick as usual, a good source of light relief. My second cousin could always cheer me up. However, after Sammie had gone and while my cousin was off, swimming somewhere deep and meaningful in Mr Deakin's gaze no doubt, our conversation had been mostly light until, when I was telling him about Detective Dennis Sapsead and the possibility of an appeal, Tristan mentioned something that made my ears prick up.

'That's funny.' He said. 'What a coincidence. I saw Detective Sapsead on Gillycote Road, not far from your house.'

'Really?' I said, both intrigued and concerned. 'When was that?'

'A couple of weeks ago.' Tristan replied, scratching his chin. 'Your Miss Hennessey called me because that Colin bloke from Starbucks that rents your house had rung her to say that the wind had ripped the felt off the roof of your garden shed. Well, I went up to your place as soon as I could to fix it, and there was Sapsead, sitting in his car just along the road.'

All of a sudden, the blood in my veins ran cold. I found myself gulping at air. However, not because Tristan had seen Dennis Sapsead parked outside my house (I could hardly have cared less at that moment), but because of what my second cousin had said about my garden shed. Suddenly, I remembered Marjorie Warton's gun and Dr Carmen's medical bag, both of which were still hidden inside under the loose floorboards. With all that had happened since I'd hidden them, I'd completely forgotten that they were still there.

'Oh... I see... well never mind.' I managed to croak through a dry throat, then, after coughing to clear it, I added as nonchalantly as I could. 'Did you manage to fix the shed?'

'It was a struggle Cuz.' Tristan said. 'I couldn't get inside. No one could find the key to that bloody great padlock you put on it. I had to nail it up from the outside, but I have to tell you that it's a ropey old lump of timber, wobbly as Old-Harry, it's not going to last much longer. Another storm like the one we had after Christmas, and I reckon the blighter will fall down.'

'Right...' I said. 'I'll have to get it dealt with it as soon as possible then.'

As always, an up and then a down, I felt like a wretched yoyo.

Back in my room after my cousin, her son, and young Sammie Gough had gone, realising that should anybody find Marjorie Warton's gun or Dr Carmen's medical bag I could forget Elaine Hennessey's suggestion of a retrial or an appeal, I did something that when I look back, for one bouncy reason or another, I seemed to do quite often around that time. Scared I suppose, I knelt on the floor in front of my shaving mirror. I didn't talk to myself at all. I just studied my reflection; I looked at my face, at my tired eyes, at the new wrinkles and the long grey hairs. I'd kneel there for hours on end sometimes, wondering how I'd ever ended up in such a terrible place and trying to fathom a way to get out.

When the answer came to me, which thank the good lord it eventually did, it was a genuine moment of epiphany. Now I know that I've used that rather special biblical term before in these pages, but it was only once I think, and then a while back when I talking about the moment when my second cousin Tristan got God, so you'll just have to forgive me that I use it again. My moment of epiphany came about as an odd, and, in many ways, indirect result of my particular prison's wonderfully slow refurbishment programme and my interviews with Elaine Hennessey's highly recommended defence lawyers, well one of them at least.

Now I'm not going to bore you by detailing each and every minute of all of the five interviews that my surprisingly generous Wing Governor and our odd legal system permitted me to hold, that would be pointless and mostly terribly dull, but what I will do is give you a brief summary of the more important points of each meeting. I shall start at the beginning, with lawyer number one, who arrived at my cell door with Mr Deakin soon after breakfast on the morning of the first Friday in February. I remember the knock, weak and ineffective, so feeble that I almost didn't hear it.

No.1

Somebody-or-other Giles, from: Buckle Bennett and Daws, in Holborn.

Tie: Dull

Shirt: Grey (supposed to be white).

Suit: needs pressing.

Shoes: Oh dear, cheap loafers (very scuffed).

Long hairs protruding from nose and ears. (I drew a little picture)

Didn't listen to me at all and then droned on for what felt like ages.

57 mins

NO

Okay, so I agree, perhaps my notes were a tad dismissive and somewhat less comprehensive than they could have been. I did write more, honestly. I gave the chap a chance, but those were the most important points.

Lawyer number two came to see me later on that same afternoon. Deakin's shift must have ended around midday, sometime before she arrived I reckoned, because rather than my senior officer escorting the attractive Asian lawyer to my cell as I'm sure his very active inquisitive gene would've preferred, my favourite dinner date officer brought her along. Just like Deakin, while we spoke, the taller, much younger, and fitter officer waited outside my cell with my door ajar.

No.2

Danni Singh Dhillon, from: Hambrough John.

Tiny, but beautifully proportioned.

Impeccably dressed – although maybe a little too floral.

Shoes: whopping heels, four inches at least... maybe Jimmy Choo - loved the

bows.

Make up: understated but cleanly applied.

Hair: long and prettily tied up but could do with softening around the face .

I like her, she speaks like Joanna Lumley... a proper fav'.

Listens well.

Obviously clever.

Body language tight... edgy...

Oh dear, she's uncomfortable.

Doesn't like me... bugger.

52 mins.

No... pity though.

A bit of a disappointment that one, I liked Danni Singh Dhillon; initially I had high hopes, but as I told the two policemen from the Internal Investigations unit before Christmas, you can tell when somebody doesn't take to you and the last thing that I needed at that point in my life was a lawyer who wasn't fully on side.

I had to wait until after the weekend, until the following Tuesday morning, for the second and third lawyers to turn up for their chat, leaving me anxious for almost seventy-two hours. While the worry helped keep my bowels active, always an issue during my stay at Her Majesty's pleasure, it played havoc with my sleep pattern ...and the worst of it? I needn't have bothered. Both of them big bloated and pompous, the first chap lasted twenty-two minutes and the second only seven. My full notes for both meetings are as follows.

No.3

OMG he looks like Winston Churchill.

David Doggydoo or something, from: frankly & who gives a stuff.

Smells like a cigar.

I must talk to Elaine about recommending this one.

Keeps scratching his groin...

Crabs?

How can I allow a man like this to represent me?

How can I get him out of my lovely clean cell?

Just say no... you know it makes sense.

God he's so boring.

Shut up man, please.

I think he thinks that I am interested in, and am writing down, every word that

he says, but I am not in fact, I am writing down the first thing that comes into my head, like big slices of sharp lemon cake, tasty toasted marsh mallows, and

Richard Gere in his white Officer and a gentleman uniform, and I am trying to

look serious, oh dear he has just taken a peek at my notes, sod it he seems to

be able to read upside down, oh well with any luck he will get the message and

hurry up and go away.

He's putting stuff back in to his briefcase.

Yes, I think that he got the message.

Byeee.

22 mins.

NO NO NO

No.4

Oh shit, it's number threes twin brother… just with glasses, more hair, and a

bigger briefcase.

Take him away Mr Deakin please.

Blah blah blah

7 mins.

How did he last so long

Definitely NO!

Lawyers hey… while I can't say that I'd necessarily been expecting to be overwhelmed by their scintillating company or their witty repartee, I think I had hoped for something a tad more encouraging. With only one more interview to hold, scheduled for the following day with Chris Tensely-Evans, John Banks substitute from Banks Banks and Windie of Surbiton, I cannot pretend that I was feeling especially positive.

However, as appeared to be becoming the norm with my life in prison, just when a 'down' moment was busily smacking me in the chops, an 'up' turned out to be only shortly round the corner.

When Wednesday finally arrived, and my senior prison officer, Mr. Lance Sourpuss Deakin, delivered Chris Tensely-

Evans to my door, hugely to my surprise, I discovered that the chap who John Banks had sent to see me in his place was in fact a woman, and, as it happened, not just any woman either, no, as soon as I saw her, a wild thought struck me between the eyes and I knew instantly that Christine Tensely-Evans was absolutely perfect.

CHAPTER THIRTY-SEVEN

An immaculately presented, striking, sturdy woman in her early forties, dressed in a long mohair coat over a clean cut dark business suit, and wearing a pair of sharp rectangular full-framed spectacles (trendy, even if the lenses were a tad on the bottle-glass side), Chrissie (as she quickly made it plain that she liked to be known), stood close to my own height (taller in heels), had gently highlighted shoulder length gold-blonde hair (a shade longer than my own) which she wore loosely tied back with a full fringe. She had blue/grey eyes, a pale skin, and what my mother would have called, strong, noble features. We hit it off immediately; she looked like me, so I knew we would. Call it chemistry. Call it what you like. Almost as soon as Deakin had pulled the door to, she reached for my hand and shook it wonderfully firmly - a good vibration buzzed up my arm – then, after slipping off her coat, she plonked herself on the end of my bed, and shot me a wide grin and said in a husky voice.

'I've never done this sort of thing in a prison cell before.'

I turned to her and smiled. 'Neither had I.' I chipped back quickly. 'Then, the other day, out of the blue, my solicitor called by, and now I seem to be doing it all the time.' While I'm not certain that Chrissie fully understood my slant on her quip – she couldn't have known that I'd already seen four other lawyers - she chuckled anyway, and it was a good sound, deep and throaty.

'As a matter of fact...' She said, 'I've never been inside a prison cell before, at least not a cell inside a real grown up prison. I was quite excited when they asked me if I minded holding the meeting up here.'

'We are being refurbished.' I said. 'In order to address prison overcrowding and the miserable conditions, at Her Majesty's personal behest I think, just very very slowly... otherwise, we'd be downstairs now, staring at each other across a table in a newly decorated but otherwise cold cube of room, with white tiled walls and nowhere to go to the loo.'

'Whereas up here we are fully facilitated I see.' Chrissie waved a hand towards my weird plastic toilet and then grimaced. 'What a truly villainous piece of modern design it is, and finished in such a splendid shade of... sludge.'

'I like to think of it as utilitarian chic, a tacky plastic crapper with just a hint of the indestructible.' I said, delighted to at last find someone in my particular prison who's natural wave-length seemed even vaguely similar my own.

While I felt that our 'Opening Remarks' were progressing jolly swimmingly, in fact we didn't banter for long, perhaps just a few minutes more, until Chrissie had sorted some papers from her cherry-red leather document wallet (embossed Dunhill I noticed, expensive but understated) and spread them between us across my bed. Then her lawyers eyes steeled and her body language stiffened. Among the papers, I spotted copies of two of the reports that Elaine had given me a week or so before, plus a print out of an email with Elaine's office header. It seemed that my favourite solicitor had been true to her word and had forwarded at least some of the case material to Banks Banks and Windie.

'You'll appreciate that as I only managed to get hold of these yesterday morning I haven't had a chance to study them properly yet, just a quick flick through.' Chrissie said peering at me over her spectacles. 'Listen; before we go any further I have to tell you that when John banks asked me if I'd take a look at your case I didn't fancy it. Several reasons, first, I am quite busy enough with my own work thank you very much, second, I don't like murder, and third, this type of case can end up bogged down in red tape for months, sometimes years, and I do so hate complicated cases that drag on.'

'No beating around the bush with this one', I thought, and I could feel my heart sinking before we'd barely begun.

Then, I think after spotting the previously hopeful smile sliding from my face, Chrissie held up a finger.

'Nevertheless,' she said. 'Yesterday afternoon I spoke to your solicitor. Now I don't want to give you false hopes because without spending a great deal more time reading through this lot,' Chrissie flipped at the corner of one of the documents on my bed, the one from the police internal investigations unit I reckoned, 'I really don't know if there's any mileage in it. However, Elaine Hennessey your solicitor seems to think that there might be, and, judging from our conversation, she appears to be a sensible girl. So… this is how we are going to play it. If you decide that you would like me to represent you…' Once again, she looked at me over her spectacles. I nodded that indeed I would. 'Then I shall take these papers away, I shall read them, then we will chat again, and then we shall see.'

'We certainly shall.' I thought, and then I added to myself determinedly. 'You're not letting this one get away.'

…And that was about it. After no more than an hour of tea and chats, and a change of the duty officer outside, Christine Tensely-Evans left my cell at 12.15 and rather than feeling that I had interviewed her as a prospective appeal lawyer, I felt that she had interviewed me. I liked her though, I think I recognized something of myself in her, maybe even of both of me, and perhaps because of that I have to tell you that when the door closed, and I was once more alone with my reflection in the privacy of my small room, after only one brief meeting with my perfect lady and my consequent fleeting epiphanal moment, I felt a twinge of guilt at what I was already scheming to do.

———————————

The few days following my meeting with Chrissie, with one providential exception that led to a near tragedy, passed slowly and largely uneventfully. Winter had taken a turn for the worse, my friends and even my family either appeared to be hiding from me or had gone into hibernation, and I seemed to have picked up a cold. In fact, feeling grotty with a thick head and disgusting sinuses, and having plenty to think about and plan for, for once in my incarcerate life being locked in my cell for hours on end with little or no interesting company suited me quite well. On the Friday after my epiphanal Wednesday, soon after breakfast but before my dinner-date officer was able to drag me from my cell to the gymnasium and enforce a stroll, not only fed up with the straggly mess but also as part of my developing plan, I finally got round to cutting my hair. It was just a trim really, but my pedantic snips took ages. I scrounged a pair of scissors and a reasonable comb from the part-time prison barber, a pleasant enough chap, a trustee orderly from another wing by the name of Dale who manned the barbershop twice weekly on Mondays and Fridays and seemed to consider us, tonsorially at least, as some kind of kindred spirits. While Dale watched closely (impressed at my nifty scissor-work I've no doubt), I sat myself in front of his solitary mirror and painstakingly cut a graduated blocky sort of bob shape that still reached my shoulders but with a gently textured fringe to keep any stray ends out of my eyes. Ordinarily not my style, but I figured the classy lines would serve my purpose well enough. Still under Dale's watchful eye, before I left the small Barbershop (no more than an ill-equipped cupboard really, but, along with the dental surgery which shared the same waiting area, one of the few newly refurbished facilities on the ground floor that had actually been completed), after I returned the scissors and comb to a disinfectant jar on a shelf immediately behind the door, rather than leaving my hair hanging down, I scraped it away from my face and then tied it back into the ponytail scrunchy band that I'd recently taken to wearing. Dale looked at me and shrugged his shoulders, I'm sure silently wondering why ever I'd gone to the bother of cutting the shape so precisely only then to scruff it up. I could see his point, but I had good reason.

'It just feels better with the ends off.' I said shrugging back, trying to fob him off as I opened the Barbershop door. 'It tangles dreadfully if I leave it hanging free.'

Dale nodded and then ah-ha'd, if not convinced then at least apparently satisfied, then, as I closed the door, I caught him glancing at me sideways and raising an eyebrow. I reckoned that trustee barber might have bought into my reasoning after all but he just thought I was a bit of a twit... I wasn't going to argue.

Saturday and Sunday turned out to be days of contrasting fortunes, both good and bad from each. First thing on Saturday morning, while trying to steal an extra toilet roll from the shower block to blot and blow my nose, I came across Edward Ewan Edwards who had - rather embarrassingly – got himself stuck with his arms tucked behind while him trying to squeeze into the solitary toilet stall.

'Whatever are you doing?' I asked seeing the big man wedged between the inward opening door and the solid looking metal toilet roll holder on the opposite wall, but before I'd actually realised that he couldn't get out.

'I'm taking a crap, what do you think?' Big Ed replied grumpily.

'Do you need a hand?' I asked.

'No I bloody don't, you pervert.' he snapped.

'Not with your crap, you Wally, with the door. You look like you're stuck.'

'No I'm not.'

'Oh… well please yourself.' I said, and I began to turn away.

'Well maybe I am… stuck… just a bit.' Edward finally admitted.

'I caught my trousers on the door handle on the way in, and my pocket on the thing on the wall while I was trying to turn round, and now I can't get my hands in to free my trousers, and I can't move backwards, and I can't move forwards, and now the door handle's digging into my skin, and I don't like it….'

'I can see.' I said, quickly spotting that the door handle had all but disappeared into a fold of his blubbery flesh. 'So… do you need a hand?'

'Oh very well then… if you insist.' Edward said begrudgingly while turning his head and rolling his eyes.

Moving closer to examine the extent of my friend's predicament, I quickly realised that Edward was simply much too wide for the stall. While, presumably, he had at sometime in the past been able to force his ever-increasing bulk in through the gap, now that his heavyweight, but fit to burst prison trousers, had caught and were compressed on the lock on one side of the stall, and hooked onto the loo roll holder on the other, there was no easy way out.

'I reckon we need a knife.' I said.

'Whatever for.' Ed Said with a gulp.

'To cut your trousers free.' I said. 'I'll go and find someone; I saw Deakin floating around on the corridor or maybe one of the officers in the landing office.'

'No!' Ed shrieked. 'Don't leave me on my own.' He squealed.

'Okay, okay.' I said. 'But we need something to cut through your trousers.'

'Can't you just undo them and pull them down?' He asked.

'Edward... Your front is in there and your back and your arms are out here... How do expect me to get your trousers down?'

'You could climb over and rip them off me.' He said.

'Edward.' I sighed. 'The walls are within two inches of the ceiling, how do you expect me to squeeze through a gap like that, we'll both end up stuck, and besides, Her Majesty has rules concerning the breaching of toilet walls, you must know that.'

'Not the walls, me... climb over me... please hurry up.'

Okay... so you know what's coming... oh very clever you...

What could I do? My friend... well... my sometime prison buddy at any-rate... was stuck and approaching panic. He had asked me for help and had even suggested a method by which I might reasonably have freed him.

Bugger!

Removing my shoes, I placed my right foot carefully into the crease between big Ed's right buttock and the roll of fat at the small of his back, I levered myself upward, and then forward, and then grabbed the squidgy mass that he sometimes referred to as hair on the top of his head.

'Youch!' He said 'Easy Tiger... easy.'

'Do you want me to help you or not?' I hissed.

'Sorry.' He said

Pulling myself further up, I took a deep breath in through my nose (which I immediately wished I hadn't) and then, careful to keep my balance and a good grip on Ed's head, I raised my left foot into a similar crease between Ed's back and his left armpit (Oh my god, my stomach still churns at the thought, I should've kept my shoes on at least), then I ducked my head under the top of the doorframe.

It was at that critical moment, with my nose wrinkled against the close-up stench of Ed, and my foot imbedded in a place that I knew to be disgusting (I could feel a rank damp heat oozing through my sock), and with most of the rest of me higher and more wobbly than felt entirely comfortable, that I discovered that even through the rolls of flab Edward Ewan Edwards was ticklish.

With each constrained and stifled guffaw, Ed's gelatinous body convulsed and quivered. My toes had barely wriggled. The very structure of the lavatory stalls heaved and then trembled. I pitched forward, then sideways, then forward again. I heard a wrenching creaking cracking noise. Realising that a tumble was imminent, I did what I think most sensible people caught in such circumstances might have done, I lunged over Big Ed's left shoulder, wrapped my legs tightly around his neck, and tried to make a grab for the toilet downpipe fixed to the wall at the back of the compartment.

Alas, I missed the pipe.

Pivoting forward and then swinging down at a rush, like an orang-utan that had dropped his favourite nuts from a branch to the jungle floor, suddenly upside down, my shoulder and chest crashed into Big Ed's belly and my head dangled to within an inch of his groin.

'Can you reach my belt?' Said Ed, as if nothing at all untoward had just happened.

I wanted to bite him really really hard.

'Yes.' I said using my most peeved tones.

'Well unbuckle it then, then undo my trousers, for goodness sake, get on with it and let's get out of here please.'

I heard laughter then... and I recognised the tones, not from big Ed in ticklish hysterics, but from Mr Deakin and a couple of the Wing Officers, who, I guess having heard the kerfuffle, had quietly entered the shower block and were obviously enjoying the show.

'Bloody hell, I've seen some sights in this place, but these two have got to take the biscuit.' Deakin said.

An instant later, after one final giggling convulsion that reached its crescendo the moment my fingers grabbed for Edward's belt buckle, the right hand wall of the toilet stall gave way. I fell in one direction, down, my head perilously close to the toilet pan, and then, thank goodness, Big Ed fell the other, backwards towards Mr Deakin and the laughter. Thankfully, neither Ed nor I were hurt; the only casualty, upon whom (conveniently I thought at the time) Big Ed had landed, was Mr Deakin, with – we learned later - a broken arm and several cracked ribs… Poor chap.

What was the good that came out of that late winter Saturday's lavatorial debacle? you might wonder, well three things actually.

Firstly, Mr Deakin would be out of everyone's hair for a while, a good many of my fellow guests must have been pleased about that, and although my senior prison officer's spell of sick leave might have upset my cousin, his absence from the wing certainly helped me.

Secondly, Big Ed and I appeared to be on speaking terms again…

'Why ever didn't you use the toilet in your room?' I asked en-escort back to our cells.

'I don't like to poo in my own loo.' He replied.

'Why ever not?'

'I don't like the smell.'

'Ed… Look… I don't like to be unkind, but there's nobody going to notice the smell of the odd poo in your cell, I'm sure that I don't need to tell you this old chap, but your cell stinks, everything around you stinks, frankly Ed… you stink.'

'I'd notice.' He said, completely ignoring the insults I'd thrown at him. I couldn't feel guilty.

'Fair enough.' I shrugged, and then after a moment or two of silence I added. 'How are you? I haven't seen you for a while'.

'I'm alright… How are you?' He said.

'I have a cold.'

'You don't eat enough, you're skin and bone.' As my cousin had only recently attested, I certainly wasn't, I think Edward was simply if imaginatively applying his own relative values. 'You need building up with goodness and vitamins.' He said.

'I need something for my sore throat.' I said.

'I think I may be able to help you with that, I have some fruit in my cell, some oranges and some lemons, with some sugar and a few aspirin from the Doc, and you could make yourself a soothing drink.'

…and thirdly, what I'd considered to be Big Ed's irritating need to vitamin-*ise* me and fatten me up, with a little ingenuity on my part, actually turned out to be jolly handy.

CHAPTER THIRTY-EIGHT

Although I had an invitation to dine out, I decided to stay in on that Saturday evening. I spent most of the time in my pyjamas in front of my shaving mirror, either discussing my plans with my reflection, revising my 'to do' list, or highlighting my hair with squirts of juice from Big Ed's lemon (a crude, but, when applied carefully and then wrapped in plastic and given warmth and a good night's sleep, a surprisingly effective bleach). I think that even then, early in my scheming, I realised that for my epiphanal moment to blossom to its fullest fruition I would need to act swiftly. Although I reckoned that Mr Deakin, the prison officer easily the most familiar with my visage, would now be out of my way for some time, I dared not bank on the refurbishment works that had so conveniently diverted Christine Tensely-Evans actually into my cell lasting much longer. Furthermore, while I was confident that my new lawyer would be back to see me at least one more time, and hopefully soon, at that point I couldn't be certain, either of the timeframe, or how frequent any further meetings might be.

At around half past nine, with my nose still dreadfully bunged up, my hair wrapped in strips torn from a Tesco carrier bag, having decided that for my plan to work I'd need to make certain that several things were in place before agreeing any further meetings, I turned my light out and went to bed.

Despite my cold, I slept well.

In the morning, woken by the familiar clatter of unfastening locks and the unpleasant feel of strips of plastic carrier bag sticking to my face, before even reaching for a sip of water, I crawled to my shaving mirror. Peeling the wrappings away from my face and then from my hair, I was delighted to discover that the first of my 'several things that needed to be in place' had turned out perfectly. Overnight, the squirts of juice from Big Ed's lemon had almost magically transformed my dull mouse with its few stray greys into shimmering highlighted golden-blonde tresses. God I was good, still wizardry in the old fingertips, my incarceration a veritable tragedy for the hairdressing profession.

After rinsing any residue of the lemon juice from my hair, leaving it wet and slick with my Christmas conditioner and thus, to the casual observer at least, looking greasy and with the colour still relatively unchanged, I tied my hair back into a ponytail, and then I dressed and headed off to meet Edward Ewan Edwards for breakfast. However, when I arrived in the dining room and looked around, maybe ten minutes later, at close to half past seven, with most of the tables occupied and when the queues at the serving hatches were always at their worst, my friend Big Ed wasn't there.

'Your mate was taken poorly last night.' A voice said quietly in my ear as I stood at the entrance to the dining room. 'Not good either, if you ask me.' I turned to see my favourite dinner-date officer on door-duty behind me, he was shaking his head and the expression on his face was even more glum than usual.

'What was the matter with him?' I asked.

'He was found in his cell just before lights-out.' The Officer said, shrugging his chin. 'Heart, the Doc' thinks. Lucky for him he passed out on the floor; if he'd bunked down early, nobody would have noticed, I reckon he'd be a dead-un.'

'Bloody hell!' I said, suddenly knocked for six at the thought of losing another friend. 'He looked well enough yesterday.'

'No... he didn't.' My dinner-date officer countered bluntly. 'I doubt if Eddie Edwards has looked well for years, and certainly not since he's been banged up in here. 'A coronary or a stroke just waiting to happen', the Doc told me.'

Quickly realising the stupidity of my remark, I raised my eyebrows in sad agreement, it was true, my friend not only kept himself smelly but also a vastly overweight unhealthy mess.

'Is he in the infirmary?' I asked. 'Will they let me see him?'

'No, he's in the county hospital... the intensive care unit... the doc says they've plumbed into the mains to keep him alive.' The officer answered matter-of-factly.

'Will he be okay?' I asked.

'Dunno…' He said. 'We'll get word if anything happens… I'll let you know.'

I didn't feel much like eating breakfast after that, instead, feeling sick as yet another friendship seemed doomed to fizzle and fade-away, at 8 o'clock, after a brief comforting chat through my shaving mirror with my reflection, rather uncharacteristically, I took myself to my particular prison's makeshift recreation-room/chapel to pray.

Whether God, or whoever might have been listening to my silent prayers on that Sunday morning, paid any heed to what I had to ask I don't know, as I have told you before, I am not a religious man nor do I spuriously claim association to any particular faith, but what I do know is that after I'd joined in with the sing-song and made my various pleas, either through spiritual means or from some unwitting inner resolution, over the next few days, a certain number of my life's recently ill fitting jigsaw-puzzle pieces seemed to slip quietly into place.

After receiving a metaphorical pat on the head from my prison chaplain (a man who, perhaps unsurprisingly – he was a vicar after all - reminded me of pasty John Cokeley, the vicar of St Michael's at home in my little town), I left the makeshift church with my spirits gently lifted to return to my cell and spent most of the rest of that Sunday concentrating on plotting my exit strategy with my reflection.

Once again, although at odds with my generally edgy state of mind, and indeed, my nasty cold, I slept well that night, waking only when the sounds of clicking locks and the usual bustle of morning on the corridor outside permeated my cell door. I got up and dressed straight away. I had plans for that most important Monday morning. I'd even written a list.

My first port of call after breakfast was the Wing Governor's office. The officer on duty at the desk, a young Asian man who I didn't recognise but who I remember thinking had the type of androgynous multi-ethnic good looks that might have earned him a better living modelling catalogue clothing, was remarkably polite and helpful, and surprisingly approved my request to make a telephone call without any hesitation at all. I took to him immediately - his dark smouldering eyes, his refined vocal tones - but for the sake of my exit plan and my need to draw as little personal attention as possible, I refrained from engaging him any more than I had to.

Elaine's secretary answered my call between the third and fourth ring and untypically, although just as with the nice young Asian man on duty in the block office, on that Monday morning she also seemed remarkably keen to help.

'Oh good morning, I'll put you through straight away.' She said cheerily as soon as I gave her my name. 'I'm sure that Miss Hennessey will be delighted to take your call.' I thanked her, the telephone went quiet, then, a moment later the earpiece beeped, and the secretary came back on the line and added even more cheerfully although now also somewhat suspiciously. 'Miss Hennessey would indeed be delighted to speak to you Sir.'

Alas, my solicitor failed to maintain the jolly trend.

'Yes.' She snapped.

'Elaine… it's me.' I said, realising instantly that her secretary had been making fun of us both.

'I know it's you… my secretary has just told me. It is Monday morning. It is barely nine o'clock. I haven't even glanced at my postbag yet.' She said, and then added frostily. 'How can I help?'

'I'm sorry.' I said, somewhat taken aback by the depth of her obviously foul mood. 'I just need to square a few things with you, and I wondered if you'd heard from Christine Tensely-Evans yet.'

'You sound as if you have a cold.' She said, her tone softening.

'Yes…' I said. '…a real stinker.'

'Me too.' Elaine said, and now I could hear the wretched Mucus-Gremlin thick in her voice too. 'I bloody well hate colds.' She grumbled.

'I can call back later.'

'No, don't worry.' She said, now, I think realising that we were fellow sufferers, sounding a tad friendlier. 'Actually, I have heard from Christine, and I think we've got her on side. She asked me for the rest of the documentation, the trial transcripts, and the full police report on Dennis Sapsead. I sent them over on Friday so that she could study over the weekend. I'm hoping to talk to her again later today, but I'm fairly confident that you can expect her office to be in touch with you shortly.'

'Just how shortly do you think?' I asked eagerly.

'Shortly shortly, I would guess, certainly within the week. She'll want to take statements and make representations as soon as possible.'

'After lunch on Thursday would be good for me.' I said.

'Well, if it matters to you, I'll mention it to her, although as you'll be playing with her bat and rule book, I suspect that the lady will want to call the first ball of the innings.'

'Thursday would be good.' I repeated.

'Then I shall do my best... Now, how else can I help you?'

'My money.' I said. 'I'm worried that if I'm not careful, I'll lose even more on the markets and that I won't have enough in my fighting fund. Those statements you brought me the other day were terrible reading; the only savings that held up were the guaranteed ISAs. I want to consolidate. I want to put everything into one accessible pot. I have a current account with Barclay's Bank... actually, it's the account that you set up for Tristan to manage the rental of my home. I know that it only pays a miniscule interest, but if you can, I'd like you to transfer all my savings and the investment capital there.'

'Well, I can't say I'm surprised that you are worried and I understand your feelings, the international markets have performed appallingly recently. I shall do whatever you want me to naturally, but we are talking about a considerable figure. In my experience, banks prefer larger sums of money to be placed on deposit and then drawn down when required... I could set something up. Also, I feel obliged to point out, that if I were to put all of your funds into that particular account, as things stand, your second cousin, Tristan Blandy, would have access to the lot.'

'I know.' I said. '…but if there's one person in this world that I'm sure I can trust, it's Tristan. Move the cash to the current account for now, the sooner the better, today would be great if you can manage it, if the bank doesn't like it we can always juggle things around later.'

After a sniffling agreement, I repeated my request for a meeting with Chrissie Tensely-Evans to be on Thursday afternoon, I ended my call to Elaine Hennessey and replaced the telephone receiver. The young Asian man in the office was looking at me. I could tell that he'd been listening in on my conversation. I was tempted to say something cutting, but then he smiled at me - all pearly white teeth and dimples – and as I wanted to use the telephone again, I smiled back.

'You are experiencing difficulties?' He asked.

'Yes, I suppose I am.' I said.

'My brother is an accountant and my father is in the legal profession, they regularly oppose each other in life, I am currently the black sheep of our family, and with my mother and three sisters the dinner table at home is often fraught with difficulty.' The young man paused, his smile morphing into a look of sincerity meant as a cryptic reassurance I guessed, but I'm afraid the dusky catalogue hunk's philosophy passed mostly over my head. I nodded and then smiled a bit wider hoping that he thought I understood.

'Always tricky…' I said and then, as if as an afterthought, I added. 'I wonder… would it be possible for me to make one more very brief call.'

'Yes… I'm sure that would be acceptable.' He said (Such a lovely chap), then he pushed the telephone a couple of inches across the narrow desk towards me. 'It is my first day on this particular wing actually. My fellow officer who has been showing me the ropes received a call from a superior. I expect he will be back shortly, but in the meantime, as I appear to be in charge, please, help yourself.'

Suddenly conscious that my luck might run out at any moment, I snatched up the telephone and punched my second cousins mobile number into the keypad as quickly as I could. Tristan's phone rang eight times before a crackly recording of his voice told me that as he was either 'busy saving the world right now' or could not 'be arsed to pick up my call', would I say whatever I had to say very quickly and clearly after the tone.

'Hi Tris, it's me.' I said, and, as instructed, I did speak quickly and very clearly. 'Hello old chap, I'm hoping that you are still coming on Thursday. It's a morning call this week, my wing is on earlys, so before ten o'clock. Listen Tris, I need you to do me a favour. Things are moving along with my case. I have to write some cheques out for my new lawyer and to pay some bills. I need you to grab the chequebook and the bankcard that Elaine Hennessey gave you and put them into an envelope, mark the envelope for the attention of Christine Tensely-Evans (I spelt the name out for him), then bring them with you when you come to visit me and leave them at the Main Gate reception desk so that my new lawyer can pick them up later. This is important Tris, thanks Cuz; I'm looking forward to seeing you.'

After I hung up I wished that I'd added 'bring your mother and Sammie… and if Mr Ripper wants to come along bring him too and maybe his wife Cindy and Colin and Julie from Starbucks and Uncle Bert… the more the merrier, it would be good to see them all,' but I didn't call back.

As luck would have it, a split second after I had replaced the telephone handset into its cradle and slid the telephone back toward my catalogue man, the real life grown-up version of the Wing Governor's office duty officer arrived back at his post. The be-stubbled hard-eyed man looked at me scornfully.

'Yes… what do you want?' He asked, and not at all politely nor with any of a hint of dimples or a pearly smile.

'Me?' I said. 'Nothing… all done thanks.' Then I grinned at him, winked at his young colleague, and mooched away.

I remember the seventy-two hours that followed those two telephone calls more clearly and in more detail than I remember any other specific passage of time during my entire stay as a guest of Her Majesty. Apprehension tinged with excitement, like a child waiting for Christmas or a birthday. Although neither Elaine nor Tristan actually ever called me back to confirm anything, somehow I always remained convinced that the third Thursday in the February of that year was going to be my day. I spent most of the time preparing, simple things mostly, I practised changing in and out of my clothes quickly, doing my hair, I manicured my nails, reshaped my eyebrows, and I even shaved my legs.

On the Wednesday morning, generally happy with my preparations but still in need of a pair of scissors and a comb, knowing that Dale the barber wouldn't be on duty again until Friday, shortly before lunchtime with only a vague idea of how I might obtain the required items, as an excuse to venture without prearrangement to the ground floor, I made the mistake of feigning a toothache. My escort for the fraudulent decent to the dental surgery turned out to be one of the few female prison officers yet employed at my particular prison. We'd not run into each other before. Although dressed much as the male officers in a white shirt, navy twill trousers, heavy shoes, and with all the glittery steel trimmings, cuffs, baton, etc, the young woman was the antithesis of what I think most people might have expected. Far from the stereotypical thickset, comic strip, lesbian screw, that I am afraid the majority female prison officers are often thought to be (it really isn't true), my escort bore a close likeness to Kylie Minogue, a trill of a girl in her mid twenties perhaps, with the fairest hair, the prettiest smile, and the bluest eyes that I'd seen in a jolly long time. Her name was Alex.

'Does it hurt badly?' She asked without any spurious prompting from me as we left my cell.

'What?' I asked, lost to thought for a moment.

'Your tooth… is it very painful?'

'Oh dreadful.' I said, peeling my eyes from her glossy hair and suddenly remembering my excuse for our little trip out. 'An abscess I wouldn't be surprised.' I clutched my cheek and winced appropriately.

'Ooh, nasty.' She said and then she screwed her face up and added. 'Get it out and done with, that's my advice.'

I smiled weakly back at her and nodded.

'I was hoping for penicillin and a filling.' I said.

'Well, you might be lucky and get the antibiotics, but Mr Macalister runs a no-frills clinic downstairs. Don't worry; I'm sure he'll have it out before you can blink.'

...And she was right; he bloody well did... the Scots Meany, my perfectly good tooth.

My bottom had barely sat in his chair for a moment.

'No point in x-raying it.' He said dismissively with a clipped highland burr. 'It's already overfilled and as it is hurting you so much you'd be better off without it.'

Stab, crunch, and yank, and in less than a couple of minutes, certainly before the anaesthetic had fully taken effect, my perfectly functional number two molar was gone. My mother would have told me that it served me right. 'The boy who cried wolf', she would have quoted. Quite frankly, I felt a bit of a twit. However, with my tooth out and my mouth sore but thankfully at last becoming numb, Mr Macalister's nurse showed me to the waiting area that the dental surgery shared with Doc Metcalf's clinic and the barbershop; I eyed my intended goal longingly. Apart from a handful of hardback chairs, a graphic poster warning of the dangers of a dozen varieties of venereal disease, and me, the small sterile room was empty.

'Sit still for a moment and keep biting on the gauze.' The nurse told me. Keen to demonstrate my obedient compliance, I sat down, and peeling my lips back from my teeth like a snarling dog, I bit hard on the wad of cloth that Mr Macalister had shoved into the corner of my mouth. The nurse smiled approvingly and then added. 'I'll call for someone to take you back to your cell in a few minutes.'

With such an obvious and, I feel now as I felt at the time, fated opportunity staring me in the face, as soon as the nurse turned back to the surgery and closed the door behind her, I didn't waste a second. Bravely ignoring the 'sit still' suggestion, I jumped up from my chair and made straight for the barbershop door. Luck or god or whatever or whoever had been listening to my prayers on Sunday still comfortable at my side, I found the door unlocked, and within a matter of less than a minute Dale the barber's spare scissors and comb were out of the disinfectant jar on the shelf behind the door and tucked safely into my sock. My heart suddenly thumping, I shut the door and returned to my seat. A moment later, Kylie Minogue arrived to take me home.

'All better?' she asked with a smile that for some reason seemed now to be a less genuine beam than she'd shared with me earlier. I didn't think to wonder why.

'He ripped the bloomin' thing out.' I mumbled instead via thick tongue and then I added miserably. 'It still hurts.'

As a price to pay? Well, in hindsight, the benefit that I gained from acquiring the pair of scissors and the comb, despite the discomfort that I suffered before, during, and after their acquisition, turned out to be far greater than my need for the innocent casualty of the episode, my poor tooth.

CHAPTER THIRTY-NINE

Although my cold had at last eased, perhaps unsurprisingly, I hardly slept at all that night, for once in my life from excitement more than worry I think. I suppose that seeing Tristan's face grinning around the visitors' room door should have calmed me down. In fact the opposite was true, my second cousins prompt appearance only served to heighten my exhilaration.

Unusually, I had arrived at the visitors' room before anybody else. Anticipating the Tannoyed announcement, I'd breakfasted late and, a touch untypically I'll admit, rather than returning to my cell only to be locked in until summoned, I offered my services to the trustees of washing up crew. Ironically, the hour I spent in the kitchens after breakfast that morning turned out to be one of the few 'fun times' that I experienced as a guest of Her Majesty. A joke here, a splash there, a slap on the shoulder for a job well done, and afterwards the rare feeling of having accomplished something worthwhile perhaps, a feeling that until then I hadn't even realised that I'd missed. In fact, that solitary glimpse of what I can only describe as jocular inmate/workmate camaraderie, taught me a lesson, that volunteering – something that for one reason or another in my life, and most certainly while I was in prison, I worked hard to avoid – might not always be so bad.

I'd chosen the table nearest the door, Tristan spotted me straight away, he was on his own, I'd thought he would be.

'Watcha Matey.' He boomed as he rounded the door.

'Tris.' I said, and I stood up and reached my hand out towards him. Leaning across the table my big second cousin took hold of my hand and unusually I pulled him towards me and gave him a hug.

'God bless you Tris.' I found myself saying.

'Oh wow.' Tristan said. 'Have you found him?' He asked.

I knew what he meant, had I found God, I didn't know what to say, I didn't know what I'd found, I had to disappoint him. 'I'm just glad to see you Cuz.' I said shaking my head. 'You've blessed me often enough, I just thought you deserved one back, it is okay for a heathen like me to wish people a blessing isn't it?'

'Well of course it is Matey, and thanks.' Tris smiled, and yes, I'm afraid his soppy eyes were already glassy. 'That means a lot to me.' He added.

I think that it was probably then that I realised that if what I had been planning over the previous week or so turned out as I hoped it would I might never see Tristan again. I looked at the big lummox sitting across the table from me, his tangled hair, his bushy eyebrows, his unshaven face, and I couldn't help thinking of our chequered history. A fast-forward clutch of memories sped through my mind. Tristan the huge bouncing baby on my mother's knee, the toddler who dragged the terrible twos into the terrible threes, fours, and fives, the teenager thug that terrorised his own mother, the young man who I felt I'd let down. Then in a snatch of time between the opening and closing of my blinking eyelids, I recalled more recent times, despite our many differences, age, interests, shoe-size, in adulthood my second cousin and I had becomes good friends I think.

We chatted casually for about twenty minutes in all; the last ten minutes of any half-hour visiting slot always being awkward to fill. Tristan told me that he had done as I'd asked and had left my chequebook and bank cash card at my prison's reception desk for Chris Tensely-Evans to collect. I thanked him. He brought news of my family; his mother – my first cousin on my mother's side – despite a sniffle was otherwise well, and would have come to visit me but for the early start on what apparently outside was an unseasonably frosty morning. Uncle Bert, on the other hand, was not so good. The old chap – my mother's elder brother - had 'had a fall'. Tristan's words not mine. In England, beyond a certain indeterminate age, people do that, they have falls, they do not 'slip over' or 'tumble' or even 'trip', no, beyond a certain age the wobbly English 'have falls'. Bert's fall had broken his arm in two places, one at the wrist, and one close to his left shoulder, both were bad breaks apparently. Tristan told me that he planned to call in at the hospital on his way home after visiting me. Feeling suddenly guilty that I hadn't spoken to

Bert properly since the day he telephoned me at my salon to break the news that my mother had died, I asked Tristan to give my regards and wish him well.

Tristan also told me that he'd been speaking to Colin, the barista from Starbucks, who, together with his girlfriend, the expectant Patchouli-oil-Julie, had been renting my home on Gillycote Road for the past few months. It seemed that Colin and Julie had gone away visiting her family somewhere dark, and cold, and north of Watford and wouldn't be back until after the weekend. Tristan asked, that as the house would be empty, would I mind if he used the opportunity to sort out some problems that the couple had been having with the central heating system, he also suggested that maybe - if he had the time - he could fix the shed. 'Sunday would be good for me.' He smiled.

'Perfect.' I said, thinking that Sundays seemed to be good for everyone, while happily logging the fact that my house might be empty for the next few days.

At about twenty past ten, with both of us getting fidgety, I started to make noises of the cheerio variety.

'It's been great to see you Tris.' I said. 'Thanks for coming to visit me, I'm sure it must've been a drag for you sometimes, just know that I've always looked forward to seeing you and your Mum, I've really appreciated the way you've both stood by me and given up so much of your free time.'

Tristan looked at me a little sideways. 'That's okay Cuz, don't worry, we're family, we'll always be there for you, just like you were always there for me.' He said sincerely. It seemed that my big second cousin remembered things differently to me. I just nodded and smiled at him. 'I'll see you later then.' He said and then he stood up to go.

'Yes… I'll see you later.' I said. Then, thinking quickly although I'll admit not altogether honestly, I'm afraid slyly, I added. 'Tris, before you go, can I ask one more favour of you?'

'Anything Matey.'

'I need to get a message to Marcus, is he still living at home?' I asked. I felt guilty almost immediately, Tristan deserved better, I didn't need to get a message to Marcus at all,

I just wanted to make certain that he hadn't moved away, that I knew where to find the Fat-Brat.

'Yes, he does, he's still with Cindy and Ripper...' Tristan said unsuspectingly, then his eyes narrowed and he took in a breath. '...but you know what Matey, I really don't think that getting in touch with Marcus is such a good idea.'

The lights in stairwell number '2' flickered and flashed on and off like a strobe lamp in a cheap nightclub. Sounds of hammering and electric saws echoed through the gratings from below. On only her second full shift on my wing, Kylie Minogue escorted me onto 'B' corridor for the second time in as many days. I could tell that something was bothering her.

'Are you okay?' I asked over my shoulder.

'I beg your pardon?' Miss Minogue replied curtly.

'I just thought you didn't seem yourself today.'

'I'm fine thank you. How's your tooth?'

'I don't know. I haven't seen it since that nasty Scotsman pulled it out.'

'You know very well what I mean.'

'It's much better today thank you ma'am.'

'You should take care of your teeth.'

'I do.'

'I'm afraid Edward Edwards died last night.'

Just like that, she gave me no warning at all. My feet froze to the spot and a sharp angry shiver ran up my spine.

'Shit.' I said.

'I'm sorry. They told me he was your friend. He had another heart attack yesterday morning. We received notice while you were having your tooth pulled actually. Then today, when I came on duty the news arrived from the hospital that he'd died during the night and I had to help clear his cell.'

'Boy-oh-boy.' I said and then I whistled.

'Yes it wasn't pleasant.' Kylie said, turning her nose up, misunderstanding me completely. That wasn't what I'd meant at all, although I didn't bother to put the stupid girl right, I couldn't have cared less about the state of Big Ed's cell, how much it smelled, or who'd had to clear it out. Although I'd not known him long and he might not have been the cleanest or most communicative soul, I reckoned that Edward Ewan Edwards was my kind of a chap; straight up and down in a wiggly sort of way, not many of us around, I knew then that I'd miss him for the rest of my life.

Seeing that I was upset, Kylie moved closer. 'Look, I shouldn't be doing this.' She said in a low voice. 'But while I was sorting through Mr Edward's personal effects and bagging up the rubbish I came across this.' She reached into her tunic and withdrew a small brown package that she then handed to me. 'It has your name written on it, and there is an iPod inside.'

Back in my room, after listening for the door to click shut, while clutching Big Ed's iPod I faced my shaving mirror and I allowed myself a moment to cry. If I'd needed some kind of ultimate confirmation that pressing on with my plan was essential not only for my wellbeing but also for my sanity, then Big Ed's death was surely it. I couldn't possible stay in that wretched prison any longer than I absolutely had to. Feeling a familiar but unexpected nervous tremble growing in my fingers, I clasped my hands together and wrung them hard stifling the twitch. I steeled myself. My reflection stared out at me for a long moment until at last it winked.

'Don't worry.' It said.

'I don't think I am worried.' I replied. 'Just sad, sad at everything that has happened, at everything that has led me to this dreadful place. It seems that only a moment ago all I needed from life was my mother's smile and a nod from my father, Santa was real and a bag of sweets the most precious thing in the whole wide world. Now, only a heartbeat or two on, grown-up too much, and that wonderful world feels like it's weighing on my chest.'

'Oh for god sake don't be so dramatic.' My reflection chided. 'We all grow up, we all have to do things that we'd rather not. Lie down now… you have some time… take a nap for goodness sake… try to stay calm.'

I knew there was no point in arguing with me. In fact, despite my reflection's doubts, I didn't need to lie down, and nor did I need to try to stay calm. Incredibly, as we spoke, with almost everything in place, regardless of the upset, I felt that I was ready, perfectly calm and able to do whatever was necessary.

I stood still in the very centre of my room for precisely one hour before the knock that I'd been expecting finally sounded at my door. I had prepared myself perfectly. My nails were clean, shaped and buffed. My hair teased ready into place and now gently patted flat into its ponytail disguise. My teeth were minty fresh. My eyebrows plucked into a classical arch. I had shaved my entire body more closely, and more thoroughly, than even an 'A' list porn star might. I had even curled my eyelashes.

'You have a visitor.' Said the officer who had now unlocked my door and was standing at the threshold to my cell. The young man appeared to be alone and wore an unfortunate expression of extreme boredom. I looked at him quizzically.

'What?' He said slowly with a lazy sneer.

'Well… where is she?' I asked.

'At reception, obviously, I suppose I'll have to take you down… hurry up and get whatever you need.'

'Down?' I said, not certain that I'd heard him correctly.

'Yes down.' He snapped, now obviously as bored with my questions as he seemed to be with the rest of his life. 'Your visitor, the lady solicitor, she's waiting for you at reception, downstairs.'

Slowly, very slowly, like the rising mist from an icy sea after a wrongly warm winter's day, realisation began to fill my every sense. Christine Tensely-Evans had indeed arrived for our meeting just as I had hoped she would, just as I asked Elaine Hennessey to arrange, day and time perfect. However, suddenly it seemed that the meeting would not be taking place in my cell where I'd carefully planned for it to be, but instead in some scruffy, half finished, but doubtless fully surveilled interview room downstairs. I cannot describe to you the depths of the devastation I felt at that moment, after all my efforts, the hope… no, the conviction that my plan was destined to succeed. Strangely, as the blood drained from my face I felt myself smile at the young man. Don't shoot the messenger. I heard the familiar idiom ring in my ears. I wanted to blow his bloody brains out. Biting my lip to stop it quivering, I nodded as calmly as I could, and then, swallowing hard at a lump in my very dry throat, I stepped towards the door.

CHAPTER FORTY

I followed my miserable escorting officer along 'B' corridor with my head bowed, my eyes fixed down, and my footsteps barely leaving the floor. Shuffling miserably, I half expected that at any moment I might hear my mother's voice telling me to stand up straight and pick my feet up. Instead, when we turned the from 'B' corridor and crossed the landing into stairwell number '2' I heard a dreamy voice that I guess right then I wanted to hear even more.

'Hullo.' the soft feminine tones came to my ears, 'Where do you think you're off to?'

I looked up from the swirling monotone kaleidoscope of floor tiles to see Kylie Minogue waiting at the top of the stairs, and standing next to her, peering out through thick spectacles beneath the brim of a woollen cloche hat and wearing a long camel mohair coat, was Christine Tensely-Evans. Bounce and bounce back, the incarcerate rollercoaster trend of lows and highs apparently alive and well. I squealed out loud.

'What?' I said... once more finding my single syllable stump, I turned to my escort and grinned. He was grinning too, not at me though, but at Kylie Minogue. I looked to Christine.

'Bloody annoying!' She said, her tone hardening, and then, hoisting her handbag and her large and obviously heavy briefcase up to her chest, she added. 'I'd just got myself settled in a grotty little room next to the building site downstairs and off go all the lights, no power, no nothing. It looks like we'll have to make do with your cell again I'm afraid, not ideal I know, but we'll just have to manage.' She shrugged at me and then shot my escorting officer and Kylie Minogue an icy stare.

I didn't know who to thank, Her Majesty for ordering my particular prison's refurbishments, the construction workers on the ground floor for being so painfully slow and inefficient, or God, whichever one of those many available had answered my prayers. Just to be on the safe side I vowed right there and then that I would pray and sing my heart out to any deity that might deign to listen to me on every single Sunday morning for the rest of my life. If I could have clapped my hands with glee without raising any suspicious eyebrows, I would have.

While the turnaround in my fortunes was fantastic, I can't pretend that, by the time that Chrissie and I had walked back along the full length of 'B' corridor to my cell, my nerves were quite as steady as I'd hoped they would be at that moment. Following instructions from my escorting officer, trembling just a smidge, I stepped into my room and waited for my new lawyer to join me. After the usual acerbic discussions between guard and brief regarding security, client confidentiality, and whether or not the door should remain open or could be closed, eventually, having won the argument, Chrissie was allowed to enter my cell. I had taken a seat on the lid of my weird plastic toilet and, as before, I offered Chrissie the use of my bed. After shutting the door firmly onto 'B' corridor leaving Kylie and my escort - who I could hear were already chatting happily - outside, my perfect woman smiled at me and sat down, laying her briefcase towards my pillow, and placing her handbag on the floor close to her feet. My inner-self grinned I'm afraid; I felt it, warm and uncomfortably self-satisfied.

'Before we start on the nitty-gritty, I received some news this morning that should make us both feel more confident.' Chrissie said straightaway, patting her briefcase. 'I'm not sure how she's done it, but somehow your friend Elaine Hennessey – the clever girl - has obtained a copy of a closed circuit video recording from one of the security cameras in the development behind your hairdressing salon. I haven't seen the footage yet, but from what Elaine tells me it's damning stuff. The recording concerned covers a five-day period around Easter last year, I don't yet know the exact dates, but apparently although it is time-lapsed the digital video clearly shows Detective Dennis Sapsead breaking into and entering your hairdressing salon.'

I'm sure not sure how I felt after I took in what Chrissie had said, she looked terribly pleased with herself, but I think I felt a mixture of emotions, surprise, concern, and anger, the most prevalent. Surprise that any of the cameras behind my salon actually worked, that the original police investigation had apparently missed them, and that any recording from so long ago was still on file. Concern that once revealed the video might open a Pandora's Box of similar clips but this time featuring me. And anger at the confirmation that Dennis bloody Sapsead had indeed set me up.

If I'd had any doubts or second thoughts concerning my need to carry out what I had been planning (which in all honesty I don't think I had), then far from convincing me otherwise, Chrissie's revelation about Dennis Sapsead only served to strengthen my resolve, now more than ever I knew that I had to get out and get even.

In fact, Christine Tensely-Evans only remained conscious for a matter of moments after she'd finished telling me the news. Once certain that she was properly away with the fairies, I pushed her briefcase to one side and laid her gently back onto the bed. There were no marks, well… a bruise perhaps, just a small one behind her left ear, but I was certain that after a day or two in bed the bruising would fade and Chrissie would be fine.

Haste being essential I couldn't afford to dally with niceties. After lifting the briefcase to the floor and the handbag from the floor onto my small chest of drawers, I rolled Chrissie over and started to remove her clothes. Although her wardrobe selection on that chilly spring morning wasn't ideal or even particularly stylish, thick woollen tights and a snug polo-neck jumper under a heavy tweed business suit, I soon had her naked and tied, and covered with blankets tucked up in my bed. Apart from her shoes, a pair of unimaginative but sturdy navy court pumps with a convenient kitten heel, which I had to loosen using the scissors that I'd borrowed from the prison barber, Chrissies clothes fitted me almost perfectly. It may sound creepy, but I put on everything, from her panties and bra - which I padded with toilet paper in the cups and a towel wrapped around my hips - to her skirt and blouse, from her long camel mohair coat to the woollen tights. Remembering my experience walking across town when wearing Cecile Ablitt's classic Chanel suit, I knew that to play the part well enough to bluff my way to freedom I'd need to feel as feminine as possible. I'd need to feel like a woman.

Inside Chrissie's handbag, I found all that I could possibly have hoped for, a fully loaded purse, a charged mobile phone, a collection of keys that included a monster for some kind of BMW, and most important of all, a small quilted Gucci bag containing the essential make-up repair kit, a small vial of Escada perfume, and a bottle of Opi Californian Raspberry nail polish. The ultimate transformation didn't take me long. My hair was a fabulous match in terms of both style and colour, Chrissie's light foundation suited my newly shaved skin well, my nails took only a few moments to dry, and with the perfume, I smelled delicious. Standing back and looking into my shaving mirror, less than ten minutes after my lawyer had entered my cell, although I say it myself, the change in the reflection was remarkable, my resemblance to Chrissie, uncanny. I knew it would be the instant I first saw her. As yin and yang, or the opposites of the same double-headed coin, I knew that regardless of gender with only a little work our basic features would be a near perfect match.

Pulling the woollen cloche hat over my freshly coiffed hair leaving just a few carefully positioned highlighted ends around my face, with Chrissie's spectacles in place on my nose, I felt that at last I was ready. Peering beneath the lenses, I looked for the briefcase on the floor by the end of my bed. Tucked just inside, I'd already spotted the envelope containing my chequebook and cash cards that Tristan had brought with him and had left at the prison reception desk for Chrissie to collect; my second cousins spidery scrawl on the front was unmistakeable. My pulse suddenly quickened. Almost everything was in place. I took a long slow breath to settle my nerves. With just one last piece of the jigsaw to fit before opening the door to face my audience I turned to Chrissie. Lying prone, tied firmly to my bed under a pile of skimpy prison blankets, my new lawyer, my perfect woman, Christine Tensely-Evans LLM, senior partner at Banks Banks and Windie, still out for the count, deserved none of this. I should have felt dreadfully guilty. I'd hit her with a homemade cosh, an old sock half filled with sand into which I'd dropped a lump of rolled up lead roof flashing that I'd found in the yard… just the one blow. I'd checked that she was breathing while I was taking her clothes off. Chrissie seemed fine, more like she was asleep than unconscious. All I needed to do now was make her look comfortable and a tad more like me.

Taking my facecloth from the washbasin, I ran it under warm water, squeezed out the excess, and then took it over to the bed. Chrissie seemed oddly peaceful and not at all troubled by her ordeal. Leaning over her, I lifted her head gently and began to wash her face. Lipstick, blusher, mascara, with only light rubbing the quality make-up came off quickly and well enough. Chrissie had a beautiful skin, soft and milky, and much younger, and more finely toned than most women of her age.

Finally, I trimmed her hair, just a shade shorter, nothing fussy, just a little closer in length to how my own would have appeared before I started tying it back. When I'd done, I gathered Chrissie's hair into a loose ponytail with my scrunchy band, ruffled it up a bit so it looked like she'd been sleeping, then I lay her head back on the pillow. Then, after arranging the blankets so that from the doorway only the back of Chrissie's head would be visible, I kissed her on the cheek and whispered three words, 'Sorry', 'thanks', and 'goodbye'.

The first half dozen steps were the worst. I thanked god for the kitten heels, stilettos would have been awful on my prison's smooth tiled floors. Fortunately, when I opened the door, I found that Kylie Minogue had gone. The officer outside my cell, the young chap who'd come to take me downstairs earlier, who I'd seen on the corridor several times before but who I wasn't particularly familiar with and thankfully didn't really know me, turned and nodded when he saw me. With Kylie gone, suddenly he looked all miserable and bored again.

'All done Ma'am?' He asked a touch more tersely than I thought he should have, he was speaking to a visiting lawyer after all.

Despite his churlish tone, I smiled inside. The fact that the young officer had apparently accepted that I was indeed who I purported to be immediately and without any quibble came as quite a relief.

'Yes thank you.' I said, both softening and raising the inflection of my voice to my best approximation of Chrissie's. Thankfully, my nerve held and I managed to say it without croaking or squeaking at all.

After calling goodbye to myself and closing the cell door behind me, I lifted the briefcase high in front of my chest as I'd seen Chrissie do at the top of the stairs when she arrived, and then I hoisted her handbag - rather deftly I thought - over my shoulder.

'Could you show me down now?' I asked.

'Of course Ma'am.' The young officer replied, still sounding bored but at least now speaking more politely.

Essentially, it was as simple as that. My escort didn't look at me closely, he didn't question that by any recent standards as a legal counsel, my visit had been brief, and he didn't so much as glance into my cell. Conveniently, on the way downstairs, the young officer seemed keen to avoid small talk, the early afternoon corridors and stairways were quiet, and apart from a leering builder working high on a stepladder on the ground floor, until I reached the reception desk at the main gate, no one paid me any special attention at all.

I suppose that good fortune smiled at me again then, although for a few tense tummy churning moments I'd thought otherwise. While I was waiting in line at the desk to sign myself out, the final hurdle, with Chrissie's briefcase still held high against my chest concealing at least the lower part of my face, my pulse jolted when I saw Lance Deakin with his arm in a sling, sitting on a tall stool, apparently on duty behind the reception office desk. I'd thought that I'd prayed and sung him out of my way. He was the last person I wanted to see. I could only assume that the man whose silly bashful grin had seduced my cousin from good sense, and who of all the prison officers I felt was most likely to see through my disguise, after his crunching encounter with Big Eddie Edwards, had returned to work on light duties as a desk officer. I had no idea. Thankfully, hampered by his broken arm and I reckon, keen not to make any silly mistakes in his new job, Mr Deakin appeared to be concentrating far harder on paperwork than on me or anybody else around him. Tucking my chin almost inside Chrissie's briefcase, although careful to avoid any eye contact, I waited my turn in the line with the fear of discovery beating in my ears. As it happened, relief from my apprehension and the impending face-to-face with my senior officer was only a moment away. While Deakin was struggling to sort out a minor issue for the two men ahead of me in the queue, an officer who was waving a medical pass in the air, and an inmate whom at the time I didn't really focus on, but who I was sure had been looking at me, a long black limousine pulled up on the courtyard outside the Main Gate office window. Everyone looked round. The air in the office instantly seemed to thicken and fizz. Deakin and the other staff on duty all began to move a great deal more quickly. Immediately the car drew to a halt, the driver and two burly minders, all three of them dressed in black suits and conspicuously wired for sound, clambered out. A moment later, the back door of the car swung open. The largest and baldest of the minders quickly made his way around the car to stand guard as a much smaller, although still tall, grey haired aristocratic looking man, wearing a long navy blue Crombie style coat, and shiny black shoes, eased himself from the back seat.

'Who is that?'

I heard someone in line behind me ask as the driver of the limousine opened the door from the courtyard into the main-gate reception area.

'That's the big-wig, Martin Hendy-Coombs, the home-office minister for prisons and the probation service. Apparently, he's on an official visit to inspect the progress of the refurbishments. Look at the place, what a joke.' Came the loudly whispered reply.

Desperate to remain inconspicuous, although remembering a flippant comment that Tristan had made to me in a The Wheatsheaf pub when I first met Marcus and Mr Ripper I recognised the name instantly as that of Cindy Dobson's father and thus the Fat-Brat Marcus Hendy-Coombs' grandfather, I didn't look around. However, a moment later I heard another door to the main-gate office open, the door that I'd used only a moment earlier when I'd left the main Prison buildings. A sharply barked series of stern commands. This time I did glance over my shoulder. Behind me and to my left, a group of two prison officers and four of Her Majesty's newest and, I'm sorry to say, most sad-faced recruits, marched into the room. I'd have known the look anywhere; the newbies were young and looked thoroughly miserable. I felt quite sorry for them.

All of a sudden, the main gate reception area was in kerfuffle. The home-office inspection party was moving in one direction, and the prison detail was moving in the other, leaving the queue to the desk, and therefore me, in the middle. Before I knew what was happening, the inmate that I'd felt had been looking at me ushered me gently but firmly towards the desk.

'Ladies first.' He said.

I glanced up at him quickly and frowned, his brown face opened into a smile, his eyes flashed, and then he mouthed the words, 'Good luck.' Suddenly concerned that Deakin might have been watching us I looked away. An instant later, before I could respond or even wonder what I might have said, or come to that, before I could worry about Mr Deakin, the four raw recruits and the two prison officers were pushing past me, a now agitated Mr Deakin as desk-officer was handing me the visitors' 'in and out' book, which although I was unable to find Chrissie's name I duly signed, and then, like an unwanted nuisance, and directly in front of Her Majesty's Government's Home Office Minister for Prisons and the Probation Service, the Right Honourable Mr Martin Hendy-Coombs, I was hurriedly shown out through my particular prison's front door.

Perhaps one day I should drop Marcus's grandfather a line and thank him for providing such a marvellous distraction to aid my escape. Would that be too cheeky?... bah!

The inmate who ushered me ahead in the queue was of course, Phillip Johnston, and at last, after all the time I'd spent with him in prison, once more caught up in a fraught mêlée perhaps, in that brief glimpse of his smiling face I recognised the wrapping paper mugger who had saved me from the sixth former beating such a long time ago. Fate really is a peculiar animal.

Silently waving goodbye to my utilitarian-chic home from home and also to my favourite prison officer Mr Deakin, walking quickly around the ministerial limousine, to complete my escape, despite the prospect of having to drive again raising my anxiety levels to silly heights, needs must etc, I headed straight for the car park to find Christine Tensely-Evans' BMW. Breathing in the cool early afternoon air, stepping into the weak sunlight out from the shadow of the main gate, as I crossed the spiritual divide from incarceration to freedom, a flashed daydream of keys and locks dragged a memory of childhood and my Grandfather to mind. My father's father's whimsical stories and boasts would hold every member of my family enthralled. I remembered one particular yarn that I heard a dozen times.

'In all the years that I was a jailer in the army not one prisoner ever escaped my jail.' My grandfather would start proudly, and then he'd wait for a moment until whoever was listening looked suitably impressed, before adding. 'Mind you, nobody ever actually tried.'

Remembering my grandfather's tease made me wonder if that was the answer. If so few prison inmates actually try to escape, so long as rules are adhered to and the obvious checked, the vast majority of prison officers' confidence is so high that they simply forget the possibility that one might. Although I'll admit to a limited survey sample, the former was certainly true in my particular prison. Of the people I'd got to know inside, by quite a wide margin most were happily content to serve out their time quietly, and I reckon some, fearful of the big wide world outside, before they'd even finished one sentence had a plan in mind to begin another. Looking back, notwithstanding my ingenuity and talent for disguise, of course, I guess the relative ease of my escape speaks for itself.

Although tucked behind a white panel van in a line of vehicles on the far left hand edge of the car park, thanks in part to the remote control device on Chrissie's car key, and in part the manufacturer's sensible decision to incorporate a miniature replica of the Blackpool illuminations into the vehicle's central locking system, I found Chrissie's BMW easily. I have to say that I was disappointed. Not so much with the make or model of the car, although it has to be said the '3' series hatchback Beamer was never a favourite of mine, but with the condition. Chrissie's car was absolutely filthy, not at all as I had expected to find it. Ignoring the muck on the bodywork, just a glance at the state of the interior, sweet wrappers on the floor, old newspapers strewn here and there, fingerprints and goo smeared on the windows, and suddenly I wondered if my bonking Chrissie on the head might not have been so undeserved after all. Looking around the car, and suddenly the thought of wearing my former new lawyer's worn panties seemed less appealing. I remember squirming in the driver's seat.

Despite my tentative driving hampering my need for haste, the journey back to my little town, including stops at a number of shops, a carwash, two banks, and a loo, and a half hour detour along the M4 to Chrissie's home in Windsor, took a little over four hours. I arrived on Gillycote Road to find my house empty, just as Tristan had promised it would be, as dusk was falling at about a quarter past six. Although still dressed as a woman, I had changed my look completely by then, gone, the business suit and snug fitting polo necked jumper, on, the navy slacks, red sailing jacket, and clean and more substantial underwear.

Remembering walking home along the farm track after meeting Colin's brother while fleeing Broughton Castle just over a year before, I parked the now gleaming BMW (new number plates courtesy of Halfords in Slough) between two cars advertised for sale, in the lay-by on the cul-de-sac behind St Michael's Church. 'Hide in plain view' I recalled hearing an expert advise while being interviewed on some news programme or another, I think the ex military sort was talking about radicals at the time, and how they pass unnoticed in their home communities, but I reckoned the concept sounded fluid.

After dumping my suitcase (a smart Louis Vuitton borrowed from Chrissie) on the kitchen floor, before allowing myself the luxury of revelling in the simple joy of being home at last in my wonderful little house, I made directly for my garden shed. Thankfully, I found the key where I'd hidden it in such a hurry on the night that Marcus surprised me when I got home after visiting Dr Carmen, immediately below the door between two parts of the cinder block step. Although the lock was stiff, the shackle opened on the second twist of the key. I took a breath and closed my eyes then pulled the shed door ajar. Wafts of air from inside smelled musty and of something a long time dead, a rat perhaps or maybe a mouse, I shuddered at the thought. Leaning my head and shoulders inside, I eased the door wider, and then slowly and bravely opened my eyes. In the half light, apart from a few more cobwebs, and I'm certain a good deal more dust that I couldn't yet see, my shed appeared to be just as I'd left it.

Crouching down in the doorway, I ran my hands along the floor. Finding the joint between the second and third boards, I wriggled my fingertips into the gap, pushing forward so that the tongue and grove separated, before sliding my hands in further and pulling hard. The floorboard came free with a satisfying pop. I lifted it to one side. In the space beneath my shed, between the floor and the dry dirt below, although the sheen on the soft leather had dulled since I saw it last, Dr Carmen's medical bag appeared to be safe and well. Reaching down, I lifted the heavy bag out, rested it by my feet on the cinder step, and then reached back down to feel for the soft velvet pouch and Marjorie Warton's small silver gun.

CHAPTER FORTY-ONE

I recall noticing a smell in my house that evening, something that reminded me of school summer holidays spent at home on my own with my mother, a familiar, and yet right there and then, an out of place aroma, of open windows, fresh fruit, and flowers cut from our garden, that seemed to emanate from somewhere around the washing machine; some kind of fabric conditioner I guessed. I don't remember minding the smell. I'd expected to find changes, to see changes, to feel changes... more probably. In fact though, like my shed, apart from the smell, my little house felt pretty much the same as it had on the morning that Dennis Sapsead had burst in and spoiled everything. Sitting at my kitchen table, (I suppose smugly absorbing the moment) it seemed to me that my favourite barista Colin and Patchouli oil Julie were doing a good job of looking after the place. I leaned back into the bentwood chair and stared at the ceiling, quietly reminiscing. Although I could never describe my home as having been a hub for social whirling, my kitchen table had seen its share of fun. We'd had good times. I imagined the sound of Tristan's hearty laughter over breakfast. I saw my cousin's happy cherub face over a steaming cup of tea. I pictured myself with my very special friend on the day that I first saw the house. I remembered sitting there alone.

That was when it happened, when the fist of sat-upon emotion smashed me in the face. My god I howled... except that actually I didn't... In fact, self-preservation jumped in and stopped me after the very first yelp. Indeed, to make absolutely certain that my anguish made no noise at all, self-preservation grabbed a grotty old tea towel from beside the kitchen sink, and shoved it firmly into my mouth.

Still the tears came... and the snot... For goodness sake, why is it that noses always have to join in. Grabbing my head in my hands, I remember slumping forward onto the kitchen table. I remember feeling the cold hard wood against my forehead and a sudden jolt of further despair as even while I battled with the thrill of being in my own home after such a long time, I realised that I couldn't stay and that this time when I left the little house on Gillycote Road it would have to be forever.

There were a dozen or more things that I would have liked to do then, soaked in a hot bath with essential oils and candles, put on some music, maybe Nat King Cole, or lounged with the lights out in my favourite chair. Instead, after wiping my eyes and blowing my nose, I crawled upstairs to my bedroom and I sought comfort in front of the mirror.

'How much time do we have, I wonder?' I asked.

'Who knows, an hour, a day, maybe more, maybe less, it depends how clever they are. Are we ready? Is everything in place?'

I looked at my reflection and nodded. We were ready, I had a bag packed, I had Chrissie's passport, I had access to money, and a fast car waiting; all we needed was luck and revenge. Leaning forward, I peered into my own eyes, I saw disappointment, I saw sadness, and pain, I saw regret, but above all, like a beacon away in the distance, despite a million lessons to the contrary, I glimpsed something brighter ahead.

Taking Chrissie's phone from my pocket, I gathered myself, then flipped the lid, and punched in the first of three telephone numbers that I needed to call.

'Two-oh-one-four-oh-two, good evening, hello.' The nasal female voice answered after only three rings.

'Pru Percival?' I asked, using my most queenly tone.

'Yes.' The sappy bottle dyed redhead squealer warily replied.

'Oh jolly good... Gladys Cox speaking.' I said giving a combination of an aged aunt's Christian name and my mother's maiden name. 'We met... ooh... several months ago,' I lied, 'at a sale in aid of Military Veterans, a charity you support in an official capacity I believe.'

'Oh... er... yes, Mrs Cox, yes I remember you very well.' She lied back. 'How are you?' She asked, now becoming somewhat less timid.

'I'm bearing up thank you very much for asking.' I said, then, my voice dropping a half tone, I added. 'You do know that my husband passed away, such a wonderful man, on his way to church, he sneezed twice, and then puff he was gone. It caused a dreadful commotion in the churchyard.'

'Oh my dear Mrs Cox I'm so terribly sorry to hear that. If there is anything that I can do to help you will let me know.'

'Well yes, actually there is, that is why I am calling you today. I am planning to move away shortly and I've been clearing the house. I've come across several items that belonged to my late husband, medals, military regalia and such-the-like, some of which I think might be rather valuable and I'd be pleased to donate it all to your charity if that would be good.'

'Oh well yes Mrs Cox, that would be marvellous.' With the promise of serious goodies for her to present to her preferred charity's most likely matriarchal committee, Prudence Percival suddenly became much friendlier. 'What a magnificent gesture, what a wonderfully generous woman you are Mrs Cox, I'm sure that I, I mean, I'm sure that the Military Veterans charity, would be delighted and able to make good use of anything that you might be generous enough to give.'

'Then it is settled.' I said. 'I've boxed everything up, including the jewelled ceremonial dagger and one or two other gifts from the colonies.'

'A jewelled dagger... gifts from the colonies... goodness me.' The silly woman sighed, obviously falling for every word.

'Yes, with a wonderful golden scabbard, from India I think. The only snag is that I shall be off first thing in the morning. I don't have my own transport. I live on Gillycote Road. Would you be able to call and collect this evening?'

'A scabbard too.' I could fairly feel Pru Percival's avarice oozing through the telephone. 'Gillycote Road... let me see... well... Mr Percival is out at Choir practice at the moment, but then, if I were to set off right away I'd have the car back in the garage long before he comes home.' She said more to herself than to me before adding in a louder more positive tone. 'Yes, why not, if it's all right with you Mrs Cox, I can call over right now.'

'Marvellous.' I said.

Moving from my dressing table stool to the end of my bed, after I'd hung up, I lay back in to the soft duvet and tried to relax my mind before punching in the next number. I wondered how Marcus would react to hearing my voice, whether he'd already heard that I'd escaped from prison, and if he too would fall for what I had to offer. Like Pru Percival, the Fat-Brat answered my call within the first few rings.

'Hiya, hello, who is it?' Marcus said too cheerily for my liking. I knew his slimy singsong voice straight away.

'Marcus it's me. Listen don't hang up. I need to talk to you. Just give me a few minutes.' I said urgently.

Silence, but at least he stayed on the line. I pressed on.

'Marcus, I need you to do me a favour, this is important, please listen to me.'

Nothing, but still the Fat-Brat didn't hang up.

'I know you think that I treated you badly and I'm sorry and if you give me a chance I may be able to make amends.'

Zilch.

'This is going to sound crazy, but I need to get money to some people fast, I have a serious problem Marcus, and I need your help.

Nada.

'Listen, a year ago, the night you came to my house and found me in the garden. I wasn't just taking the evening air; I'd been hiding a large stash of cash in a bag under my garden shed. The money is still there Marcus, thousands of pounds; I need you to get it for me.'

I heard an intake of breath.

Bingo.

'You are in jail, what do you need money for?' Marcus asked, and immediately I knew that I had him.

I made the last of the three telephone calls from the bathroom downstairs; I wanted the echo from the hard tiled walls to help disguise my voice. Sitting on the closed lid of my toilet gave me a strange feeling of something unpleasantly and recently familiar. I looked around my bathroom, although four squarish walls, about eight feet by eight, mostly white with grey trimmings, it reminded me not one bit of my prison cell. Bugger. Closing my eyes and steeling myself against the bleak world that I'd thrown myself into, after taking a long, slow, steadying breath, I counted to ten, and then punched the number that I'd taken from Elaine Hennessey's notes only a few weeks earlier into Christine Tensely-Evans phone. Unlike Pru Percival and the Fat-Brat both of whom at least had the civility to answer my call promptly, Detective Sergeant Dennis Sapsead raised my pulse somewhat more than was entirely comfortable by keeping me hanging on for eleven and a half rings.

'Yes.' He grunted, when at last he picked up.

I swallowed hard before speaking, then, lowering my voice and adopting a gravelly country burr, I asked. 'Am I speaking to Detective Sapsead?'

'You are.' Came the clipped reply.

'Good, this is Tristan Blandy, I don't know if you remember me or not but my Second cousin is…'

'I know precisely who you are Mr Blandy.' Sapsead cut in quickly.

'Right, well… the thing is, I've been carrying out some repairs to the central heating system in my cousin's house and I've just bust through a wall in the bedroom and I've found a gun and a bag with doctoring things in it, I thought I'd better let somebody know.'

'I see… Tell me… where are you now Mr Blandy?' Sapsead asked, his voice suddenly sounding strangled.

'I'm in my cousin's bedroom.' I said.

'Right.' Sapsead breathed, and then, after clearing his throat twice he took a deep draw of air and said slowly and clearly. 'I want you to stay exactly where you are Mr Blandy. Do not move. Do not touch anything. Do not talk to anyone. Please do not even breathe unless you absolutely have to. I will be with you as soon as I possibly can be. Ten minutes tops; okay?

'Okay.' I said calmly, and then I hung up and allowed myself a smile.

In hindsight, it might have been wiser to leave longer between handing out my invitations, but then in hindsight perhaps I should have taken the afternoon that my mother died off work.

Having already placed Marjorie Warton's gun loaded with its five small bullets, a dozen or so large and very strong cable ties, and a small bottle of Mace CS spray, neatly on my kitchen table, when I'd finished with Chrissie's cell-phone, after scrunching the SIM card into little pieces, I turned the lights out in my house and sat down quietly and waited to see which of my guests would be the first to arrive. As it happened, I didn't have to wait long for any of them. Prudence Percival turned up first. The snivelling little woman eagerly clip-clopped up my garden path looking exactly as I remembered her, wearing the same ridiculous 'Iced Bun' outfit that she'd worn on the morning that poor Cecile Ablitt fell down the stairs. I answered the door promptly with Marjorie Warton's gun in my pocket, the bottle of CS gas in one hand, and a yellow duster in the other. Dear Pru didn't notice anything untoward at all.

'Good evening Mrs Percival.' I said with a wide smile. 'My my, what a very fast car you must have. Please, come along in.'

I have to say at this point, what a truly marvellous invention the cable-tie was; I wonder now how bank robbers, and serious villains, and even the police service, ever managed before, as a replacement for handcuffs the flexible thin plastic strips are marvellous. I'd like to say the same for the Mace spray, but while as a chemical sledgehammer, the product is jolly effective, I find the noise that some people make when caught by the fumes, quite frankly, disgusting. Just one tiny squirt of the stuff and Prudence Percival was grunting, and squealing, and wriggling on the floor like a little ginger pig.

Fortunately, before my doorbell rang again, once I'd trussed her up and popped her into my bath for safe keeping (empty naturally), after a relatively few minutes, although I am sure that she remained overcome, she did quieten down. Detective Sapsead was the next to arrive, and true to his word, only nine minutes and forty seconds after I'd hung up from our call. The brute fairly battered my bell push, ringing the doorbell four times just while I was walking across my hall. I opened the door, and as I'd done with Pru Percival, I gave him a nice big smile.

'Where is Tristan Blandy?' He snapped immediately.

'Ooh… dear me… upstairs I think.' I said - all flustered like - kind sir 'ish - and I really don't know I'm just a poor defenceless woman. I wrung my hands and looked up towards the lord.

Sapsead pushed past me without another word.

Actually, the grouchy detective bursting in full of adrenaline as he did, highlighted another failing in the Mace spray, it took six squirts full in the face to knock him down, and even then the brute struggled like hell when I tried to bind him with the cable ties.

Infuriatingly, within only a few seconds of settling the deceitful policeman to his penultimate fate, under a series of more substantial nylon luggage straps that I'd wrapped around my bed, I heard a noise from downstairs. Still breathing hard from the unnecessary exertion that Sapsead had caused me, I tiptoed down the staircase and then peered across the hall towards my kitchen. Standing in the doorway looking directly up at me, silhouetted against the brighter kitchen light was Marcus Fat-Brat sneak Hendy-Coombs. He saw me and through my disguise straightaway.

'What on earth are you doing here?' he said, as calmly and as matter of factly as you like.

I shook my head, but at the time, I couldn't think of anything to say, so as I stepped into the hall, I sprayed him too. Like poor dear Pru, but thank goodness without so much of the dreadful grunting and squealing, Marcus went down like a sack of spuds. Stupidly, seeing the Chubby Creep writhing on the floor and obviously terribly distressed, suddenly and, considering what for the last several weeks I'd been planning to do with him, inexplicably, I felt rotten. For some daft reason, seeing the boy's pudgy face all screwed up and uncomfy, an overwhelming pang of guilt… well… it overwhelmed me. Only a moment after I'd pointed the wretched bottle of Mace at Marcus, I found myself crouching on the floor apologising to him for what I'd done.

I am such a twerp sometimes.

Marcus, of course, hadn't a clue what was going on. Temporarily blinded and completely disoriented by the noxious vapour, he could barely hear me; he just kept thrashing around, and swearing, and calling for his Mum. Finally, grabbing his shoulders, I turned him towards me. His face looked a mess, already red, and puffy, and wet with tears.

'I'm sorry.' I said. 'I know it's horrible, I'm really sorry.'

'What did you do that for?' He sputtered at me through the river of slime that was now oozing from every orifice.

'Because I have to kill you Marcus and I don't want you messing things up.'

'Kill me?' He wailed. 'Why do you want to do that?' Then tried to wipe his eyes so that he could see me.

'Because you told tales on me Marcus, you grassed me up, you split, you spilled the beans… you butted in when you weren't wanted and ruined my bloody life Marcus.' Suddenly I was shrieking, pulling away from the Fat-Brat and standing up, I wrapped my arms around my chest and stared down at him.

'No I didn't, I didn't tell anyone anything. I never said a word, not even to that bloody copper.' He cried, and then suddenly calming down, to my total shock Marcus took a breath, and added. 'I love you, you bastard, I'd never let you down, I'd never do anything to hurt you.'

Crap, Bum, and blast… shit, shit, shit. How bloody well dare he? The little sod. He chose a moment like that to say the one thing that I'd always longed to hear. To utter the one phrase that other than my mother, in almost forty-six years… well maybe closer to forty-seven, nobody had ever had the decency to say to me before. Pathetic though it sounds now, but my knees gave way and my eyes suddenly filled with tears.

Such a crybaby.

Unfortunately, God or fate, whichever of the pair had been listening to my singing and prayers on the previous

Sunday morning, also chose that moment as a special time... the time to revoke my good luck credit card. The crash from upstairs sounded like a thunderclap. The light fitting above my head rattled. A cloud of dust appeared from nowhere. I quaked in my proverbial boots. A second and then a third bang followed almost immediately and then came a roar; a guttural noise that sounded, I imagine, something akin to a pissed-off Grizzly bear.

Having somehow freed himself from my bed (my praise for the cable-tie inventor perhaps a tad hasty), a moment later Detective Dennis Sapsead made his appearance on my staircase; he did not look a happy chap.

'Hey bitch!' He shouted from the second step down looking ruffled and furious although apparently still not recognising me.

Again crouched on the floor in the hall, terrified, I squirmed towards Marcus. I looked at him, he looked at me, and then we both looked at Dennis Sapsead. The swarthy policeman, the liar and cheat, and now the central focus of my revenge, snarled like a dog then launched himself from the stairs.

Whether I had Marjorie Warton's gun in my hand before he jumped or if I pulled it from my pocket while he was in mid air I don't know, but when the shot exploded from the barrel no one could have been more surprised than me. In the confines of the small hallway, the noise was incredible, not so much a boom or a bang, but a sharp ear-splitting crack that I actually felt inside my head. Alas, regardless of the blast or any impact, Dennis Sapsead's flight towards me continued unabated. I tried to roll out of the way. In fact, I think Marcus tried to pull me, but before I could move more than a few inches, the detective came crashing down and the lights went out.

CHAPTER FORTY-TWO

'Are you okay?' I remember hearing Marcus as if he were a ghostly memory in a restless dream. 'I think you've killed him.' He said.

I also remember a weight being lifted from my chest, and then being dragged by my ankles into somewhere where the lights were bright... my kitchen. I suppose that I came round only a minute or two after Sapsead had landed on me, but at the time, it seemed much longer.

Something cold and wet sploshed on my face.

'What are you doing?' I said, suddenly once more conscious of where I was and more or less aware of what had just happened.

'It's just a facecloth and some cold water.' Marcus said, his voice still sounding hoarse. 'I thought it might help, but if you don't want it, I could certainly use it.'

'You'll ruin my make-up.' I said.

'What?' Marcus chided. Squinting at me through watery eyes, he shook his head.

'Forget it, where is Sapsead?' I said.

'In the hall... I think he's dead.'

I rolled onto my side, and then stood up slowly. My head spun immediately, I toppled forward into Marcus's legs.

'Careful.' He said grabbing my arms and helping me up, then he looked me in the eye. 'You have to get out of here. After all the din, and the shouting, and the shot, I 'm sure that somebody must have called the police.'

'Are you sure he's dead?' I said.

'I think so, you definitely hit him, and although you cushioned his fall his head hit the floor with a terrible crack. It didn't look nice.' Marcus said shaking his head and pursing his lips, and then he added. 'It wasn't your fault though.'

'Bloody hell Marcus, don't be daft, of course it was my fault... everything is my fault.' I closed my eyes as a flood of useless feelings and painful regrets bombarded my poor worn out brain. I thought of the dentist in prison for a fleeting moment and I wondered if the stupid man had pulled out the wrong thing. A shiver ran up my spine. I thought of my home,

I thought of my shop, of my life, of the people I loved, and of the people that I'd believed I hated. I thought of my mother, and Tristan, and my cousin, and everyone else that I'd let down.

…and then, thank goodness, I thought of me.

'You have to go now.' Marcus said.

'I know.'

Quickly, I glanced around the kitchen. Chrissie's suitcase and shoulder bag were on the floor close to the back door and her Camel coat folded neatly over the back of a chair.

'I'm not going back… I won't be caught again.' I said.

I picked up the coat and put it on, I felt Chrissie's car keys rattle against my leg. After throwing the smaller bag across my shoulder, I picked up the suitcase and opened the back door.

'I'm sorry Marcus, I really am. If it's any consolation, I don't think I'd have had the courage to shoot you.'

Marcus didn't say anything; he just looked at me with a vacant expression and then glanced at the door. Turning to leave, I paused for an instant in the doorway, and then turned back.

'Oh… Marcus…' I said speaking quickly. 'Just a couple of things, there's an old lady in my bathtub, be nice to her, she's had a bit of an upset… and… well… tell me… do you really love me?'

Marcus nodded twice, neither of us smiled, and I left.

The fresh night air felt sharp against my skin. A breeze had picked up since I arrived home. I remember that the moon seemed particularly large that evening, large and rather inappropriately, cheerful. Staring up at the sky, apart from the wind flustering the leafless trees on the south side of Gillycote, and Chrissie's kitten heels clip clopping on the pavement, I realised that for the first time in many months, my world was wonderfully quiet. Although still in some pain after Sapsead's crash landing, and feeling shaky on my feet, I savoured those few moments walking along Gillycote Road, those last few minutes in my town. I knew that, whatever happened, I would never be there again.

Turning into the narrow lane that led to St Michael's Church and to the cul-de-sac where I'd left Chrissie's BMW, I met a young woman who was walking quickly in the opposite direction. Both of us stopped abruptly and then stepped aside to let the other pass. I smiled, the young woman didn't. Suddenly I realised that I was facing Sammie Gough, Tristan's girlfriend, the sweet waitress who'd walked me home from the Franglaise Fusion restaurant in town and who'd made Marcus jealous. I'd forgotten that she lived so close by. My heart jumped into my throat. Sammie glared at me as if I were a monster, and then after pulling her dark overcoat up around her ears, quickly hurried by. Panicked that the girl had recognised me and after her reaction to me in prison was bound to call the police, foolishly I started to run. Chrissie's kitten heels suddenly felt like a pair of roller-skates. On the lane's unmade surface, I could barely keep my feet. Struggling with the suitcase and shoulder bag, wearing a long camel coat, and moving like Jajabinks from Star Wars on heeled shoes that barely fit, far from escaping quietly in the night, I could scarcely have exposed myself more.

As it happened, the moment I reached Chrissie's BMW and glimpsed my sorry reflection in the car window I understood why Sammie had run off, not that she'd recognised me as I'd feared, but because I looked truly awful, more like the battered caricature of a nightmare clown that the sophisticated woman that I aspired to be. Feeling dreadfully conspicuous, I wrenched the car door open, flung the shoulder bag and suitcase onto the back seat, and then clambered inside and hit the locks.

After starting the engine and peering into the rear view mirror while catching my breath, before setting off, I was about to affect some running repairs - maybe brush my hair - touch up the lipstick - and wipe the globs of mascara from my cheeks, when my reflection decided that we needed to have a chat.

'Chicken shit.' It started.

'What?' I said.

'You heard me… Chicken shit, yellow belly, coward.'

'Shut up.' I said.

404

'Just three quick shots that's all it would have taken.'

'Leave me alone.'

'…and you managed just one, and then only because I took over. You really are the pits.'

'Oh go away.' I pleaded.

'You let them go on purpose didn't you? You lied to me. I think you knew that you'd never do it. I can excuse the Fat-Brat, but that bloody snivelling old bag deserves everything she gets.'

'Enough…' I said. 'I've heard enough, we haven't the time for this, we have to get away.' I shut my eyes tightly and grabbed hold of the rear view mirror, pulled it away from the windscreen, and then opened the window and hurled it outside.

As the mirror hit the ground and smashed, and my reflection at last shut up, an almighty thud came from the other side of the car. I spun in my seat horrified to see a bloodied and raging Dennis Sapsead pulling on the door handle and attacking the passenger window of Chrissie's BMW with his fist. Startled, stupidly, rather than knocking the already nicely purring car into drive and simply pulling away leaving the mad policeman behind me and even madder, for some insane reason, the law of the land probably, I felt a need to put on my seatbelt. While Sapsead pounded on the window, first with his left fist and then with the right, although I knew that I didn't have long, that eventually the glass simply had to break and Sapsead's hands would soon be around my neck, incredibly, I sat fiddling and fumbling with an irritating metal clasp.

Fortunately, about then, Chrissie's BMW decided that it wasn't too thrilled with Sapsead bashing it about. An alarm began, a piercing, screaming, pulsating siren. Actually, inside the car the noise wasn't too awful, but outside, Sapsead immediately grabbed his ears. Quickly realising that I had a chance, like an obsessive-compulsive tic, my daft need to wear the wretched seatbelt having to be satisfied, I pulled the camel coat from under me, away from the clasp and concentrated solely on the job in hand. When at last I felt a clunk, and then a click, sucking in air through my teeth like Mr Dyson's very best dual-cyclone, I slammed the gearshift forward and then hit the throttle as hard as I could.

Of course, BMWs being the 'Supreme driving Machines' that they are, Chrissie's 3 Series should have rocketed me forward at the terrific rate of nought to sixty in under seven seconds. Instead, after one bouncing lurch, the experienced and skilful driver that I am not, I managed to stall the damn thing in less than two seconds. Although the lurch forward threw Sapsead to the ground, hearing the engine die, and the alarm stop, the enraged man was up like a shot and this time I saw that he had something in his hand, a house brick I thought. I grabbed at the key desperately trying to start the engine. First turn... nothing, second turn... nothing. Then wham! The brick came at the window like a mortar shell; I couldn't believe that the glass didn't burst. Wham again; alas, this time something gave. Although in the darkness I couldn't see the crazing in the window, this time the sound was different, duller, and softer, more compliant, the glass had almost given up. With my anxiety levels reaching dizzying heights, as Sapsead drew his arm back for what I knew would be a third and a final fling, I ducked down and reached to turn the key one more time. Crouching low between the seats looking forward, suddenly I spotted the problem, I'd left the gearshift in drive. I lunged with my hand stretched out. Knocking the stick forward with one hand and twisting the key for all my life was worth with the other, at last the engine fired. Hearing the sudden roar, Sapsead's brick arm paused, not for long, but the split second was all I needed to throw the shift into drive and start the car moving at last. Suddenly the momentum was with me. Caught off balance Sapsead was falling backwards, his arms flailing in the cold night air, the brick fell from his hand. Pulling down on the steering wheel hard left, the BMW swung round, out onto the narrow road, and I was heading straight for Sapsead with murder quite definitely in mind.

When I was a lad, and Starsky and Hutch were on TV, when they squealed their tyres to chase a baddie, the result was a foregone conclusion, S&H-1 Baddies-0. On that Thursday evening, I was Paul Michael Glaser and Sapsead was David

Soul's consummate foe. Unfortunately, the deceitful Detective Sergeant didn't seem to know the rules of my game. Instead of dutifully throwing himself beneath the wheels of Chrissie's BMW to meet a suitably gruesome end, as the car charged towards him, the wretched man leapt in the air, landed on the bonnet, and then grabbed hold of the windscreen wipers.

After promising faithfully to whoever was listening that I'd pray again and even sing as loudly and as joyously as I could on the very next available Sunday morning, I kicked the throttle pedal down to the floor. With the engine roaring and wheels spinning, the BMW fishtailed out of the cul-de-sac, sped along the narrow lane, and with Sapsead's ugly bloody mug screaming threats and obscenities at me through the windscreen, burst onto Gillycote Road at over fifty miles an hour. Once again terrified, with my knuckles white on the steering wheel, in danger of losing control, I clung on for grim death, and after thumping into a kerb, swung the car hard right towards town. I passed my little house before I really noticed it, I didn't have time to say goodbye, although from the corner of my eye I did see that somebody was standing outside, Marcus I think. Keeping my foot flat to the floor, not knowing what to do, but hoping that Dennis bloody Sapsead would just bugger off and let go as soon as possible, I sped toward the end of Gillycote and the junction with the roads in and out of town.

I only saw the double-decker bus as it began to round the corner. I hit the brakes just in time. Alas, for Dennis Sapsead, the combination of basic human physiology, stress engineering, and the flimsiness of the windscreen wiper fixings that he was clinging to, didn't work terribly well. Of course, it might have been better if the bus driver hadn't tried to get out of my way. That way when the BMW screeched to a halt, and Dennis flew the fifty feet or so from the bonnet, he might simply have landed on the road, a sore head maybe, but he might have survived. As it was, I reckon after spotting the BMW swerving towards him, the bus driver took evasive action, and instead of following the corner round, as he should have, doubting my incredible reflexes, he tried to veer right, straight across the junction. Sapsead hit the bus, or the bus hit the flying detective, whichever you prefer, more or less halfway, and more or less head-on. It wasn't nice.

Unfortunately, the worst was still to come.

With the policeman now spread fairly evenly, if somewhat thinly, across the front of the bus, I think the driver decided to get out. Covering his eyes with his hands, I saw the ashen faced man spin away from the steering wheel and leap for the door. Suddenly out of control, the double-decker bus was no longer heading either onto Gillycote Road, or for the road north out of town, but directly for a house on the opposite corner of the junction. Sitting in the stationary BMW, I watched it happen, the final sandwiching of Detective Sergeant Dennis Sapsead.

CHAPTER FORTY-THREE
A very short epilogue.

So here I am, relaxing on my small balcony enjoying the view over the western reaches of the Amalfi coast in southern Italy, my very most favourite place in all of the world. It is lunchtime, a CD of Mike Oldfield's Tubular Bells is playing quietly behind me. Today is Sunday, I have been to church, and although I'm still not certain of my target audience, I have sung, and I have prayed.

Appropriately, the sun is shining, and while there are one or two large fluffy clouds in the sky, and there has been a southerly breeze for a day or two that the locals tell me always picks up when summer is nearing its end, I can't say that I'm particularly worried, the autumns and winters are not so bad on the peninsula.

I've been here for quite some time now, since I left home in the early spring of the year before last in fact. I've been using my mother's name, maiden of course, I wouldn't want to give the game away too easily now would I? While necessity demands that for the sake of my personal safety and liberty, for the time being, and for the foreseeable future at least, I continue to live as a woman, I still think of myself as very much a man.

I have a small job, here in town, just three days a week, not that I need the money – thanks to dear Enid Fulton – but because I like to keep myself busy and these days I recognise that company is good for me. The salon is small and rather shabby, and is owned and run by a wonderful elderly gentleman of whom I have grown particularly fond, Signor Domenico Patrizio Del-Porto Esconlio-Milio, youch, try saying that one quickly after a half bottle of the local wine.

Mr Dom has been terribly kind. I think secretly he is in love with me, or at least, he is in love with my female alter ego. Alas, with my still faltering Italian and his patchy English and his increasingly suspicious sun-wrinkled wife, we don't get to talk as often or as deeply as I think either of us would like, but I recognize the looks, I know the signs. In recent weeks, Mr Dom's health has not been so good. A heavy summer cold he says, but after listening to his wracking cough for a while now - I'd say months where he says weeks - I worry that it's something more serious. Since the cough has worsened, Mr Dom has taken to leaving me to work by myself in the salon. I don't mind. In many ways, it reminds me of the old days, at home in my own salon, in my own town. Mr Dom's customers maybe older on average than mine were, and a touch more sun-kissed, but a head of hair is a head of hair the world over. Despite the odd linguistic difficulty and the lack of Starbucks sharp lemon cake to fuel my creative juices, the rules are broadly the same, and together with my - although more recently less attentive - reflection, we manage.

Enough about me, what of those I left in my wake, I hear you ask, what of my small family and my few friends?

Well... whilst via various avenues of communication I do try to keep up to date, I am sure you will understand that since my unfortunate exile, news from home tends to be scant and infrequent.

However, among recent despatches...

Alas, although I have been unable to speak with my second cousin Tristan directly since the morning before I discharged myself from Her Majesty's pleasure, only this week I caught up with his more recent movements and learned that he and Sammie Gough are no longer an item. My sources told me some time ago me that shortly after I departed, eager to add some spice to his life (I don't think), Tristan began studying to become a minister of the gospels with an obscure church based somewhere remote in Scotland. Should I blame myself for not being there for the Lummox? I don't know. Although my second cousin asked his fiancée to move with him as his wife, Sammy Gough - sensibly in my opinion - declined, postponing their wedding and suggesting that their relationship needed time, and presumably distance, to blossom and bloom. Only a year on and obviously she was wrong. I miss Tristan dreadfully.

My cousin, on the other hand, Tristan's mother, has apparently had a happier time. A month or so ago, while anonymously rummaging on the internet, quite coincidently I stumbled across my policewoman niece's facebook page. Okay, the truth... in fact, I spent over two hours searching through hundreds of profiles on the wretched site before finally I found the silly girl. Anyway, after clicking a few buttons and sneaking this way and that, I came across a photograph that she'd posted online that fairly blew my socks off. Of my cousin and Mr Deakin, taken in June this year, on the day they were married. Unfortunately, apart from being present during their undeniably romantic first meeting, although I think of myself as something of an accidental Cupid, I remain deprived of all the of the more interesting details.

Sadly, last winter, Uncle Bert died. I never did call in to see him. Guilt haunts me.

Of my favourite barista Colin and Patchouli oil Julie, I haven't heard much. I don't know where they live these days. I know that Julie gave birth to their son something over a year ago. Apparently, they called him Freddie. A good strong name Freddie, my father's name, I wonder if the baby is a redhead too.

Cindy Dobson is well, although as she is no longer married to Mr Ripper she has probably reverted to her maiden name. I don't suppose that the divorce comes as much of a surprise. Despite his laudable work at the local tip, the man was an ignorant oaf, while the lady... well... the lady is the daughter of my favourite member of parliament for goodness sake.

I am sure that you will be relieved to know that Christine Tensely-Evans survived her dreadful ordeal in that horrible prison cell. In fact, I read an extracted report from a high court journal printed in an overseas English newspaper no more than two or three weeks ago, that Chrissie is presently considered to be among the finest defence lawyers in the country and that her name is frequently mentioned in high places.

As for my very good friend, well... although things haven't worked out for us as at one time I'd hoped they would, as far as I know, as I write today, she is alive and healthy, and still happily living her small life in my small town, back in dear old Blighty.

Marcus, however, is another matter, no longer the selfish Fat-Brat stalker who I now realise I had so cruelly misjudged, but now a svelte, sun bronzed, grown-up and conscientious companion, Marcus is currently somewhere inside our apartment fixing me a long cool Ginger Cosmopolitan.

How he got here?

Well, that's a tale.

The truth of the matter.
In truth.
Truthfully.
I knew that I had done wrong the instant I glimpsed Marjorie Warton's lifeless eyes.
I am a murderer after all.

THE END

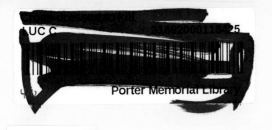

Made in the USA
Lexington, KY
10 March 2012